WALLS OF TERROR

Also by Frank Simon
in Large Print:

Veiled Threats

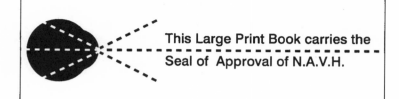

This Large Print Book carries the
Seal of Approval of N.A.V.H.

WALLS OF TERROR

FRANK SIMON

Thorndike Press • Thorndike, Maine

Published in 1998 by arrangement with Crossway Books, a division of Good News Publishers.

Thorndike Large Print ® Christian Mystery Series.

The tree indicium is a trademark of Thorndike Press.

The text of this Large Print edition is unabridged. Other aspects of the book may vary from the original edition.

Set in 16 pt. Plantin by Minnie B. Raven.

Printed in the United States on permanent paper.

Library of Congress Cataloging in Publication Data

Simon, Frank, 1943–
    Walls of terror / Frank Simon.
      p. (large print) cm.
    ISBN 0-7862-1303-5 (lg. print : hc : alk. paper)
    1. Large type books. I. Title.
  [PS3569.I4816W35   1998]
  813'.54—dc21   97-32570

For Les Stobbe
author, editor, agent, and friend

ACKNOWLEDGMENTS

My sincere thanks to:

LaVerne, my life companion, prayer warrior, and first editor.

Dr. Charles H. Dyer, who provided information on the archaeology in Babylon.

Dave Dickinson, who helped me keep the AK-47s and Uzis straight.

Carl Hammert, who told me about the Cessna U-27A from a pilot's point of view.

Eitan and Orit Kashtan, for their wonderful hospitality and background information on Israel.

Les Stobbe, who helped smooth out the bumps on another road.

John and Jan Simon, who provided valuable suggestions.

The fine people at Crossway who made it all possible: Jill Carter, Leonard Goss, Lane Dennis, Ted Griffin for his sure editing touch, and Cindy Kiple for her cover art.

CONTENTS

1

LONDON HONEYMOON

Mustafa Mirza staggered over the hard-packed dirt floor and out the door into the predawn stillness that surrounded his village in northern Iraqi Kurdistan like a shroud. Waves of dizziness swept over him as he looked around. The dirt paths of Parakh were deserted and silent. People should have been up by now, but as far as he knew, he was the only one left alive.

In eighteen years of hard living, Mustafa had seen illness, injury, and death, much of it caused by fighting the Iraqis or enemy Kurdish groups. And he had suffered through his share of misery.

Two days ago a helicopter had swept low over the village. Mustafa had not thought much about it at the time, but hours later the mysterious plague struck. The villagers staggered about until they collapsed, choking and coughing, unable to breathe. He had been among the last to catch it. He watched in horror as his family and friends fell, their heads burning with fever, writhing in pain as they gasped for breath. Then he had succumbed as well.

Mustafa's father had been murdered by an Iraqi army patrol several years earlier, leaving Mustafa to take care of his mother and seven brothers and sisters. He brushed now at the tears as a profound sadness swept over him. His mother had died in the first few hours. He would never forget the agony on her face when she curled up on the dirt floor. He wanted to help but didn't know what to do. Mercifully, she passed quickly. Then Mustafa succumbed to the plague at the same time as his brothers and sisters.

He had finally come out of his delirium several hours earlier, and his head still pounded from an excruciating headache. He had checked the pitiful clumps of rags that had been his brothers and sisters. All dead.

He shook his head to clear it as he leaned against a stone fence. The only noise in the village was the wild whistle of the wind as it carried the stench of death away from the dead villagers and the carcasses in the sheep pens.

He turned to the south as a new sound made itself heard above the wind. Mustafa felt icy pangs of fear settle suddenly in his stomach. It was a jet plane approaching at low altitude. This, he knew, was a very bad sign.

In spite of his weakened condition, he began running through the corpse-strewn streets. The whining shriek of the fighter grew louder behind him as he willed himself to keep going. Every joint screamed in pain, and his head felt like it would split open. The jet was close now. Mustafa saw the end of the village approaching ever so slowly. He knew he would never make it. He tripped and almost fell. He struggled to maintain his balance, somehow knowing that if he went down, he would never get up — at least not in this life.

A flash of light enveloped him just as he reached the last hut on the edge of his village. A moment later the loud *whump-whosh* of exploding napalm swept over him. He felt the intense heat the same moment he looked over his shoulder. He stood there, rocking unsteadily on his feet as his eyes swept over the devastation. The first pass had taken part of the southern half of the village, the nearest flames a scant fifty yards behind him.

Mustafa paused only a moment. To his horror, he saw three more planes angling in behind the first one, and more off in the distance. The Iraqis obviously intended to wipe out the village, unaware the job had already been done.

He turned again to the north and somehow used the energy of desperation to resume his flight to safety. He stumbled up the rocky ridge and over the top as the Iraqi fighter-bombers finished their grisly task. Mustafa tripped over a rock and fell. He blacked out momentarily, providing a brief respite from the excruciating pain and numbing weakness. Sounds came back first, the wind overlaid by the booming crackle of the napalm-fed flames. Then vision returned, heralded by an explosion of stars.

Mustafa's head was turned to the west as he lay sprawled on the rocky ground. As he watched, a bright ball of red and black fire shot into the air several miles away. He struggled into a sitting position as he watched the destruction of the village nearest to his. As he saw the flickering flames reach into the brightening sky, he prayed that Allah would annihilate the murdering Iraqis. The scouring fingers of napalm sprang up once more, this time a little more to the south and about five miles away. All villages within thirty miles were now history.

Mustafa crawled back to the ridge to look down on what had been his home for eighteen years. All he could see was a continuous sheet of flames, and the Iraqis were still not done. Fighter-bombers were spreading their payloads of death beyond the village perimeter as if to wipe out everything remotely associated with it. When Mustafa saw the strikes continuing up the hill he hid behind, he struggled to his feet once more and staggered off to the north, hoping the pilots would not notice one lonely Kurd trying to remain alive.

Before him, only a few miles away, was the Turkish border. He hoped he had enough strength to make it.

It was September 3rd. The travel alarm was set but had not gone off yet, and the room in the Jerusalem King David Hotel was quiet except for a gentle snore. Anne Enderly awoke from her pleasant dream and found reality even more enjoyable. There on the pillow next to hers lay a sleeping face topped with an unruly thatch of brown hair. The hair, the head, and the body underneath belonged to her husband of one day, Mars Enderly. Her eyes drifted to his right arm, raised as if seeking recognition. Hard, white plaster wrapped the arm and the upper part of his chest, the result of a gunshot wound to his elbow — how long ago? It had only been about three weeks, but it seemed like forever. She felt like she was sharing her husband with this monstrosity, but they managed. It bothered Mars far more than it did her, although it had posed an interesting problem last night. She gazed lovingly at his stubble-darkened cheek and ran her forefinger across the roughness. The face twitched and smiled. The eyes opened.

"Good morning," she said as she snuggled close to him.

Disorientation flitted across his eyes as wisps of sleep swept quickly away. "Hmm," he sighed as he pulled her close with his left arm. She laid her head on his chest below the cast, listening to the rapid beating of his heart. *Yes,* she thought to herself, *he's awake. This is the one God gave me, and I love him more than I can say.* He moved slightly and gave her a bristly kiss on her soft cheek. She turned toward him, and he kissed her lips gently, then with feeling. She melted into his arms as her love so perfectly and fervently matched his, enjoying the marriage bed God had given them.

Later she watched him as he awkwardly shaved with his left hand. He was six feet tall, such a contrast to her petite five foot two. And at twenty-six, he was trim with a figure most would call wiry. Although she admired it, she suspected he would fill out sooner rather than later. At thirty, she was grateful she had avoided the battle of the bulge thus far. As long as they both remained active in field archaeology, perhaps it would stay that way.

He caught her greenish-gray eyes looking at him. "Taking inventory?" he asked, a smile appearing in the middle of the shaving cream.

"Um hmm," she said with a grin.

His eyes took in the details of her nightie.

"Back to your shaving," she said with a blush. "We're due at Hadassah in about an hour to have that cast removed. That doesn't leave us much time for breakfast."

"Do you think . . ."

"No, I don't. I have to get ready also. So press on with your scraping."

"Yes, ma'am," he drawled as he turned back to the mirror. "I can see sharing the facilities is going to take getting used to."

"I'm sure you'll figure out the basic rules soon enough."

He glanced around at her through his wire-rim glasses. "Ladies first?" he asked.

"Let's just say it takes me longer, and it's in your best interest if I do a good job."

He laughed. "You can have it right now." He waved her to the lavatory, his shave half done.

"No, you finish up. Then I'll put my face on."

"I never take mine off," he muttered.

"What was that?"

"Nothing. I'll be done in a minute."

She let her eyes linger on him for a few moments, then returned to her dressing.

It was almost 8:30 when they walked, hand-in-hand, into the King David restaurant. The waiter seated them quickly, provided menus, and departed. When he returned, Mars and Anne ordered dry cereal and bagels with coffee. Anne smiled at her new husband, her eyes prominent behind the large, round lenses of her glasses. Mars thought she looked a little like an owl — a lovely owl with beautiful green eyes.

Mars glanced at his watch a little after 9:00. "What time did Dad say he would be by?"

"9:30," Anne replied. "Don't worry, he'll be here. He's as anxious for you to get rid of that cast as you are."

An impish grin creased his face. "Oh, I doubt that."

She laughed. "Mars, will you be serious."

"I assure you, I am."

She ignored his remark.

He shrugged and signed his name to the MasterCard bill, pulling off the guest copy.

He then poured them another cup of coffee and tried to enjoy it with Anne as they waited.

At precisely 9:30 they heard a deep, rumbly voice approaching the dining room entrance. The newlyweds turned in time to see the stocky figure of Moshe Stein enter along with Joe Enderly, Mars's father, and Bob and Flo McAdams, Anne's parents.

Moshe stopped when he saw Mars and Anne, his round face looking smug. He arched his eyebrows and stroked his bushy, black beard as if not quite sure who they were. "A marriage made in heaven, true? Of course true."

Anne stood up. Mars maneuvered his right arm clear of the table and joined her, eyeing Moshe suspiciously. "I thought you said your *yenta* duties were over."

"Oh, they are," the Jewish archaeologist assured him with a smile. "I am no longer the matchmaker. But you will forgive me if I admire my handiwork."

"Do we have a choice?" Anne asked.

Moshe paused for only a moment. "No, I am afraid you do not."

Joe beamed at his daughter-in-law as he hugged her. "After all these years, I'm so glad to have a daughter. I couldn't be happier for you both."

17

Mars shook hands with Bob but was not quite sure what Anne's mother expected. Flo decided for him by throwing her arms around him and hugging him. He dutifully kissed her cheek and decided he liked having a mother again.

"So we're off to Hadassah Hospital to get that ugly, white thing hacked off," Joe said. "Who all is going?"

"I promised Bob and Flo Yad Vashem," Moshe announced. "We'll meet you back here."

"Sounds good." Joe turned to his son and daughter-in-law. "Shall we go?"

They walked out to the parking lot and got in the GMC Safari. Joe drove through the heavy morning traffic as they made the short trip up Mount Scopus. They parked and entered the hospital's lobby.

"Are you sure Moshe said Dr. Kohn would meet us here?" Joe asked as he held the door for Anne.

"That's what he said."

A thin man of less than average height stood up and came toward them. Mars recognized him immediately, which brought back painful memories. The doctor executed a skillful left handshake with his patient.

"Mars, so nice to see you."

"Hello, Dr. Kohn. I'd like you to meet my

wife, Anne, and my dad, Joe Enderly."

"Meir Kohn. Pleased to meet you both." He paused. "Under better circumstances this time."

"Infinitely," Mars agreed. "Dr. Kohn, I really appreciate everything you've done for me."

"That's my job, Mars. Now, Moshe filled me in on what has transpired since we last met. He said your medical apparatus will play havoc with your honeymoon if I don't do something about it."

Mars looked down at his right arm stuck out in front of him like a white battering ram. "Er, yes. It is a little bit of a bother."

"What Moshe said was stronger than that," the doctor said with a broad smile.

Mars laughed. "That sounds like Dr. Stein all right."

' Meir grew serious. "I'll take that off shortly, Mars. But I have to warn you to be careful for about the next six weeks. The bone is going to be weak for a while, and it would be very easy to break it again. After I remove the cast, I'll take an X-ray and give you a padded sling for that arm." He tried not to smile when he saw Mars frown. "Listen to me, now — I want you to wear the sling most of the time for at least the next four weeks. You can take it off from time to time — as long as you're very careful. The inconvenience is not intolerable — the sling is lightweight and quite comfortable."

Mars looked doubtful.

Meir turned to Joe. "I think you will find the lobby more comfortable than the examining room." He looked at Anne. "However, if Mrs. Enderly wishes to come . . ."

She grabbed her husband's left arm.

Meir smiled. "If you will excuse us," he said to Joe.

Mars noted the prompt response Dr. Kohn got to his every request. He had a quiet authority that commanded respect. Everything was done with precision and economy of motion.

Meir operated the hand-held saw deftly. In minutes the cast was in dusty pieces, and Mars was gingerly moving his right arm. A quick trip to radiology was next. After Meir examined the still-wet film, he extended a parting gift.

"My wedding present to you both," he said with a smile, holding out a blue sling padded with foam rubber. "Wear it in good health." He helped Mars put it on.

"Thank you, Dr. Kohn," Mars said. "I appreciate everything you did for me — for us."

"You're welcome. Please give my regards to Moshe."

"We will."

The Enderlys walked arm-in-arm down the corridor to the lobby.

"That looks a whole lot better," Joe said when he saw them.

"Feels a lot better, too," Mars said.

They joined Moshe and the McAdamses for lunch at the American Colony. The early afternoon they spent touring the old city of Jaffa, south of sprawling Tel Aviv. Moshe treated them to freshly baked bagels at a thriving Arab bakery. They finished a little after 3.

"Well, shall we head to the airport?" Joe asked.

"We'd better," Anne replied. "Mars is beginning to get anxious."

Joe glanced at his son. "I'm afraid he comes by that honestly. It's a congenital defect among the Enderlys."

"Let's hope it's recessive," Moshe observed under his breath.

"What was that?" Mars asked.

"Nothing, nothing," Moshe replied quickly. "Time to get you two lovebirds off to London." He motioned toward Joe, who was on his way to the car.

Mars, Anne, and Moshe got in the back, and Bob and Flo got in the front. Joe guided the GMC Safari out of Jaffa and through Tel Aviv toward Lod.

Mars had his arm around Anne as they looked out at the passing scenery. His sigh of contentment was clearly audible even to those in the front seat. Anne glanced at her husband in embarrassment as they both struggled with what was still very new to them. When Mars sighed again, Anne applied her elbow where she thought it would do the most good. He turned his head in obvious surprise, not yet understanding that the misdeeds of husbands are not always apparent to the perpetrators.

Moshe looked out his window. "It would seem the previous evening was satisfactory," he observed quietly.

Joe cleared his throat but said nothing.

"Mars . . ." Anne whispered.

"Yes?" he asked, a puzzled expression on his face.

"Quit it."

"Quit what?"

Moshe turned his head, his eyes locking with Mars. The bearded face broke into a broad smile. "I am afraid you are embarrassing your young bride, my friend. Perhaps she is self-conscious about the source of your obvious contentment?" The dark brown eyes blinked at him.

"Oh," Mars said. "You mean . . ."

"The penny's dropped, as the Brits would say."

Mars turned his head further. Anne was treating him with a rather warm, accusing gaze, something she was very good at, Mars knew from experience.

Mars looked away, a smile coming to his lips. "Ah, I see it now." He gave a shrug as best he could considering the sling. "Would it be better if I said I had a lousy time?"

Anne applied her elbow with even more feeling.

"Oof," Mars gasped. He knew she really meant it.

"True love," Moshe observed. "Now, you two play nice."

Joe took the exit for Ben Gurion International Airport, stopping at the terminal. Mars, Anne, Moshe, and the McAdamses got out. Joe went to park the Safari. Moshe helped Mars and Anne carry their bags to the security area, where a young Israeli lady asked them countless questions about their luggage. After the inquisition they carried the bags to the British Airways counter. Mars gave the agent the tickets and waited for official confirmation that the airline was indeed expecting the honeymooners. The agent smiled at the newlyweds and told them the flight was on time.

Mars and Anne said their good-byes and passed through passport control. Minutes later they were in the departure lounge. Mars glanced at his watch, noting they had over two hours to kill. An impatient scowl crossed his face. Anne lifted his left arm and slid hers through. He smiled as he squeezed her soft hand. He couldn't help sighing.

Fadel Barrak stepped lightly off the tube train at the Picadilly Circus station after the long trip from Gatwick Airport. He was six feet tall, smooth-shaven, and had a moderately heavy build, none of which was fat. Never having been outside Iraq before, he was finding England a puzzling and delightful place. The subway platform was crowded even at 8 in the evening as people rushed around him in the dim subterranean light. Up ahead he saw the tallest escalators he had ever seen, obviously the way to the surface. He joined the long line and inched along until he could step on the mechanical stairs.

He stepped out into nighttime London on a sidewalk framed by the famous traffic circle. The buildings and gaudy signs were vaguely familiar, the real Technicolor scene a contrast with the pictures he had seen. The circus was clogged with traffic — cars and taxis along with a few red double-decker buses.

He pulled his itinerary out of his pocket and consulted the hastily penciled directions he had received at the airport. Orienting himself, he waited for the light to change, then shuffled across the road along with the crush of pedestrian traffic. Upon reaching the other side, he continued walking until a thin, wedge-shaped building appeared, looking as if it wanted very much to reach Picadilly Circus, but this was the best it could do.

He entered the front doors of the Regent Palace Hotel and walked up to the registration desk. The clerk took in his dark complexion, brown eyes, and black hair and waited. Fadel greeted her in heavily accented English, pulled his Iraqi passport out of the breast pocket of his well-tailored western suit, and extended it along with his payment voucher.

She smiled at him. "Mr. Amir Ali," she read from his passport. "One moment while I check your reservation." Her practiced fingers ran over the computer keyboard. "Yes, here it is. One week, paid in advance."

She returned the passport and extended a plastic key to a room on the fifth floor. Fadel thanked her, grateful that his forged passport and the deceased Amir Ali had not let him down.

Fadel took the elevator to the fifth floor, inserted the plastic key in the electronic lock, and swung open the door. The room was small and lacked a bathroom, although it did have a lavatory. When he saw the bed, he remembered how tired he was.

Even in a proper western suit, Avraham Abbas was obviously not a German. His dark complexion and black eyes and hair marked him as Middle-Eastern even though he had no beard or mustache. He eased his six-foot frame into an airport lobby chair, finding it as uncomfortable as it looked. The former leader of the Palestinian Revolutionary Force (PRF) had escaped into Syria with his lieutenant, Abdul Suleiman, after an ill-fated Syrian invasion of northern Galilee. Since this had made them odious to Syria's president, Hashem Darousha, they soon found themselves on a one-way flight to Baghdad with the clear understanding they were not to return. Fortunately for them, Iraqi president Hammad Talfah was quite impressed with their reputation for accomplishing difficult missions. Avraham had been pleased with that situation, though he had not expected to be pressed into service so soon.

"Flight's on time," Abdul reported, taking the seat beside Avraham's. "We can board in about fifteen minutes." Avraham nodded.

Abdul had roughly the same build as his boss and the same black eyes and hair; he too was clean-shaven. There the similarities ended. Avraham had a round face, while Abdul's was more characteristically hawk-like. But these appearances were misleading. No one, including Abdul, understood Avraham's wild, almost maniacal execution of terrorist operations. Suleiman was a strong, effective fighter, but he lacked the frenzy of his long-time boss.

Their Lufthansa flight was announced in German followed by English. "That's us," Abdul said.

The two got up and walked to the gate. Even they had no understanding of the maelstrom their actions would unleash.

2

OLD ENEMIES

Mars and Anne snuggled as best they could deep in the heart of the coach section of the packed British Airways 737. Anne leaned her head on Mars's shoulder, aware of the sling but doing her best to ignore it. When she squeezed his hand, he turned and smiled.

"It was sweet of your dad to offer us first-class tickets," she said.

"Yeah, I guess it was."

"What do you mean, 'you guess'?"

Mars sighed. "It's a long story. Dad has tried to run my life ever since I was little — or at least I thought so. But to be fair, I might have been wrong, at least a little bit." He tried to suppress the uncomfortable lump in his throat. "I'll never forget his coming to Israel after they kidnapped you." He wiped away the sudden tears with his left hand and cleared his throat. "So I guess you're right — it was sweet of him to offer."

28

She smiled. "But you still turned him down."

"I felt it was best to stand on our own feet. Do you think I made a mistake?"

She looked up at him. "No, dear. I don't mind at all. I'm used to traveling this way."

"He also offered to put us up at a five-star London hotel. Perhaps we should have . . . I don't know anything about the Regent Palace, but five-star it definitely isn't. The travel agent said the bathrooms were in the hallways."

"We'll survive."

"I know. And besides, the agent did say it's right in the heart of London. Who hasn't heard of Picadilly Circus?"

She squeezed his arm. They didn't notice much about the rest of the trip but were glad when the pilot with a proper British accent announced their final approach to Gatwick Airport. A fine mist beaded the window as Mars looked out at the black night-time sky. He glanced at his watch.

"Almost 10," he said. "It'll be late by the time we get to the hotel."

"That's all right, dear. I don't care as long as I'm with my hubby."

His good humor returned.

The 737 touched down with loud chirps, then taxied to the appropriate gate. When

Mars stood, Anne was already on her feet and retrieving their carry-on bags from the overhead bins. After a long wait, they filed out into the aisle for the snail-like procession out of the aircraft. Finally they approached the flight attendants flanking the door and tirelessly telling each passenger good-bye and sincerely wishing that they fly with British Airways again in the near future.

Mars and Anne said their thank-yous and plodded up the tunnel to the gate. Mars pointed out the direction to passport control, and they resumed their journey. The exercise felt good as they walked through a long series of large metal tubes that seemed to lead nowhere. Finally they arrived in a large hall where Commonwealth passengers passed through quickly as officials took only a cursory glance at their passports, while foreigners languished at the ends of long lines. About twenty minutes later Mars and Anne were finally able to present the landing cards they had filled out on the plane. The agent asked them how long they were staying in England, then stamped their passports. Mars glanced briefly at his before stuffing it into his shirt pocket, noting he was allowed to stay for six months but was prohibited from employment.

They proceeded to baggage pickup and

waited for the metal monster to disgorge their luggage. After another short wait, they claimed their wheeled suitcases, extended the handles, and headed for public transportation. They purchased tickets on the British Rail Gatwick Express train to London's Victoria Station and walked to the tracks. A train pulled in, and all the doors opened. As Anne started forward, someone familiar passed through her peripheral vision. She stopped so suddenly that Mars bumped into her.

"Look over there," she gasped, nodding toward the front of the train.

"Where?"

"Three cars down — those two men behind the big lady in pink."

Mars followed her gaze. "Avraham and Abdul." His voice automatically dropped into a harsh whisper. "What in the world are they doing here?"

"Who knows. Should we wait for another train?"

Mars thought for a moment. "No. But we've got to do something about this — after we get to the hotel."

They pushed their way aboard and sat down. The doors whooshed shut, and the train pulled out. The British Rail promise of a thirty-minute trip was reasonably accurate,

Mars noticed. The train pulled into Victoria Station at 11:30.

Mars and Anne trekked through the vast terminal until they found a subway ticket booth. After a certain amount of confusion, borne reasonably well by the agent, they purchased two tickets on the Victoria Line to the Green Park interchange station with transfers to Picadilly Circus. When Mars asked where the Regent Palace Hotel was, the agent assured him it was right on the Circus — they couldn't miss it. They descended to the interchange station beneath Victoria and waited.

The trip to Green Park was easy since it was the next station. The Picadilly train was packed. Mars and Anne struggled aboard with their luggage, and the other passengers grudgingly gave way. The doors closed, sealing the Americans in the midst of a mass of uncomfortable bodies.

The train pulled out of the station and continued its voyage far beneath the streets of London. Minutes later it slowed for the Picadilly Circus Station.

"Excuse us please," Mars announced as he and Anne turned toward the doors.

No one moved as the two Americans struggled to keep their footing despite the train's sudden braking. Mars put his bag in his right hand. He reached down and grasped his suitcase with his left hand as the train stopped and the doors popped open.

"Are you ready?" he asked over his shoulder.

"I'm coming," she said grabbing her bag and suitcase.

Mars advanced toward a tough-looking young man in front of the door, who grudgingly gave way rather than risk a collision with the determined American. The couple dodged between two Londoners who were trying to board and made it out onto the platform. Free of the train, they stopped for a moment and looked around at the dimly-lit, cavernous station. In the distance they saw the tallest escalators they had ever seen, emphasizing how far underground they really were.

"There they are again," Anne said pointing.

"Yeah," Mars agreed, knowing there was no way he could ever mistake those two men for anyone else. Not after all that had happened. "I hope they don't look our way."

Anne shivered violently, remembering her recent captivity by them. "Me too."

But the terrorists were only interested in leaving the station. They waited their turn for the escalator, got on, and were soon out of sight. The two Americans exhaled in relief.

: They pulled their suitcases to the line, which Mars knew he must refer to as a queue. They inched forward, then struggled onto the moving steps while holding onto their luggage as best they could. They stepped off at the top and walked out into the dark bustle of Picadilly Circus in the heart of Soho. Multicolored lights flashed all around them as heavy traffic struggled through the Circus.

"See 'em?" Mars asked anxiously as they looked around.

"No, but they could be anywhere in this crowd."

"That's true enough."

They gawked at the strange traffic patterns, both vehicular and pedestrian, as night-life Londoners made their way around them in irritation. Mars scanned the surrounding buildings, a scene somewhat familiar and yet strange. "I don't see the Regent Palace — the ticket clerk said it was right on Picadilly Circus."

Anne looked about as well. "I don't see it either. Maybe we'd better ask." She almost smiled as she saw her husband's anxious look. "I will, if you want."

"No, that's all right," he replied quickly.

Mars looked around. He feared that the hurrying Londoners would simply ignore him. Then he saw the black uniform of a bobby topped by his conical cap. Mars approached cautiously. "Pardon me." The officer turned his head to see who owned that awful accent. "Could you tell us where the Regent Palace Hotel is?" Mars inquired, trying to maintain his smile.

"Yes, sir," the bobby replied, all business. "It's just off the Circus over there. Cross here and go around that building, an' you can't miss it."

Mars thanked the man and walked to the crosswalk with Anne. When the light changed, they crossed the street in a sea of people and made their way around the indicated building. And there, as the officer had promised, stood the thin, wedge-shaped Regent Palace Hotel.

They entered the lobby and proceeded to the registration desk where a smiling clerk received them. Mars extended his passport together with the voucher for their stay. Anne pulled her passport out of her purse and gave it to the clerk.

"Very good," the clerk said after verifying the reservation. She handed Mars the plastic door key and asked if they needed help with their bags. Mars politely declined, which seemed to surprise the clerk.

The Americans pulled their bags to the elevator, then rode up to the fifth floor and found the room after a brief search. It took several tries before Mars could get the plastic key to work in the electronic lock, but he finally heard a click and pushed open the door. He flipped on the light.

"Well, the travel agent warned me the room would be small," Mars said with a sigh. He entered, parked his suitcase at the foot of the bed, and perched his bag on top of it.

"It will be just fine," Anne said. She placed her suitcase and bag beside her husband's. She smiled as she continued to get used to being a wife.

"What are you smiling about?" Mars asked with a grin.

"I was just thinking how glad I am to be Mrs. Mars Enderly."

His grin grew wider. "I'm so glad you said yes."

She remembered his asking her to marry him, immediately after she had been rescued from the Palestinian terrorists. "I'll never forget your proposal. I wouldn't anyway, but *especially* under those circumstances. It was while I was a prisoner that I really understood how much I loved you."

Mars nodded, wiping away a sudden tear. "I thought I'd die when they kidnapped you. And then when I couldn't get anyone to help . . ."

She stroked his cheek. "It's all over now."

A frown clouded his face. "Except that Avraham and Abdul have popped up again. We need to contact the authorities."

"Yes, I know. Where do we start?"

"London police, I guess."

Mars picked up the phone and made the initial call to the police with the assistance of the operator. From there, it took three more calls to locate someone who was willing to discuss the problem of Palestinian terrorists on the loose in Britain. That someone was Dennis Hastings of British Intelligence.

"You are sure this Avraham and Abdul are terrorists?" Dennis asked.

"Very," Mars replied. "Do you want specifics?"

"Not over the phone," the agent said quickly. "It's late. Can you and your wife come by in the morning?"

Mars held his hand over the mouthpiece. "He wants us to come to his office tomorrow." Anne nodded.

"Yes, Mr. Hastings. When and where?"

"Shall we say around 9 in the morning?

That'll give you time for breakfast."

"I guess so. How do we get there?"

"Where are you staying?"

"Regent Palace."

"I will have a car waiting at the front entrance at 8:45."

"We'll be ready."

Mars frowned as he hung up the phone. "I don't like this spook business." Looking at Anne lifted his spirits, but even that didn't entirely chase away the dread he felt.

"I don't either," she agreed. "But we can't let those madmen do whatever they're planning to do without at least saying something."

The Baghdad Hotel was a dilapidated, four-story structure on Berwick Street in the middle of Soho. Even though it was quite late, the knock on the door of number 405 came as no surprise to Avraham and Abdul.

Avraham stepped to the door. "What is it?"

"The tour package you ordered, sir," came a voice with a distinct British accent.

Avraham opened the door. A tall, middle-aged man hurried in with a large box. He looked the two Palestinians over carefully as if memorizing every detail. He opened the box and placed it on the closest of the twin beds. He pulled out two Makarov 9mm semiautomatic pistols, checked to make sure they were loaded, then handed them to his clients.

"Careful with those, my dears," he said with a smile. "Authorities frown on people carrying such, don't you know." He pointed to the box. "Two spare clips and a box of cartridges."

"We know what we're doing," Avraham snapped.

"I hadn't the slightest doubt. I don't know what you two are about, and I don't care to find out. I am just doing my job."

"You have something else for us?"

"Quite so." The man pulled a wrinkled scrap of paper out of his pocket and gave it to Avraham. "Henry Box works as a driver for the London fish market — you can reach him at this number. When you're done, he'll take you to Cornwall where you will meet a fisherman. Any questions?"

"These men know what to do?"

"Oh, I assure you they do. Enjoy your stay in London."

The man turned and let himself out of the room.

Mars and Anne got up at 7 the next morning and had a leisurely breakfast in the hotel's grill. They walked through the lobby to the front doors and out into the cool September morning. It was mostly clear, with only a few white clouds under a bright, blue sky. As promised, the car was waiting at 8:45, and the driver knew who they were without asking.

The drive through the crowded center of London was quiet and comfortable. Although the driver was silent, he obviously was expert in what he did. Before long they pulled up before an imposing stone building. Mars thanked the driver and noticed what might have been the slightest nod of acknowledgment.

Mars and Anne looked the building over for some indication of what it housed, but there was no clue. They pushed through the heavy brass doors and entered an austere lobby.

A heavy-set man in a tweed suit approached them. "You must be Mars and Anne Enderly," he said, shaking their hands. "I'm Dennis Hastings, British Intelligence. Shall we retire to my office?"

He led them to a small office on the first floor. After they were seated, he sat heavily in a well-worn swivel chair behind a cluttered desk.

"I did a quick search on Avraham Abbas

40

and Abdul Suleiman and didn't find anything, but that doesn't mean much." Dennis
paused as he considered the young couple
with his piercing blue eyes. "Mrs. Enderly,
I would presume your maiden name to be
McAdams."

"Yes, it is," Anne confirmed.

"I recognized your face. I confess I was
skeptical when Mars first called — I usually
don't expect Americans on their honey-
moons to know anything about Palestinian
terrorism. Now, I know the major points
about your experiences, but not the specifics. Could you kindly fill me in?"

Mars took a deep breath and let it out
slowly. "That's a long story, Mr. Hastings."

"You will find me most patient," he replied with a hint of a smile.

Mars and Anne gave him a concise but
complete description of their recent experiences with the two men and the PRF. Dennis made rapid notes on a pad and looked
up sharply when Mars mentioned Ya'acov
Isaacson of the Israel Defense Forces (IDF)
Military Intelligence. He had filled several
pages by the time Mars finished.

"Nasty business," Dennis said as he toyed
with his pencil. "And now these lovely gentlemen are gracing our shores. How delightful. I don't suppose either of you has any

idea what they are doing here?"

"None," Mars answered for them both. "They were the last people on earth we expected to see."

"You are positive it was them?"

"Definitely, Mr. Hastings," Anne said. "I'll never forget them as long as I live."

"Same here." Mars agreed.

"That's what I thought," the agent said. "One can only hope." Dennis eased his bulk out of the chair and stood. "So nice of you to come in. We will follow up on this." He gave Mars a business card. "If anything else comes up — though I'm sure it won't — you can reach me at this number. However, I imagine you two have better things to do than chat with British Intelligence."

Mars pocketed the card. "Thank you, Mr. Hastings. You will forgive me if I hope I do not have to call you."

Dennis laughed. "I understand perfectly. The driver will return you to your hotel."

They shook hands, and Dennis ushered them to the front doors and saw them out. The driver drove them through the heavy traffic. Pedestrians thronged Picadilly Circus as he turned off it and dropped the Enderlys at the Regent Palace. He then drove away, without having said a single word during the entire trip.

"That guy talks too much," Mars observed as the nondescript car disappeared.

Anne shivered. "Intelligence people give me the creeps."

"I agree."

After a quick trip to their room, they left the hotel for what Anne called an orientation tour. They walked down to Whitehall, past the Horse Guards to Downing Street. They peered down the narrow street at Number 10, over a barricade manned by a solemn police guard. Satisfied this was as close to the Prime Minister as they were likely to get, they swung around to St. James Park, took a trip down The Mall, and strolled by Clarence House. They had lunch at a hotel off Hyde Park and afterward toured the Victoria and Albert Museum, which took the rest of the afternoon.

Taking a leisurely walk back, they pushed through the Regent Palace's front doors around 6. After a short time in their room, they went to the restaurant. The *maitre d'* seated them at a table for two and gave them their menus. Mars peered over the top of his as Anne studied hers with her usual thoroughness. He watched her large, round glasses tilt this way and that as she explored the offerings. She caught him smiling at her and lowered her menu.

"And what are you looking at?" she asked.

"Why, you. Am I breaking one of the rules?"

"It depends. I never know when your sense of humor has slipped its leash."

"If you really must know, I was thinking how much I love you . . ." He paused and swallowed. "And how very lucky I am to have you — especially after what happened." He didn't elaborate — he didn't have to.

"I love you too, Mars." She thought back to her captivity. "I know exactly what you mean."

Mars caught a glimpse of the waiter out of the corner of his eye. "Ready to order?" Anne nodded.

"I think I'll try the steak and kidney pie," she said.

Mars peered at her over the menu. "You've got to be kidding."

"No. I've always wondered what it tastes like."

"Probably like kidneys. Wonder if it comes with a spleen on the side."

The waiter cleared his throat. "The steak and kidney pie? Very good, madam. And for the gentleman?"

Mars thought he put an unusual inflection on "gentleman" but decided to let it go.

"Oh, I guess I'll have the grilled chicken dinner."

"Very good, sir." He took the menus and left.

The service was prompt. Anne bowed her head and silently thanked the Lord for her food. She looked up to see Mars watching her. She flushed as she saw the tension around his eyes.

Finally he smiled and tasted his chicken. The food was excellent. Mars couldn't detect anything wrong with the way Anne's dish looked or smelled. But he turned down her offer to try a little.

"It could be worse," Anne remarked with a grin.

"How's that?"

"We could be in Scotland eating haggis."

"What's that?"

"Minced internal organs boiled and served in a stomach."

Mars frowned. "That sounds terrible. I'm glad we're in England."

They topped off the meal with apple cobbler, vanilla ice cream, and coffee. Mars paid the bill with his MasterCard, and they left the restaurant. They paused in the lobby and looked through the front doors.

"Care for a walk?" Mars asked.

Anne could tell he was not enthusiastic.

She shook her head. "It's been a long day. I think I'd rather go to our room and discuss what we're doing tomorrow."

They took an elevator to the fifth floor. After a few irritating tries, Mars got the plastic key to work and swung the door open. Anne entered and stepped to the window. Mars looked over her shoulder, but it was not much of a view.

"If I had taken Dad up on his offer, that would be Hyde Park."

She turned back to him. "I'm glad you didn't. This is fine. I've got exactly what I want."

He gathered her awkwardly in his left arm and pulled her close. She wrapped her arms around him. He leaned down and kissed her gently, and she returned it with a fervency that surprised and delighted him.

"Mmm, my sentiments exactly," he gasped as he came up for air. He looked deep into her eyes. "Anne, I love you more than I could ever say. I'm so glad you came into my life. I had no idea what true love was like."

She beamed up at him.

"Shall we make ourselves comfy?" he suggested, arching his eyebrows at her.

"Let's," she agreed.

Mars struggled to get out of his sling.

"Could you help me with this, dear?"

She unfastened the sling and pulled it off. "Need help with your pants?" she asked as she gave him a gentle poke in the ribs.

"No, I can manage."

3

MEETING "AMIR ALI"

Lieutenant Ari Jacovy of IDF Military Intelligence rounded the corner nearly at a run. His boss had said, "Immediately," and Colonel Kruger was not in the habit of saying things he didn't mean. Ari was almost at the door when his friend Captain Ya'acov Isaacson appeared from the opposite direction, obviously out of breath, his ample middle shaking in a most unmilitary manner.

"What's up?" Ari mouthed silently.

Ya'acov shrugged impatiently and waved his hand toward the door. Ari opened it and walked in. Ya'acov entered and closed the door without being told. "You sent for us, Colonel?" he asked.

Colonel David Kruger looked up at them from his neat desk. "Come in, gentlemen. Have a seat." He waited as they made themselves as comfortable as the circumstances permitted. "Yes, I sent for you. Both of you have landed in the middle of something interesting, but that's not unusual."

"What is it, sir?" Ya'acov asked.

"Our old friends Avraham Abbas and Abdul Suleiman have popped up again."

"Where?" Ari genuinely wanted to know.

"London."

"London?" Ya'acov asked in amazement. "How in the world did they get there? The last we heard they were cozying up to Hashem Darousha in Damascus. Does Syria have some terrorist op going on in England?"

"President Darousha apparently didn't like their odor after the recent embarrassments and sent them packing to the peace-loving president of Iraq."

"I didn't hear about that," Ya'acov said without thinking.

David nodded. "Because you didn't have a need to know. Well, now you do. Dennis Hastings of British Intelligence wired our foreign service when he found out about our involvement. The Mossad jumped on it, of course, until the PM reminded them of *our* involvement. As you might expect, this caused a major flap between the Intelligence services. However — to shorten this — we won."

Ya'acov whistled as he remembered his previous encounters with the PRF terrorists.

"Maybe we should have let *them* win."

David rapped a thick envelope with his pen. "Ya'acov, I didn't ask you down here for your opinion. We've been assigned this operation, and we'll handle it like the professionals we are."

"Yes, sir. It's just that the worst experiences of my life are tied up with those two."

"I know, and some of the most unorthodox operational moves as well. I won't dwell on it, but what you did during the Syrian invasion went beyond bizarre. You are very lucky the PM was impressed with your *chutzpah* — and the final results. General Levy was ready to can you, as you probably know."

Ya'acov noted that David did not offer his opinion. "Yes, sir, I know. What's the plan?"

"You are operating according to plan for a change?" David glanced toward Ari. "Take note of this, Lieutenant."

Ya'acov sighed. "Colonel, you know I do my best for you. And my methods *have* paid off."

David thought this over. "Yes, Ya'acov, I have to admit they have. But they also scare the pants off me. Do you think we could strike a happy medium?"

"I will do my best, Colonel."

"I will accept that. The general says we

are to assist the Brits — this is their show, at least for now. Bring Hastings up to date on what our friends have been up to over here. You two are at his disposal, and if there are any questions, call me. If they catch the terrorists, we will press to have custody, but that's out of our hands." David handed the envelope to Ya'acov. "Here is everything you need. Change into civilian clothes and get packed. Your flight leaves at eighteen-fifteen hours."

Ya'acov started to get up.

"Oh, one more thing," David added. "Guess who tipped the Brits on this?"

At first Ya'acov had no idea. Then he snapped his fingers. "It has to be Mars and Anne. Didn't they just get married?"

"You've got it. They're on their honeymoon in London."

Anne peeped through the curtains to see the narrow street below, still in morning shadows. She watched Mars shave as she waited for her turn at the tiny lavatory. He caught her stare as he rinsed soap off the razor. "I didn't know I was so fascinating," he said as he resumed his work.

"Oh, I'm sure you'll like the things I have to do also. But for the record, everything my hubby does fascinates me."

He looked to see if she was kidding him. She wasn't. "Thank you, dear. Everything about you fascinates me too. I guess that's one of the neat things about marriage."

"Um hmm."

"The lady has a Ph.D., and all she can say is 'um hmm.' "

"I'll ignore that. What are we doing today?"

He thought for a moment. "Breakfast at the hotel's grill, only I think the Brits say 'brokers.' I need to check our itinerary, but I think today is free. I thought maybe we could take one of those bus tours. The agent said it was the best way to see as much of London as possible."

"Sounds good to me. Do you know what sights?"

"There are different tours, most of them all day. It depends on what you want to see. The one that sounded good to me goes to Westminster Abbey, St. Paul's, Buckingham Palace, and London Tower, with lunch at a pub that is supposed to be pure cockney."

"That does sound good."

Mars finished and relinquished the lavatory to his wife while he dressed in casual clothes. His stomach let out a yowl of anguish as he was buttoning his shirt.

Anne looked around in amazement. "Are we getting hungry?" she asked as she turned back to the mirror.

Mars looked down at his belly as if it were a traitor. "Apparently so. That's something you'll have to get used to. When it gets on a tear, there isn't a thing I can do about it."

She glanced at him as she worked on her mascara. "That's O.K., dear. It's part of togetherness." She waited until she caught his eye. "I love you just the way you are, and I wouldn't want anything to be different."

They finished getting ready and went down to the lobby. The breakfast buffet was all laid out when they arrived. They made their way around the tables, picking up whatever looked interesting. They set their loaded plates on a vacant table and returned for juice and coffee.

As they ate, the dining room gradually filled. Mars quickly cleaned his plate and went for seconds. When he returned to the table, he noticed a young man looking around the room. Their eyes met as Mars sat down.

"Excuse me," the man said with a heavy accent. "I do not mean to intrude, but all tables are taken. Might I . . ."

Mars's first reaction was irritation, which

quickly changed to sympathy. "Sure. Please join us."

The man smiled in gratitude as he put his plate down and pulled out his chair. He sat down and smiled nervously at the two Americans. He shook Anne's hand solemnly, then Mars's. "My name is Fad . . ." He paused in obvious embarrassment. "Excuse me, you would not understand an Iraqi nickname. My name is Amir Ali. I am in London for an international trade show on oil well servicing equipment. I work for our government in oil field production."

"Pleased to meet you, Mr. Ali. I'm Mars Enderly, and this is my wife, Anne McAdams." He stopped suddenly as his face flushed crimson. "I mean, Anne Enderly. We just got married. We're on our honeymoon."

Fadel appeared flustered. "Oh, I did not mean to intrude. Let me find another table."

"Oh, no," Anne said quickly. "We'd be delighted for you to have breakfast with us. I don't believe I have ever met anyone from Iraq before."

Fadel looked at her guardedly. "Iraqis do not travel much — except for business, which is why I am here. We like to be as self-sufficient as possible, but the best oil well equipment is made elsewhere. So, what do you two do, if I may ask?"

"My husband and I are archaeologists," Anne answered. "We just finished a dig in the Old City of Jerusalem."

"Yes, I remember hearing about that. Quite a find. And that horrible kidnapping that came after. Was it you who . . . ?"

Anne shivered. "Yes. Neither Mars nor I will never forget that."

Evidently wanting to change to a more comfortable topic, Fadel went on, "You would probably find Iraq interesting. We have many archaeological sites. There is much work being done in the ancient city of Babylon, for example."

"I've read about that," Mars interjected. "There has been a lot of controversy among archaeologists about building new structures on top of ancient foundations. Rightly so."

Fadel held up his hands in a helpless gesture. "I am sure there are many in Iraq who would agree with you on that, though not publicly."

"What part of Iraq are you from?" Mars asked.

"Al Hil . . ." Fadel began. "Excuse me, I keep forgetting the problems with Arabic translations. I am from Al Basrah, the seaport at the head of the Shatt al Arab — our access to the Persian Gulf."

"I would have thought Baghdad."

"No, the petroleum center is in Basrah."

Anne finished her breakfast and savored the excellent coffee while Mars and the Iraqi continued sampling what the buffet had to offer. She smiled at her husband. His appetite was no surprise to her since she had observed it during the long Jerusalem dig. To her, it seemed the two men were engaging in an eating contest. Finally it appeared Mars had won. The Iraqi parked his knife and fork and sipped his coffee.

"Will you be seeing any of the sights while you are here?" Anne asked him.

"I do not know. I would like to, but I will be quite busy. What do you plan to see?"

"Mars and I are doing the typical tourist thing, I guess — bus tour of London, visit Windsor Castle and Hampton Court, see a play, go shop in Harrods." The last item caused Mars's eyebrows to lift. "Later this week we plan to rent a car and tour the Midlands and Wales."

"That sounds wonderful. But I suppose anything would at this time in your lives."

Anne blushed.

"I would agree with that," Mars said as he squeezed her hand.

"I must be going," Fadel said as he got up. "Please stay seated," he added as they started to stand. "Enjoy your coffee. Thank you for allowing me to share your table. I wish you every happiness."

He turned and left the dining room.

"Interesting guy," Anne observed.

"Yes. From an interesting country — interesting, bizarre, and brutal. Wouldn't you hate to live there?"

"There or most anywhere in the Middle East."

"What did he say his nickname was — Fad?"

"That's what it sounded like to me. I wonder what it means?"

" 'Chief choirmaster to the president'?" Mars offered.

"You're hopeless."

"Well, he does work for the government."

"Finish your coffee."

"Yes, ma'am."

It was a cool, pleasant morning. Avraham and Abdul waited on the edge of Picadilly Circus as a sea of humanity swept past them. Their taxi driver read the paper to the accompaniment of his clicking meter. The Palestinians watched the narrow entrance of the Regent Palace Hotel as morning rush hour went on without them.

"There he is," Abdul said, pointing.

"I see him," Avraham snapped. "Get your hand down."

Fadel Barrak stood on the sidewalk while the doorman flagged a cab. Avraham and Abdul pointed out the other taxi, and their driver folded his paper and waited for the other car to enter traffic.

Fadel paid the cabby, pushed through the heavy doors to the American Embassy on Baker Street, and walked past the Marine guard to the receptionist.

"May I help you, sir?" she asked.

Fadel opened his Iraqi passport and showed it to her. "My name is Amir Ali. I have sensitive information vital to your government, and I would like to speak to someone in your Intelligence service."

The young lady tried, unsuccessfully, to look like she handled situations like this every day. She studied the passport as if it might hold an important clue, then handed it back. "Yes, Mr. Ali. I think you probably need to see Alex Morton. Let me see if he is in." She punched in the extension number and waited while it rang. "Mr. Morton, could you come down to the lobby please? There's someone here I think you should see." She pushed a button to disconnect and looked up at the Iraqi. "Mr. Morton will be right down."

A few minutes later a medium-built man with black hair opened a door and looked into the lobby. Spotting the nervous man standing in front of the receptionist, he smiled as he walked toward him. "Mr. Ali, I'm Alex Morton with the CIA. Would you like to come back to my office?"

"Yes, thank you." Fadel smiled at the receptionist and followed the agent to a small office on the second floor.

Alex offered the Iraqi a seat, then sat heavily in an old but serviceable swivel chair. "Now, what can I do for you, Mr. Ali?"

Fadel cleared his throat. He looked around the small room before returning his gaze to Alex. "I will make this brief. I can give you the location of a secret Iraqi laboratory — something your government knows nothing about, I assure you. For this, I want money and sanctuary in the United States."

Alex whistled. "What kind of laboratory?" he asked.

Fadel smiled. "I will be more specific later. I will tell you now there is a good reason why the lab is secret. Your government has shown great interest in such things in the past. Time is of the essence, so are you prepared to deal?"

Alex tapped his pencil on a pad. "As you probably know, I must pass this on to my superiors." He saw Fadel shift impatiently. "But I'm sure they will be interested. Where can I reach you?"

Fadel hesitated but finally said, "I am at the Regent Palace. You may leave a message at the desk. Will it be long?"

Alex glanced at his watch, calculated the time in Washington, and tried to estimate the reaction time of the senior spooks. "I should receive word by sometime tomorrow."

"I was hoping for something today."

"This requires approval near the top. That does not come immediately."

Fadel nodded. "Leave me a message," he repeated.

Alex showed the Iraqi to the front door, then returned to his office to compose the secret message.

Abdul tapped on the cab driver's shoulder, pointing to the man emerging from the American Embassy. The driver nodded as they waited for Fadel to attract a taxi. Finally one swooped to the curb. They followed the cab back to the Regent Palace Hotel, where Avraham jumped out while Abdul hurriedly paid their driver.

"Hurry up," Avraham growled.

They rushed across the street and through

the hotel entrance not far behind the Iraqi.

"Where do the tours leave from?" Anne asked as she and Mars waited for the elevator.

"A Ph.D. ending her sentence with a preposition?" Mars asked in mock dismay. "Whatever will the University of Texas president think?"

"Nothing if you don't tell him. Now, where do we go?"

"Actually, I haven't the foggiest. The concierge will probably know."

The doors opened, and they went down to the lobby. Mars started toward the concierge's desk when a familiar face rushed past them.

"Hello, Amir," Mars said as the man dashed for the waiting elevator.

Fadel glanced at the American as he scurried by but said nothing.

"He sure was in a hurry," Mars said as the elevator doors closed.

"Mars, look!"

He whirled around to see Avraham Abbas and Abdul Suleiman ram through the front doors almost at a dead run, slowing abruptly as they entered the lobby.

"Over here!" Mars grabbed Anne by the arm and guided her quickly around the corner, then turned back and peeked out. The terrorists hurried toward the elevators, trying very hard not to draw attention to themselves. They stopped short and stood motionless for almost a minute. Then they left the hotel.

Mars left their hiding place and looked secretively through the glass doors. Avraham and Abdul hesitated for a moment before walking off.

"What do you suppose that was about?" Anne asked.

"I don't know. Looked like they were after Amir."

"Lucky they didn't catch him. Do you suppose he knows they're here?"

"Assuming we're right, I don't think so. Avraham and Abdul didn't seem worried about anyone seeing them."

Anne shivered, and Mars put his arm around her. "You don't think they saw *us,* do you?" she asked.

He gave her a squeeze. "No, dear. They never looked this way."

"Good! I want it to stay that way. Why did they wait so long before leaving?"

"I would guess they wanted to see what floor the elevator stopped on. Wait here. I'd better phone Hastings and tell him what happened."

He went to a pay phone and made the call, taking what seemed like a long time.

Anne watched him return. "What did he say?"

Mars laughed. "He wanted us to come to his office." He saw the look of protest on her face. "Don't worry — I said no. He asked me a lot of questions about Mr. Ali, then said to 'carry on.' I told him we'd do our best."

Mars checked in with the concierge and found that there were several tour bus offices within walking distance of the hotel. They strolled out the entrance and walked hand-in-hand toward Picadilly Circus. They made their way along the crowded Westminster streets until they came to one with several tour offices. They picked one using the scientific criterion that it was the closest and checked with the clerk at the counter. Mars paid for two tickets, and they went back outside to wait.

About twenty minutes later, a large bus pulled up. Mars and Anne boarded with the other tourists and picked out a seat about midway back. Ten minutes later, the tour guide bounded aboard, and the driver pulled into traffic. The guide pointed out sights in the city of Westminster as they traveled toward their first stop.

"Look at that magnificent church," Anne said. "Wonder which one it is."

Mars gazed at the sweeping flying buttresses. "Don't know," he said helpfully.

The bus turned the corner, revealing the familiar soaring entrance of Westminster Abbey, the view most favored by photographers. The guide led his flock through the arched doorway and into the nave. The Americans were surprised to find that there were no pews and that folding chairs were used for services. The elaborate choir loft formed the center of the church, while the perimeter held countless nooks and crannies and chapels.

The guide pointed out all the famous people buried in the abbey, giving special emphasis to Poets' Corner, where some of England's greatest writers were buried.

"This gives me the willies," Anne whispered to Mars.

"Why is that?"

"It's a big, indoor graveyard. I never thought of Westminster Abbey that way before."

"Neither did I. But look at all this history."

They continued on to Edward the Confessor's Chapel where they saw England's Coronation Chair, used for every coronation since William the Conqueror in 1066. Mars tried to connect what he was seeing with the pictures he had seen of Queen Elizabeth II's coronation but failed.

"That looks kinda clunky," he observed.

The guide shot him a nasty glance.

"Hush, Mars," Anne whispered in embarrassment.

"Well, it does," Mars whispered through clenched teeth while he smiled at the guide.

The man concluded the tour and led his charges out through the choir area. The organist began playing a hymn, startling everyone with the sudden sounds. The music sounded familiar to Anne, and she finally placed it.

She stopped to listen. "Oh, Mars, that's one of my favorite hymns. It's called 'Immortal, Invisible, God Only Wise.' I remember hearing it as a girl growing up in West Texas. Only it means so much more to me now. The words speak so eloquently of the majesty of God."

The angry scowl Anne saw on Mars's face wiped the smile off hers and out of her heart. She glanced down as she remembered her husband's private war with God, one she so wanted to help him end.

He spoke softly as he looked at the top of her downturned head. "If this helps you through life, O.K. But it's a crutch — I wish you could see that."

She shut her eyes, allowing her tears to run freely down her cheeks. "That's not how it is, Mars, dear — I wish you could see that. I love you so much, and I want what's best for you."

"I know that. Now please drop the subject. Wipe your eyes. His lordship is about to descend on us for being tardy. We don't want two more people to be buried in here, now do we?"

The tour guide paused in the abbey's great doorway and looked back at them uncertainly.

"Come on," Mars urged. "I don't think it would take much to cause him to leave us here."

She pulled a tissue out of her purse and patted her eyes. They walked out of the abbey and up to the waiting bus. Mars gave the guide his best Texas smile as he followed Anne up the steps and to their seat.

Anne tried hard to put the hurt aside, but she couldn't. She wanted to say more, but she sensed Mars's tenseness and did not wish to upset her husband further. He sat there through the ride to The Mall, not saying a word. After the bus dropped the tourists off, the guide led them past Clarence

House and down to the circle in front of Buckingham Palace. The crowd continued to swell as the time for the changing of the guard neared. Anne watched the magnificent red-coated parade as it echoed the British Empire's history, but somehow it all seemed pastel to her.

They ate lunch in the cockney pub and resumed the tour afterwards. When they returned to the hotel in the early afternoon, Anne was feeling a little better. She resolved to pray for Mars on a continuing basis. Somehow this seemed inadequate to her, but it was all she knew to do.

4

QUESTIONS AND
MORE QUESTIONS

It was late afternoon, and Mars and Anne had been in their room for a half-hour when the phone rang. Mars picked it up. "Hello?"

"Mr. Enderly, don't say anything please. It's imperative I see you and your wife as soon as possible."

Mars recognized the voice immediately. He struggled with conflicting emotions, made stronger by the unfortunate incident earlier that day.

"Who is it?" Anne asked, seeing the look of concern on his face.

He motioned for her to wait, then spoke into the phone. "I'm surprised, but I guess I should have expected this. O.K., where do you want to meet?"

"Leave your hotel now, and walk toward Picadilly Circus."

"What then?"

"I will contact you. Please."

"O.K."

Mars hung up.

"Who was it?" Anne asked again.

"Captain Ya'acov Isaacson. He wants us to meet him."

"What's *he* doing here? Why does he want to meet us?"

"It's got to be about Avraham and Abdul. I guess we'll find out the rest when we meet him — *if* we meet him. I said we'd do it, but are you up to it? I could go alone."

She was struggling with what she very much wanted to forget. "I think we should both go, dear."

"You sure?"

She smiled at him and took his hand. "Yes, I'm sure. I'm moderately durable."

He grinned. "I can certainly agree with that."

They left the hotel and walked toward Picadilly Circus. Mars looked around, trying to spot the overweight Israeli. The sidewalks teemed with the less conventional people Soho was famous for, but the IDF officer was nowhere to be seen.

"Hey, mate," came a nearby voice.

Mars stopped and turned his head. A cabby was smiling at him as he pointed to a rear door. "You an' the missus want to go to Hyde Park?"

"I don't . . ." Mars began to answer, then ducked down to look in the backseat. "Yes, I believe we will."

The cabby smiled as Mars opened the door for Anne and helped her in. She slid in beside Captain Ya'acov Isaacson as Mars got in and pulled the door shut. The driver immediately pulled into traffic and turned onto Picadilly.

"What . . ." Mars began.

"Shall we enjoy the view," Ya'acov suggested. "This is the first time I've been to England. This is all so new to me. Are you two having a good time?"

Mars glanced at Anne and smiled. "Yes, a very good time. I believe that's expected on a honeymoon."

Ya'acov smiled at them. "I would expect so. I am very happy for you two."

Mars looked at him, wondering how much was sincere and how much was Intelligence smoke screen. "Thank you, Ya'acov. I believe you, although I don't think either my country or yours cares enough for individuals."

Ya'acov hesitated, his brow furrowed in thought. "This is off the record — and my boss would shoot me if he heard me say it — but I agree with you." He held up a hand to prevent an interruption. "But we both —

I'm sorry — all *three* of us have some unfinished business to take care of. And in this case I think we can take care of it in a way that's best for you two and the countries involved."

Mars nodded. "O.K., I think I agree with that. What do you want to know?"

Ya'acov nodded toward the driver. "Shall we wait for our destination?"

The cabby made his way through the congested traffic until he turned right onto Park Lane. He continued down the block and stopped just short of Marble Arch. Ya'acov paid the fare while Mars and Anne scooted out.

They entered the restful, green sanctuary of Hyde Park and walked past a man speaking to about a dozen people.

". . . imperative that we unleash the hidden power in us all. Life is an endless circle, turning in on itself and us, bringing forth the best, if we let it, heralding the lighthood that will make us one with all things. You, sir, . . ."

The unlikely trio drifted out of range before the speaker's argument could be completed. Mars looked at Ya'acov, who couldn't help smiling.

"I believe that is Speakers' Corner," the Israeli explained.

"Oh, yes," Mars said. "I wondered what was pegging my bizarre meter."

Ya'acov led them deep into the park toward a man who was obviously waiting for them.

"Mars, Anne, this is Ari Jacovy. He works with me in Military Intelligence."

Mars and Anne shook his hand while Ya'acov checked to make sure they were alone.

"O.K., Ya'acov, what's going on?" Mars asked.

"I'm sorry this ugly mess has reared its head again, I really am. As I'm sure you've guessed, British Intelligence contacted us after you talked with Dennis Hastings. It's their operation, but we have had more experience with these two hoodlums. We offered to help, and they accepted. Ari and I are here to provide liaison."

"So what do you need to see us about?"

"There are some things you need to know, and we need your firsthand recollections. I'm sure I don't have to convince you of the necessity of putting Avraham and Abdul out of the way."

"No argument from us on that," Mars confirmed.

"Good. After Avraham and Abdul escaped into Syria, President Darousha booted them out of Syria, and President Talfah of Iraq took them in. At that point we lost sight of them until they materialized here."

"What about this Ali guy?" Mars asked.

"Good question. Hastings has checked him out as much as he can without spooking him. Obviously this has something to do with him, but we don't know what." Ya'acov saw Mars's expression change. "Really, we don't. All we can guess is that the Iraqi government is suspicious about Ali for some reason. But the Iraqis are about the most paranoid people on earth and often persecute their own people for no reason. We don't know any more about Ali than what you told Hastings. An oil field production manager doesn't sound too threatening to the state, unless he walks around with dynamite in his pockets."

"So what do you need from us?" Mars asked.

"Please tell us everything. Maybe we'll see something that Hastings missed."

Mars and Anne went through it all again. When they finished, Ya'acov checked over his notes. "This Ali guy is obviously involved. If we only knew more about him . . . I'd be willing to bet that 'Amir Ali' is an alias."

Mars snapped his fingers. "Wait a minute.

There was a bobble when he told us his name. Anne, what exactly did he say?"

Anne wrinkled her brow in concentration. "I think he said his name was Fad. Then he told us that was an Iraqi nickname and said his name was actually Amir Ali."

Ya'acov looked at Ari. "What do you think?"

"I think he made an error and started to tell you his real name."

"So you think his first name is Fad?" Mars asked.

"Or part of it," Ya'acov said. "Did he stop suddenly when he noticed his mistake?"

Mars looked at Anne.

"As a matter of fact, I think he did," she said.

Ya'acov snorted. "That gives us several possibilities — Fadel maybe. But it still leaves us without a last name. You said he told you he was from Al Basrah?"

"That's right," Mars replied. "Wait . . . He said something like 'Al Hil,' then explained that the proper Arabic translation was 'Al Basrah.'"

Ya'acov looked at him oddly. "That doesn't make sense. I'm fluent in Arabic. The pronunciations and spellings vary when translating into English, but 'Hil' and 'Basrah' are in no way related."

"So he meant to say Al Hil?"

"Maybe. Or some place that begins that way — Al Hillah comes to mind. Are you positive that's what he said?"

· Mars looked at Anne. "Not for sure. It sounded something like that, but it was noisy in the restaurant. Dear?"

"I'm not sure either."

"This is awfully thin, folks."

"That's all we know," Mars said. "What do you want us to do now?"

"Continue with your honeymoon."

"Oh, we intend on doing that. Hastings told us the same thing."

Ya'acov laughed. "Well, that makes it unanimous." He paused, and his expression grew serious. "I'm sure I don't have to tell you to be careful. Let us know if anything else happens. This is a British show, so you need to go through Hastings, but you can call us in a pinch. You can reach us through the Israeli Embassy." He gave them a card.

"Oh, and one more thing," Ya'acov added, "please stay away from Ali. This is not for amateurs."

"Don't worry, we will," Anne answered for both of them.

It was cool for early September. Mustafa Mirza shivered and pulled his worn jacket closer about himself. He had only one goal — to escape from Iraq. He had bypassed the northern village of Zakhu early that morning. As far as he and the neighboring people felt, the entire area — northern Iraq, southeastern Turkey, and northwestern Iran — was Kurdistan. The formality of a border meant a lot to the majority peoples in those three lands, but not to the Kurds. Mustafa knew that his travel plans wouldn't be acceptable to Iraq or Turkey if they knew about them. But that didn't concern him, unless they caught him.

By midafternoon he knew he had to be in Turkey, although there were no indications of any border crossings in this windswept area of central Kurdistan. It was time to start looking for a village. He was exhausted and almost at the end of his energy, since he had not dared grab any food as he fled, even if it had been safe to do so. All he wanted to see were some sympathetic faces and a place to lie down.

He noted a small goat herd on a hilltop off to the northwest. He stumbled toward it, knowing there had to be a village nearby. He forced himself to keep on, desperate for shelter and food. He finally reached the hill and started up it. He looked for the shepherd but didn't see him. Tinny bells sounded as the sheep wandered aimlessly over the barren knob looking for something to eat.

He reached the top and looked down. At the base of the hill stood the shepherd surrounded by a small Turkish army patrol. Despite being so exhausted in body and mind, Mustafa knew he had to avoid the Turks at all costs. He turned and started down the hill the way he had come. The unmistakable sound of an AK-47 being cocked froze him in his tracks. He glanced to the right and saw the Turkish soldier who had circled around the hill from the west. He felt hate well up inside him as the soldier motioned with his rifle to start moving down the hill.

Mustafa plodded down the rocky incline and into the midst of the patrol. The officer suspended his interrogation of the shepherd and watched the new subject approach. He fired off an imperious question in Turkish, which Mustafa did not understand.

The man quickly switched to heavily-accented Kurdish. "What are you doing here?"

Mustafa clenched his fists but controlled himself. He knew from experience how brutal Turks could be, especially to Kurds. "Everyone in my village was dying; only I got out. Then the military burned it and the nearby villages as well."

"This was in Iraq?"

Mustafa knew the Turk did not recognize Kurdistan. "Those in Baghdad say so."

"And so you have illegally entered Turkey." It was not a question.

"I had no choice. All my relatives — everyone in my village — are gone. The sickness or the military would have gotten me."

The officer paused, his brow marked with concern. "Do you know what napalm is?"

Mustafa snorted. Turks and Iraqis thought Kurds knew nothing. "Of course I know what napalm is."

"Is that what they used on your village?"

"Yes. They bombed the entire village with it."

"Describe this sickness that ran through your village."

Mustafa took in a deep breath and let it out slowly. "It started with choking and coughing — I could hardly breathe. And there was a high fever. As far as I know, everyone died except me. I got it, but I am mostly over it now."

The officer looked like he wanted to be elsewhere. "Guard him until I return," he told one of his men.

He took the patrol's truck and drove off toward the west.

Fadel checked with the desk after breakfast, but it was not until afternoon that a message appeared in his box. A short note informed him that his U.S. visa had been approved and requested that he come by the Embassy with his passport.

He left the hotel unaware that he was being observed by two terrorists and a British Intelligence agent. He took a cab to the American Embassy and found Alex Morton waiting for him in the lobby.

"Mr. Ali, come on back," he said as they walked toward the agent's tiny office.

"You wanted to see me about a visa?" the Iraqi asked.

"Forget that — just something for prying eyes. Now, I think we're ready to do business. First of all, what is your real name?" The agent clicked on a recorder without asking for permission.

"What is your government offering?" Fadel countered.

"You'll like it, believe me. But first you have to tell me your real name, and don't lie. This agreement has two conditions: You must tell us the truth, and the lab must be what you say it is. Otherwise, everything is off, and you'll be on your own. Are we clear on that?"

The Iraqi nodded with a shiver. "My real name is Fadel Barrak."

"Good." Alex pushed a single sheet of paper toward the Iraqi. "That's the agreement. Look it over, but essentially the U.S. government is guaranteeing, with the stipulation I just mentioned, to relocate you anywhere in the U.S. you choose. All your needs will be met — housing, a car, food, health care, whatever. That and an annuity of $100,000 a year."

Fadel took his time reading it. "I agree to this," he said finally.

"Good. All we need at this point is your signature and the information you promised — as soon as possible. I'm sure you want to get to your safe haven without delay."

Fadel signed the paper. "The lab I told you about is located near the ancient city of Babylon."

"What is the lab used for?"

Fadel hesitated. "I am not sure."

"Mr. Barrak, you'll have to do better than that or there's no deal."

"No, you don't understand — you have no idea how secret this installation is. I am almost positive the lab is used for either nuclear research or bomb assembly. Everything I know about it fits in with other labs that have been discovered and destroyed."

"Which brings us to an important question: How is it you know about this?"

"You are familiar with Adnan Talfah?" It was not really a question.

"Your president's son? Of course."

"I am his double and thus useful to my president when it was inconvenient for his son to appear publicly."

Alex leaned forward and examined the Iraqi closely. Finally he uttered a graphic curse. "I thought you looked familiar — not that I'm that much of an Iraqi expert. When did you shave off the mustache?"

Fadel's face turned sour. "When I decided to get out of my country."

"Since you brought that up, why did you leave?"

"You know of Adnan's reputation?"

"It's common knowledge — wild in the extreme."

"He's a monster!" Fadel paused and cleared his throat before continuing. "He found out about my . . . my girlfriend. He raped her and then killed her. This happened over a year ago, and still I can hardly talk about it. His father, of course, did nothing. After that, I swore I would have revenge."

"But even with your closeness to Adnan, you are not sure what the lab is used for?"

"Being his double and so being close to high levels of power does not mean I am an insider. If Adnan did not have such a big mouth, I would not know anything."

"I suppose being close to the power made it easier for you to escape also."

"It did."

"You said the lab is near Babylon. Where exactly?"

"I have a map."

"With you, I hope?"

Fadel shook his head. "No. It is in my room."

Alex whistled. "We have to get it right away. We can't take any chances on it falling into the wrong hands."

The barest smile crossed Fadel's lips. "Iraqi hands or others?"

This flustered the American. "No need to go into that. When can we get it?"

"Do not worry. No one knows I am here. I will go get it and bring it back."

"Why didn't you bring it with you? That would have saved us much time."

"I did not know if we would have a deal."

"Let's get it. I'll go with you."

Fadel folded up the agreement and put it in his coat pocket. "No. I will go by myself."

"O.K., O.K. But *please* be careful."

"I assure you, I will."

Abdul leaned forward as he saw Fadel leave the American Embassy and wave down a cab. "That's him, driver."

The cabby nodded and pulled in behind the other taxi.

"Follow him up to his room," Avraham whispered as Abdul sat back. "When you discover his room number, come get me, and we'll pay him a visit." Abdul nodded.

The two cabs crept through the congested London traffic using tricks known to cab drivers the world over, pulling up in front of the Regent Palace at virtually the same moment. Abdul jumped out, leaving Avraham to pay the driver. Fadel got out of his cab and hurried through the doors, unaware of the Palestinian right behind him.

A crowded elevator waited in the lobby, its doors beginning to close. Fadel squeezed past as Abdul grabbed the left door, stopping it long enough to board. When the Iraqi turned around, he inadvertently brushed against Abdul's coat and felt the hard object near his armpit. Fadel felt cold sweat on his forehead as he faced forward. His confidence vanished as quickly as an interrupted dream. He watched the indicator creep toward the fifth floor, not daring to look at the man beside him.

The door opened, and Fadel stepped out, rounded the corner, and walked briskly to his room. His heart hammered as he pulled out his plastic key and inserted it. He saw distant movement out of the corner of his eye as he opened the door and walked in. He closed and bolted the door as his mind raced frantically. He knew he had only moments before the man would return with help.

He pulled the folded map from under the mattress and stuffed it in his coat pocket. He then grabbed his laptop computer, unbolted the door, and stepped out. The corridor was empty. He turned toward the stair exit and started toward it when a door further down the hallway opened. Just as Anne and Mars came out of their room, they saw their new acquaintance.

Mars stiffened. "Amir," he said quickly, "how are you?"

The Iraqi looked as if he wanted to dash past. "I am fine . . . I am late for a meeting, a presentation on pipeline pumping equipment. I really must see it."

"Don't let us hold you up," Mars said with a nervous smile. "Business before pleasure, I guess."

"Yes." He started to walk past, then stopped. "Would you two do me a favor? I hate to ask it, but I really do not know anyone else in London."

"What is it? We'll help if we can." Mars traded a quick glance with his wife.

"Hold my laptop until I get back from my meeting. I shouldn't have taken it out of my room — habit, I guess. I forgot they don't allow recorders, cameras, or computers at the presentation. I'm already late, and I don't have time to fight with my blasted card key. Would you assist me?"

A thousand questions raced through Mars's mind.

"Of course we will," Anne answered for them, surprising Mars. "We'll lock it in our room. Give us a call when you get back."

Fadel's gratitude was obvious as he handed Anne the laptop. The Enderlys watched him dash down the corridor and push through the stairway exit. Mars re-opened their door, and Anne entered and put the laptop in the closet, Mars closed the door.

"Why did you do that?" he asked.

"Because he asked us to. Didn't you see him? He was scared of something."

"He was nervous all right. But remember what Ya'acov said — to stay away from Amir?"

"Yes, I know. What do you think we should do?"

"I don't know. I suppose we should call Hastings, but that feels like betraying Amir."

"Do you think Amir's really in trouble?"

"He'll be all right," Mars said without any conviction at all. He pulled out the British agent's card and punched in the number.

The agent answered on the second ring. "Hastings here."

"Mr. Hastings, this is Mars Enderly."

"Yes, Mr. Enderly. Is this something we can discuss on the phone?"

"I hope so 'cause we're about to drive to Hampton Court."

"Hmm. Well, carry on."

"Someone we know left his computer with us."

"I see. And you're due for Hampton Court, I take it."

"Yes, we are."

"Very good. Leave the computer locked in your room."

"What's he saying?" Anne whispered.

Mars waved her to silence. "That's all?" he asked Dennis.

"That's all. I will see to it."

They said their good-byes, and Mars hung up. "He said to leave the computer in our room and go to Hampton Court."

"Did he say what he was going to do?"

"No, he didn't. Shall we go?"

5

DOUBLE DANGER

As Abdul rushed back into the first-floor lobby, Avraham arched his eyebrows at him.

"Did you learn his room number?" he whispered.

"Yes, but I think he's spooked."

"Why? What happened?"

"Don't know. He was in a hurry to get to his room. I think he will run."

Avraham looked toward the elevators. "We'd better get up there and take him in his room before he bolts."

A swift movement down the corridor caught Abdul's eye. "Look," he said pointing. "He came down the stairs."

Fadel barged through the side exit. The two Palestinians raced down the corridor, past startled guests, and on through the door before it had time to fully close.

"There he is," Abdul shouted, pointing toward the front of the hotel.

Fadel dashed across the street nearly a

block ahead of his pursuers. "He is in good shape," Abdul muttered as he led the way down the side of the hotel. As he and Avraham crossed the street, they struggled to keep the fleeing figure in sight.

"He is heading for the subway," Abdul said with conviction. "If he beats us to a train, we will lose him."

They arrived at Picadilly Circus out of breath. They looked across the street, but Fadel was nowhere in sight. Only the watchful eyes of nearby bobbies kept the terrorists from zigzagging daringly through the abundant traffic. The light changed, and they quickly crossed the street, then raced for the stairs leading down to the subway. They rushed to the ticket office and waited impatiently for those in front to pay their fares. Finally Abdul stood in front of the cage.

"Two for Earl's Court," he nearly shouted as he tossed down a ten pound note.

The clerk passed him two tickets and slowly counted out the change. Abdul grabbed it and stuffed the money into his pants pocket. He and Avraham dashed for the escalator and jumped on.

"See him?" Avraham demanded from behind.

"No. He could already be on the platform."

A train pulled into the station, bringing panic to the two terrorists' hearts.

"Get moving!" Avraham shouted. "If he gets on that train it is all over!"

Abdul ran recklessly down the moving steps, shoving the other passengers aside as he went, Avraham coming right after him. Startled shouts followed them all the way to the bottom as the two watched the train sitting there with all its doors open. They were finally down, but the doors were beginning to close. Abdul grabbed the ones on the nearest car and held them until Avraham arrived. The two men pushed onto the already crowded car, earning the disapproving glare of the rest of the passengers. The doors closed, and the train began moving.

The car rocked gently back and forth as the train picked up speed. Abdul looked around but did not see Fadel. But he knew, as crowded as the car was, the Iraqi could easily be hidden from view.

Several minutes later the subway pulled into Green Park Station and lurched to a stop. The two men jumped out the moment the doors opened. Abdul turned toward the front of the train while Avraham observed the rear cars. The departing and boarding passengers merged under the watchful eyes of the terrorists.

"I think he is still on the train," Abdul said.

"Are you sure?"

"No. But I think we would have seen him if he got off."

"Do you think he saw us?"

"I don't know. But I believe he will stay on until he is further away."

"Unless he spots us."

"Yes. Shall we change cars?"

Avraham nodded. They hurried to the next car forward and dashed in just as the doors were closing. They looked around carefully but again saw no sign of their quarry.

Fadel tried to make himself as inconspicuous as possible as he huddled in the corner of the car, hoping his pursuers had missed the train. His memory of the man on the elevator made his blood run cold. He didn't know him, but he would never forget those chilling, shark-like eyes. And he had glimpsed a second man during the mad dash for the subway. He knew what they were after.

The train began to slow, then ground to a stop with screeching brakes. Fadel looked between the heads of passengers as about the same number got on as off. He was waiting impatiently for the doors to close when he saw a familiar face. The man pushed his way aboard followed by someone who was evidently his partner. They were obviously searching each car. Fadel ducked behind a taller man and crouched as much as he could. The doors closed, and the train pulled out of Hyde Park Corner Station.

He expected to be confronted at any moment, but the train clattered on as it had before. Fadel hoped the men would miss him in the crowd. His future relied solely on the swarm of humans who shielded him from certain death.

His heart skipped a beat as the train began to slow for Knightsbridge Station. The car screeched to a stop, and the doors opened. Fadel glanced around the tall man. Hope swelled in his heart as he saw his two enemies step out of the train.

"Excuse me," the tall man said as he started for the door, leaving Fadel exposed.

Abdul glanced toward the speaker, and his eyes locked on Fadel's. Abdul punched Avraham and pointed. The two men waited for those exiting to clear, then got back on and began working their way back toward Fadel. They surrounded him as the train lurched into motion.

"Well, we finally meet," Abdul said in

Arabic. "You will get off with us at the next station. All we want is the map. Give us that, and we will leave you alone."

Fadel shook his head.

Abdul gave him his shark-smile. "You will or we will kill you right here. You cannot escape from us."

Fadel's mind raced. Perhaps he could get away from them in the crowd somehow. He nodded.

"Good. You will follow my partner, and I will be right behind you. Don't try anything foolish."

The train pulled into South Kensington Station and stopped. Avraham headed for the doors as soon as they opened.

"Move," Abdul ordered.

Fadel started forward as Avraham led the way through the crowded car and out onto the platform. The Iraqi's heart hammered in his throat. He knew he had to do something or they would kill him, no matter what they promised. He glanced around without moving his head as they approached the escalator leading to the surface. Hoping his timing was right, Fadel barreled into Avraham, hitting him hard from behind with his shoulders and shoving as violently as he could. The terrorist caromed off the side of the escalator and fell onto the dirty concrete.

"Stop!" Abdul shouted.

Fadel shoved his way past a middle-aged man, throwing him onto the moving, metal steps. The Iraqi bounded up the escalator and past the passengers heading for the street, indignant shouts roiling in his wake. As he hoped, his assailant had not fired his weapon. He glanced back. The other man was charging up the escalator right behind him.

Fadel reached the top and raced out across Thurloe Place and down to Cromwell Road. He rushed across the street and up Exhibition Road past the Victoria and Albert Museum. He gasped for breath as a knifelike pain stabbed his side. He ran through the bewildered pedestrians as he looked desperately for help. He stopped at Kensington Road and glanced back. Abdul was gaining rapidly. Fadel dashed across the street, dodging traffic, and made his way into Kensington Gardens. He forced himself to slow to a fast walk as he cut diagonally across the open park. He looked back and did not see his pursuer, but the park offered many hiding places. Hearing a sharp sound, he snapped his head around just as Abdul launched himself through the air. The Palestinian grabbed the fugitive's waist and knocked him down.

Curious faces turned toward them from nearby walks. Abdul rolled Fadel over and felt quickly in his coat pocket. He grabbed the thick, folded map and pulled it out. One glance told him it was what he was looking for. Abdul stood and jerked out his pistol. He aimed and fired two quick shots, one in the center of Fadel's forehead, the other through his heart. The Iraqi died instantly. The onlookers knew they should do *something* but, frightened by the smoking gun in Abdul's hand, could not bring themselves to make a move.

Abdul dashed out of the park to the north and circled back around to Kensington Road, making sure he was not being followed, meeting Avraham across from the Royal Albert Hall.

"I have it!" he said, handing over the map.

Avraham opened it and scanned the detailed drawing. "What about Fadel?" he asked as he folded the map and stuck it in a pocket.

"Dead."

Avraham flagged a cab, and they began the trip back to their hotel.

Begun by Cardinal Wolsey on the banks of the Thames, Tudored by King Henry VIII, and accreted by Sir Christopher Wren for William III, Hampton Court Palace seemed in a disjointed slumber above its graceful and generous gardens, dreaming perhaps of its long and illustrious past. Mars and Anne marveled at the discordant collision of Tudor architecture with the more graceful renderings of Wren. There was no overall harmony, as the famous architect probably realized after having done his best for the court of William and Mary.

Mars and Anne toured the many great rooms, marveling at the paintings and weapons displayed on wall after wall. They admired the magnificent Great Hall with its hammer-beam roof. They saw the treelike grapevine planted in 1769 and listened in awe as the guide showed them a tennis ball in the indoor courts that had been pulled from the rafters during a renovation. The ball, he explained, could have been hit there by Henry VIII himself.

It was late afternoon, and their last stop, after the formal tour, was the Maze, a hedge planted in a bewildering series of loops, twists, and dead-ends. Mars and Anne eventually made their way through and out onto the Palace grounds.

"That was stimulating," Anne observed as she walked hand-in-hand with her husband. Mars gave her hand a squeeze.

"The Maze, the palace, or me?"

"Fishing for compliments? I meant the palace. Believe me, dear, you're in a class by yourself."

"I'm not sure how to take that."

She released his hand and put her arm through his, resting her head on his shoulder. "That give you a hint?" she asked.

He smiled down at her. "Yes, ma'am. Forget Wolsey. Forget Henry. Forget Wren."

"What about William and Mary?"

"Forget William."

Anne looked up at him. Mars made every attempt to keep from smiling but was unsuccessful.

"I ought to poke you one," she whispered.

Mars reveled in the benign threat as his glance drifted over to the small restaurant that shared the grounds with the Maze. He peeked at his watch, noting it was a little past 4. "What say we get a little snack? I need some energy for the trip back to London."

"Is that all you ever think about?"

"I'm still a growing boy," he protested.

"Well, if you're not careful, you'll start growing out."

"Perish the thought. What do you say? Shall we give it a go?"

"Yes, dear."

They entered and noted pictures of the

royals who apparently thought highly of the place. The hostess guided them to a table looking out over the Maze. In moments their waitress appeared.

"Will it be two for tea, sir?" she asked Mars.

"I, ah, well — tea?"

Anne tugged at his sleeve. "Mars, it's time for high tea."

He beamed at the waitress. "Oh, that. Why, yes. Two teas, please."

"Yes, sir. You will be wanting scones with that, am I right, sir?"

"Oh, yes, definitely."

"Very good, sir."

She left for the kitchen without making any notes.

"What makes me think this is going to be a disaster?" Mars whispered.

"Steady, dear. I'm enjoying being with my hubby."

"You know what I mean, Anne. I want everything to be just right."

"I know, dear. As far as I'm concerned, everything *is* just right."

He looked around until he could find some of his good humor. He smiled. "You're right, dear. I love you."

"I love you too, Mars — more than I can tell you."

They concentrated on themselves and quit worrying about what was going on in the kitchen. About fifteen minutes later, the waitress returned with a metal tray. She placed a dish with four scones to the side and set the two teacups before her guests.

"Sir, would you and the lady care for cream?"

Mars glanced at Anne, who only smiled.

"Er, yes, we'd love it."

This appeared to be the correct answer. The waitress picked up the teapot and the cream pitcher and poured both at the same time into the cups. The cream portion was generous, and she stirred it in carefully.

"And will you be having brown sugar?"

Mars figured he understood the system now. "Yes, please."

She scooped coarse brown sugar into the cups and carefully stirred, making sure all the granules dissolved.

"Clotted cream and jam for the scones, sir?"

"That sounds wonderful."

The waitress smiled at him and placed a dish of what looked like butter and a separate container of grape jam on the table. She checked the scene quickly and left them to their tea.

The scones looked like large, oblong biscuits, and they were piping hot. Mars and Anne each took one, split them, applied liberal amounts of clotted cream and jam, and tried a taste.

"This is marvelous," Mars said in amazement. "These are the best rolls I've ever tasted."

"Scones," Anne corrected.

"Yeah, right. There's certainly nothing like this in the United States." He glanced down at the murky tea in his cup. "I don't know about cream in tea, however."

"You told her you wanted it."

"Yeah, I know. It seemed expected."

"High tea is an English tradition, and it is done in a certain way."

"When in Rome, *et cetera, et cetera?*"

"Something like that."

He frowned and took a cautious sip. "Hey, this is good."

Mars ate both of his scones while Anne nibbled on her first one. He looked at her second one covetously. "You want that one?" he asked hopefully.

"Aren't you afraid of spoiling your appetite?"

"Never seen it happen yet."

"I'll split it with you." She divided the scone with her knife and placed half on Mars's plate.

He spread a generous amount of clotted cream on it and slathered it with grape jam. He took a healthy bite and watched as the smile left Anne's face. He turned to see where she was looking and almost dropped the rest of his scone. Ya'acov strode toward their table, and he wasn't smiling. The IDF officer glanced at the table.

"Sorry to intrude," he said softly. "Hastings told me where I could find you. Believe me, I wouldn't be here unless it was extremely important."

"Please sit down," Anne offered. "What happened?"

"Not here." Ya'acov remained standing. "Would you return to London with me — right now?"

"Ya'acov, we're on our honeymoon," Mars complained, as if this were not known to the Israeli. "Besides, we've rented a car and drove ourselves here."

"Give me your keys, and I'll get Ari to take care of it. Now, please, we must be going."

Dennis Hastings came out and met them when they arrived. "Mr. and Mrs. Enderly, Captain Isaacson, please come with me to the conference room."

He took them back to a room near the

middle of the first floor. As they entered, a man they didn't recognize stood.

"Everyone, this is Mr. Alex Morton of the CIA, who is as surprised to be here as we are to see him. Seats, everyone, and I will try and bring all of us up to speed." He turned to Mars and Anne. "I regret you two being in this sticky mess. This is our line of work, and we try not to involve outsiders. But you have been drawn in, I'm afraid, by your earlier run-in with Avraham Abbas and Abdul Suleiman. Now that this is getting more sensitive, I must remind everyone that this is covered by the Official Secrets Act. Absolutely nothing may be repeated outside this room. The penalty for disobeying is a very long prison sentence. Are we all clear?"

He waited until he had gotten affirmatives from every person. "Very good. Now, we have some bad news. Mr. Amir Ali is dead, shot twice by a 9mm gun, presumably a Makarov semiautomatic pistol. Only it would appear that his real name was Fadel Barrak, and he was attempting to play patty-cake with Mr. Morton."

"He came to us of his own free will," Alex objected. "I had no idea he was in the middle of your op."

"Wouldn't have made any difference, don't you know," Dennis observed matter-of-factly. He hurried on when he saw the CIA agent puff up. "I'm not trying to give you a hard time — I'm just bringing out the facts. The agreement among all our bosses, I have been told, is that from now on we share and share alike. You first, then we will take our turns."

Alex gave them a succinct but complete summary. "He was going after the map when he was killed," he concluded. "I take it the map was not on him."

"No, but your agreement was."

"Yes, we've already been through that. So I guess that makes it your turn."

Dennis explained what they knew or suspected about Avraham and Abdul.

Alex leaned back in his chair. "So, the president of Iraq's son's double gets hacked off, steals a map of a secret nuclear lab near Babylon, bugs out of scimitar-land, and makes it to London. Meanwhile, daddy-dear commissions the two Palestinians voted most likely to blow up the world to go after the double, bump him off, snatch the map, and boogie on back. Is that it?"

"You do have a way with words, don't you?" Dennis commented dryly.

Alex gave a pained smile. "So, what's next?"

"The only thing new is that Mr. Barrak

gave his laptop computer to Mr. and Mrs. Enderly before he was killed."

"What?" Alex exclaimed. "Where is it?"

"Steady, old boy. The Enderlys called me, and I sent a man around to get it." He looked at Mars and Anne apologetically. "He was very discreet, I assure you. Go in, take the computer, get out."

· "What's in it?" Alex demanded.

"Don't know. Our experts are looking at it now."

"You'll tell us . . ."

Dennis cut him off. "That's covered in the agreement, Mr. Morton. Whatever we get will be shared between all three Intelligence services. Besides the computer, the only loose end is — that is, *are* the two Palestinians."

"You can forget about them," Ya'acov said. "You won't catch those two."

"How can you be so sure, Captain? We are quite thorough in what we do."

"Past experience with them. It's my guess they will be out of England by tomorrow at the latest."

"I hope you're wrong. But the big thing is the nuclear lab. What we need more than anything else is to find out where it is."

No one asked why. No one had to.

6

THE FUTILE SEARCH

Avraham and Abdul looked uncomfortable and vaguely displeased sitting beside the driver of the refrigerated truck as it rumbled down the A30. They were heading south-west out of London on their way to Cornwall, a little over 200 miles away. After a sleepless night in their hotel room, the terrorists had appeared at the London fish market as instructed and found Mr. Henry Box. The man had told them to change into coarse and worn work clothes and gave them a pair of filthy, full-length coats before directing them to the truck, all without saying a word. Within minutes they were fighting the London traffic as they headed for the dual carriageway.

They drove through the North Downs of Hampshire and past the town of Basingstoke before entering Wiltshire and the southern Salisbury Plains. They passed through Salisbury itself and proceeded further about eight miles south of Stonehenge, oblivious of the history and beauty of the English countryside.

In addition to a taciturn personality, Mr. Box also had a cast-iron bladder as he made no stops and did not inquire into his passengers' comfort or lack thereof. He kept up a steady speed and carefully observed all the laws. He was the very picture of a courteous trucker.

᾽ They entered Somerset and kept on A30 until they came to Devon, changing to A38 at Exeter, which took them to Plymouth. Avraham shifted on the broad bench seat as they drove through the historic seaport, knowing their destination was at hand They passed over the River Tamar at Saltash and entered Cornwall. From there it was a little over fifteen miles through East and West Looe until they came to the tiny Cornish fishing village of Polperro.

The driver turned off the highway and onto progressively more narrow roads until he could go no farther. He stopped, leaving the engine running, and set the brake before stepping down from the cab. Avraham and Abdul got out and stretched their legs. Mr. Box nodded toward the narrow street in front of them while drawing an imaginary line with his right forefinger. The line went straight, then turned abruptly left. His duty done, the driver climbed back into the cab and backed up the hill until he could turn around. Avraham watched the trail of black diesel smoke until it disappeared in the fresh sea breeze.

"Couldn't wait to get rid of us," Avraham observed.

"He did his job." Abdul pointed down the narrow, cobbled lane that passed between whitewashed, two-story, stone houses. They walked down the street until they came to a path leading toward the small harbor. "We should find our guide down there."

Avraham nodded as they started down the steep slope of the uneven alley. Far down the hill they saw a narrow slice of Polperro Harbor and a few small fishing boats bobbing gently on the nearly-calm water. An orange tabby licked a paw and eyed them warily as they passed by on their way to the sea. A minute later the terrorists reached a small stone jetty hovering just above the high tide behind a two-story house. A long line of homes extended for some distance in both directions, the Channel water lapping at their foundations. Seagulls screeched as they sailed parallel to the shore, looking for anything edible, alive or otherwise. Avraham and Abdul looked all around, hoping only to attract the attention of their contact. But no one seemed interested in them.

Avraham pulled his stained coat about his neck as the chill sea breeze blew inland across the compact harbor, sheltered between its two sea walls. Somewhere nearby a door opened and closed. Avraham turned toward the sound and saw a man standing outside the wheelhouse of a small fishing boat tied to a buoy about a hundred feet offshore. The man looked directly at them but gave no invitation to approach. Avraham hesitated, then led the way to a rowboat tied to the jetty. Abdul waited a moment before clambering into the boat, almost capsizing it. Avraham stepped in and sat in the stern-sheets, while Abdul cast off the line. Abdul pulled the oars out from under the seats and awkwardly fitted them to the locks. He sat on the center seat and pulled the boat toward the fishing boat on a meandering course. A few minutes later they were bobbing below the stern of the *Plover*. The water lapped gently against the hull of the larger boat.

The sailor looked down over the transom at them. "Might I help you, gentlemen?" he asked, giving the impression he did not want to. He was a short, stocky man with a ruddy, weather-beaten face. He wore a heavy, wool coat, and his eyes were shaded by a wool cap pulled snugly over his head. Experienced gray eyes examined the two strangers and seemed to maintain a cautious distance.

"Is your boat for hire?" Avraham asked.

The man scratched the stubble on his chin. "Well now, that would depend. What did you have in mind?"

"To see the Channel. We have heard that ships from many nations steam by here."

"That is true. Vessels sail from here to all over the world — the United States, European countries, and many other places."

"Even places as far away as Iraq?"

The man continued to examine them for a few moments. "Come aboard," he said finally. "Mind your step."

Abdul pulled alongside the *Plover* and grabbed its low side near the stern. Avraham threw his arms over the side and scrabbled over the top.

"Throw me the painter," the sailor commanded before Abdul could move. "The rope in the front," he added in irritation when he saw the other did not understand.

Abdul climbed aboard as the sailor led the rowboat to the *Plover*'s stern and made it fast. "You'll be more comfortable in the wheelhouse," he said as he led the way forward and through the port door. He nodded toward an out-of-the-way back corner as he closed the door. "That'd be a good place to stand, me bein' by meself."

The terrorists took the hint and stood where they were told as the man turned to the wheel. He checked the gear lever, turned a key, and pressed a red button on the console. A distant motor whirred for a moment before the diesel rumbled to life. The man adjusted the throttle slightly, coaxing the engine into an uneasy idle that seemed destined to die at any moment. He then sauntered out on deck, took in the bowline, and coiled it neatly. He returned to the wheelhouse, pushed the gear lever into forward, and pushed the throttle to cruising rpm.

He then spun the wheel all the way to the right and pointed the boat toward the jetty. Avraham and Abdul watched in horror as the stone platform rushed toward them. When disaster seemed imminent, the sailor swung the rudder sharply left, centering it when the boat was heading for the jetty at a 45-degree angle. He then pulled back the throttle, engaged reverse, and ran the throttle back up to full power. The propeller dug in, thrashing the water into white foam as the wooden hull shivered from the exertion.

The prow stopped a few inches short of

the jetty. The sailor pulled the throttle back to idle and swung the rudder full right, swinging the stern toward the dock in a docile arc. The water burbled and popped as it repeatedly covered the engine exhaust. The captain untied the rowboat's painter, jumped to the jetty, and returned the borrowed boat to its place.

• Jumping back aboard, he shifted into forward and waited for the stern to walk away from the dock. Then he centered the rudder, shifted into reverse, and backed smartly away. He glanced quickly for traffic as he shifted back into forward. He spun the wheel rapidly to the left and advanced the throttle to cruising rpm, pointing the *Plover*'s prow almost due south. Soon they were past the sea walls and into the English Channel.

The *Plover* took on a pronounced roll, and Avraham felt the beginning twinges of motion sickness as they entered the swells and waves rushing in from the Atlantic. He glanced at Abdul, who appeared unaffected. Their guide stared straight ahead through the spray-drenched windshield, oblivious of his passengers. He checked the bulkhead chronometer and nudged the wheel slightly to the left, bringing the boat to a heading of 170 degrees magnetic. He held it there as the sturdy craft routinely climbed up and down the swells, plodding its way toward the coast of France.

About an hour later they sighted a smudge in the distance. Slowly, like a metal sun, the superstructure of a freighter climbed above the horizon. As the fishing boat approached, the creamy white line at the freighter's bow diminished, then disappeared as the ship stopped dead in the water. Avraham peered up at the rusty black hull as the *Plover* crossed the freighter's bow. High overhead, dingy white letters announced the name of the ship: *Ville du Havre*. The fishing boat pulled alongside the portside accommodation ladder that had been lowered.

Avraham watched the wooden platform at the ladder's base approach. "How do we get aboard?" he asked.

The sailor turned and smiled. "You jump."

Avraham walked to the port door and looked out. The seas, gentle by Atlantic standards, nevertheless rose and fell alarmingly on the freighter's sides, engulfing the bottom platform one moment and leaving it several yards in the air the next. He was too concerned about his own safety to appreciate the fisherman's skill in keeping the *Plover* from crashing into the ship.

"But we will be crushed — or drowned."

' The sailor's smile disappeared. "Get a move on, mate. Either you jump or it's back to England wi' me — take your choice."

Avraham threw the wheelhouse door open with a crash that rattled the glass as he stormed out to the stern. Abdul joined him but said nothing. Avraham watched the surging water and tried to time his jump. He leapt as a gray wave was cresting. His feet skidded on the slick wooden grating, and he had to grab the broad handrail to keep from falling. The wave swept upward, stopping at his knees, threatening to sweep him into the icy Channel. He shivered as the wave retreated, allowing the bitter wind to cut through his drenched pants. He struggled awkwardly up the ladder before the next wave hit. Abdul made a surefooted leap and rushed nimbly up the ladder before a wave could catch him. The captain of the *Ville du Havre* waited for them at the top of the ladder.

Mustafa Mirza slouched in the beat-up wooden chair, his right eye blueblack and almost swollen shut from the beating he had endured the previous day. The small room had a single, naked bulb that hung from an electric cord directly over his head. A small, tipsy table stood on wobbly legs, not for *his* use, but for his inquisitors. The Turks had interrogated him continuously since transporting him to Ankara. Obviously, since he was a Kurd, they suspected he was up to no good. What did Kurds want except an independent Kurdistan? He had told them everything, but it had been to no avail.

The lock in the ancient door clicked, and a crack appeared, then widened, revealing the dimly lit corridor. A Turkish officer wearing a neat uniform entered. About five-ten and of average build, he had olive skin and a large, well-trimmed mustache. He carried a single file folder, which he placed on the table. The officer glanced at his chair as if determining its cleanliness, then sat down. He opened the folder and quickly skimmed the two typewritten pages inside. This man, Mustafa knew, was not an ordinary security thug.

"You are Mustafa Mirza?" the officer inquired in excellent Kurdish.

Mustafa nodded, wondering, not for the first time, why interrogators insisted on asking questions to which they already knew the answers. But he knew it did not pay to be flippant.

"And you are from Parakh in northern Iraq." The officer twitched his mustache slightly as his dark brown eyes bored into the Kurdish teenager.

Mustafa was aware his interrogator knew the difference between Iraq and Kurdistan. "Yes," he said, his voice barely audible.

The officer tapped the folder. "According to this report, a strange sickness swept through your village about a week after a helicopter flew over. The sickness killed everyone except you, and you were very ill. Then bombers came back and destroyed your village with napalm. After that, they destroyed the two villages nearest yours — everything within roughly thirty miles. Is that correct?"

Mustafa nodded.

The officer raised his voice slightly. "I said, 'Is that correct?' "

"Yes, sir," the Kurd answered quickly. He knew the Turks were as impatient with Kurds as the Iraqis were. "That is correct."

The officer's scowl changed to something Mustafa could not read. "Do you know what biological warfare is?"

Mustafa fumed but was very careful not to show it. Why did the Turks and Iraqis believe Kurds were incapable of understanding anything? "Yes, I know what it is, just as I know about chemical and nuclear warfare. The Iraqis have used chemicals and biological weapons against us many times."

The Turk considered this for a few moments. "Yes, they have — against Kurds and against other peoples as well. But this is new. This agent, whatever it is, incubates quickly, is extremely contagious, and is nearly 100 percent lethal." He paused as lines of worry etched deep furrows in his brow. "I suspect this agent works better than expected. So good, the Iraqis were afraid of what would happen if an epidemic got started."

A chill ran down Mustafa's spine as he considered this. Then his thoughts turned back to more practical problems. "Sir, when will you let me go? I have done nothing against your people or your laws."

The officer regarded the pleading brown eyes for only a moment. Then he closed the folder, got up, and left the room.

"Thank you for coming over," Dennis Hastings said as he got up.

Mars shook hands with the MI5 agent as he and Anne took their seats before his desk.

"After yesterday, I thought we were all done," Mars said, his tone verging on irritation.

Dennis attempted a laugh, but it betrayed his nervousness. "I wish we were. Believe me, nothing would please me better than for you two to enjoy the rest of your honeymoon and leave the spook work to us. But somehow you keep popping up."

. "Why are we so lucky?" Mars asked dryly.

Dennis chose to ignore the comment. "One more question, if you don't mind. Did Fadel Barrak give you anything besides the computer — a piece of paper, an envelope, anything?"

"We answered that before. All he gave us was the computer."

"Well, did he say anything?"

"As we said before, he told us he wanted us to keep his computer for him for the screwball reason he gave. We've been over this more than once, and I've seen you take it down, and it's all on tape. What more do you want?"

"Please forgive me," Dennis said, obviously distressed. "I assure you, this is extremely important, so we must make absolutely sure we have all the information. I can't take anything for granted."

"I don't see what the problem is," Mars observed.

Dennis prodded a folder on his desk with a pen as he thought. "Since you know about the secret nuclear lab, I suppose there's no harm. I was sure we would discover its location somewhere on the hard disk. After all, that's what he was trying to sell to the Americans."

"*We're* Americans," Mars pointed out.

A red line crept up Dennis's neck. "Er, yes, of course you are. You know what I mean. But blast it — the information isn't there, and we have looked *everywhere*. We've dissected all the files, even looked in the boot sector and all the system and hidden files. We even took the computer apart to see if anything was hidden among the parts — and found nothing!"

"I presume you have looked for encryption," Mars said.

"I assure you, we *do* know how to do this," Dennis said in irritation.

"Just checking."

"What would you know about that anyway?"

"I'm a pretty good hacker. I spent a fair amount of time probing the secure areas on the Southern Methodist University computers, seeing if I could get past security."

Anne's mouth dropped open. "Mars, I didn't know you did things like that."

He glanced at his wife, wincing at her obvious shock. "I don't anymore. That was during my undergraduate days." The tension lines changed to a smile. "I'm a good boy now." He recognized the look on her face. There would be further discussions about this later.

Dennis considered the young man as he continued tapping nervously on the folder on his desk. "Would you like to talk to our man who headed up the investigation team?"

"The chief wizard?"

"I guess you could call him that. Man by the name of George Foxworthy. Brilliant chap, but a little eccentric. Knows his stuff, I assure you. I could take you to his lab — save you a trip back in."

Mars glanced at Anne. He could see she was resigned to this further encroachment on their time together. It clearly wasn't what they wanted, but he couldn't quite talk himself into not helping.

"I guess so," Mars said finally. "I doubt there's anything I can add, but it can't hurt."

Dennis threw the pen down. "I'm sure you're right, but we do want to be thorough. Please come with me, and I'll take you back to meet George."

Dennis led them through narrow corridors to the back of the building, to a door with a frosted glass panel. He rapped once on the glass and pushed on the door without waiting for an answer. The door swung open, revealing a brightly-lit laboratory with long workbenches cluttered with disemboweled electronic devices and sophisticated test equipment hovering over them.

"Ah, you're in," Dennis said. He introduced George Foxworthy to the Americans and told the technician why they were there. "Now, since I am the leading technophobe in MI5, I will leave you people to discuss what I don't understand and don't wish to know. George will show you out when you're done." The relief on his face said he was glad to escape. "It's good-bye then." He shook Mars's hand and left.

George rounded up two tall work stools. Anne struggled up into hers, while Mars sat down with ease, propping his feet on the circular band that went around the legs. The swivel bearing squealed a little as he turned to the side.

George could not hide his contempt. "So, the Yanks are here to save our bacon, as you would say."

"I didn't say that, and this was your boss's idea, not mine. If we can help, well and good. But it's *your* problem, not ours."

"Quite so," George said, drawing back some. "So, word has it you two are archaeologists. Might I ask what your computer expertise is? Writing word processor macros perhaps?"

Mars let out a laugh of understanding; he

knew what was bothering the Englishman. Many people believed themselves to be computer experts if they could boot the machine or install a new application without calling the manufacturer's help line.

"I said something funny?" George inquired.

Mars's eyes narrowed. "I bet you have a T-shirt that says 'Real Programmers Write Assembler.' "

"As a matter of fact, I do. Do you speak Hex?"

"Hexadecimal," Mars intoned, as if reading from a dictionary, "adjective: 1, of, relating to, or based on the number 16; 2, a number system used by people with sixteen fingers. In answer to your question: Hex seven nine, six five, seven three."

Mars grinned as George tilted his head back in thought. He wondered if the man would whip out a programmer's calculator or a chart of computer codes. To his credit, he did neither.

"Very good, Mr. Enderly."

"Please call me Mars."

"Mars," the other repeated. "Hexadecimal codes for y-e-s in lowercase, from memory. I'm impressed. And do you program in assembler?"

"Microsoft Assembler, yes."

' "Ah, an Intel bigot, I take it."

"I prefer the PC, yes. And I don't believe the computer Fadel Barrak gave me had a Technicolor apple on it with a bite missing."

"Right you are, old thing. Well now, I do believe we speak the same language. Done a bit of hacking in your time, have you?"

Mars glanced at Anne, who was obviously having trouble keeping up. But the word "hacking" had registered, he saw.

"Not anymore," he said quickly. "Undergraduate days, don't you know."

"Hmm, I see. Shall I give you a rundown on what we've found, or rather not found?"

At Mars's nod, George described the computer and what they had done to it. The computer was an IBM ThinkPad, the latest in a long line of popular Big Blue portables. This one had a bright active matrix color display, a CD-ROM drive, a 10.2 gigabyte hard drive, a built-in fax modem, and all the other necessities required by those with larger than average pocketbooks. One glance at the screen told Mars it was running Windows 2000, the latest 32 bit protected mode, multitasking operating system from Microsoft.

George played with the pencil eraser pointing device before pushing the Think-Pad away. "Mars, we've boldly gone where no techie has ever gone before — and found nothing. We've looked in every file, and I mean *every single one.*" He emphasized each point with a tap from an oscilloscope probe. "There's nothing on that ten-gig drive except the operating system and Microsoft Office 2000, and not even the Professional version of that. As far as we can tell, there are no user files and only a few leftover temporary ones. Our friend Fadel wasn't really using this laptop for anything useful."

Mars puffed out his cheeks as he thought. "According to Dennis, Fadel was trying to sell the location of a secret Iraqi nuclear lab. Logically, the location must be stored in the PC."

"Show me where. There's nothing in the files. We even took the computer apart, including removing all the chips — even the soldered-in ones. We examined every square millimeter with a microscope. There's nothing there — no microdots, no inscribed rice grains, nothing. Now, what can you add to that?"

Mars whistled. "Nothing probably. And I must say I'm impressed with your thoroughness. But there's one thing that bugs me — if there's nothing in the PC and Fadel wasn't really using it for anything, why did he bring it out of Iraq?"

"Good question. The only reason I can think of is camouflage. The PC fit his ostensible reason for being in Great Britain."

"Makes sense, I guess."

George saw the American's hesitation. "But you don't buy it."

"No, I don't feel comfortable with it," Mars admitted.

George swiveled his chair back and forth. "I don't either," he agreed.

Anne looked at the flying toasters flitting across the PC screen. She started to say something, then stopped.

"What is it?" Mars asked.

"This isn't my field, but I was wondering if the technicians noticed anything unusual about this PC. I know it's a silly question, but . . ."

"Not silly at all," George replied. "That's exactly what we were looking for — something out of the ordinary. We've checked this thing out right down to the serial numbers on the parts. It's true Blue, as they say."

"What does that mean?"

"It's stock IBM," Mars translated.

"And it performs according to spec," George added, "give or take."

"What do you mean by that?" Anne wondered.

"All computers have minor variances from

technical specifications. You know — timings slightly off, a defective transistor or two, those sorts of things. This PC has its share of those, but nothing to keep it from working. The most serious problem is some kind of defect in one of the video chips. The display adapter won't operate in a few of the more unusual video modes. But those modes are almost never used, so it doesn't affect how the PC works."

Anne frowned. "Isn't that unusual?"

"Not at all," George replied with a laugh. "Video adapters are very reliable, but they sometimes break, like anything else. When they do, they sometimes keep working in some of their modes."

Anne tried to hide her uneasiness. "What if it's broken because something is hidden inside it?"

George scrunched up his face. "As I said, we checked each board and chip, right down to the manufacturer's labeling. All the parts are authentic."

Anne looked into his eyes without flinching. "But what if someone took off a chip and put something inside it?"

Mars swiveled his stool and looked at his wife. "That's an interesting thought. I wonder if you *could* dig into a chip and put something in it without breaking it — or at least not breaking it completely."

George watched them both for a few moments. "I don't think so," he said cautiously. "But lest we be accused of not turning over every stone . . ."

He grabbed the phone and punched in an extension number. Moments later a thin man in a white lab coat came in, took the computer, and disappeared without a word.

"He didn't look too happy," Mars observed.

"Can't really blame him," George said. "He's already taken that thing completely apart once. He's not looking forward to doing it again." He forced a smile and stood. "Right. Well, there you are — we'll either find something or we won't. Thank you ever so much for your help."

As George escorted the Americans to the receptionist, Mars suspected their host was in a hurry to get rid of his guests. The good-byes were polite, and the young lady at the desk was prompt in calling for a taxi. Mars and Anne finally relaxed as they sat down in the backseat and tried to enjoy the ride back to the Regent Palace Hotel.

7

THE BABYLONIAN WALL

Mars looked past Nelson's Column on Trafalgar Square at what he had assumed was their destination. The pigeons swirled away as he and Anne walked past the hulking bronze lions guarding his lordship's slim pedestal. Their brisk pace faded to an uncertain stroll, and the warm afterglow of sunset was unfortunately overlooked. Mars knew they were lost, but he didn't want to admit it.

"Is that St. Martin's Theater?" Anne asked, pointing at the stone building across the street.

Mars stopped in disgust. "No. It's St. Martin-in-the-Fields. Blast it!"

"Now, dear, we'll find it. There's still time. Perhaps we should ask someone where it is."

Mars's glance told her this was not what he wanted to hear. "Why can't they be more explicit when they print their tourist maps?

All it said was 'St. Martin.' "

Anne pointed to a figure standing in front of the National Gallery. "There's a policeman over there."

"They're called 'bobbies,' " Mars said in irritation.

But she had already turned around, and he had to hurry to catch up. They waited for the traffic to clear, then dashed across the street. The bobby, stationed securely beneath his high, black hat, seemed to tower over Mars. Stern eyes evaluated the Americans as they approached, reminding Anne of God's pronouncement on Belshazzar: "You have been weighed in the balances and found wanting." This tickled her, and she gave a short, startled laugh before she could stop it.

"I fail to see what's so funny," Mars snapped in irritation. "I can't help it if the stupid map is wrong."

Anne ducked her head. She hoped Mars would not see the tears brimming in her eyes. "I wasn't laughing at you, dear — I would never do that. I *love* you."

Mars sneaked an embarrassed glance at the bobby, whose manner had become even more severe. He tried to forget the man as his eyes drifted back to his wife. Though he had not meant to, he knew his temper had wounded the one he loved most in all the world. "I'm sorry, dear. Could we discuss this later?"

She nodded without looking up.

Mars sighed and turned back to the policeman. "We're looking for St. Martin's Theater."

The steely gaze remained. "Bit off our track, are we?"

"Do you know where it is?" Mars asked, biting off each word.

"Yes, sir," the man admitted.

"Would you be so kind as to tell us where it is?"

The man rattled off directions that Mars only half comprehended, paying more attention to the bobby's darting forefinger as he jabbed in the rough direction of their destination. Mars thanked him through clenched teeth and guided Anne off.

They found the theater without further trouble and were seated a few minutes before the curtain went up. The house lights went down, and Agatha Christie's *The Mouse Trap* began yet another presentation.

Mars turned to Anne when the curtain came down for the intermission. "Want to get up and . . . ?" He stopped when he saw a familiar face. "Oh, no. What did we do to deserve this?"

"What is it?" Anne asked, but she immediately understood. Ya'acov Isaacson was standing in the aisle.

"Do you suppose he'll go away if we ignore him?" Mars asked.

Ya'acov motioned for them to come out.

Anne couldn't help a short giggle. "I don't think so. We'd better see what he wants."

The IDF officer headed for the exit as soon as he saw them following. He waited for them in a pale pool of light below an iron streetlight.

"How did you find us? We are supposed to be on our honeymoon," Mars said, anxious to get the first word in.

"I am well aware of that," the Israeli said with a laugh. "Your travel agent was kind enough to fax me your itinerary. Just thought you'd like to know that your idea about something being hidden in a computer chip turned out to be right. The Brits found a ROM circuit containing a map of the secret lab. Whoever put it in the chip really knew what he was doing — they said it was impossible to tell by looking at it."

"I suppose Dennis will be wanting to see us again."

Ya'acov chuckled. "You have much to learn about Intelligence, my friend. You won't hear from any of the services now that they have what they want. You two have served your purposes. So you are completely free to continue your honeymoon."

Mars looked at the man, trying to read his expression under the feeble light. "Then why are you here?"

Ya'acov glanced around. "I'm not here officially. This is FYI, so please don't mention this to anyone."

"No, of course we won't."

"You two enjoy yourselves."

He shook their hands and walked into the night.

Avraham Abbas pushed open the door to the bridge, strolled in, and took up his station beside the helmsman as if he had every right to be there. Abdul Suleiman joined his boss in front of the large plate-glass windows. The *Ville du Havre*'s master viewed them with Gallic disdain but said nothing. He had been well paid for their passage, and he would be rid of them soon enough. He ordered the engines ahead one-third as the French freighter entered the Shatt al Arab, the 120-mile river channel formed by the confluence of the Tigris and Euphrates Rivers, long contested by Iraq and Iran but now grudgingly shared by both. In a little more than sixty miles they would be at Al Basrah and he would see them no more.

It had been a long and boring trip for Avraham. The small freighter had taken a leisurely week in navigating through the Mediterranean, the Suez Canal, the Red Sea, the Gulf of Aden, the Arabian Sea, and finally the Persian Gulf. What the ship was carrying, besides the illegal passengers, the Palestinians had no idea, though they guessed, from the presence of the guards, that it was not a peaceful cargo.

The faithful diesel engines thudded away below decks, transmitting a barely perceptible vibration up into the superstructure. The captain gave occasional terse orders to the helmsman as they forged their watery trail up the ship channel, making frequent course corrections to stay clear of the occasional ship and the much more common *dhows*, which appeared to have no understanding whatsoever of the naval rules of the road. These encounters occasioned fierce blasts of the ship's whistle and vigorous observations delivered in heated French punctuated by a flailing fist.

Hours later, in the slanting rays of the setting sun, the *Ville du Havre* tied up at Al Basrah. Avraham's concern that they would not be met at the dock evaporated when he saw the black limousine pull onto the pier. President Hammad Talfah was expecting them. Avraham smiled in anticipation. He had good news for the president.

The drive to Baghdad was long but comfortable, the powerful Mercedes relentlessly chewing up the desolate miles as it plunged through the darkness. They roared past Babylon around 11 and not long after pulled into the capital itself. The traffic was light, and the driver wove the limousine through it with no regard for signals or speed limits. After making a final turn, he brought the car to a rapid but smooth stop at the front entrance to the Presidential Palace.

A man rushed up to Avraham's door and pulled it open. The Palestinian recognized him as one of Talfah's aides.

"The president is waiting for you," the man said in a rush.

Avraham and Abdul rushed into the palace after him and up to the second floor. They entered a large room that had chairs around the perimeter and several low tables. Hammad Talfah stopped in mid-pace and turned on a smile that partially obscured his earlier scowl.

"Well," he said striding toward them, "you're finally here. Welcome back." He hugged both men and nodded to the aide, who promptly disappeared. "Please have a seat."

Hammad took a large, straight-backed chair in the closest corner. Avraham and Abdul sat across from him. "I have the reports, but I want to hear it from you," the president said. "This traitor, Barrak, is dead?"

"He is, Your Excellency," Avraham responded.

"Good. And you have the map."

Avraham pulled the map from his coat pocket and extended it to his superior. Hammad opened it, scanned it for a few moments, then stuffed it into a pocket.

"Did you look at it?" he asked casually.

"No, Your Excellency. In strict obedience to your instructions, we found the traitor and killed him. Fortunately he had the map on him."

"Good work, my friends. And now I am sure you are ready for your next assignment."

"How may we be of service?" Avraham asked.

"I am assigning you to special duty with the security forces in Babylon. With all the plans I have for restoring Nebuchadnezzar's capitol, it is essential that we maintain the highest security. I know your backgrounds, and you are both perfect for the job. I promise I will take excellent care of you — in payment for what you've already done and for this new work."

"You are most kind," Avraham answered for both of them.

"I assure you, I will not forget your accomplishments. Now, I'm sure you will want to get settled in as soon as possible. My driver is waiting downstairs. He will take you to the Presidential Guest House at Babylon. You will both have rooms there for this tour of duty."

It was after midnight when the limousine entered Babylon. They made several turns, continuing on until Avraham and Abdul could see the security lights reflecting off the Euphrates River. The heavy car turned into the parking lot behind the Guest House. Two Toyota Land Cruisers and a four-wheel-drive pickup were parked at the curb under the harsh mercury vapor lights. The driver helped the Palestinians with their bags, then drove away.

"Nothing like feeling welcome," Avraham grumbled.

The door at the back of the Guest House banged open, and a guard carrying an AK-47 came down the steps.

"Are you Avraham Abbas and Abdul Suleiman?" the man demanded.

"Did you get a call from Baghdad about us?" Avraham asked.

"Yes."

"Then who else do you think would be arriving at this hour in the president's limousine?"

The man started to say something but decided not to. "Come with me please."

He operated the keypad on the door, entered, and punched the elevator button for the second floor.

"Except for the rear entrance, the entire first floor is reserved for the president," the man said as they waited.

The door opened, and they rode up to the second floor.

"The second floor is ours," the man continued as they stepped out. "We have offices and sleeping quarters here. You two will share an office and will stay right here."

The man opened two doors, revealing small but neat rooms. His duty done, he departed. Avraham nodded to Abdul and entered his room. He threw himself down on the small bed fully clothed. Moments later he was fast asleep.

Ghanim Jassim tried to relax as the Toyota

Land Cruiser ate up the short distance between Baghdad and Babylon. The impatient passenger squirmed around trying to arrange the ample girth suspended from his five foot ten frame in a somewhat comfortable posture, but he failed in the attempt. A full frown settled on his pockmarked face, and his thick mustache twitched. His dark brown eyes glowered out at the desert landscape as if it were to blame. But it wasn't. President Hammad Talfah was.

Only yesterday Ghanim had been happily supervising a promising dig near the ancient site of Nineveh in northern Iraq — Kurdistan, according to the local inhabitants. The Iraqi archaeologist snorted when he thought of the location. The Kurds, although they weren't being particularly troublesome at the moment, still tended to keep the government away from the site. And so far President Talfah had shown no interest in rebuilding Nineveh on its ancient foundations as had been the case with Babylon, at least not on a large scale. Ghanim let out an unusually pungent oath that the driver wisely chose to ignore.

The Land Cruiser made a screeching turn off the highway and onto the main entrance to Babylon. They drove past the Greek Theater and the Hammurabi Museum and turned right on Procession Street. They turned left before Nebuchadnezzar's Southern Palace and drove across the nearly empty parking lot, down to a mound of dirt near the back of the huge building. The driver brought the vehicle to a sudden stop and waited for his passenger to get out.

Ghanim tugged the door open and stepped heavily to the pavement. He glared at the palace for a few moments, then stalked to the edge of the pit. He put his hands to his bulging hips and looked down, finally removing his sunglasses so he could see into the shadows. Only then did the earlier irritation begin to melt away as he looked down on the ancient remains of a wall, amazingly preserved except where the backhoe bucket had smashed through it.

The archaeologist looked around with renewed anger. There at the edge of the parking lot was the cause of the scientific desecration. The idiots had been in the process of laying a fiber-optic cable across the pavement, that being more important than any archaeological finds underneath, at least as far as the government was concerned. And whatever else was buried under all this modern construction, he grumbled to himself as he knelt beside the hole.

"Hold this," he ordered.

A worker dropped his shovel and grabbed the top of an aluminum ladder. Ghanim stepped gingerly onto the top rung and descended slowly into the pit. He examined what little he could see of the wall, fingering the kiln-fired brick. One side of the wall was covered with a thick coat of plaster. He looked at the ancient masonry for a long time, not saying anything, but his eyes were moving constantly. Finally he decided, *Yes, this is worth putting Nineveh off for a while.*

The British Airways 737 arrived at Ben Gurion International Airport at 5:10 P.M., precisely on time. Passengers all around Mars and Anne tugged their possessions out of the crammed overhead bins as they prepared to stagger down the narrow aisles. Mars and Anne joined the slow-moving line as it crept forward. They forced smiles for the cheerful attendants at the door. Then they were down the ladder and onto the waiting tram for the trip to the main terminal.

In minutes they were inside and ready to present their landing cards. They made it through passport control, collected their luggage, and headed out into the arrival area. It was impossible to miss the beaming face behind the bushy black beard. Moshe Stein grabbed Mars's left hand and pumped it vigorously, giving Joe Enderly a chance to hug his daughter-in-law.

"So how was the honeymoon?" Moshe asked.

Mars's smile disappeared. "Dad told you what happened, didn't he?"

Moshe traded glances with Joe. "Yes, he called me right after you phoned him the first time," the Israeli replied. "That really scared me. I thought we had seen the last of those two after the tank battle below Golan."

"I wish," Mars said with feeling.

Moshe fell in step with Mars as Joe led the way toward the parking garage. Anne struggled to match the long-legged strides of her husband. Abruptly he remembered to slow down. Quickly, like a little bird, her soft hand darted into his. He gave it a quick, contented squeeze.

A dark scowl settled on Moshe's face. "I wish we were done with them too, Mars. This new run-in kept Joe and me busy for quite a while."

Joe cleared his throat nervously.

"Wait a minute," Mars said slowly. He tried to catch Moshe's eye but couldn't. "You didn't have anything to do with the IDF sending Ya'acov and Ari to England, did you?"

"They are both very good at what they do," Moshe replied.

"The influential Dr. Stein strikes again," Mars announced, trying to keep a straight face.

"Ya'acov helped us when no one else would," Anne reminded them, remembering her kidnapping. It seemed like something from another lifetime, but it was all too recent.

Mars took a deep breath and let it out slowly. "Yes, he did," he admitted. He smiled at his new wife. "I have him to thank for getting you back."

"Him and a few others," Anne reminded him.

A line of red crept above Mars's collar. "Yes, I know. Moshe, I appreciate all you did." He glanced at his father as he struggled with old feelings. "And, Dad, I especially appreciate you dropping everything and coming to help."

Joe shrugged. "You're welcome, Mars. After all, we're talking about my sweet daughter-in-law." He paused, watching the complex emotions race over his son's face. "I don't know what else to say except that I love you, son — and I love my new daughter too."

"I know that, Dad. Thank you."

They walked out of the terminal into the late-afternoon sun.

"Your father and I had a long discussion on which vehicle to bring," Moshe reported. "Naturally, I knew you two would expect to see my van." He watched their look of horror as they remembered the battered, blue Volkswagen bus. "But since Joe still has the Safari, we came in that."

Anne sighed in relief.

"It's a good thing my feelings aren't hurt easily," Moshe said.

The Israeli put the bags in the back of the big GMC while Mars and Anne got in the backseat. Joe wheeled the Safari onto the highway to Jerusalem.

"I kept my suite at the American Colony," Joe announced as he maintained his pace with the aggressive Israeli drivers. "Got a room for the two of you until you decide what you want to do."

"Dad, you didn't have to do that," Mars grumbled.

"Oh, hush up," Joe said, careful to keep his tone light. "I did it for Anne. You can sleep out on the street if you want."

"I can put a cot in the van," Moshe suggested.

Mars glanced at Anne, who was trying not to laugh.

"I think that's sweet, dear," she said.

"I guess I'm outvoted," Mars conceded.

Joe craned his neck until he could see his son in the rearview mirror. "Son, you have my respect. Believe me, I'm not trying to run your life. I just want to do something for the newlyweds. But if you would rather make your own arrangements, I understand."

Mars sat there thinking as the big American car ate up the distance to Jerusalem. "Thank you, Dad," he said at last. "We accept." Anne squeezed his hand.

Joe slowed down as Sederot Weizmann brought them into West Jerusalem.

"Oh, Anne," he said, "I had a wonderful time visiting with your folks. We did the tourist thing after we got you two packed off on your honeymoon. I'm glad they were able to take the extra time. Gave us the chance to get to know each other. You have some fine parents. I see character runs in the family."

Anne blushed. "Thank you. The older I get, the more I appreciate them. They're just hard-working country people."

"That's the kind of people our nation was built on. I told them I would like to come visit sometime."

Anne couldn't help laughing. "Lorenzo

isn't exactly the garden spot of Texas." A gleam came to her eye. "Do you know where it is?"

Joe's smile grew wider. "Touché, young lady. When I first heard it, I didn't — I had to consult an atlas. Now I know it's a small cotton farming community east of Lubbock. But it's real enough now — I know three people from there. Bob and I had some good discussions about farming and life on the high plains."

"You enjoyed it?"

"Yes, I did."

"I would call it fascinating," Moshe interjected.

Anne turned to him. "Why is that? Growing up, I found it anything *but* fascinating. It was so flat — nothing between you and the horizon — hot in the summer, cold in the winter, and windy all the time. It was a hard life for the small farmers, and that's all there were around us."

"Ah, but the wide, open spaces are what make it fascinating. You took it for granted. Look at Israel. It's a little over 250 miles from Metulla in the north to Eilat on the Gulf of Aqabah, and only forty-five miles from Tel Aviv to the Jordan River. How does that compare with Texas, let alone the United States? We are a tiny country surrounded on all sides by those who at best tolerate us and at worst want to destroy us, regardless of what the peace treaties say."

"I seem to remember something about that," Mars grumbled as he remembered Anne's abduction.

Anne frowned. "Having been through that, I see what Moshe means. It was peaceful where I grew up, and there certainly wasn't any lack of space. I remember going out at sunrise with nothing between me and the horizon but clear air. I could turn all around the compass and not see anything but flat land and an occasional tree."

Moshe nodded. "As the Brits would say, 'There you have it.' "

Joe maneuvered the large GMC through the heavy Jerusalem traffic with the aggressiveness of a native, the other drivers showing due respect for the massive vehicle bearing down on them. Joe turned north at Derekh Shekhem and a few blocks later into the American Colony's drive.

"Care to come up to my room?" he asked Moshe. "I'm sure the young folks don't want any company."

"Dad!" Mars said in embarrassment.

Joe looked him in the eye. "Do you?"

Mars cleared his throat nervously. "Er, no, I guess not."

"I assure you, as your former *yenta,* I understand," Moshe rumbled before turning to Joe. "I would like to join you, but I have some unfinished business at the *geniza.* We're about to turn the site over to Samuel Kretzmer's group so they can start building their hotel."

"So that's still on?" Mars asked.

"Oh, yes. They had to change the plans to accommodate our find, but the hotel will go up. The entrance to the *geniza* will be in a little courtyard, and part of the first floor has become a portico to preserve the marble floor and wall. The model I saw was quite attractive. The designs do as much as possible to protect and enhance the find."

"It could have been worse, I guess," Anne said with a sigh.

"Indeed it could," Moshe agreed. "We're not building on top of ancient foundations like they're doing in Babylon, for example."

"I'd rather forget Iraq after what's happened," Mars said.

"I don't blame you. Like to see the site one more time? I'll be there tomorrow around 9 — if that's not too early." His face took on a serious look that was betrayed by the twinkle in his eye.

Anne glanced at her husband, remembering their two lives were one now. He smiled and nodded. "We'd love to."

"See you then." He pulled their bags out of the Safari and looked at Mars's good arm.

"We can make it," Mars assured him.

Moshe shrugged and walked to his battered blue Volkswagen bus. He struggled with the driver's side door, which finally opened with an agonized groan of unlubricated hinges. He had to slam it twice before the latch caught. The engine ground for several moments before it came to life and settled into a noisy idle. A substantial blue cloud formed around the engine compartment. Moshe waved at them as he drove off.

"Some things never change," Mars said.

"We can hope," Anne said.

8

A NEW OPPORTUNITY

"Looks a lot different, doesn't it?" Moshe asked as Mars and Anne made their cautious way through the plywood door guarding the construction site. A high wooden barrier sealed off the ancient tile floor and the *geniza* from the Street of the Chain, which led to the Wailing Wall.

"I'll say," Mars said as he dodged a worker pushing a wheelbarrow. "They move fast."

"Once I told Samuel we were done, his crews were here the following morning."

"But you're *not* done," Mars said, looking to the Israeli for confirmation. "Are you?"

A tight smile came to Moshe's face. "Near enough. Everything has been removed from the *geniza*. We'll be busy analyzing and cataloging it all for several years, but it doesn't have to be done here. And Samuel does a fairly decent job of protecting the architectural artifacts. It's not a perfect situation, but I can live with it."

"It's hard giving it up, isn't it?" Anne said quietly.

Moshe sighed and nodded. "Yes, it is. Like to take one final look at the *geniza?*"

He turned and led them across the familiar black and white pavers. They descended the 2,000-year-old stairs and entered the cool recesses of the huge room cut out of Jerusalem limestone. The *geniza* was empty now except for work lights and a half-dozen director's chairs.

"Wow!" Mars exclaimed. "When you said 'everything,' you meant it. How did you get the stone boxes out?"

"It wasn't easy," Moshe admitted as he motioned for them to sit down. "But every time I thought about complaining, I remembered the first-century Jews who brought them down here. If they could do that without modern machinery, surely I could get the confounded things out."

"So that's that," Mars said.

"Except for writing the papers, yes," Moshe confirmed. He propped his chin on his hands as he regarded the Americans. "I had planned on asking a certain question when we got to this point, but your sudden marriage tangled up my picks and shovels, so to speak."

"Regretting your job as *yenta?*" Mars

asked. "If you're looking for sympathy, forget it."

Moshe lifted his head and sprawled back in the chair, causing the canvas back to make ominous popping noises. "Me regret that? Ha! Let me tell you, Mars Enderly — and Mrs. Enderly — that gave me more pleasure than you will ever know." He shrugged. "But with the blessing comes the consequences. True? Of course true!"

"What question were you going to ask?" Anne inquired.

Moshe's eyes took on a faraway look. "I just wanted to know if you two would like to join an ancient Jewish archaeologist on another dig sometime, before he retires to the nursing home." He rocked his head back as if he had decided to examine the ceiling. Anne noted the glistening eyes.

She turned to her husband. "Dear, we really need to discuss our career plans soon. There's no reason we can't start now, especially since we have Moshe's expert advice. Your degree plan is the most important consideration, but we both need to plan our next dig."

"Yeah, I know," Mars replied. "I didn't really want to think about it — er, especially right now."

Anne smiled. She considered poking him

with her foot but decided not to.

"Having a good time, are we?" Moshe asked with a wide grin, his composure fully restored.

"What can I say? You did good, Dr. Stein."

Moshe rocked back in his chair again. "That's what every *yenta* longs to hear."

"If we could get back on the subject?" Anne reminded them.

"Which is?" Mars asked.

"Your degree plan. I think we can say you passed your course, although I don't know what Southern Methodist University is going to say about us getting married."

"Yeah, I doubt they expected that."

"That's probably putting it mildly. But the question remains — what next?"

"Back to Dallas and start cranking out the courses and working on my thesis, I guess."

"That would be a reasonable course," Anne admitted.

Mars caught the hesitation. "Did you have something else in mind?"

"You have enough elective hours for another dig, don't you?"

"Yeah. In fact, I had sort of planned on one next summer."

"The suspense is killing me," Moshe whispered.

Anne ignored him. "Well, we could continue here." She cocked an eye at Moshe. "I know an Israeli archaeologist who would probably help us. He's eccentric and crotchety, but he really knows his stuff. Want me to check?"

"First the students turn on me, now my colleagues. What have I done to deserve this?"

Mars squeezed Anne's hand. "Please do."

"Did you have something in mind?" she asked Moshe.

"As a matter of fact, I did. How would you two like to join a dig at Tell Kuyunjik — Nineveh?"

"What?" Mars exclaimed. "You mean in Iraq?"

"I believe that's where Nineveh is. Are we having trouble with our geography?"

"My geography's just fine. There's a certain bozo that hangs out in Baghdad that I'm not too fond of."

"Well, I wasn't planning on visiting *him*. There are some very important sites in Iraq. And things are much better now that the UN embargo's been lifted."

"I would be uneasy working on a site with the government breathing down my neck," Anne said.

"I understand," Moshe agreed. "But

Nineveh is in Kurdistan. The Iraqi government doesn't bother the sites up there — at least not now." He saw a spark of interest light up her eyes.

"Hmm. What exactly are we talking about?" she asked.

"Don't know for sure. They've found something near the Palace of Ashurbanipal. And I have this friend . . ."

"Is there anyone you *don't* know?" Mars asked.

Moshe tugged at his beard. "I do fairly well. The man's name is Ghanim Jassim, and he's absolutely top-notch."

"Could you let us think about it?" Anne asked.

"Of course."

"How long would it take to arrange, if we decide to do it?"

Moshe pursed his lips. "It's already arranged."

Anne rolled her eyes back.

"But nothing's cast in concrete," he added hurriedly. "If you two can't go, I will ask someone else. It's just that . . ."

Anne looked at the man as she wrestled with his complexity. "Thank you, Moshe. We feel the same way about you. We'll get back to you as soon as we can sort out the details."

"Dinner at my place?" he suggested.

Mars's grin saved Anne a question. She nodded.

"Good. I will invite Joe also." He fixed them both with a concerned expression. "And do not worry. We will not keep you there late. I know you have important things to take care of, and I certainly wouldn't think of interfering."

"How considerate," Mars remarked.

"Think nothing of it," Moshe assured him.

Joe, following Mars's directions, drove to Moshe's apartment on French Hill and parked. Mars looked out over the stair-step stone homes that clung to the gentle slope of the hill as memories of his last visit swept over him. His romance with Anne had been fresh and new, and it had seemed that everyone else was more interested in it than he and his fascinating teacher were. Now she was his wife. That was less than a year ago — much less, though it seemed ages. Mars led them to the second floor.

Moshe answered the door and brought them inside. The apartment had not changed. Mars and Anne saw the same worn couch and mismatched chairs surrounding the small coffee table. Large bookcases still covered most of the wall space, the shelves bowed by the weight. A framed photograph of Moshe's deceased wife and two boys looked down on the room, silent testimony to the peace that still eluded Israel. Anne glanced at the smiling faces in the grainy print and had to look away. She said nothing, and Moshe pretended not to see.

"Well, I see you remembered the way," he said to Mars.

"Spotting the blue bus helped."

"Hmm, it is rather conspicuous, isn't it?"

"Definitely. Whatever you're cooking smells wonderful."

Moshe beamed. "It's what we had last time. I find it hard to improve on. And since it's ready, shall we sit down?"

He led the way into the small dining room and seated his guests. They started with *humus* and pita bread followed by *shashlik,* grilled sliced lamb. The conversation was polite but subdued as everyone concentrated on the food.

Moshe cleared the table when they were through. He disappeared into the kitchen where he hummed to himself as he prepared the dessert and arranged it on a metal tray. He returned to the dining room and set large crystal parfait glasses at each place.

"Mars and Anne know the story behind

this," he told Joe. "Suffice it to say, this is chocolate mousse the way it should be." He rescued a large dollop of whipped cream that was trying to escape from his glass. He closed his eyes as he licked his finger. "Heavenly," he pronounced.

Joe stared at the mound of high-octane sweetness.

"Did I give you enough?" Moshe asked in mock alarm.

"This looks wonderful," Joe replied.

"It is," Moshe admitted. "Enjoy."

Spoons clicked repeatedly against the glasses as the mousse quickly disappeared. Moshe waited for the last person to finish, which turned out to be Anne.

"Seconds?" he asked as if this were a reasonable question.

"None for me," Joe said. "That's the best dessert I've ever had. Not even a five-star hotel can top that."

"Thank you," Moshe said. "I see we think alike."

"Moshe, do you really have more of that?" Mars asked.

"Of course," the Israeli replied, seeming hurt by the question. "It won't keep, you know, so I will have to finish it before I go to bed. Would you care for a refill?"

"No, thank you. Just checking."

"I see. Shall we retire to the living room? Make yourselves comfortable while I bring in the coffee."

Anne sat on the couch. Mars positioned himself next to her and, after a moment's thought, put his arm around her. Deciding he liked that, he settled back. Joe took one of the side chairs as Moshe brought in cups of Turkish coffee. After serving his guests, the Israeli took his cup and settled back in his well-worn chair opposite the couch.

"How are you finding Israel?" Moshe asked Joe.

"Delightful, as always. My company, Dallas Heuristics, has a contract with IAI — Israel Aircraft Industries. So after we got the newlyweds packed off on their honeymoon, I decided to put in a little close coordination time. We've done quite a bit of work for them over the years."

"Good. What's IAI up to now?"

"Afraid I can't say — highly classified. Highly classified and very stuffy. I'd rather hear about the dig you just finished." His eyes tightened slightly before he continued. "With everything that was going on, I never did hear many details."

Moshe told him how Mars had detected the hidden staircase leading down to the subterranean room and the magnificent mosaic of Herod's Temple, and also his persistence that had led to the discovery of the *geniza*. Inside had been a treasure-trove of Temple artifacts, stored because they were no longer fit for service — artifacts that had last seen the light of day early in the first century.

"You found the actual Temple veil?" Joe asked. "Put in there around — let's see, when did Titus sack Jerusalem — 80 A.D.?"

"It was 70 C.E.," Mars replied as if he were instructing a child. "The proper term is 'Common Era.'"

Moshe saw Anne flinch. "I think we all understand *'Anno Domini.'*" His broad smile defused Mars's momentary look of irritation. "In my professional opinion," he added slowly, "the veil was probably stored in the spring of the year 33. Stored in the *geniza* because it was torn in two — torn in two by God, according to three of the Gospels."

Anne looked at her Israeli friend, trying to fathom what was going on in his mind.

Joe could not hide his surprise. "Surely you don't believe that. Science has finally raised us above the need for superstition and fairy tales, thank goodness." His daughter-in-law's stricken expression troubled him.

Moshe's eyes roved the room, touching quickly on each of his guests. "As I teach my students, the Bible — the Law and the Prophets plus the Christian New Testament — is a pretty good book of history. It's the most reliable ancient book there is." He stroked his beard as he centered on Joe. "No one could offer a plausible explanation for how the veil got torn, other than what the Bible says."

"The guy who was investigating it . . ." Mars snapped his fingers as he tried to remember the name.

"Dr. Yitzhak Yadin," Moshe supplied.

"Yeah. He didn't think much of that explanation."

"And I believe we concluded he was not exactly an unbiased observer, especially after he hid the veil and tried to destroy it." Moshe watched submerged emotions ripple across Anne's face. "What are your thoughts?" he asked her.

"I remember you telling us that the Bible was a good book of history, but I didn't believe you. But then we found the veil, torn in two just like the Bible said. After the terrorists kidnapped me, I read the Bible Zuba Rosenberg had given me. I finally came to the conclusion that what the Gospels say is true — the only way to escape

God's judgment is to believe in His Son, Jesus Christ."

"Zuba has told me the same thing, on more than one occasion," Moshe said.

Anne looked at him in surprise. "He has?" She paused. "What did you make of it?"

"I don't know. At first it made me mad. *Why is this Jewish heretic trying to push his views onto me?* I said to myself. But I've gotten over that — he's a very good friend. I still don't know what to make of it, but I know it's a serious subject."

"Depends on your point of view," Mars grumbled.

Moshe frowned at him. "You have a precious wife, my friend." He started to say something else but stopped himself with obvious difficulty. "Come, come, we are all very good friends. You two don't know how much you mean to me — and I am getting to know Joe as well. Let there be peace — *shalom*."

Mars looked at Anne as if remembering who she was. The anger was gone, instantly replaced by sorrow over his callousness. "I'm sorry, dear. I didn't mean that."

She nodded as the tears trickled down her face. She pulled a tissue from her purse as she tried to assure herself that he was not mad at her. But somehow that was no comfort. In fact, it made her blood run ice-cold.

"Are you all right?" Mars asked.

Her first impulse was to lash out in anger. But something still and quiet seemed to urge caution. "I'll be O.K. Mars, I love you so much. I want you to find what I've found." She knew she was breaking their informal agreement not to discuss spiritual things, but she couldn't help herself.

He momentarily stiffened but then relaxed. "I love you too, Anne, you know that. And I *am* sorry I hurt you. Will you forgive me?"

"Of course I do," she said, wiping her nose.

Mars turned to Moshe. "I think we'd better be going."

"I understand. Take care of that sweet wife of yours."

They all stood in the awkwardness of a pleasant evening gone sour as each struggled for the socially proper way of dealing with the embarrassment. They said their good-byes as Joe led the way to the door.

Anne turned back as Joe opened the front door. "Oh, I almost forgot. Mars and I discussed the Nineveh site. We'd like to go."

A smile chased away Moshe's frown. "Wonderful. I was hoping you would join me."

"We still have to touch base with our universities, but I'm sure they will agree. Have you heard anything new from Dr. Jassim?"

The smile vanished. "No, I haven't. I called the Nineveh site, but he wasn't there. His assistant said he didn't know where he was, which struck me as odd. But not to worry — I will find him. You young folks have a nice evening — yes, I know it's just starting. Ah, the wonders of youth and love. I will call you tomorrow."

He turned to Joe. "Thank you for coming. I look forward to getting to know you better."

Moshe stood in the door until his guests were out of sight.

It had taken two days for Mars and Anne to contact their schools. After phoning ahead, they took a taxi to Moshe's Hebrew University office on Mount Scopus. They took the stairs to the second floor, where Mars rapped on the door with his left hand.

A deep "Come" sounded from within.

Mars turned the knob and pushed open the door. Moshe sprang to his feet and removed a beat-up cardboard box from one chair while Anne picked up a tall stack of books from the other.

"Where do you want me to put these?" she asked.

Moshe glanced around the jumbled office. Books were everywhere, including most of the floor. "Anywhere you find a place."

"That may not be easy," she said as she moved toward a stack near the door. She deposited the displaced books on top, squaring the unstable tower the best she could. She took her hands away and was amazed the books did not fall over.

"Very good," Moshe said. "Now please sit down." He returned to his swivel chair and rocked back. "I presume this visit is good news."

Mars nodded. "We called our schools. SMU said fine, and so did the tea-sippers."

Moshe smiled at the gentle gibe until he saw the look Anne delivered her husband. "Er, how did the University of Texas students get such a nickname — if that's not too personal a question?"

"I'm not sure," Anne admitted. "I think the Texas A & M students did it to get even for the Aggie jokes."

Moshe shook his head. "You people from Texas are feisty."

"We have an image to keep up," Mars agreed. "Anyhow, Anne and I have mailed confirming letters. They're going to treat the

Nineveh dig just like the one in Jerusalem. Have you found Dr. Jassim yet?"

Moshe made a steeple with his hands and peered out over them. "As a matter of fact I have. He is in Babylon."

"What's he doing there?" Mars asked.

"The Iraqis were laying a fiber-optic line across the parking lot beside the reconstruction of Nebuchadnezzar's Southern Palace when they cut across a wall. The local head archaeologist called in Ghanim. Ghanim's fairly certain the find dates from near the end of the Babylonian period, but he won't be certain until more work's been done. He wants us to join him there instead of Nineveh. Frankly, it sounds like a more promising site."

"Except that old Neb the Nut Junior will probably ruin it by building on top of whatever foundations they find, just like they've done in the past," Mars predicted gloomily.

"You are referring to his excellency, President Hammad Talfah?" Moshe asked in mock surprise.

"The very one. I don't know if I want to put in all that work and have some idiot mess it up."

"He seems to feel strongly about this," Moshe said to Anne. "How about you?"

Anne glanced at her husband. "I can't

accept if Mars is uncomfortable with it. I guess we need to discuss it."

"As your former *yenta*, I agree completely. But maybe I can reassure you a little. It won't be a perfect dig, but what dig is? We all have to deal with politics nowadays. But if Ghanim is right, this site has more potential than any other I know of right now. And Ghanim has enough clout to make sure we can document and report whatever we find."

"You keep saying 'we,' " Mars pointed out.

Moshe shrugged. "I'm sure we will all see eye to eye on this. We always have."

Anne looked at her Israeli friend and pursed her lips. "Something about this has puzzled me ever since you brought it up. Iraq isn't exactly Israel's friend. How . . . ?"

"How do we get this overweight Jew into Iraq without something unpleasant happening to various body parts?"

"I wouldn't put it quite that way," Anne replied.

Moshe laughed. "I know you wouldn't, but I can. It's a good question. Let me just say that I have an understanding with the Iraqi archaeological powers that be, and they have an understanding with the government. These digs are important, so it's quite possible to arrange for the official eye to be pointed elsewhere when I tiptoe past immigration. And getting out is not a problem, as long as you don't have the Ishtar Gate in your suitcase."

"Is there anything you *can't* arrange?" Mars asked.

"As long as it doesn't get political, I do fairly well," Moshe admitted. "And this, fortunately, is not political. So, does that reassure you? The important archaeology will get done, and Ghanim is fairly successful in protecting his sites."

"It *is* a fascinating period," Anne said.

Mars sighed and smiled as he saw Anne's interest. "O.K., I agree. If Dr. Stein says it will work, who am I to say no?"

"That's never stopped you before," Moshe observed. He held up his hands in surrender before Mars could rejoin. "Enough of this. We have planning to do, children."

9

EYES OF SECRECY

The captain in charge of the IDF photo intelligence lab shrugged. It was 2 in the morning, and his crew had long since left — there was nothing else to do. For a solid week the best analytical minds had pored over the digital image map liberated from the dead Iraqi's PC. It had been a week of absolute frustration as they had tried to pin down where in Iraq this secret lab was. But there just weren't enough details, and the Iraqis had not been considerate enough to include the longitude and latitude.

Ya'acov Isaacson nodded and watched in dejection as the officer departed, leaving the Intelligence officer alone with the sentry at the door. A few minutes later the buzzer sounded. The guard glanced at the security monitor, noted that the officer's security card had been accepted, and opened the door. Ari Jacovy slipped in and took the high work stool beside Ya'acov's.

"Find anything?" Ari asked without much hope.

Ya'acov groaned and pushed the map blowup away from him. "Not a thing."

"Too bad."

"So how come you're still up, Lieutenant? Having trouble sleeping?"

"As a matter of fact I am. Somehow I don't like the thought of President Talfah playing nuclear patty-cake without adult supervision."

"The General Staff doesn't care for it either, from what I've heard. I've been hearing a lot of talk about our raid on the Osirak reactor. Some of our hawks would love to do it again, if they knew where this thing was."

"Are you a hawk?"

Ya'acov's round face took on a semblance of a smile. "My, aren't we nosy. I don't know, to answer your question. I sure don't like unhinged dictators having nuclear weapons."

". . . or chemical or biological agents."

"True. But the nukes scare me more."

"The talk I hear about biologicals sounds pretty grim."

Ya'acov nodded. "You're right about that." He looked down and tapped the large map in front of him. "But this is a nuclear lab — it has all the earmarks."

He tapped the drawing with his pen. "Heavy containment wall with a vault-type main entrance. The whole thing is underground. And if this line is a river, that would allow for the transportation of heavy devices off the highway system, or water coolant in case they want to run a reactor."

"Could also be chemical or biological," Ari persisted.

Ya'acov tried not to get irritated with his friend. "Yes, I suppose it could. We certainly can't rule that out."

"Got any theories on where to look?" Ari asked, pushing his luck.

"It's somewhere in Iraq," Ya'acov snapped. He regretted it as soon as he saw his friend's reaction. "Sorry. It's been a bad day. O.K., it's in Iraq next to a road that ends at a river or a stream or a dry *wadi* or whatever that squiggly line is."

"What about the theory that Barrak almost told the Americans he was from Al Hillah?"

Ya'acov sighed. "Neither Mars nor Anne is sure what he said or if it really was a slipup. But let's say he said Al Hillah. If that's where the lab is, is it a base of operations or something totally unrelated? Ari, this is worse than looking for a needle in a haystack."

Ari nodded. "I know, I know. But let's assume it *is* Al Hillah. How does that — or something near there — fit the map?"

Ya'acov pulled the map back and compared it to the large-scale map on the wall. "O.K., if the lab *is* near Al Hillah, and if that *is* a river, it could be the Euphrates, I suppose."

Ari grinned at his friend's lack of confidence. "Or a dry *wadi*," he offered.

"Yeah, or a dry *wadi*. Ari, whose side are you on?"

But the lieutenant was studying the wall map. "Let's say it's the Euphrates. So, where could you hide a nuclear lab near Al Hillah?"

"Al Hillah itself comes to mind. It's near Al Kufah and Al Hindiyah. There are lots of rocks and sand around there. No lack of hiding-places."

"Being close to Baghdad would appeal to Talfah's lust for control."

Ya'acov nodded. "You've got a point there."

Ari's eye slid down the map. "Al Hillah's also near Babylon."

"I don't think a tourist attraction would fit the bill."

"Could be near there though," Ari persisted.

"It could. The Euphrates goes right by the site, as I recall."

"You *did* pay attention during geography."

That brought a feeble smile. "Lieutenant, I can find something else for you to do if you want."

Ari ignored the remark. "So, are the visual spooks going to keep looking?"

"Officially, yes. They're going to keep scanning the satellite shots for unusual traffic around rivers, but I know they feel it's a waste of time. But I think I'll direct their attention toward Al Hillah. Can't say I hold up much hope, but it's worth a shot."

Ari leaned forward to study the map. "What do you make of the drawing?"

Ya'acov sighed and rubbed his gritty eyes. "A large rectangular underground lab with an east-west road running by it dead-ending at a north-south river. The Euphrates? Who knows? I think these faint lines are probably the sidewalks on the surface."

"What about these tiny circles?"

Ya'acov shrugged. "Posts? Fountains? Light poles? Your guess is as good as mine. But where is that lab?"

Ghanim Jassim smiled at the male receptionist as he settled his bulk in the chair and mopped his round, pockmarked face with his sweaty handkerchief. It was a pleasant, cool day outside, but the office was stuffy and warm. He had chafed at Mohammed Faroun's summons during the entire drive up to Baghdad. Although Ghanim had more freedom of activity than any other Iraqi archaeologist, he was still subject to the president's bureaucracy. He smoothed down his thick mustache with the damp cloth and returned it to his pocket. He looked down at his rumpled shirt and stained khaki trousers and noticed his ripe aroma. He needed a bath. *Oh well,* he thought, *Mohammed said to come immediately.*

The intercom buzzed on the receptionist's desk. The man listened for a moment, then told Ghanim he could go in. The archaeologist grunted as he got to his feet.

Mohammed stood to greet his guest. He was five-eleven and had a solid build with no flab. He had a full black beard and intense brown eyes that were locked on the nervous archaeologist. "Thank you for coming, Ghanim. How are you?"

"Quite busy, thank you. When I got your message, I of course came at once. Please forgive my appearance — I did not have a chance to clean up."

"I understand completely," Mohammed said as he sat down behind his large desk.

Ghanim sat back with a sigh. "Now, how may I help? Is anything wrong?" His question had a slight edge to it.

"No, nothing is wrong." Mohammed paused for a moment. "But something has come up."

"What, if I may ask?"

Mohammed consulted a memo on his desk. "You know the team you asked for — ah, Moshe Stein, Anne Enderly, and Mars Enderly?"

"Yes, of course I do. Moshe is an old friend. He's one of the finest oriental archaeologists alive. There's no one better to help me on this find. And he assures me these two Americans are top-notch. They helped him with that Jerusalem site. Is there a problem with his . . . ?"

"Ethnic background?" Mohammed supplied. "No. I assure you, Dr. Stein is most welcome. No, the problem is something else entirely." When he saw the archaeologist shrug in helplessness, he continued, "We have canceled their visas. They cannot enter the country at this time."

"What? This is preposterous! I can't work this site without their help. It was all agreed!" He knew better than to ask why. These things were *never* explained.

Mohammed waved his hands helplessly.

"I know that. For what it is worth, I think this is temporary. And I am afraid that is all I can say."

"What do you want me to do?"

"Go back to Babylon and continue your work."

"And what am I to do for help?"

"Carry on for now. I think it likely the visas can be reissued."

"When?" Ghanim knew he was treading on dangerous ground.

Mohammed glared at him for a few moments. "You will be told." He stood, indicating the meeting was over.

Moshe held the door open as Mars and Anne entered the small university conference room. "I thought this would be more comfortable than my office." The Americans had gotten an unexpected call at the American Colony Hotel as they were preparing for the first leg of their journey to Iraq, an El Al flight to Amman, Jordan, scheduled for early afternoon.

"What's happened?" Anne asked as she sat down.

"That's a complex question," Moshe grumbled with unusual irritation. "The short answer is that the Iraqi government has canceled our visas. Ghanim was kind enough to call before I got the official word from their bureaucrats. Something has happened, and the government doesn't want to let us in. Ghanim did what he could, but he couldn't get them to change their decision. The good news is that he's sure it's temporary. He thinks we will be able to enter in a day or two."

"Does he know why?" Mars asked.

"No," Moshe replied. "And it's dangerous for him to pry."

"This is great!" Mars grumbled. "We've made all these plans, and the Iraqi government arbitrarily wrecks them. When it comes to politics and people, the people always lose."

"That is mostly true," Moshe agreed. "But this is a temporary setback. Ghanim said we will be able to enter in a few days. It won't affect the work schedule that much."

"Are you sure of that?"

"Fairly sure. Ghanim is plugged in to what's going on. His estimate on when we could get in probably came from an Iraqi official. If so, I think we can count on it."

"I hope you're right," Anne said.

"So do I," Moshe said with a smile.

A knock sounded at the door. It opened a crack, then more fully. Captain Ya'acov

Isaacson peered in. "May I enter? I need to see the three of you — now, if possible."

Concern creased Moshe's brow. "Come," he said.

The IDF Intelligence officer entered and carefully closed the door. He remained standing by it. "I understand your Iraqi visas have been canceled." It was not a question.

"That is not what you came to say, is it, Captain?"

"No, Dr. Stein. I need to talk to all three of you."

"Then please sit down — move those books anywhere. You are making me uncomfortable standing there. We have no communicable diseases, as far as I know."

Ya'acov ignored the gibe. "I have a car downstairs. It's a beautiful day. I was thinking how lovely the Old City looks from the Mount of Olives. Perhaps an outing would do us all good."

Moshe looked at the Americans and shrugged. "Ya'acov has a point. The view up there is wonderful. I think it would do us good indeed. And I believe it would relieve Captain Isaacson, true?"

The officer nodded. "Thank you. I appreciate your cooperation."

Ya'acov drove the Ford station wagon to

Derekh Yeriho, around the curve where it meets Ha-Ofel, partway up Olivet's slope. When he pulled over next to the Jewish cemetery, they got out and walked among the horizontal tombstones, many with stones of remembrance on them. The weathered, cracked stones seemed ancient, the flowing Hebrew inscriptions partially erased by age. In the distance stood the Old City's wall with its sealed-up Golden Gate.

"I remember this," Mars said. The tears came before he could stop them. He wiped them away with the back of his left hand.

"I do too," Moshe said somberly. Then he brightened. "But the circumstances are much better this time, my friend."

Mars squeezed his wife's hand and nodded. Anne looked at him, wondering what was going through his mind.

"I didn't mean to bring back bad memories," Ya'acov said. "I have always liked this view — and it's handy if you want to make sure you are not overheard."

"I understand," Mars said, the pensive look turning into a smile. "And it *is* much better this time. The former distress has passed."

"I am glad it worked out, Mars," the officer said. Mars could tell he meant it.

"Thank you."

"So, we are here to admire the view," Moshe observed less than sincerely. "IDF Military Intelligence has apparently had a mission change."

Ya'acov snickered in spite of his training. "Would you care to work in Intelligence, Moshe? Your keen sense of observation would be very valuable to us."

"I know, I know. But I am afraid my present colleagues cannot spare me."

"How unfortunate. But to get to business . . . I repeat, we are aware that your visas were canceled. It probably surprises you that we know this — or that we care. But we do. And we're very curious."

"What a coincidence," Moshe said. "We are curious also. Are you saying Intelligence doesn't know why or that it is something you can't talk about?"

"We don't know why for sure, but we suspect it's tied in with something else we're working on. Before I continue, I must ask each of you to assure me you will say nothing about this."

After they agreed, he continued, "We think this has something to do with the incident in London. One possible location for that map is Al Hillah, which is located south of Babylon. We're trying to either confirm or disprove the location. And for this we need help."

"Why do I feel an urge to run?" Moshe asked. "I suspect we are not going to like what comes next."

"Please hear me out. This is a most unusual situation. Normally we do not involve civilians in our operations. We do so only when we have no other choice. If President Talfah does have a secret nuclear lab, we must find it."

"And after you find it, what then?"

"Others will decide that. But consider this — would you rather see Talfah have nuclear weapons?"

"No, I would not. But I still fail to see what this has to do with us." Moshe's solemn words echoed the thoughts going through Mars's and Anne's minds.

"We believe the visa problem will be resolved soon — don't ask how we know this. Assuming you will shortly be in Babylon, we want you to observe on our behalf. If you see anything suspicious, we want you to report it to us."

Moshe's eyes flashed. "How can you even think of such a thing! We are scientists, not spies! Besides, you know what a closed and paranoid society we are talking about. Even if we agreed, which is doubtful, there's no way we could snoop around and report to you without getting caught by their security people. You know more about these things than I do. You surely understand the unacceptable risk you are asking us to undergo."

"Let me take that one piece at a time. First, no snooping — just observing. You have eyes and ears, and as archaeologists your business is observation and analysis. Second, there is a way of reporting that involves nothing outside the ordinary and is absolutely undetectable by the Iraqis. And please remember why we want you to do this."

"I'm with Moshe," Mars said. "But I'm curious, what's this magic communication thing you've come up with?"

Ya'acov smiled. "This will appeal to you, Mars. This is the information age. Everyone uses computers. Even archaeologists are taking notebook computers into the field. You use them for notes, for drawing sketches, for sending E-mail to colleagues." He turned to Moshe. "You use them on your digs, don't you?"

Moshe glanced nervously at Mars and Anne. "Hmm, well . . . Not as yet. However, I have given it some thought."

"Oh," Ya'acov said trying to hide his surprise. "Well, ah, how about Mars and Anne?"

Anne came to Moshe's defense. "Ya'acov, archaeologists were using notebooks and pencils before computers and E-mail were invented, and they still work quite well, thank you. But to answer your question, computers are coming into use in the field and are proving quite valuable. I've used them on a few digs, and I know Mars has also."

This seemed to reassure Ya'acov. "We want to provide your expedition with a computer. You will use it exactly as you normally would. However, should you observe anything that would be helpful to us, all you have to do is make a few cryptic archaeological notes using a special file name, and the rest will happen automatically. And I promise, this is absolutely undetectable by the Iraqis. All you will be doing is exactly what the other archaeologists are doing."

"Exactly how does this work?" Mars asked.

"I probably shouldn't say, but I really need your help. We've modified an IBM ThinkPad running Windows 2000. A special dynamic link library looks for that special file at all times. If it finds it, a circuit hidden inside the CD-ROM adapter transmits a tight beam to a geosynchronous satellite we will position in line of sight to Babylon. It's all automatic and undetectable."

"You hope," Moshe grumbled. "We are the ones who will be in the line of fire."

"I understand that. I have always been straight with all of you. And once that was quite painful to me." He looked at Mars before continuing in a softer voice, "Not that I regret it."

Mars managed a self-conscious laugh. "You're what we Texans call a straight shooter. I appreciate what you did for Anne and me. How sure of this are you?"

"I am positive. I have seen the tests myself. We compress and encrypt the data and send it out on a highly directional, low-power link. The cyberspooks tell me it is about as hard to detect as a normal computer, which is exactly what this appears to be — what it is, actually."

"You mean the radio frequency energy that escapes from computers?" Mars asked.

"Yes. Despite your government's FCC regulations, some RF does escape computers. Even if the Iraqis did pick up something from the ThinkPad, it will look exactly like these stray radiations. Believe me, Mars, I saw the tests with my own eyes. It works."

Moshe and Anne looked at Mars.

"Makes sense," he had to admit. "This is ingenious. As long as our notes pertain to the dig, I don't see how they can detect what's really going on. I presume you have some archaeological code words for us?"

Ya'acov smiled. "I thought you would never ask. It so happens I do." He pulled out a high-density diskette and handed it to Mars. "The computer you ordered on the Web will be delivered from Tel Aviv later today. Install this, and you will have everything you need. Memorize the words before you quit the application. When you exit, the application will completely deinstall itself and format the floppy."

"Very thorough," Mars commented.

Ya'acov took a deep breath. "All of you know what we are trying to prevent. You may not hear or see anything, and we definitely do *not* want you doing any snooping. Keep to these guidelines and it will be perfectly safe — I'm convinced of that. But if you *do* find out something, you could save the world from a nuclear disaster. Will you help us?"

"Let us think about it," Moshe replied.

"That is all I ask," Ya'acov said. "You will have the computer this afternoon. I want you to keep it regardless of your decision. Oh, it comes with a CompuServe account for Doctor Stein. I bet if Mars snoops around in the address book, he might see a familiar entry.

If you agree to help in the way I have described, send an E-mail thank you for the wedding present."

"If we accept, what are we looking for?" Anne asked.

Ya'acov pulled two pieces of paper out of his pocket and unfolded the first one. "This is a copy of the map the Brits took out of Barrak's computer. This over here is the lab — almost certainly underground. It has thick concrete and steel walls, including an armored entrance."

"What are these faint lines?" Mars asked, pointing to the side of the lab.

"We don't know. Our best guess is that it's a surface building. Those narrower lines could be walks, but we have no idea what those small circles are. The two parallel lines are probably a road, and the wiggly line could be a river or a *wadi* — or something else entirely."

"That's a lot of unknowns," Anne remarked.

Ya'acov laughed. "You can see why we need some help."

"So the surface building, if that's what it is, sits to the side of the lab."

"Yes. It's entirely clear of the lab."

Anne pointed to a small room near the center of the map. "What about that?"

"Probably some auxiliary room. It's outside the lab itself."

Ya'acov folded up the map and returned it to his pocket. He unfolded the second piece of paper and handed it to Moshe.

"There is one other thing. You are familiar with Iraq?"

"Somewhat," Moshe confirmed.

"Study this on the way back, then give it to me before we part. It shows the location of the emergency extraction site east of Babylon."

"What's this 'emergency extraction site' business?" Mars demanded. "I thought you said this was perfectly safe."

"It is, but with the Iraqis it is wise to be cautious. As Moshe will tell you, perfectly innocent people occasionally disappear in Iraq. It's rare for foreigners, but it happens. You face this danger, however slight, no matter what. We are allowing you an extra margin of safety."

"Is there something else you are not telling us?"

"No. You know what we are looking for, and my estimate of your safety is the truth. Mars, I believe in being extra-cautious with these people. In fact, I was the one who suggested the emergency extraction option."

"O.K., so it won't come to that. But if it does, how does this emergency extraction thing work?"

"One of your code words is 'Mount Ararat.' If you send that across the link, we will send a plane to the location on that map."

Moshe snorted. "Our ark, so to speak."

Ya'acov smiled. "Not very subtle, but yes. I guess if it came to it, which it won't, that ark would probably look very welcome."

"I guess it would," Mars admitted.

"One other thing, and then we can go. If you see a telephone icon on the desktop, it means we have sent you a message. Click on it and an innocuous note will pop up — it means nothing. Hold down the alt key, and press the *a* key. Then key the two-digit month followed by the two-digit day of the month. The program will then decrypt the message and display it. Press any key and the program will exit, deleting the message and icon."

"Under what circumstances would you send a message?" Mars asked.

"Only in an extreme emergency. Now, let's get this in perspective — there will be no emergency. We are just trying to allow for every possibility. And you know I don't play games."

Mars nodded. "No, you don't. I appreciate that."

"Very well. Shall we be going?"

Ya'acov drove them back to the Hebrew University.

10

MYSTERIES IN BABYLON

Ghanim Jassim replaced the telephone with a bang. He wondered whether he should be glad about the news he'd been given or continue nursing his grudge with the idiots in Baghdad. Only this morning Mohammed had told him the visas were canceled. Now he'd called saying everything was fine, with of course no explanation of what had caused the problem in the first place. "The visas are reissued. Tell them to come whenever they want." Ghanim sighed and waited for his pulse rate to slow. The dig was the important thing, he knew, and now it could proceed. The politics he would leave alone — it was safer that way. He picked up the phone to call Moshe.

The phone rang while Moshe was signing for the computer. The delivery man waited impatiently for the archaeologist to write his name on the indicated line. Moshe picked up the phone and cradled it on his shoulder.

"Yes?" he said.

Mars and Anne saw his eyes grow wide with surprise. The pen remained poised above the receipt list as the delivery man shifted from foot to foot. Moshe's eyebrows shot up as he listened.

"Wonderful news, Ghanim."

The delivery man tapped the signature line with his forefinger. Moshe ignored him.

"So it's back on, is it? Marvelous." He nodded during the other party's reply. "Shouldn't be a problem. The travel agent said we could rebook for almost any day, and I will get her right on it. I'll call you when I know for sure, but I think you can assume we will be in tomorrow at the same time as originally scheduled." A barely audible buzz came from the phone. "Right. Thank you; we are looking forward to working with you as well." A few more nods. "Very good. Bye."

Moshe hung up and looked past the delivery man at Mars and Anne. "The Iraqi government has reissued the visas."

"Sir, I need your signature," the delivery man announced just a bit crossly.

Moshe looked at him as if he had magically appeared. "Oh, yes, of course." He scribbled across the line quickly. The man grabbed his pen and clipboard and vanished.

"It's decision time," Moshe announced. "Do we help the Intelligence people or not?"

Anne looked at Mars.

"I can't say I'm entirely comfortable about this," Mars began. "But I think we should. We're already involved, in a way. I don't think we can walk away if there's a chance we can help prevent nuclear terrorism."

"I feel the same way," Anne replied. "I don't think we have a choice."

"And I will make it three," Moshe said. "It worries me, but I think to do nothing would be worse." He glanced toward Mars, and a gleam came to his eyes. "Your husband is salivating," he told Anne. "I'd better let him open our toy or he will not be able to help us plan."

Mars grabbed the box, slit open the plastic tape, and started pulling boxes and manuals out of the packing material. He took out the notebook computer itself and opened the lid, admiring the understated simplicity of the keyboard. He flipped the computer on, noting, as he expected, that the battery was low. He found the charger and began his search for an outlet. Finding one behind a mound of papers, he plugged the computer in.

Moshe regarded all this from the safety of his cluttered desk. "Everything shipshape?" he asked.

"The battery needs charging, but the computer works. Mind if I take the rest of this back to the hotel later so I can study it all?"

"Yes, of course. As long as your wife does not object."

Anne giggled.

"What's funny?" Mars asked, his enthusiasm temporarily dampened.

"You are, dear."

"Well, I need to get checked out on this." His appreciative eyes drifted over the computer. "This is one nice machine. I'd love to own one."

"I couldn't tell," Moshe rumbled.

They spent the rest of the afternoon planning. Around 5:30 Mars turned on the notebook computer again. After it booted up, he installed the diskette Ya'acov had given him. All three archaeologists studied the list of words and their code meanings. The associations were obvious, so it did not take long. When they were sure they had it memorized, Mars exited the program. As promised, the application deinstalled itself and thoroughly formated the diskette, which took ten long minutes.

"Man, there's not anything left on that," Mars commented as he popped it out.

"That's what we expected, I guess," Moshe said. "I think it's time we thanked someone for your nice wedding present."

"What?" Mars began. "Oh, I suppose it is. Got a phone jack I can use?"

Moshe pointed one out, and Mars connected the notebook's modem to it. He started the CompuServe Information Manager and tapped the Enter key when the Connect button appeared. A few moments later he was connected to CompuServe. He clicked on the Create/Send Mail menu entry and selected the only address in the book: Yitzhak Jacob with an address of 750521,2121. He keyed the subject line and then composed a two-sentence message. Clicking the Send Now button, he sent it on its electronic way. Anne peered over his shoulder.

Address: TO: YITZHAK JACOB, 750521, 2121
Subject: THANKS FOR THE WEDDING PRESENT. WE WILL THINK OF YOU EVERY TIME WE USE THE PERSONALIZED NOTEBOOK.

★ ★ ★

The following afternoon, Mars, Anne, and Moshe flew to Amman, Jordan on El Al and then on to Baghdad on Royal Jordanian Airline. The 737 landed only thirty minutes late and taxied to the terminal.

Mars struggled to rise from his window seat. He grabbed the IBM ThinkPad and held it out to Anne. "You take the computer. I'll get our bags."

Anne took the computer while he struggled with the overhead bin. The stuck latch gave suddenly, and the door opened with a bang. A bit embarrassed, Mars pulled out their two bags. Moshe grabbed his own and struggled into the aisle after the Americans.

A flight attendant opened the forward cabin door, and the passengers began creeping toward the exit. Once inside the terminal, they found themselves in a long line waiting to pass through Customs. Mars and Anne stepped to the side to see what was happening. The man at the head of the line, apparently an Iraqi businessman, was standing docilely by his luggage while two uniformed men pawed furiously through the bags, throwing personal items onto the large table. When the agents had examined everything, one of them stamped the man's passport and gave it back to him. The hapless traveler then repacked his belongings as quickly as possible and walked toward the exit.

The Americans looked worriedly back at Moshe. He shrugged and seemed unconcerned.

"Moshe, my good friend," an overweight Iraqi wheezed in heavily accented English as he rushed up. He shook the Israeli's hand vigorously, then mopped his brow with a wadded-up handkerchief.

"Ghanim," Moshe responded. "So nice to see you." He turned to the Americans. "I want you to meet my colleagues, Mars and Anne Enderly. Mars, Anne — this is Ghanim Jassim, my dear friend and a world-class archaeologist."

The Iraqi shook their hands with the same enthusiasm he had used on Moshe.

"We are looking forward to the dig," Moshe said. "I am so glad our difficulties were resolved so quickly."

Ghanim looked around cautiously. "So am I," he whispered. He looked down the nearly stationary Customs line. "We seem to have a problem. Come with me."

He ducked under a rope and looked back, waving for the others to follow his example. Mars, Anne, and Moshe passed under the cord that Ghanim was holding up. The waiting passengers buzzed angrily as they watched the linejumpers pass by. One of the agents looked back to see what the problem was. His mouth fell open as if he could not believe anyone would attempt such flagrant contempt of authority. He left his station and rushed to deal with this threat. He thundered at Ghanim in rapid-fire Arabic. The archaeologist did not appear intimidated, which puzzled the agent so much he stopped in mid-diatribe. Ghanim pulled a carefully folded letter from his shirt pocket and opened it for the man. The agent scanned the document, and his eyes grew wide when he saw the signature. He gave the letter back and said something with considerably less volume.

"This gentleman would like to see your passports," Ghanim said with a smile.

The three foreigners pulled out their papers and followed as the man led them to the examining table. The agent glanced at the bags and the computer but didn't ask to see inside anything. He brought a nearly worn-out stamp down on each passport and gave all three to Ghanim, who thanked the agent and distributed the documents. The angry rumble from the other passengers continued until the agent put his hands on his hips and glared at them. The murmuring quit as if someone had flipped a switch.

Ghanim led them out of the terminal and over to a Toyota Land Cruiser parked illegally in a loading zone. He drove them through Baghdad without any comment on the city, instead describing what had been found in the parking lot in Babylon and what he hoped it was. The car flew down the highway, past the arid landscape. The rock and sand were broken up by low desert brush that had somehow managed to survive. These were augmented by palm trees in the villages through which they passed.

Finally they arrived at Babylon. Mars and Anne gawked at the rebuilt Marduk Gate on their left as Ghanim turned right into the main entrance. They drove past the Greek Theater and the Hammurabi Museum and made a hard right onto Procession Street with its high stone walls before finally turning left into the vast parking lot beside the reconstruction of Nebuchadnezzar's Southern Palace. The Americans looked out the windows, admiring the massive brick building, realizing it was built on ancient foundations.

Ghanim parked beside the first of three temporary buildings. "Here we are," he announced. "No tents for this dig. These are our offices, dining hall, and sleeping quarters. We have power, running water, even air conditioning." The wide grin indicated that roughing it had lost its charm. "The buildings were already here for the construction crews, so I commandeered three of them. Might as well be comfortable if we can."

Ghanim spent the rest of the afternoon showing his colleagues the extent of the restoration. He took them through Nebuchadnezzar's Southern Palace, the Ishtar Gate, the Lion Monument, and the Ninmah Temple. The walking tour led them down Procession Street where they made a right turn and followed the road down toward the Euphrates River. About halfway there the Iraqi told his guests that they were passing over where the Euphrates had flowed in Nebuchadnezzar's day.

"What's that?" Mars asked, pointing to the left.

"That's our president's Guest House," Ghanim replied. "Great view of the river. I can take you by it, but I am afraid we cannot go inside."

They stopped outside the cube-like main entrance. The front door hid under a high arch, and the windows were tall rectangles, providing a dark accent to the light stone exterior. The back of the building was set higher and had large openings framing other doors. Globular street lamps were posted all about, each supported by slender poles. Attractive shrubs dotted a side garden. Beyond that flowed the ancient Euphrates. On the far shore, stately palm trees formed a dense line, drawing life from the river.

"It fits in with the reconstruction, I guess," Anne said.

Ghanim smiled when he saw her obvious distaste. "I see that the president's looking over our shoulders runs against your principles as an archaeologist. I would have to agree, but not too loudly, you understand. We do the best we can."

"Half a loaf is better than none?" Moshe asked.

"Exactly," Ghanim replied. "I think it will be a good dig."

It was a long, quiet walk back to the temporary buildings.

Ya'acov turned the corner and saw the CIA agent standing at the security entrance. "Mr. Morton, what brings you to Israel?"

"To see you," Alex replied. "Could we go back to your office?"

"Just as soon as we get you signed in."

"Do I have to?"

Ya'acov tried hard not to smile but was

not entirely successful. "I am afraid you do. Not to worry. We are at least as good at keeping secrets as Langley is."

Alex glanced at the IDF officer, wondering if that was a hidden criticism. He bent over the clipboard and scrawled his name and organization.

Ya'acov glanced over his shoulder. "There, that wasn't so bad. Come on back. There's someone I want you to meet." He led his guest to a first-floor office. He followed the agent in and closed the door.

"This is Lieutenant Ari Jacovy, Mr. Morton."

"Please call me Alex," the agent said as he shook hands with the younger man.

"We prefer the informal as well," Ya'acov replied as the three sat down. "Ari was with me in London but was otherwise occupied when I met with you and Dennis — and the Enderlys. Now that we are comfortable, I believe you are going to tell us the purpose of your visit."

"We were wondering what you have found out about the nuclear lab."

"As your superiors should know, we are following the agreement we have with you and British MI5."

"But we haven't heard anything. My boss sent me to see what's going on. The White

House, I understand, is quite interested."

"There is nothing to report. We are analyzing our satellite shots and checking with our sources, but we haven't uncovered a thing. Believe me — when we find something, we will let everyone know."

"Hmm," the American replied, obviously not impressed.

"Since you are here," Ya'acov continued, "do you have anything to share with us?"

"As a matter of fact we do. That's the other reason I came. We have a report that the Turks are holding a Kurd who supposedly escaped from northern Iraq."

"What do you mean 'supposedly'?" Ari asked.

"The Turks aren't sure he's telling the truth. The man could be from Iran or even Turkey, since the Kurds live all through that area."

"What's your assessment?" Ya'acov asked.

"Our man talked to him. We think he's telling the truth, at least about where he came from. But the scary thing is, he claims to be the only survivor from some mysterious illness that swept through his village."

"Natural plague of some sort?" Ya'acov asked hopefully.

The agent frowned. "Not a chance. This has biological warfare written all over it —

if it's true. We haven't been able to confirm this part of his story, but that's not unusual. It's difficult to get hard information out of Iraq, especially when it concerns the Kurds. But if it *is* true, it means that President Talfah is working on biological weapons again, and that's very bad news. If this plague or whatever it is is as deadly as this Kurd says, we could be in serious trouble, and I don't just mean Iraq's immediate neighbors. If terrorists get hold of this . . ."

"I don't want to even think about that," Ya'acov replied with a shudder. "Thank you for telling us. Anything else we need to know?"

"That's all I have. You'll keep us informed?"

"As I said, we will keep our side of the bargain. Where will you be going next?"

Alex sighed as he glanced at his watch. "It's gonna be a long day. I fly to Cairo in about an hour and then on to Ankara."

"Well then, we need to get you packing. I will escort you back through Security."

The combination truck stop and cafe was a little over a mile south of Babylon and about seven from Al Hillah, which is where most of the scientists and technicians came from. This mecca of desert commerce saw many people in the course of a day. Most were driven by a spouse or friend, although some came by bus. The only ones who knew about the subway were those who used it and the establishment's owner, who was also a minor official in Iraqi security.

The early-morning rays of the sun slanted across the ground. Nadhim Shakir waited with the others in the junkyard behind the cafe. He was six feet tall and a trim 150 pounds, still too young to be plagued by the weight problems that come with middle age. He had short-cropped brown hair and was smooth-shaven. His brown eyes were serious most of the time, not without reason.

The yard had a high, chain-link fence around it and was heavily patrolled. The lab personnel all came through a secret entrance in the back storeroom, and then only under the close supervision of the owner. Nadhim snorted. He didn't even know the man's name.

The guard patrolled the yard with his Doberman pinscher as Nadhim and the others waited on the shift supervisor. Nadhim didn't know him either. In fact, there were not many of his fellow workers he did know. This was partly due to Nadhim's lowly status, since he was assigned to maintenance while most of the others were scientists and technicians. But it was also due to an all-pervasive obsession for security throughout the facility. What you don't know, you can't tell.

Nadhim smiled as a pleasant thought interrupted his somber reflections. He *did* know one of the scientists, quite well in fact. He had known Lama Hamdani ever since they were little. They had become sweethearts at an early age, and their love had continued through their maturing years. Nadhim had expected her to break off the relationship when he could not pursue a university degree, but she had not. She really loved him, which was a great comfort. Her parents had not approved, of course, and this had prevented their marriage thus far. But Nadhim hoped this would change. That his uncle was a famous archaeologist gave him hope. He knew Uncle Ghanim was on his side.

Lama worked on the next shift, so he never saw her at the lab, nor during shift change when he was on his way home, since whoever was in charge of security had decided there would be no contact between shifts.

The supervisor arrived and led his charges back to the rusty hulk of a bus that was sitting flat on the ground, having long since lost all vestiges of an undercarriage. He opened the front door, waited for everyone to enter, followed the last man in, and closed the door. It was pitch black. The man flipped on a switch. All the seats were gone, leaving a bare shell. He walked through the dim interior and pulled up the trap door. The workers trooped obediently by and on down the concrete steps leading into the cool earth beneath. At the bottom, the supervisor punched in a code and opened the door.

· Nadhim hurried down to the small platform. As he habitually did, he estimated the alignment of the narrow gauge tracks based on his sense of direction. As close as he could tell, they pointed almost due west, so their destination was several miles into the barren desert. The small electric train with its painted windows was waiting to take them away.

Nadhim waited respectfully for the others to board before taking his seat in the corner. The supervisor closed the door and walked to the control panel in the front. He picked up a phone handset and mumbled a few words into it. He listened to the reply, hung up the phone, and pressed a button on the panel. A large red light winked on, and the train lurched forward, its electric motors whining.

Nadhim tried to imagine what the journey looked like beyond the black-painted windows, but this only made him dizzy. All he knew for sure was that the trip took about five minutes at a speed he estimated to be around thirty miles an hour. Where that placed their destination, he was unsure. Several times he had looked out to the west from the cafe, searching for some sign of his workplace. But all he had seen was sand interspersed with scraggly desert plants. Finally he had decided the entire facility had to be underground.

The train finally slowed and growled to a stop. The doors hissed open, and the workers filed out. Nadhim followed them across the small platform and up to the security entrance. He looked up in dread as he walked under the heavy steel door that he knew was designed to seal off the lab.

He waited his turn to pass through Security. He routinely passed his ID card through the magnetic reader. When it winked green, he moved on to the retina scanner, looking into the lens as the strobe flashed. Again getting the green light, he passed through the electric door and into a long corridor. His boss, a harried scientist, was waiting for him. In the two years Nadhim had worked in the secret facility, he had never heard the man's name. If he had to call him during the day, he always asked for the maintenance supervisor.

"It's about time you got here," the man grumbled as soon as Nadhim entered the lab's small workshop. "I have a thousand other things to do today. I don't have time for this stupid maintenance."

He threw the list he was holding onto the worktable. Nadhim picked it up and quickly scanned it.

"Can you handle it?" the scientist asked.

Nadhim tried to keep his rising irritation out of his voice. "I see no problems. Lab A has an electrical circuit problem. The problem is most likely in the power distribution room. I'll check there first. If it's not there, I'll have to check the lab itself."

"Can't go in the lab," the scientist snapped. "Call me if you decide the problem's in there."

Nadhim nodded. He had expected that. Only once had he been as far as the double airlock doors leading to the access rooms. He had never been inside the lab.

"I will call if I can't fix it from outside. The security camera problem is probably caused by a break in the fiber-optic line. I can check it out in the power room since all the cables go through there. It is just a matter of tracing the cable until I find what's wrong."

"Fine. Do that first. The security people are having a fit because they can't see what's going on inside the labs. There will be consequences if it's not fixed quickly."

"That should be easy to repair. When did the monitors go out?"

"That's none of your concern. Get busy fixing it."

The scientist waited until he saw Nadhim nod, then stormed out.

Nadhim folded the work orders and stuffed them into his shirt pocket. He then pulled out the diagnostic tools he needed and placed them in a large plastic toolbox. The guards nodded at him as he passed back through Security and out onto the subway platform. To the left were double doors opening to the large utility room that also housed the main workshop. He unlocked the right-hand door and pushed his way inside. The heavy door closed with a thump that echoed throughout the room.

Nadhim pulled out the cabling schematic and located the fiber-optic cable that carried video signals from the closed-circuit TV cameras in the labs to the banks of monitors in the security offices. He was reaching for his diagnostic tools when he noticed the cable end had come loose. He reached down and reattached the cable and made sure the connector was tight.

The circuit problem to Lab A was almost as simple. Nadhim tested the circuit and found it sound, except there was no power even though the breaker switch was on. When he pulled the breaker and replaced it, the circuit was live again. A rare smile crossed his lips. He wished all maintenance problems were that easy.

He returned to the lab workshop with thoughts of delaying his report until after a break, but his scientist supervisor was waiting for him.

"Everything fixed?"

Nadhim struggled to remain calm. "Yes. Would you like a report on what was wrong?"

"No, no . . . No time for that." He nodded toward a large wooden box on top of a cart. "This needs to go into the incinerator immediately. When you finish, call me." The scientist hesitated. "Be careful with that. And make sure it burns *completely*. Understand?"

Nadhim nodded and pushed the cart back out into the corridor. He strolled past Security again and out to the incinerator next to the utility room. He unlocked the door and pulled it open. Inside were the heavy steel walls of the oven and a few charred remains from its last use. Nadhim ran his hands over the well-constructed wooden box as he wondered what was inside. He thought briefly about unscrewing the heavy wooden lid but decided not to. He lifted the box off the cart and slid it onto the grate and deep into the oven. He closed and locked the door and pushed the red button to begin the automatic cycle. The blower started, and the gas burners lit.

Nadhim looked through the heavy quartz window as the box ignited and quickly turned black as the red flames raced up the flue. He watched in fascination as the box burned and finally collapsed. Nadhim gasped as he caught a glimpse of what was inside. He only saw it for a moment before the flames obliterated it, but a moment was enough. Inside was the unmistakable shape of a monkey, its face contorted in pain. This, Nadhim knew, was something he must keep to himself.

11

A *YENTA* IN IRAQ

Mars held the door as Anne and Moshe stepped out of the combination dining hall and meeting room. The sun was low in the east, giving the Southern Palace and the parking lot a warm, golden glow. The archaeologists walked across the asphalt toward the lateral trench that crossed the interrupted cable ditch. Ghanim, standing on the far side of the trench, looked up as they approached.

"Good morning," he said with a cheery smile. "Enjoy your breakfast?"

Moshe patted his ample middle. "Of course, my friend. Just the thing to get us started on a busy day."

"Busy? Yes, I imagine it will be. Take a look at this."

Moshe and the Americans looked down into the deep shadows of the trench. The ancient wall ran parallel to the Palace its entire length.

"Late Babylonian period, you think?" Moshe asked.

"Most probably," Ghanim confirmed. "But don't just take my word. I want you to examine the bricks yourself."

Moshe waved his hand. "It will only confirm your opinion. What do you want to do first?"

Ghanim pointed in the direction of the Euphrates. "Let's see how far the wall goes."

"What do you think it is?" Anne asked.

"From the thickness and style, I'd say it's part of a large building." Ghanim glanced at the IBM ThinkPad Mars was holding. "I see you brought along an electronic spade."

Mars grinned. "Yeah, they sure help in the documentation."

"That they do, although I have to make do with something a little less elegant." He pointed toward a small, open tent not far from the trench. "You can put it in there, if you like. It will be safe."

Mars hesitated a moment, then hopped over the trench and took the computer to a worktable inside the tent. When he returned, Ghanim was down on his knees scanning the top of the wall.

"Moshe, I think the bulk of the building

is toward the river. What do you think?"

Moshe looked all around, then down into the trench. "Sounds reasonable. Only way to find out is to start digging."

"Couldn't agree more." Ghanim nodded to a large group of workers gathered around a backhoe. "I've marked the parking lot in line with the wall. There is some urgency, so I'm going to have the backhoe dig down about three feet for a distance of about 200 feet. Then our workers can take over."

Moshe nodded. "Wish we didn't have to use it, but I understand. How long before we start digging?"

Ghanim shrugged. "Oh, a couple of hours at least. We can't do anything until the backhoe is done."

It was well into midafternoon when the backhoe operator finished and parked his machine. Anne observed the nervous Iraqi archaeologist as the work progressed, noting the differences between his approach and that of the seemingly imperturbable Dr. Moshe Stein.

Ghanim scanned the trench extension. "Doesn't look like we hit anything new, thank goodness. Now if I may suggest, let's set up three teams at equal distances along the trench. I will take one, Moshe can take the second, and Mars and Anne the third."

They all nodded. "Good, good. Two of my supervisors speak reasonably good English. If you approach, they will come forward. Just tell them what you want, and they will see that it's done. If there are any problems, see me, but you will find them excellent at their work."

"Shall we?" Moshe asked, motioning for Mars and Anne to proceed.

"Go ahead, Mars," Anne suggested.

"Oh, no, dear. You're the Ph.D."

She turned an intense gaze on him, but he stood his ground. She walked toward the Iraqi workers as the other archaeologists trailed behind. One of the men stepped forward. He looked past Anne to see if Mars was going to approach. When he didn't, he nodded to Anne.

"It is time to start?" he asked her.

"Why, yes," she replied. "Your English is very good."

There might have been a smile. "Thank you. Where do you want to dig?"

"Please come with me, and I will show you." She glanced back. Mars smiled, and Moshe and Ghanim were both noncommittal.

The supervisor called out names in staccato Arabic. Anne led the group to the area closest to the original trench. "Start here.

Dig down until you come to the wall. When you find it, stop work and let us know." The man nodded at each point. "You have sifting equipment?"

"Yes." His tone said that was a silly question.

"Good. I was sure you did. Then you know everything coming out of the trench must be sifted."

"This I know," the man replied.

Anne knew it was time to get out of the way. "Well then, I guess we are ready. Please begin."

The supervisor barked out strident orders and watched with an eagle eye as they were carried out. The slightest deviation was corrected instantly. Anne looked down the trench and saw Moshe and Ghanim standing far back from their work crews. Mars and Anne retreated an equal distance.

"These guys really know what they're doing," she remarked to her husband.

"Obviously," Mars replied. "Ghanim has his trained people just like Moshe does."

They watched as the workers tirelessly dug the dirt and rock out of the trench while others carted it over to the large screen sifters. There was nothing for the archaeologists to do. Ghanim's crew, at the end of the trench, was the first to reach the wall. Mars and Anne looked up when they heard the shouts.

"Must be nearer the surface," Mars remarked.

"Probably. It looks like the ground slopes off toward the river."

Fifteen minutes later Moshe's crew found the wall as well. Anne's supervisor glanced up at her. She smiled and nodded. The man barked more orders, and the workers tore into their labor with increased vigor.

"Apparently our honor is at stake," Mars whispered.

Anne poked him in the ribs. "We're doing just fine."

Mars grinned. "If you say so, dear."

A shout came up from the trench. Mars and Anne hurried forward and got down on their knees. The supervisor brushed off some clinging dirt with a work-hardened hand and looked up. Anne shaded her eyes against the late-afternoon sun and tried to see into the shadows.

"Can't see," she said.

The supervisor positioned an aluminum ladder and helped her and Mars down into the trench. The Americans knelt beside the top of the exposed wall and examined the bricks.

"Kiln-fired brick with heavy plaster on one

side," Anne said. "Of course, that's what we expected to find."

"Assuming the wall extended this far."

"Seems it did, and much farther." She nodded toward the other crews.

"Might be more than one building," Mars pointed out.

Anne looked at the thickness of the wall. "Could be, but I rather expect Ghanim is right. This is one large building."

"What do you suppose it is?"

Anne smiled. "It's a little early to be speculating on that, but it must be some sort of official structure."

"Palace, do you think?"

"Palace, temple — who knows?"

They heard the crunch of heavy footsteps up above. The Americans looked up and saw Moshe.

"So," the Israeli said, "it looks like we all get prizes today. I was beginning to worry about you two, but I see there was no need." He glanced at the crew. "I think Ghanim is ready to call it a day. Is there anything you need to finish up?"

"Don't think so," Anne replied.

"Good, good. Ghanim said we're going to have some guests for dinner."

Mars scrambled up the ladder and held out his hand to help Anne up. The supervisor shifted the ladder to the other side of the trench and got his men and equipment out of the hole.

Mars waited until they were out of earshot. "What you're saying is that we reek a bit and we might want to do something about it."

"Why, I would never say such a thing," Moshe replied. He glanced at Anne. "Well, I might say it about you, but not your lovely wife. Women do not reek."

"Who's visiting?" Anne asked, ignoring both men.

"Ghanim's nephew, Nadhim Shakir, and someone very dear to Nadhim's heart, I understand — Lama Hamdani."

"Moshe?" Mars asked.

"Yes, my friend?"

"Is your *yenta* license good in Iraq?"

A hurt look came to his face. He regarded Mars sadly for a moment, then turned to Anne. "I treat him like a son, and this is the thanks I get. Such doubt . . ."

Anne snickered. "You didn't answer his question," she pointed out.

"So *that's* the way it's to be. Two against one. What am I to do?"

"I take it you know these two," Anne said.

"I met them on a previous visit, yes."

"And there is a romantic interest."

"Yes, that would be a fair statement."

"So?" Anne said pointedly.

"Well, naturally I was interested, of course," Moshe admitted. "Ghanim is such a good friend. Nadhim is a fine young man, and very much in love with Lama. The feeling is very mutual, I am happy to say."

"Sitting ducks for a competent *yenta*," Mars observed.

"There is a problem, unfortunately."

"What's that?" Anne asked.

"Lama's family is against it. She has a Ph.D. in biochemistry, while Nadhim is a working man. Nice job, I understand, but no university education."

Ghanim walked up. "I see you have told them," he said with a nervous smile. He looked all around and lowered his voice. "But there is something else I need to tell you all. It is no secret that the government is very concerned about security. I want us to all have a good time this evening, but I must warn you not to ask any questions about Nadhim's and Lama's work. They both work for the same government facility, and what they do is secret."

"We understand," Moshe answered.

Ghanim appeared somewhat relieved. "Thank you. I do want us to have a good time. Nadhim and Lama are wonderful people, if I do say so myself."

"And Nadhim is lucky to have you for an uncle," Moshe said.

"Thank you. Shall we get ready?"

It had taken Mars only a moment to dub the temporary building that housed their sleeping quarters the Ritz, which Moshe accepted as completely reasonable. But Ghanim failed to see the humor and went along only in the interest of professional harmony.

After quick showers in the Ritz's tiny bathroom, the archaeologists were ready for their guests. Ghanim checked his watch and led the way to the dining hall/meeting room. The cook and his crew had prepared the dinner, then left. Ghanim checked each stainless-steel pan simmering above its paraffin flame.

"Excellent," he proclaimed.

A quiet knock sounded at the door.

"And our guests are on time."

He opened the door, brought Nadhim and Lama into the room, and introduced them to Mars and Anne. Moshe greeted them warmly. The two young couples began exploring their common interests, circumscribed by what they knew was off-limits. Mars and Anne were surprised at how well their new friends spoke English. Ghanim and Moshe held their own conversation until it was time to eat. The Iraqi ushered his guests through the impromptu buffet line and to their places at the battle-scarred camp tables.

They all sat down before heaped plates. Ghanim speared a large chunk of chicken with his fork and put it in his mouth. But he froze when he saw Anne quietly bowing her head and praying over her food. Mars felt his face grow hot as the others directed embarrassed gazes toward her. Finally she looked up.

"I was thanking God for my food," she said, feeling the need to explain.

"Er, yes, I see," Ghanim responded. "Being thankful is a good thing, I guess."

Mars stared at his plate without saying anything.

"Convictions are important," Moshe said softly. All heads turned toward him. "If all things come from God, and many earnestly believe this, is it not right to thank Him?" He looked down the table at Anne.

Anne caught the Israeli's gaze. *What did he mean by that?* she wondered. What was the source of Moshe's expressed interest in things of a spiritual nature, an interest that obviously fell short of a readiness for an ultimate commitment? She felt a lump grow in her throat as she became aware of her husband's contrasting embarrassment. *Why can't Mars at least consider spiritual matters?* she thought, not for the first time.

Finally everyone began to eat, and the tension eased but did not disappear. When they finished, they cleared the table and sat down again. Ghanim brought hot tea in tiny cups.

Anne took a sip. "This is delicious."

"Something we Arabs do quite well," Ghanim said with a smile.

Anne glanced at Nadhim and Lama, understanding completely what she saw in their eyes. "Your uncle tells us you've known each other for many years."

Nadhim smiled. Lama looked down.

"Since we were children," he answered. He hesitated, then continued, "Uncle Ghanim tells us you two were recently married."

Anne blushed.

Mars cleared his throat. "Yes, we were." He looked at the earnest young man, familiar with what he was going through despite the cultural differences. "When you meet the right one, nothing is more important." He glanced at Anne and was puzzled by her expression. She was pleased, he could tell, but there was a tension as well.

"Oh, I understand this," Nadhim replied. "I am completely devoted to Lama."

She smiled at him. "And I to him. But . . ."

"But there is a problem," Nadhim finished. She squeezed his hand. "Lama is an important biochemist, and I am proud of her. I, on the other hand, have a good job but never attended university."

"I understand," Mars said. "What do you plan to do about the situation?"

Nadhim sighed. "We want to marry. Uncle Ghanim is helping us. We believe he will be able to persuade Lama's parents in due time."

"What if . . ." Mars began but stopped when he felt a shoe tap his.

"It's important that the families be with you," Anne said. "You're not just marrying each other — you're joining two families."

"You are right," Nadhim agreed. "And Uncle Ghanim can be very persuasive. Lama's parents are coming around."

"Yes, I believe they are," Lama said. "I hope so, with all my heart."

"I will pray for you," Anne said.

Lama looked momentarily startled. Then she said, "Thank you. I appreciate your interest in us. Could I ask you something?"

Anne hesitated. "Well, yes. What do you want to know?"

"Did marriage greatly change your professional lives?"

Anne glanced at Mars. "Yes, it did. We no longer have separate lives. Our two lives have become one, and that changes everything. For the better, I might add. It complicates things, but in a sweet way."

"Yes, it does," Mars agreed. "I highly recommend it."

Nadhim grinned. "I am glad to hear you say that."

Mars cocked an eye at the far end of the table. "Now, the person we really need to get involved in all this is Dr. Moshe Stein."

Moshe looked over when he heard his name.

"Why is that?" Nadhim asked.

"He's a *yenta*. He's the one responsible for us getting married."

"What is a *yenta*?"

Moshe looked up at the ceiling and closed his eyes.

"A *yenta* is a Jewish matchmaker," Mars replied. "And believe me, he's the very best. I bet if we get him involved, everything will be resolved in no time."

"I would like that," Nadhim admitted.

"I have an idea he's already on the job,

but I'll make sure."

"You children are not being disrespectful of your elders, are you?" Moshe asked.

"Oh, no," Mars replied. "You're getting all the respect you deserve."

"That is what I was afraid of," Moshe grumbled.

Nadhim, apparently a bit uncomfortable with the direction the conversation was taking, looked toward the head of the table. "Uncle Ghanim, what have you found in your dig here?"

"It would be unscientific for me to speculate at this point."

"I'm not an archaeologist. What do you *think* you've found?"

Ghanim smiled at his nephew. "An official building dating from the late Babylonian period, but do not quote me."

"Nebuchadnezzar's time?"

"It's possible. But I think somewhat later, around the time when Cyrus the Second took Babylon without a fight — say, near 539 B.C.E."

"The time of Nabonidus or Belshazzar?" Anne asked.

"That's what I think," Ghanim admitted. "We will have to see if the dig confirms that."

"I've studied Babylonian history," Anne

went on, "but I also remember reading about Belshazzar in the Old Testament book of Daniel. It was around . . ."

Moshe tapped his fingers on the table. "It's in chapter 5."

Anne looked down the table at him. "Thank you, Moshe. The most accurate ancient book there is, to quote someone famous."

Moshe nodded. "That it is."

Nadhim glanced at his watch. "We'd better be going, Uncle. It is a workday tomorrow for both of us."

They said their good-byes and left.

"Well, I guess it's back to the Ritz for us," Mars announced.

"It's early yet," Moshe replied. "There's much we could discuss about the Babylonian period."

"Not tonight," Mars said.

"I fail to see what the rush is." Moshe tried to keep a straight face but couldn't. "Aren't you glad I talked Ghanim into giving you two the suite?"

Anne felt the heat of a blush. The Ritz, like the other two temporary buildings, was not very large. It was divided into a small room at one end, a somewhat larger midsection, and a tiny bathroom at the other end. The small room was the "suite," and it contained two cots pushed together and not much else. Moshe and Ghanim shared the cluttered midsection.

Mars coughed. "That was very thoughtful. Thank you."

"You are most welcome," Moshe said. "You young people are excused. Ghanim and I will be quiet when we come in. See you two in the morning."

The couple left under the approving smiles of their elders.

12

THE HANDWRITING
ON THE WALL

The next morning, which was cool and cloudless, the work supervisors were waiting at the trench. Mars and Anne peered into the hole. The bottom was almost black in the slanting rays of the sunrise.

"We will continue where we found the wall," Anne told the patiently waiting supervisor. She glanced toward the north at the imposing mass of the reconstructed Southern Palace. "Keep on the north side of the trench and dig down, but stay back a little from the wall face. We will expose it later."

The man nodded and issued his orders with loud claps of his hands. The workers stormed down the ladder with their picks and shovels. They crossed to the side nearest the palace and began digging.

"I don't know about you, but I'm impressed," Anne whispered to Mars.

He nodded. "Ghanim has them well trained. So, Dr. Enderly, what do you think we'll find today?"

She smiled. "A wall."

"Think I ought to go warn Moshe and Ghanim? They might want to issue a press release."

"Let's wait. It might get even better."

"Whatever you say, doctor."

She jabbed him in the ribs with her elbow.

"No fair," he complained. "I'm injured." He waggled his sling in front of her.

"Wait until you get out of that and see what you get."

"Oooo, that sounds menacing. But seriously, I can't wait."

She looked up in his face. "Me too. I feel like I'm sharing my husband."

"Well, you're not."

He put his left arm around her and squeezed.

The workers seemed absolutely tireless as they dug down through millennia of dirt and rock. By midafternoon they were four feet below the top of the wall for a distance of more than thirty feet.

"That's deep enough for now," Anne called down into the trench. "Move the workers down to the west so we can examine this part of the wall."

The supervisor nodded. He gave the orders and waited while his workers climbed out of the pit and took up their new positions. Their picks and shovels were swinging again before Mars and Anne could get to the base of the wall. The supervisor kept his eye on what they were doing while maintaining a constant stream of orders to his men.

Anne reached into a beat-up plastic bucket and pulled out two small spades and a wide brush. She handed one of the spades to Mars and turned to the wall.

"Shall we see what's under there?" she asked.

"By all means."

They worked side by side, carefully pulling down the thin layer of soil left by the workers. Anne brushed away the clinging dirt to reveal the thick coat of plaster underneath.

"It's in beautiful condition," Mars remarked.

"Kiln-fired bricks plus a desert environment, I guess."

He nodded. "Still, this is 2,500 years old."

They worked slowly down the wall face, revealing the beautiful workmanship of craftsmen who'd been dead for millennia.

"Nice work," Mars remarked as he picked at the dirt. A large clod fell away, revealing a deep impression that cut through the plaster and into the underlying brick. "What's this?"

Anne stopped and watched as he continued to scrape the dirt away. Other gouges appeared as he worked to the side.

"Seems to be some kind of design," he said.

Anne used a fingernail to pick a small lump of earth out of one of the depressions. She resisted the urge for a closer examination as she and Mars concentrated on removing the surrounding dirt. Finally an area about two feet long by one foot deep was uncovered. They got down on their knees for a close look. The incisions were almost an inch deep and had smooth, even lines.

"What in the world cut that?" Mars asked.

"Don't know," Anne replied. "I've never seen anything like this before. It's not chiseled. The surface is smooth. See those small bubbles there? It looks like it was cut by a laser."

Mars examined the spot and whistled. "Belshazzar had lasers?"

She ignored the comment. "Do you suppose a fire could do this? Perhaps it was cut with a chisel, and then the building burned down."

Mars examined the surrounding wall.

"And leave the rest of the plaster untouched? I don't think so." He stepped back as far as he could. "Those look like letters of some kind. Let's uncover the rest."

They worked down and to the side until they could see what appeared to be a single word. It was almost a foot tall and three feet wide.

"So what is it?" Mars asked.

"I'm not sure," Anne replied. She glanced up and saw the supervisor of their crew looking down.

"You need Dr. Jassim?" It was polite but not exactly a question.

Anne nodded. "Yes, and please get Dr. Stein as well."

The man trotted off to the west. Less than a minute later Ghanim and Moshe were looking down from the parking lot.

"What have you found?" Moshe asked as he peered into the pit.

"Come on down," Anne suggested. "I think you and Ghanim need to tell us."

The two men hurried down the ladder and took their time as they examined the smooth, even letters. Finally Moshe turned to Ghanim. "What do you think?"

The Iraqi took a deep breath and let it out slowly. "I yield to the expert."

"What is it?" Mars asked.

"It is an Aramaic word."

"In Belshazzar's Babylon?"

"So it would appear. Aramaic was in common use then as a language of commerce and diplomacy."

"Right, but burned into a wall?" Mars persisted.

Moshe stroked his beard. "There it is," he said.

"What does it say?"

"I would transliterate it as *'mene,'* which means 'numbered, evaluated, or measured.'"

"What does that mean?"

Moshe rubbed his hand over the inscription. "Let's see if there's more. Let's clear away the dirt to the left of this word."

He waited while Mars and Anne uncovered more of the Aramaic. A second word appeared, a duplicate of the first, then a third. But the fourth was obliterated after the first letter.

"The wall's busted away at this point," Mars announced. He brushed away enough of the dirt so the letters that were left could be clearly scan.

Moshe nodded. " *'Mene mene tekel.'* 'Numbered' is repeated, perhaps for emphasis. *'Tekel'* can be translated as 'weighed' or 'put on a scale.' The remaining Aramaic letter is properly transliterated as the letter *u*."

"So we don't know how it ends," Mars said.

Moshe shook his head. "Actually, Mars, we do know how it ends. The last word is *'upharsin,'* which means 'divided.' "

Mars frowned. "But the rest is missing. How do you know what it said?"

"Because it's in the Bible. The fifth chapter of Daniel describes a hand writing these words on the palace walls: *'mene, mene, tekel, upharsin.'* Daniel told Belshazzar that God had numbered his reign and brought it to an end because he had been weighed on the scales and found wanting. Because of this, his kingdom was divided and given to the Medes and Persians. And we know from other sources that this is exactly what happened when Cyrus the Second took Babylon without a fight." Moshe pointed at the wall. "And there are the words, right there."

An angry flush suffused Mars's face. "The Bible said it was on the palace wall? There's the Southern Palace over there! You can't rely on what the Bible says."

"Most archaeologists agree that's Nebuchadnezzar's Southern Palace, but is that the extent of it? Could we be standing in another wing of the palace? Did one of the kings following Nebuchadnezzar build a new palace? We don't know. But I agree with Ghanim. This wall dates from the time of Belshazzar. And there right in front of our eyes is a quote right out of Daniel."

"I'm not buying it," Mars grumbled.

"I'm not your enemy," Moshe said softly.

Mars glanced up. The Israeli's deep brown eyes were looking into his with an emotional depth he could not deny. He glanced at Anne. Her face was completely drained of color. She looked down quickly.

"I know you're not," Mars said softly.

"There's something else we have to deal with," Moshe added.

"What's that?" Mars asked.

"What was there in the time of Belshazzar that could burn letters into plaster? I've never seen anything like this before. I don't even know how it could be done today, at least without affecting the surrounding plaster and brick. The heat source, whatever it was, was obviously intense, and applied very precisely." Moshe looked at their Iraqi host. "Have you any suggestions, Ghanim?"

"No. I have no idea."

Anne traced one of the Aramaic letters as if to reassure herself it was real. "Moshe?"

"Yes?"

"On our last dig we found the torn veil, just like it said in the New Testament. Now we find something mentioned in Daniel. What do you make of all that?"

He hesitated a long time before answering. "These are special cases of what I have told my students for years. We know the Bible is an accurate book of history — we've found many ancient tels by digging where the Bible said they were." His serious expression melted into a smile. "Isn't this what *you* would expect?"

She glanced at Mars. "Yes, I guess it is."

"But?" Moshe prompted.

"It still surprises me."

"And of course there's more," Moshe continued. "If we keep verifying the accuracy of the Bible, then what about all the other claims it makes, especially those in the New Testament?"

Ya'acov Isaacson knocked on a guest office at Israel Aircraft Industries' Ben Gurion International Airport installation.

"Come in," the voice inside said.

Ya'acov entered and closed the door quickly.

"Ya'acov, what are you doing here?" Joe Enderly asked.

"I am here to see you."

Joe waved toward a side chair. "Please sit down." He paused and sat up suddenly. "Is anything the matter?"

"No, nothing like that. I need to ask your opinion on something."

Joe relaxed a little. "I'll help if I can. I hope it's not connected with my company's work with IAI. That I can't talk about, even to you."

"Nothing like that. But I need your assurance that you won't say anything about what we discuss."

"Sure. Most of what I do I can't talk about." He smiled. "I think you have my complete dossier."

The Israeli returned the grin. "That I do. But I still have to say it. O.K., what do you know about what Mars, Anne, and Moshe are doing in Iraq?"

"All I know is that it's some dig at Babylon." He paused. "Why do you ask? — and let's cut to the chase if you don't mind."

Ya'acov sighed. "I asked them to watch for anything unusual in Babylon, since we suspect the nuclear lab is near there."

Joe pointed a finger at the IDF officer. "If they are in danger because of you, so help me . . ."

"I wouldn't do *anything* that would endanger them. I can't give you the details, but what I asked them to do cannot get them in trouble."

"How can I be sure of that?"

"Because it only involves doing what archaeologists do anyway. And the reporting mechanism is absolutely undetectable."

"So you say."

"Joe, I saw the tests myself. Besides, they were explicitly told not to snoop, and I know them well enough to know that they won't. We haven't received any reports, and frankly I don't expect any. They aren't going to hear anything about a super-secret lab — you know what fanatics the Iraqis are about security."

"Then why recruit them?"

"I wouldn't exactly call them recruits. But to answer your question, it's possible they could notice *something* unusual — something that might indicate unusual activity nearby — heavy traffic, whatever."

Joe rocked back in his chair. "So, they probably won't see anything. Why are you here?"

"As I said, to ask your advice."

"So ask."

"I know your background in nuclear weapons: clearance and all that."

Joe whistled. "So you know about my nuclear clearance. I'm not commenting on that."

"We've been working on the assumption that we're looking for a nuclear research laboratory near Babylon. Everything points toward it." Ya'acov pulled some copies from a large envelope and pushed them across the desk. "Here is the drawing of the underground lab. The other papers are summaries of our analysis and selected intelligence reports related to Iraq. Look it over."

Ya'acov tried to relax in his chair as Joe studied the documents. The American looked up a few minutes later.

"O.K. A drawing of a lab, how you got it, and what you think it is, plus the story of some poor Kurd the Turks are holding and what may or may not have happened to his village, which might or might not be located in Iraq."

Ya'acov nodded. "What do you make of it?"

"Everything points to a nuclear lab for either research or possibly the assembly of crude weapons. Then along comes what seems to be an example of biological warfare against a Kurdish village. Are they related? Despite everything, could this be a lab for developing biological agents?"

"That's my question, Joe."

The American thought about it a long time. Finally he pushed the papers back to Ya'acov.

"This information is about as thin as it gets. But if it were me, I think I'd be looking for a biological lab. And of the two possibilities, I think the biological threat scares me more."

"Me too, if this bug is as nasty as this report says. I'm still not sure what's what, but if the lab is biological, somebody had better do something."

He put the papers back in the envelope and stood up.

Joe's steel-hard eyes followed him. "Ya'acov, don't keep me in the dark. You'd better do everything in your power to take care of my boy and Anne and Moshe."

"I will, Joe. Believe me, I will."

Lieutenant Colonel David Kruger nodded toward two side chairs in front of his desk. Ya'acov took one as his friend Ari Jacovy took the other.

"Bring me up to date, gentlemen," David ordered.

"Colonel, the only thing new is my visit to Joe Enderly at IAI. Within the guidelines, I shared the information we have on the lab and asked for his opinion."

"Including the summary on the Kurd the Turks are holding?"

"Yes, sir, including that."

"Showing him that implies you think there's a connection."

"Sir, you know Joe's background. He's capable of making up his own mind, including filtering out what he thinks is irrelevant."

David nodded. "I'll buy that. So what was his opinion?"

"He's leaning toward the biological possibility."

"Despite all the evidence to the contrary."

"Yes, sir. He's not positive, but I'm convinced he thinks it's the most likely answer."

"What do you think?"

"It took a while, but the more I analyze the reports, the more I suspect a connection between the Kurd's story and what we're looking for. And if that's true, we have a potential problem every bit as scary as the nuclear threat — maybe more so when you consider the terrorist angle."

David shifted his attention to Ari. "Do you agree?"

"I think it's possible. Like the other analysts, I'm having a hard time shaking all the indications that it's a nuclear lab. Why not assume it could be either?"

David slammed his fist on the desk. "Because it makes a difference in what we do if we locate the blasted thing! We no longer have any leverage to make President Talfah do what we want. If the lab is nuclear, the favored option is a stealth attack with smart munitions." He paused as they saw the implications. "If the Kurdish story is true and this is really a biological lab, blowing it up would be the very worst thing we could do. We could end up killing everyone in the Middle East."

"Or worse," Ya'acov added.

David nodded. "Or worse. Ya'acov, I want you and Ari to keep on top of this. I don't want either of you doing anything else until this crisis is over. Understand?"

"Yes, sir," Ya'acov answered for both of them.

"Good. Heard anything from the archaeologists?"

"No, sir."

"I wasn't so sure that was such a good idea when you first suggested it. But I'm glad they are there, especially now. Well, keep me informed."

Ya'acov and Ari hurried out.

Nadhim smiled as he saw the familiar blue Honda Accord pull up in front of the small restaurant in Al Hillah. The sun was down now, and the reds and oranges of the sunset were beginning to fade into deep blue. Nadhim waved as Lama got out of the car and hurried toward him. They entered the restaurant, and the waiter guided them to their reserved table.

"Glad you could get away," Nadhim said after they were seated. "That makes two nights in a row." He looked into her deep brown eyes.

"I told Father I had research to do."

"That's what you said last night. Do you think he's suspicious?"

"I don't think so. My job really does require a great deal of research."

The waiter came, and Nadhim ordered for them. The man wrote it down and disappeared into the kitchen.

Nadhim reached across the table and took her hands. "I miss you so much when we're apart. Do you think your father will eventually . . ."

Lama smiled and squeezed his hands. ". . . allow you to court me?" she finished for him.

"Yes. I know Uncle Ghanim is doing all he can, but this sneaking around is making me crazy. We've known each other for years. I want to marry you, Lama."

She looked down. "I know. He will come

around. His attitude is changing — I can see it. It is just a matter of time."

"It can't come soon enough for me."

The waiter brought out a selection of plates containing vegetables, *humus,* and pita bread. Lama and Nadhim took some bread and tested the *humus.*

"Believe me, I understand," Lama said after the waiter departed. "I feel the same way. It's hard on me also."

Nadhim cut up a tomato and put a large chunk in his mouth. "It would all be different if I had been able to go to the university. Then I would have been somebody."

"But you *are* somebody. You are my darling Nadhim. You have been my heart's desire for longer than I can remember."

His sour expression softened into a grudging smile. "I love you too, dear. I guess that is what bothers me the most. We know what we want, but your father keeps standing in the way."

"I know. But he is still my father."

"So. There we are."

The waiter arrived with the sliced lamb. Lama served them as they ate under the flickering candlelight.

"Maybe I could save up enough to go to the university," Nadhim said as he reached for more pita.

"Why? I am proud of who you are and what you do."

"You are?"

"Yes," she answered in exasperation. "Now, why is that surprising?"

He shrugged. "Well, what are we to do then?"

"Try a little patience," she suggested. "Things *are* working out, dear. Father is coming around. Once he permits you to court me, we can start making our plans." She smiled at him. "You have no idea how much I look forward to that."

"Me too."

She rolled her eyes. "I could hardly tell."

He laughed as some of his natural humor returned. "I will try to have a positive outlook."

"Good."

"Lama, have you thought about what you want to do if — I mean, when your father permits us to marry?"

She frowned. "Some. I want to look for a research position with a university."

He looked into her eyes with concern, knowing there was little he could safely say. "You want to leave your present job?"

She shook her head. "Yes. I would feel much better in an academic community."

Nadhim nodded. "I would feel better also,

and as soon as possible." He shivered involuntarily.

"Yes."

Another thought occurred to him. "That would take you away from here." A new prospect brightened his disposition. "I would quit also and find a job close to yours."

Finished with the main course, they ordered sherbet and coffee. Nadhim felt the familiar glow return as he regarded the object of his love. They ate the sherbet and savored the coffee. After Nadhim paid the check, they stepped out into the night.

It was fully dark now, and the light breeze was becoming quite cool. He took Lama's soft hand in his, and they strolled along the streets of Al Hillah. Nadhim noticed that she was unusually quiet. They walked for several minutes before he finally spoke.

"Something wrong?" he asked. "You are so quiet tonight. Have I done something?"

"No, no. I am worried about something."

"About us?"

She forced a laugh. "No, not about us."

"What then?"

She looked around nervously. "Not here." She stopped. "Nadhim, I need to talk to you, but we can't do it here."

He tried to see her eyes, but it was too

dark. "Where would you like to go?"

"Let's take my car."

He followed her back to the restaurant. She gave him the keys, and he opened the door for her. He took the wheel and drove them out of town to the south. He turned onto a narrow dirt road, drove a little ways off the highway, and parked. He rolled back the sunroof and waited.

"What do you know about my work?" she asked him.

"We're forbidden to talk about what we do — both of us, you know that."

"I *know* what they tell us," she snapped with uncharacteristic irritation. "I'm sorry, dear. I have to talk about this to someone — it is more than I can carry. I think you know more than they think you do."

He cleared his throat. "I know that my future wife is a brilliant biochemist." He lowered his head. "As to your job, I don't know exactly what you do, though I suspect it has to do with research in biological hazards."

"Very good," she admitted. "How did you come to that conclusion?"

He told her about incinerating the monkey.

"That probably came from my lab," she confirmed. "Nadhim, they tell us one thing, but it's obvious to me that what we're doing is really something else. I'm experimenting with a strain of anthrax we obtained from the Chinese. It's the deadliest bacteria I've ever seen, and the hardiest. It's nearly 100 percent lethal, and the spores remain viable for many years, even in desert climates. Anthrax is a nasty disease in humans, but I've never seen anything like this."

"So, if it got loose . . ."

"Exactly. I was told we are conducting these experiments so we will know how to protect our people from an outbreak."

"But you know better."

"Yes, I do. The truth is unavoidable. We are not looking for ways to control a disease — I am testing the effectiveness of a weapon. This is biological warfare."

Nadhim felt an icy chill settle in his stomach. "What are you going to do?"

"What *can* I do? If I complain or try to quit, they will put me in prison. I can only hope for a chance to transfer to some government-approved position sometime in the future."

"I suppose you are right."

She put her head on his shoulder. "Thank you for listening to me. Somehow that makes it more bearable."

Ordinarily, Lama by his side with her head

on his shoulder was something Nadhim dreamed about. But this evening it brought no pleasure, just nameless dread.

13

TRAGEDY IN THE LAB

It had been five days since Lama Hamdani's date with Nadhim. She tried to relax as the subway sped toward the underground lab. It was late afternoon outside, but she would spend the next eight hours like a mole. She looked at the black-painted windows as she thought about her current job and what her future career might be. She understood the need to protect the public from disease, a need that made dangerous research like hers necessary. But she also knew she was not doing work like that done by the famed Centers for Disease Control in Atlanta, Georgia. The directors *said* that was the purpose, but she knew they were actually developing raw materials for biological weapons with unprecedented power. She shivered as she recalled her latest experiment with the Chinese strain of anthrax. Every exposed laboratory animal — several monkeys, as well as dozens of rats — died within hours. She had no doubt what the effect on humans would be.

The train slowed and pulled up at the lab's platform. She filed out with the other scientists and technicians and made her way past the vigilant guards. Although she was used to the government's extreme security precautions, the working conditions at the lab still bothered her. At first she had not known the names of any of her fellow workers. The directors had relented on that a little when they realized that socializing increases scientists' productivity. Still, outside her closest associates, Lama knew no one else in the lab, except Nadhim, of course. She smiled as she thought about him.

She felt a familiar heaviness as she turned right at the center corridor and walked between the clusters of research laboratories. She stopped in front of the airlock door that provided access to the four labs on this side of the building. She looked up at the TV camera and waited. The electric lock buzzed, and she entered and closed the door. It locked, and the inner door to a narrow passageway clicked. She opened it and hurried to the central room that provided suit storage, decontamination, and final access to the four working labs. She felt a slight pressure in her ears, evidence of the slightly lower air pressure in each succeeding room, a precaution designed to prevent lethal biological substances from escaping in the event of an accident.

She entered the suiting room and saw she was the first to arrive. She stepped into the heavy, blue plastic suit and sealed it. Making sure the air hose was connected and operating, she tested the suit for air-tightness. The other three scientists drifted in and got into their suits as well. As lead scientist, Lama conducted the mandatory intercom check with her associates and the duty security guard. Satisfied, the man she could not see unlocked the doors leading to the four separate labs. The suiting room was now considered "dirty" and would require a thorough decontamination when the scientists finished their first work session.

Lama pushed through the door and reconnected her air line inside. She closed the door and heard the reassuring whistle of air rushing through the filter as she breathed. She shuffled toward the locked cabinet that contained live samples of the Chinese anthrax. The plastic air line uncoiled behind her as she walked along. It was time to start her next experiment.

"I am ready to unlock the incubator," she announced into the helmet microphone.

"Proceed," the unseen guard replied.

Lama picked up a large key and unlocked the heavy door. She replaced the key and slowly opened the door. She took down a red canister that looked like a small ice bucket. She pried off the tight lid and looked inside, noting the familiar yellow vial that she knew contained enough deadly bacteria to kill half a continent. She lifted the vial out with her gloved fingers and placed it in a holder by itself.

She walked to the large, sealed hood and peered inside. Steel cages lined the back wall. Two small monkeys watched her, their fingers wrapped around the thin, steel bars. Laboratory rats scampered about in the cage beside the monkeys. They were all doomed, Lama knew.

She checked to make sure the laminar air flow was working and the pressure differential was correct. This would keep the deadly bacteria out of the lab while she prepared the experiment. She pressed the red button to raise the hood's heavy glass and steel door. It retracted and locked with a loud thump. She leaned far under the hood and removed the stainless-steel cup from the aerosol dispenser. She then carefully placed the anthrax vial next to the cup. The next step always made her nervous.

"Ready to open vial," she announced.

"Wait for check," came the expected reply. Several seconds later the guard continued, "Lab cluster integrity verified. All pressure gradients and sensors are nominal. Proceed."

She felt rather than saw the TV monitor observing the delicate operation. She bent over beneath the hood door and opened the lethal vial. She heard a metallic clunk from somewhere overhead as she reached for a pipette. She had just begun to turn her head when the hood door broke loose from its latch and came crashing down. She cried out in agony as the heavy slab slammed into her back, crushing her against the hood's work surface.

She closed her eyes as she endured the pain. A few moments later she opened them, screaming when she saw what was right in front of her. The vial was lying on its side, its contents spilled out scant inches from Lama's face mask. It was then that she first noticed the hissing sound. She looked back and saw the jagged tear in her suit where the door had ripped through it. She also felt the wetness that she knew was her blood.

For a brief moment Lama lay under the weight of the door, vaguely aware of the loud Klaxon that announced a severe accident.

"Get me out of here!" she screamed into the mike.

She heard muffled thuds from the direction of the suiting room. She knew the other three scientists were attempting to go through the decontamination process. But no one would be leaving the cluster of four labs until Security was sure containment had not been breached.

The only sound in her earphones was static.

"Security! Get me out of here!"

She tried to wiggle out from under the door, but it was too heavy. Why doesn't the guard answer? Can't he hear me?

"Security! I need help! The hood door has fallen on me!"

"We are working on it!" came an obviously irritated reply. "We can't do anything until we verify containment!" And a few seconds later, "Verify the state of the sample."

A clammy chill ran down her spine. She knew the guard could see the sample on his monitor. She knew he had been recording her every move right up to the accident. She tried to still her racing heart. "The sample is exposed." She looked back at the gaping rip in her suit. She knew she was exposed too. She choked back the tears.

"The sample is spilled under the hood."

"Stand by."

Lama moaned. She was fully aware there was no antidote for the Chinese anthrax. She closed her eyes as the tears flowed. She knew only too well what this bacteria would do, and how fast it would do it.

The duty lab director stormed into the main control room as the warning Klaxon continued to sound.

"Do we have a breach?" he demanded of the security chief.

The man scanned the monitors and gauges.

"No, sir. The lab pod is locked tight. All air pressure readings are nominal and holding, so all the seals are working. We have containment."

"Well, shut that blasted thing off."

The chief hit a big red override button, and the Klaxon shut off.

"That's better. Now, what happened?"

The chief hit a button and brought up Lama's image on the large monitor. "The latch on the hood door apparently broke. When the door fell, it ripped her suit." He took a deep breath. "She spilled the sample, so she's exposed."

The director cursed. "What shape is she in?"

"She's injured, and naturally she is frantic to get out of there."

The director scanned the other monitors quickly. "What about the other three labs in that pod?"

"Green as far as I can tell. No samples exposed, and the suiting room door to the affected lab is sealed. Once we go through decontamination, they can come out."

"You're absolutely positive?"

The chief pointed to the relevant gauges. "No doubt about it. And as security chief, I'd like to get them out so we only have to worry about the contaminated lab."

"I will be making that decision!"

The chief nodded.

"She's exposed," the director stated.

"No question about it. It's your call. What do you want to do?"

The man shook his head in disgust. "Not a blasted thing we can do except leave her in there."

"Until she dies?"

"You idiot! What do you want to do — go in and shoot her?"

"She's really going to suffer."

"Look, I'm the scientist, not you! You think you're telling me something I don't already know?"

The chief rocked back in his chair as he

struggled to keep his temper. He looked at the crumpled figure on his monitor. He tried to remember the beautiful woman he had admired so many times — admired without any response from her. He shook his head.

"Couldn't you send someone in to put her out of her misery?"

The director sighed. "No," he said softly. "No one goes in there until that lab is decontaminated. But there is something we can do."

"What's that?"

The director looked up at the monitor. "Decontaminate the suiting room and get those other three out of there. Then start venting nitrogen into the contaminated lab. Better asphyxiation than coming down with the anthrax. Once she's dead, we can decontaminate and dispose of the body."

"Yes, sir," the chief replied. He was glad the responsibility was not his. "What do I tell her?"

The director sighed. "Whatever you think best."

The chief scowled at his boss as he left the control room.

"Can anyone hear me?" Lama shouted.

"I hear you," the earphones said.

"When are you getting me out of here?" Her voice was low and flat.

"We are working on it. Rest easy, and don't exert yourself. We'll get you out as soon as possible."

Silent tears flowed down her face. She knew she was dead. They would not try to get her out. And even if they did, there was no cure for the Chinese anthrax she had already breathed into her lungs. She knew that better than anyone in the whole complex, including the directors.

She thought of Nadhim. Wracking sobs shook her body as she realized she would never see him again. What would he do? He would never know what had happened. Her family would be told something, and that is what he would hear. They would probably blame her death on some accident. Nadhim would never know the truth.

She listened for a moment. Something was out of place. Then she recognized it. The recirculation blower was off. She heard a hissing sound.

Five hours after the accident, the director called a meeting in the conference room. He and the chief of personnel watched as the scientists, technicians, guards, and maintenance personnel filed in.

"Is this everyone?" the director whispered to the chief.

The chief glanced at his clipboard. "Except for one guard at the entrance. And he will be watching us on one of the monitors."

The director nodded. He got up and closed the door, then returned to the head of the table in front of the rear-projection screen and the large-screen monitor.

"Before we begin, I must remind everyone here of our security regulations. You are forbidden to discuss anything that happened here today. Anyone violating this will be executed. You all heard the alarm. We have had an accident, but it has been contained."

A murmur of relief passed around the room.

"The research we do here is, unfortunately, dangerous, even with all the safety precautions we take. One of our scientists was careless and tore her suit while she was handling lethal bacteria. Knowing she was exposed and would die an excruciating death, she committed suicide before we could reach her.

"The contamination was limited to the lab, which has been thoroughly decontaminated. The anthrax sample has been sealed and safely stored. Our colleague's body has been safely incinerated. I witnessed it. I know this is upsetting, but we had to prevent the escape of the anthrax."

He scanned the room, making eye contact with everyone there. "Remember, because of security regulations, none of us can discuss this incident with anyone, under any circumstances. Are there any questions?"

They waited expectantly.

The director nodded. "Very well. We are dismissed."

He and the security chief waited until everyone else had filed out.

"Do you see any problems?" the director asked.

"No. They understand. You handled it well. There will be no repercussions," he answered matter-of-factly.

"What about the parents?"

"That's a security matter. My boss will take care of it."

It was late at night, and Lama was long overdue. Hasim Hamdani received his guest with great respect, because that was the Islamic way and because the new black car spoke of a government connection. Hasim took the man into a small room off the entrance and waited for him to sit down. Then Hasim took the chair opposite.

"I will be brief," the man began, savoring

the fear he saw in the other's eyes. "I am sorry to say there has been an accident where your daughter Lama works. A fire started in the room where she was working, and the whole thing went up before anyone could stop it. It was extremely intense." The man paused when he saw the old man's tears. "Are you all right?"

Hasim nodded, wiping at his eyes with his hands.

"There was nothing anyone could do. I am afraid not much was left. Because of the circumstances — the secret nature of her work and what happened — the state cremated the remains." The man nodded at the small box at his feet. "Of course, nothing more can be said about this matter. Your daughter served her country well. Please accept our government's sympathy."

The man got up, leaving the box where it was. Hasim escorted him to the door and bade him good night. He returned to the living room, sat down on the couch, and started crying. What he didn't know — what he would never know — was that Lama had agreed to meet Nadhim Shakir that evening after work.

Nadhim hesitated before punching in the telephone number. Besides it being late, he tried to avoid ever phoning Lama at her parents' house. But she had missed a date with him the previous evening, and that was not like her. In fact, she had never done that before. He had thought briefly about coming to the truck stop early to catch her coming off her work shift but immediately discarded that dangerous idea. No, it was more than dangerous — it was fatal. He punched the number and waited as the phone rang.

"Hello," came a weary voice. It was Lama's father.

"Hello, this is Nadhim Shakir," he mumbled into the mouthpiece.

There was a short pause. "What do you want?"

Nadhim thought frantically. What could he say? "Is Lama there?"

There was such a long pause that Nadhim wondered if he had been cut off.

"Hello?" he repeated.

"She is not here," her father replied. The line clicked dead.

Nadhim slowly hung up the phone.

Mars and Anne stood in deep morning shadows at the base of the trench, eight feet below the parking lot. The trench was a little longer now but still had a long way to go before joining with Moshe's. The floor, what little they could see of it, was made of large, fired tiles, many broken when the room had been destroyed. Earlier they had found several broken pitchers and a crushed table with an ivory inlay top. Ghanim and Moshe had examined them, confirming again the late Babylonian dating.

"This place is huge," Mars remarked.

"Convinced this is one building?" Anne asked.

"Yeah. Now that I've seen what's in the other pits, I'm sure."

"So, do you think it *is* a wing of the palace?"

"I'm not sure where this is going, but yes, I believe so. It's certainly not a Babylonian McDonald's."

She laughed. "I think that's safe to say. But I guess the real question is, is this where Belshazzar spent his last night before Cyrus sacked the city?"

Mars looked at her suspiciously. "Maybe here, maybe in the Southern Palace."

She nodded. "But no matter what else we find, this discovery will add tremendously to what we know about ancient Babylon."

Mars glanced at the inscription. "Has any of this been reported yet?"

"No. I asked Ghanim when you were making notes over in the tent. Nothing gets out until we finish this season and our notes are shared with the Iraqi archaeological authorities."

"Security?"

"I think so."

Mars made a face.

It took two more days to join the three trenches. Although Mars and Anne had not uncovered the eastern end of the palace, Ghanim's crew had rounded the western corner. The building seemed to be as long as the Southern Palace. They would apparently never know how wide it was because the structure was obliterated at that point, even down to the original foundation. Ghanim offered the opinion that this part of the site had later become a quarry for building materials, and the stones and bricks, if they still existed, were incorporated in various houses and buildings in central Iraq.

The southwest corner had provided Ghanim's crew with a surprise when the palace floor revealed a large cistern completely full of dirt and debris. A high, arched tunnel led away from the cistern toward where the Euphrates had flowed in Belshazzar's day. The crew had excavated about thirty feet of the stone tunnel before Ghanim directed them to continue clearing the palace floor. The cistern would have to wait, since it would take a great deal of labor to dig it out. Anne made some preliminary sketches and measurements on the cistern and tunnel before returning to her work with Mars.

The palace wall was around eight feet tall near Procession Street to the east but less than four at the western end. But what was left of the thick, kiln-fired brick wall was in excellent shape. Even the thick plaster on the inside surface was in remarkably good condition. It was smooth and had an even off-white color, except where the Aramaic words cut deeply into the wall.

At the eastern end of the pit, Mars got down on his knees and read the measuring tape for Anne.

"Got it?" he asked.

She made one more mark on the clipboard. "I think so. Ready to transcribe it to the computer?"

He grinned. "Ready."

She gave him the clipboard.

"See you later," he said as he started up the ladder.

He walked around the end of the trench and started toward the open tent, where he quickly transcribed the notes into the IBM ThinkPad and reviewed the most recent entries. The only other thing he and Anne had to do that day was precisely locate the wall with reference to the nearby buildings. He looked back toward the trench and saw the surveying equipment had been set up. Ghanim's crew were certainly thorough. He walked back to the trench and looked down.

"Anne? Can you help me with the transit?"

"Sure. Be right up."

She joined him as he was checking the instrument.

"Know how to operate that?" she asked.

He shrugged. "Enough to get by. But I'm sure Ghanim and his crew will double-check our results anyway." He looked down the trench toward the river. "There's our man at the end. We need a series of elevations plus some angles to the Southern Palace and the Nabu Temple."

The measurements went quickly, with Anne listing each elevation and angle as Mars read it off. Finally they finished, and Mars waved to their helper, who put down his stick and returned to the workers helping Ghanim. Mars looked back in the eyepiece and panned the transit around to the west again.

"This makes a pretty good telescope," he remarked.

"Having fun playing?"

"I'm not playing. This is scientific . . ."

"Scientific what?" Anne asked, wondering why he hadn't finished his sentence.

He moved the transit a little to the right.

"I've found it," he said.

"Found what?"

He stood upright and looked all around. "I've found the nuclear lab," he whispered.

She stepped closer. "What do you mean?"

"It's under President Talfah's Guest House."

Mars stooped down again and peered through the transit. "Those surface details on the map match what I'm looking at. The lines are sidewalks, and the small circles are outdoor lights. They match exactly. That and the fact that I just saw an armed guard through one of the second-floor windows."

"You can't be sure."

"Not positive, but I'd be willing to bet you anything that the lab the spooks are looking for is under that house. What a perfect location."

"How do they get in? We haven't see any unusual traffic."

"I don't know — some kind of a secret entrance, I guess. But that has to be it. The location is right, and the walks and lights are perfect. Here — take a look."

Anne looked through the transit for several minutes. Slowly she took her eye away.

"Sure looks like it."

"I think I need to get our notes up to date."

She shivered, knowing what he meant. "Yes, I am afraid you are right."

They walked to the open tent near the center of the parking lot. No one else was around as Mars opened a new file and made some notes on the palace wall construction. He very carefully inserted the proper code words, saved the file, and exited the program. He watched the ThinkPad. After a moment the hard disk accessed for a few seconds, then stopped. Nothing changed on the screen's desktop.

"I believe that little thing works," he said.

14

QUESTIONS AND ANSWERS

Ya'acov entered the communications office within five minutes of the call. He didn't recognize the duty officer, but there were many in Intelligence he did not know.

"Ya'acov Isaacson," he announced. "You called about a message."

"Yes, Captain," the man replied, all business. "Please sign here." He pushed a clipboard forward on the counter and retrieved a thin envelope from a cubbyhole.

Ya'acov signed his name and took the envelope. He was surprised to feel the familiar shape of a diskette inside until he remembered the communications people had no way of decoding the text of the message. The message address, he knew, was in the code in use for that day, but the message itself was in the special code reserved for this project alone.

Ari Jacovy was already in his office when Ya'acov got back. "First message from them?" he asked.

"Are you suggesting I've been holding out on you, Lieutenant?"

"Oh, no, sir. Just making conversation while my boss gets his act together."

"Bring your chair around."

Ari moved his chair until he could see the IBM ThinkPad centered on the desk. Ya'acov tore open the envelope, pulled out the diskette, and put it in the laptop's drive. He then clicked on the decrypt icon and waited. The hard disk access light winked, followed by the one for drive A. A window popped up asking for confirmation on file A:\babylon.bmp.

"They sent an image file?"

Ya'acov smiled. "You weren't included in this part of our planning."

"I know, I know . . . I didn't have the need to know."

"That's right, Lieutenant. But now you do. Technically that's an encoded Windows bitmap, although it would look kind of weird if you displayed it. After we decode the file, the message is buried inside the bitmap."

"A code within a code."

"Exactly."

Ya'acov clicked on the OK button and watched as the program read the diskette file and began processing it, using a decoding algorithm based on a very large prime number, a technique considered virtually unbreakable by most cryptographers. Five minutes later the application opened up a maximized text window. The two officers slowly read the message.

"Looks like archaeology notes," Ari remarked.

"That's what it's supposed to look like. But see these words?" He pointed out a series of ordinary terms spread throughout the notes. "This one means the location of the lab follows."

Ari whistled.

"My sentiments exactly. We didn't actually expect to receive that."

"So, where is it?"

"In Babylon," Ya'acov said, pointing to a keyword.

"Where in Babylon?"

Ya'acov smiled. "In the interest of not getting our friends killed, their code is not that precise."

"What is all that?" Ari asked, pointing to the text following the code for Babylon.

"I'm not an archaeologist, but it looks like measurements to locate a wall — elevations, angles to other structures, and so on."

"The first one is a bearing to the right

wing of President Talfah's Guest House?"

"So it would seem," Ya'acov agreed.

"Does Talfah really have a guest house in Babylon?"

"That he does. It's on the banks of the Euphrates, not far from the reconstructed Southern Palace of Nebuchadnezzar."

Ari looked up at the large map of Iraq on the wall. "You don't suppose?"

Ya'acov felt a cold chill race down his spine. He yanked open a drawer and pulled out a large black-and-white photo of Babylon. He then found a copy of the lab map and set them side by side.

Ari traced the sidewalks on the photo. "Couldn't those be the faint lines on the map?"

Ya'acov thought about it for a few moments. "Could be. But this satellite photo doesn't have enough detail to say for sure."

"But you think so?"

"Yes, I do. Time to see the boss."

Ya'acov was a little surprised that David Kruger was in and could see them immediately. They gathered up the PC, the photo, and map and hurried to his office. Ari knocked.

"Come in."

They entered and approached warily.

"What have you got?" David asked.

"The location of the lab, maybe," Ya'acov replied.

"What?"

"May I, Colonel?"

When David nodded, Ya'acov placed the PC on his desk and flipped up the screen.

"We just got our first message from the archaeologists. The code word identifies the lab location as Babylon, and this note mentions President Talfah's Guest House. Now, that doesn't necessarily mean that this is the exact location because our code isn't that sophisticated. But if you compare this photo with the map we have of the lab, you can see that the sidewalks appear to match these faint lines."

"Hmm, hard to tell from that photo," David remarked.

"Yes, sir. Could we get a high-resolution satellite photo of the house?"

David rocked back in his chair. "Something came in this morning that you two haven't heard about. This thing is red-hot. The Americans are apparently convinced that what we're looking for is a nuclear bomb factory, and that President Talfah is getting ready to start supplying Islamic fundamentalist terrorists. They want the thing destroyed, and cost and resources are no object."

Ya'acov paused, then said, "Colonel, what if this turns out to be a biological research lab? I don't think we want to be spewing death over half the world."

David frowned at him. "You do have a way with words, Ya'acov."

"It's the truth, Colonel."

"But everything points to a *nuclear* lab, including the opinion of the man who died trying to get this map to us."

"Everything points to it except one thing."

"You mean our mystery Kurd who is the guest of the Turks, we think?"

"I've seen the analysis. The likelihood that there has been limited biological warfare in northern Iraq is high. It's a good report."

"But that still doesn't mean the lab we are looking for is biological."

"No, Colonel, it doesn't, but that's certainly a possibility — a strong possibility, in my opinion. Joe Enderly thinks so too."

David laughed. "So, it's two against the IDF General Staff and the Americans?" He pointed to his side chairs. "Seats, gentlemen." Ya'acov and Ari sat down. "The time for discussion is over. The first order of business is to nail down that location. Ya'acov, get off a message to the archaeologists. Have they seen unusual traffic near the Guest House — yes or no? Next, I'm ordering your satellite shot as soon as we're done here, and I'm including surveillance of the surrounding area for a radius of twenty miles — the people working in that lab have to get in and out somehow. Let me make this absolutely clear — this *must* be a positive identification because we'll undoubtedly bomb the site once it's identified. I want you two parked in photo intelligence waiting for the shot, and I want your report ASAP. Any questions?"

Ya'acov knew there had better be none. "No, sir."

"O.K. Get moving."

Ya'acov grabbed the PC while Ari picked up the photo and map. They left the office as David was dialing Communications. They made a trip to Ya'acov's office long enough to compose the message to the archaeologists and send it on its electronic way.

Ya'acov and Ari sat in high stools at a long workbench in IDF photo intelligence as they waited for the promised hi-res satellite photo. A few minutes later a middle-aged sergeant brought it in and placed it before the captain.

"Here's the shot from the bird," he said.

"Thank you," Ya'acov replied. "Any news

from the area surveillance?"

"No, sir. Our interpretation people are studying the stills and video as they come in, but nothing yet. They know where you are."

"Thank you, Sergeant."

The man nodded and left.

Ya'acov placed the map copy beside the photo.

"Well, now we know what the tiny circles are," he said.

"Outdoor lights," Ari said.

"Right. Every last one of them is in the photo, right where they're supposed to be."

They quickly measured the walks and the distance between the lights on the photo and the map.

Ari whistled. "Adjusting for scale, they match exactly. This can't be a coincidence. The lab is under the Guest House."

"I'm afraid you're right," Ya'acov said.

Ari noted the lack of enthusiasm. "This is what we're looking for, isn't it?"

"That depends on what the lab is and what we do about it."

Ari nodded toward the phone. "Time to talk to the colonel again?"

"Right."

Less than five minutes later they were back in David's office with the photo and map on his desk. The colonel looked them over quickly and glanced at Ya'acov's notes.

"No doubt in my mind," he said at last. "Ya'acov? Ari?"

"It's the lab, all right," Ya'acov agreed. "But we still don't know if it's nuclear or biological."

"We've already been through that, Ya'acov, and I don't want to hear any more about it. Do I make myself clear?"

"Yes, sir."

"Very well. Now all we need is confirmation of how they're getting in and out of the lab. Anything to report on that?"

"No answer from the archaeologists. And nothing from photo intelligence yet."

"O.K. Let me know immediately when you hear anything further."

"Yes, sir."

Ya'acov was on the verge of suggesting a quick trip to the snack room for coffee and something sweet — some habits are hard to break — when a communications courier delivered a diskette. The man obtained the necessary signature and left.

"Suppose that's our reply?" Ari asked.

"We'll know in a moment."

Ya'acov inserted the diskette in the PC, started the decrypt program, and clicked the

OK confirmation button. A few minutes later they were looking at archaeological notes. Ya'acov scanned down the text.

"And the answer is no."

"Somehow that's not surprising. If Talfah really did put that lab under the Guest House, I don't think he'd be crazy enough to have the employees go in and out through there."

"Not for all the world to see, no."

The phone rang. Ya'acov picked it up and listened for a few moments. "Be right there," he said before replacing the receiver.

"The photo spooks think they have something."

The captain in charge of the IDF photo intelligence lab was waiting for them as they came through Security.

"Come look at this," he said, leading the way to a large video monitor. "I had the guys do a quick edit on this. Watch."

He stabbed the Play button on the remote as Ya'acov and Ari sat down on a pair of high stools. After a few seconds a series of cars began pulling up in front of a building.

"That's a truck stop on the highway between Al Hillah and Babylon. There wasn't a lot of traffic when we started, but all of a sudden it picked up — about forty or so cars in a five-minute period. Then it dropped back down, and thirty minutes later the same thing happened again."

"Rush hour Iraqi style?" Ya'acov asked.

"Nope. The overall traffic on the highway didn't change at all. I know — we counted all the vehicles. Only these two groups of cars were out of the ordinary. When the first group arrived, people came out of the building and got in the cars, and the cars drove off. With the second group, people got out of the cars, went in the building, and didn't come out."

"Curiouser and curiouser," Ya'acov remarked.

"Right. And look at this."

"Is that a junkyard?" Ari asked.

"That's what it looks like. Now watch that guy. See him leave the building and start across the yard? Watch where he goes."

"He disappeared inside whatever that is," Ya'acov said. "What is that thing anyway?"

"Don't know for sure. According to its size and shape, it's probably an old bus or trailer. But the people all go in there, and they don't come out."

"Like a roach motel," Ya'acov remarked.

The photo intelligence officer smiled. "I guess that's an apt simile."

"How far is this from the Guest House?"

"A little over a mile."

"So you think this is how they get in?"

"If that lab is really in Babylon, it has to be. There is no other traffic anywhere around that can account for the necessary personnel. Underneath that junkyard is a subway — depend on it."

"Thanks," Ya'acov said as he got up. "Keep an eye on it."

"Oh, we will. I predict we'll see another flurry of traffic in about eight or nine hours. Care to bet?"

Ya'acov laughed. "Not a chance."

David looked up as Ya'acov and Ari entered. "Have something?" he asked.

"Yes, sir," Ya'acov replied. "The archaeologists report no one going in or out of the Guest House, but the photo spooks have found the rat hole, I think. High traffic at a truck stop between Al Hillah and Babylon. Two groups separated by thirty minutes. The first group of people leaves the building without first going in; the second goes in and doesn't come out."

"Shift change," David commented.

"Sounds like it," Ya'acov confirmed. "But there's more. The people in the second group go in this junkyard behind the truck stop and enter what looks like a bus or trailer, and that's the last you see of them.

Looks like they're using a subway."

"How far away?"

"A little over a mile — mostly open desert."

David rocked back in his chair. "That's the lab — it has to be."

"Yes, sir. The only question now is exactly what the lab does."

David scowled at him. "I don't want to hear any more about that, Ya'acov. Do I make myself clear?"

"Yes, sir."

David's frown softened. "You two have done excellent work. I want you to prepare a full report on this and a one-page executive summary." He glanced at his watch. "And I want it in an hour."

"Yes, sir," Ya'acov answered for them. He and Ari rushed out to comply with the order.

It had been three long days since Mars had discovered the lab's location. Ghanim had cut back his workforce to one small crew since the majority of the grunt work had been completed. When Mars saw a man standing outside the tent, he assumed it was one of the remaining workers until he came closer. Then he recognized Nadhim Shakir.

"Hello, Nadhim," Mars said as he approached. "Come on in. Looking for your uncle?"

"Yes," the man replied nervously.

Mars entered the tent and put the clipboard down.

"Is something wrong?" he asked.

Nadhim glanced around. "No, no. Do you know where Uncle Ghanim is?"

"I believe he's at the west end of the wall. Want me to go with you?"

"No, I will find him. Thank you."

Nadhim hurried down the long trench until he came to the end. He looked over the edge and saw Ghanim down on his knees examining the base of the wall.

"Uncle?"

The archaeologist squinted as he looked up. "Yes, Nadhim?"

"I need to talk to you. It is important."

Ghanim glanced around at his workers. "I will be right up."

After struggling to his feet and making his way to the ladder, he clumped his way up the rungs and joined his nephew. They walked into the center of the parking lot, away from the workers.

"Now, what are you doing here?" Ghanim asked.

"Something bad has come up, Uncle. I need your help."

Sweat broke out on Ghanim's round face. He pulled a wadded handkerchief from his pocket and mopped his brow. "Nadhim, you know the dangers of security better than I do. What if . . ."

"Of course I know the dangers, Uncle. You know my work is secret. But I don't know what else I can do."

"Very well. What's wrong?"

Nadhim struggled to keep his composure. "Something has happened to Lama."

"What do you mean?" Ghanim asked.

"I had a date with her over a week ago. I waited for her at the restaurant for over two hours, and she never showed up. And she didn't call me. She's *never* done that before. I called her father the next day. All he would say is that she wasn't there, and then he hung up on me."

"Did you call back?"

"Uncle, it's been a week, with no word. I can't exactly call Mr. Shakir and ask the same question."

"She could be in the hospital," Ghanim suggested.

He shook his head. "No. Mr. Shakir would have told me. He has softened a little toward me. And one other thing — he sounded scared."

"But it still could be something simple —

an illness, a sudden trip to relatives."

"She would call me."

"What if she is too sick to call?"

All the color drained out of Nadhim's face. Tears filled his eyes, and he had to look away.

"What's wrong?" Ghanim demanded.

Nadhim strained to maintain self-control. "I think I know what happened to her," he said in a voice barely above a whisper.

"If you know . . ." Ghanim started.

"Uncle, you don't know what it is I do. I work in an underground lab not far from here. Actually, I'm not supposed to know what it does, but I found out — at least I am fairly sure."

"What is it?"

"Biological warfare stuff. I know I'm not educated, and I have a menial job, but I'm not stupid. They don't tell me anything, but I've seen things. I think I know what they're doing — what Lama was doing."

"With a Ph.D. in biochemistry, it's not hard to guess."

"True."

"So, you think she had an accident."

Nadhim felt the tears come. He wiped his eyes with the back of his hand. "Yes, I do. Her father won't talk to me, and I don't dare ask at work. What am I to do?"

Ghanim sighed. "You're sure there's no other explanation?"

"None."

Ghanim put his arm around his nephew. "I am sorry, Nadhim. I am truly sorry."

"But what do you think I should do?"

"You have to keep on. There's nothing else you can do. I don't need to tell you about the danger at your work. You know that better than I do. Life goes on. You will have to bear up." He tried a smile, but it was a weak effort. "I am here for you. I will be glad to see you anytime, you know that."

"Yes, Uncle. I appreciate that."

"Did you see anyone when you came here?"

"Just Mars. He told me where you were."

"You didn't tell him anything?"

Nadhim shook his head. "No."

"Good. My friends are good people, but I think the fewer who know about this, the better."

Nadhim hugged his uncle and left.

15

FORTY-EIGHT HOURS!

"Another one," Mars remarked as Anne entered the tent.

"Another what?" she asked. She looked over his shoulder and saw the telephone icon. "Oh, I see."

Mars clicked on it and entered the password. A window opened with a copy of some archaeological notes they had sent Ya'acov, with some subtle additions. Mars scanned the document looking for keywords.

"Wow," he said suddenly.

"What's the matter?"

He pointed to the word followed by two digits. "We're to leave here within forty-eight hours."

Anne nodded. "That's what it says. What happened?"

Mars took a deep breath. "I think it's obvious. They're going to bomb that lab. It can't mean anything else."

"We'd better go find Moshe."

Mars exited the application and closed the ThinkPad's lid. "Right. Where is he?"

"I think he's doing some work in the meeting room."

"Well, we can't talk in there. Let's go."

They forced themselves to walk slowly. Mars led the way up the steps and through the door. Inside, he and Anne were surprised to see Moshe and Ghanim embroiled in an animated discussion in Arabic. The Israeli looked up as they entered.

"Well, our lovebirds have returned," Moshe observed.

Mars cleared his throat as he wondered how to proceed. "Are you and Ghanim busy?"

"No, no. We were having a friendly discussion concerning the finer points of Babylonian dating. I was winning."

"I do not believe so," Ghanim said.

"Perhaps it was a draw."

"No."

"Oh. To be stabbed by one's own colleagues."

Ghanim grinned. "I'm right, and you know it."

Moshe shrugged. "Sit down, you two. What's up?"

Mars and Anne remained standing.

"I need your help in finishing the notes

on that pitcher you found today," Mars said. "Could you come over to the tent and show me on the map where you found it? I'm not sure the location's right."

Moshe looked puzzled for a moment but finally nodded. "Yes, of course. Will you excuse me, Ghanim?"

The Iraqi waved toward the door with a smile. "Of course. I have to load a find in the car anyway."

Moshe waited until they were a safe distance away from the temporary buildings. "What's going on?" he asked.

"Was it that obvious?" Mars asked.

"Yes. I only hope Ghanim didn't notice."

"To answer your question, we've received a message telling us to get out within forty-eight hours."

"What!" Moshe demanded.

"That's all it said."

They stopped and looked off in the direction of the Guest House.

"So they're going to bomb it," Moshe said.

"That would be my guess," Mars agreed.

"Yes, but how in the world can we do this?" Moshe grumbled. "And what about Ghanim and the other people in Babylon?"

"I'm sure the only ones in danger are those near the Guest House."

"Fine. So, do I tell Ghanim we have to leave because *my* government is about to blow up a nuclear lab that *his* peace-loving president has hidden in Babylon?"

Anne shrugged. "That would be the truth."

Moshe stroked his beard. "Assuming we can trust Ghanim, if any of this somehow leaks out through someone else, we're dead. President Talfah is quite efficient in dealing with enemies of the state."

"That brings up an interesting question," Anne said.

"Which is?"

"*Can* we trust Ghanim?"

Moshe thought about it. "He's been a friend for a long time, and I know he dislikes the oppressiveness of his government. I think we can, but I would rather not stake my life on it unless I have to."

"We may have to," Anne persisted. "As you said, what reason *can* we give for packing up and leaving?"

"I could say I was sick, and, with all due respect, I want to be treated in Israel."

"But that would be a lie."

"Yes. And I doubt he would buy it either." Moshe looked at her. "What do you think we should do?"

"Tell him the truth," Anne said.

"Mars?" Moshe asked.

"I wouldn't mind telling him a lie if I thought it would work. But I don't think it will."

Moshe extended his hand toward the temporary buildings. "Then I suggest we invite Ghanim for a walk."

A few minutes later the Iraqi was with them in the middle of the parking lot. Moshe looked all around, making sure they were alone.

"My friend, there is something very serious we need to discuss with you."

Ghanim looked at the Israeli suspiciously. "What is it?"

"What is your opinion on President Talfah's habit of working on nasty weapons?"

"I stay out of politics, Moshe. You, of all people, should know that. That's how I've managed to stay an active archaeologist rather than a prisoner. You didn't bring me out here to discuss what President Talfah does."

"Not exactly, but it is related. Mars, Anne, and I have a real problem, and only you can help us."

"What is it?"

"We have to leave Iraq — now."

"Why? What is going on?"

"This must go no further," Moshe warned.

"You know I don't betray trusts. Now, what is it?"

"President Talfah has a nuclear research lab under the Guest House down by the river. My country is going to bomb it in less than forty-eight hours. We have to leave before then."

Ghanim's mouth fell open. "You — an agent?"

"It's not like that."

"Then please explain it to me because that's surely what it looks like!"

Moshe patiently explained their involvement and why they had agreed to do it. As Ghanim listened, his hard face gradually softened.

Finally Moshe concluded, "I can't say I always agree with what my country does." He nodded toward Mars and Anne. "I wish there were time to tell you what happened to these two. But I have to tell you honestly, the thought of President Talfah making nuclear devices either for himself or for terrorists — scares me to death."

"Surely you knew what your government would do if they found such a lab."

"*If* we found it, yes, I had a good idea. I don't like it, but what other choice is there? You know what Talfah is like."

Ghanim sighed. "Yes, I know what our

illustrious president is like. And yes, I guess I understand. I would be happier if our country did not have nuclear arms." He looked pointedly at his friend. "Just as I would be happier if Israel did not as well."

"I can understand your concern."

Ghanim looked all around. Several workers were busy in the distance, but no one seemed to be interested in what the archaeologists were discussing.

"Moshe," he continued, "there is one very serious problem with what Israel plans to do. The entire Middle East is in grave danger if they bomb that lab."

"Why is that?"

"It isn't a nuclear lab. It's being used for biological warfare research."

Moshe looked at him in shock. "Our people are sure it's nuclear."

"I know for a fact it is not."

"May I ask how you know this?"

Ghanim thought this over for a long time. "My nephew Nadhim works in it. And until she died, Lama did as well."

"Lama is dead?" Anne gasped. "What happened?"

"An accident, apparently. Nadhim is not sure."

"Oh, I'm so sorry," Anne said, tears coming to her eyes. "How horrible for Nadhim."

"Yes, it is. But you can see we have a terrible problem here. If the Israelis bomb a biological warfare lab, who knows how many people will die as a result. So, you had better tell them to call this off."

Moshe glanced at Mars and Anne. "We will take care of that right now. Mars, is the computer in the tent?"

"Yes," he replied. "Let's go do it."

The others followed him into the tent. Mars flipped up the screen, opened a new Word document, and composed a quick report on the pitcher Moshe had found earlier. He then inserted a code keyword.

"What does it mean?" Ghanim asked, looking over his shoulder.

"The keyword tells them to cancel the operation."

"Because the lab is biological?"

"No, it only says to cancel. The code isn't sophisticated enough for me to say why, and I don't have a code word for 'biological.' " Mars thought for a moment, then added to his message.

Ghanim scanned the text quickly. "Oh, I see. The reference to carbon-14, calling it a *biological* dating method. Not a very scientific statement, but do you think they will understand?"

"I did the best I could. But, yes. I think

they'll understand."

"I sure hope so," Ghanim grumbled. "So, now what? Connect it to a phone line? I hope you understand that none of them is secure in Iraq."

"No phone required," Mars said with a smile. He exited the word processor and watched for the expected access to the hard disk. When nothing happened, he opened the document again. "Something's wrong."

"What?" Moshe asked.

"The document didn't send — it's still here. The comm program doesn't delete the message until it's successfully sent."

"Can you tell what's wrong?"

Mars held both the control and alt keys down while he pressed a long series of keys. The Word Tools menu came down. He pressed the escape key, and it disappeared.

"The transmission link is not in service."

"Momentary problem, do you think?" Ghanim asked.

"No. They've shut it down on purpose. Ya'acov told me how reliable the link is because I was worried about it. This thing does what it's told, and it does not fail. And the computer is working perfectly as well. No, this is deliberate. They don't want to talk to us."

"But why?" Anne asked.

"I don't know, but I have my suspicions. I think they don't want any communications with us because they know where to lay their eggs."

"I'm afraid he's right," Moshe said.

"So what do we do?" Ghanim asked.

"I don't know," Mars said. "But unless we do something, that lab is going to be bombed about forty-eight hours from now."

The Iraqi turned and looked at his Toyota Land Cruiser parked next to the Ritz. "I'll be back in a minute." He got in the car and drove it to the parking lot beside the Neb-uchadnezzar Museum. He waited impatiently as workers unloaded the wall section from the back of the vehicle. Then he locked up and returned to the dig.

The phone on Avraham's desk rang. Abdul looked up from the small table that served as his work space. The two shared a small office on the second floor of President Talfah's Guest House in Babylon. They were both bored with their new assignment but knew better than to complain about it.

"Yes?" Avraham answered. He listened for a few moments, then said, "We will be there in a moment."

"Who was it?" Abdul asked.

"Our master calls," Avraham grumbled as

he got up. "Wants to see us in his office."

They hurried to the large corner office, which looked toward the restored buildings of Babylon. Inside, Akram Rashid tilted back in his swivel chair, gazing off in the distance. Akram was middle-aged and had a large, round head with cruel, intense brown eyes. He had a thick, black mustache that he frequently checked for proper grooming. Although he was a little under six feet tall, he weighed over 200 pounds, and none of it was fat.

When Avraham rapped on the door, Akram turned from the window. "Ah, yes. Avraham and Abdul, come in and sit down."

He stood slowly as if not quite sure it was necessary. The two Palestinians frowned at this slight and took the offered chairs. When they were all seated, Akram motioned toward the large monitor on his desk and the elaborate keypad that allowed him to switch to any of the TV cameras around Babylon or inside the lab.

"What do you think of our security operation, now that you've had a chance to study it?"

Avraham smiled his approval. "The equipment is better than I have ever used. Abdul can speak to this better than I, but I think procedures are quite sound and should ˌˌective."

"Oh, they *are* effective, I can assure you of that," Akram snorted. "Have you and Abdul had a full rotation of all the major security sections?"

"We have. Are you ready to assign us?"

"Yes, that's why I called you. I think enforcement would best utilize your talents. Investigation of possible security risks and handling verified security violations — does this appeal to you?"

Both men nodded.

"Good. As you know, my security division is responsible for both the lab and Babylon. The lab I think you saw yesterday. And I'm sure you know what we're doing in Babylon. Big tourist site and ongoing restoration of Babylonian buildings. What you may not have heard about is the team of archaeologists who are working on a new find in the parking lot next to the Southern Palace."

"No, I had not heard," Avraham said.

"It just started very recently. We found a wall when we were digging a trench for a new fiber-optic cable. Ghanim Jassim, one of our leading archaeologists, is running it." Akram made a face. "He brought in some foreigners to help him. An Israeli by the name of Moshe Stein and two Americans,

Mars and Anne Enderly."

Avraham gulped. "What?"

"Is something the matter?" Akram asked.

The Palestinian struggled to maintain his composure. "We know them. They interfered with our operations in the PRF."

Akram nodded. "Oh yes, now I remember. I thought their names were familiar."

Avraham snorted. "Not only that — they were involved with IDF Intelligence in some way. The officer who gave us so much trouble was with them when we escaped into Syria."

"You are sure of this?" Akram demanded.

"Absolutely."

The Iraqi rubbed his mustache with a finger as he thought. "I must look into this," he said at last.

Nadhim waited impatiently for the elevator to make its leisurely trip from the maintenance shop in the research lab to the basement of the building above. What the building itself was, he didn't know, even though he had complete engineering drawings of its basement. He knew the basement was used for storage and had a conference room, but its most important function was to serve as the main nerve center not only for the lab but for the surrounding area. A large portion of the basement was occupied by a security communications control room. All the video, digital network, and alarm lines converged on this room from the lab and the surface above.

Nadhim had often wondered exactly what the lab was under, but there had never been an opportunity to find out, and he certainly knew better than to ask. When he had received the maintenance call, he had thought he might find out at last, but he had been directed to meet a man in the basement. He had been there many times but never above. During his ride, Nadhim looked down at the elevator panel. There were buttons for the first and second floor, but they would not work without a key. He snorted in amusement. All he had to do, if he wanted to, was open the control panel and bypass the switch. So much for security. But he knew what would happen to him if he ever did such a foolish thing.

The elevator stopped with a jolt, and the door opened. A large man with intense brown eyes and a black mustache was waiting for him.

"Come with me, Nadhim," he said without preamble.

Nadhim followed him to a small office

adjacent to the communications control room.

"Do you know who I am?" the man asked when they were seated.

"No," Nadhim replied.

"I am Akram Rashid, chief of security." He smiled at the look of fear this instilled. "I see you recognize the name."

"Yes, I do."

"Good. Then you probably understand that if I call for you, it is quite important."

"Yes, of course. How can I help?"

"Your supervisors tell me you are very good at what you do. You have the best understanding of how our security network functions and work well with state-of-the-art equipment."

"Thank you," Nadhim mumbled.

Akram raised an eyebrow. "I am not handing out compliments, only stating the facts. I need help on a security problem, and my people tell me you are the one I should ask."

Nadhim nodded.

"Now, here is the problem. A short distance from here some work is going on that poses a security threat. We are going to close the site with a fence and install some TV cameras on poles. And, of course, the telephone lines are already tapped. But I want audio surveillance as well. Do we have any equipment for listening to conversations from long distances?"

"There are two ways. We can plant microphones and transmitters for close-in work and use parabolic mikes where that is not possible."

"We probably need to do both. The crew is using three temporary buildings; we need to bug those. But the workers are outside most of the day. Perhaps the parabolic mikes would be best for that. Do we have any here?"

"No. But we can get some quickly enough from Baghdad. Is this site close to here?"

"Why do you want to know?"

"I presume you want to monitor from here. I need to know if short range transmitters can be used or if I have to arrange for long-range communications."

Akram thought this over. "The site is within a mile of here."

"Then the short-range transmitters will work fine."

"Good. Do you know how to set up this equipment and train our people to use it?"

Nadhim struggled to hide his irritation. "I am quite familiar with these devices. They are easy to use."

"Very good. Order what you need. Let me

know when the equipment arrives."

"I will."

Akram conducted him back to the elevator and punched the button. "I am depending on you, Nadhim," the man said as the doors opened. "Do not fail me."

Nadhim shivered. "I will not," he said as the door closed.

He returned to his utility room maintenance shop and sat down at the long workbench. He filled out a requisition for three parabolic microphones plus the extra equipment required to use them. Then he sat up straight. Something Akram had said sounded familiar. They were going to bug three temporary buildings. Uncle Ghanim's site in Babylon had three temporary buildings. Nadhim tried to visualize a map of the local area. Yes, he decided, the lab could be close to Babylon if the subway tracks curved after leaving the truck stop. He put down his pen. That had to be it. He knew where he was for the first time since he had begun working here. He also knew he had to see Uncle Ghanim, and he had to see him quickly.

It was after dark when Nadhim approached the temporary building that housed the dining room. He opened the door and went in. The archaeologists looked around in surprise. Ghanim started to stand, but his nephew grimaced and motioned for him to stay seated. Nadhim hurried over and held a scrap of paper where his uncle could read it.

Don't say anything! Come outside! it said in bold Arabic.

Ghanim stood and followed. Moshe hesitated for a moment, then got up as well, as did Mars and Anne. The archaeologists followed Nadhim out into the parking lot and over to the expanding excavation.

"Uncle, I need to speak to you alone," he whispered.

Ghanim tried to see his nephew's eyes, but it was too dark. "What you have to say, you can say in front of them."

"But, Uncle . . ."

"Please trust me. Whatever it is, they need to hear it also."

"Very well," Nadhim whispered. "Come close." He turned in a slow circle before continuing. "Uncle, you and your friends are in trouble."

Ghanim felt something cold settle in his stomach. "Where did you hear this?"

"That doesn't matter. I found out today that our security people are going to put a fence around your dig. Also, they're going to bug your buildings, put up surveillance cameras, and set up parabolic mikes so they can hear what you talk about outside. Your phones are already tapped." He looked at Moshe and the Americans. "I don't know why, but I would guess it has to do with your friends."

Ghanim sighed. "I suppose we should have expected this."

"Why?"

"Ghanim, should we be discussing this?" Mars asked.

"It's a little late for caution," the Iraqi snapped. "We are all in this together, it seems to me. We might as well be honest with each other." He turned to his nephew. "We all know what your lab does and where it's located."

"How? I only found out where it was today. It's under some building right here in Babylon."

"It's under President Talfah's Guest House."

Nadhim looked toward the west. "So that's where it is." He turned back toward the highway. "And that's where the subway goes. I finally know where I work."

"There's more, unfortunately. The lab is going to be bombed in less than forty-eight hours."

"Uncle," Nadhim hissed, "this is crazy. If anyone bombs that lab, it will kill everyone for hundreds of miles around — maybe thousands. There may be no stopping some of the things they deal with down there." He turned to Moshe. "It's the Israelis, isn't it?" he demanded in anger. "It's your answer to everything you don't like. Just bomb it."

Moshe took a deep breath. "I will not attempt to defend my country's actions. I do not always approve of what they do. But do you really believe it is in the best interest of peace to sit idly by while President Talfah builds terrorist bombs, whether nuclear or biological?"

Nadhim was silent.

"Well, is it?" Moshe persisted.

"No. But don't you realize what will happen if a biological warfare lab is blown up?"

"Yes, we do. But the Intelligence people think it is a nuclear lab."

"Your brilliant Intelligence people are wrong."

"That they are. But we can't do anything about that now. We have already tried to warn them to call off the mission, but our communications link isn't working."

"What can we do?" Ghanim asked.

"There's nothing we can do," Nadhim said. "Our security people will be here tomorrow to put up the fence and install the snooping gear."

"Maybe we should take the Land Cruiser and get out while we can."

"Where would you go? The noose may not be tight now, but it will be soon. If you run, they'll kill you all for sure. There's a chance if you stay here."

"That won't matter two days from now."

"No, I guess it won't. But you won't be able to do anything from jail — or the end of a noose."

"Nadhim, do they know you are my nephew?" Ghanim asked.

"I'm sure they do. The security people are very good at what they do."

"Do you think they could have followed you?"

"No. I was very careful. And now I have to be going."

"We have to do *something*," Ghanim said.

"But what?" Nadhim asked.

"I don't know. I just don't know."

16

UNDER HOUSE ARREST

The following morning, before Ghanim's workers arrived, security crews showed up at the parking lot with the supplies to erect the perimeter fence. Ghanim peered through the blinds inside the Ritz. He let the slats fall back in place.

"They're here."

Mars hurried to the window.

"Stay away from that," Ghanim ordered. "Moshe, I want you, Mars, and Anne to stay inside. I'm going to talk to the security people."

He opened the door and hurried out. He immediately saw the man he needed to talk to and went directly to him.

"Good morning," Ghanim began. "Could you tell me what is going on?" He hoped he was showing the proper amount of ignorance and irritation.

"Certainly," the large man replied with a confident smile. "I am Akram Rashid, chief of security at Babylon. This is only a security precaution. It will not affect your work at all. We felt it wise to protect your find from thieves and to prevent interference in your work."

"But I have never had those problems on any of my digs. I appreciate the concern, but this is unnecessary."

Akram looked him in the eye. "It *is* necessary."

Ghanim flexed his hands as he wondered what to do. Finally he turned around and retreated to the Ritz. All eyes were on him as he entered the building.

"What's happening?" Mars asked.

"Exactly what Nadhim said. The chief of security himself — Akram Rashid — is supervising it. They're putting up the fence." He looked around the room. "I suppose the bugs will be in place shortly. From now on, no more sensitive discussions inside. And not outside either — don't forget the parabolic mikes."

"What will we do?" Anne asked. "We have to be able to talk about this."

"I know one place that should be safe," Mars said.

"The tunnel," Anne said.

"That should work," Moshe added. "But we need to be careful they don't miss us.

Maybe only two at a time."

"I agree," Ghanim said. He glanced at his watch. "Time for breakfast. Remember, people, everything has to look normal or we'll be arrested."

He led the way to the dining building.

Ya'acov and Ari cleared the final security check and walked into a tightly closed hangar on a secret Israel Air Force base near Beer-sheba. Inside, under the hangar's bright mercury vapor lights, sat three dull black aircraft, each an angular series of flat surfaces defying most accepted standards of aviation aesthetics. They didn't look like they could fly, and in fact they were not highly efficient or maneuverable. But they were hard for enemy radars to see, and this made all the difference in the world. They were United States Air Force F-117A stealth fighters.

An Air Force officer in a khaki uniform detached himself from a group in the center of the hangar and hurried toward the new-comers. Ya'acov and Ari traded salutes with the man as he approached.

"Gentlemen," he said, "I'm Colonel John Barker, 37th Tactical Fighter Wing, commander of this detachment."

"Colonel, I'm Captain Ya'acov Isaacson,

and this is Lieutenant Ari Jacovy. We are with IDF Military Intelligence."

"Ah, the gentlemen who found Talfah's nasty little toy box."

Ya'acov smiled. "We had a little help."

"Great work, whoever did it. What do you think of my birds?"

Ya'acov and Ari scanned the planes again.

"To tell the truth, Colonel, they look like something out of an aircraft designer's nightmare," Ya'acov said, eyeing the odd-looking canted tail fins.

The American laughed. "It wasn't beauty we were after. Those birds are pure stealth. A flock of geese has a bigger radar cross-section."

"I imagine the pilots appreciate that," Ari offered.

"That's a roger on your last," John confirmed. "Now, my boss said you were coming for a briefing on our operation."

"Yes, sir," Ya'acov confirmed.

"Good. Glad to do it. Let's do a walk around the aircraft, then we'll do the magic show."

They took their time walking around the nearest F-117 as the American colonel pointed out each feature of the state-of-the-art aircraft.

"How are they controlled?" Ari asked.

"Quadruplex fly-by-wire. The pilot's controls are actually inputs to computers that figure out how to make the plane do what the pilot wants."

"I have heard this plane sacrifices aerodynamics for stealth," Ya'acov commented.

"That's true. We're limited to high subsonic airspeed, and the bird's performance is somewhat less than most fighter pilots want. In fact, someone gave the one-seventeen the nickname 'Wobblin' Goblin.' "

"What ordinance will you be using?" Ari asked.

John pointed to three large white bombs resting on yellow carts. "The latest in laser-designated munitions. Those are brand-new. Note the long, slim shape. They're built to penetrate heavy concrete or even a limited amount of armor steel. After penetration, a charge in the tail propels the main explosive down through the casing where it detonates. We borrowed the idea from some of the tank-penetrating munitions. But I expect that the operational briefing is what you're mainly interested in."

"Impressive hardware," Ya'acov agreed, "but the basic plan is what we were sent for."

"Right this way. I have my dog-and-pony show all set up for you." The American led them into a small conference room. He closed the door and pulled a cloth off a large map of the Middle East.

"There's the route, gentlemen. From the Negev into Jordan below the Dead Sea, across Jordan well south of Amman, and into Iraqi airspace about ten miles north of the southern border with Saudi Arabia. From there, it's pretty much due east, staying well clear of known missile and anti-aircraft artillery sites and Iraqi air bases."

"To enhance your invisibility," Ya'acov could not help remarking.

John's confident smile disappeared. "Roger that, Captain. The stealth works, but there's no point in stretching our luck. Now, to continue, three separate passes on the target, spaced two minutes apart, and whatever is under that house on the Euphrates will be history. I guarantee it. Egress will be via the same basic route, with allowances for evasion if necessary. We have informal permission to be in Jordanian airspace, and we have the same agreement with the Saudis if we need to evade hostiles. We will have tanker assets over Jordan for refueling on entry and again on egress. Any questions, gentlemen?"

"Yes," Ya'acov replied. "I've seen the reports on the accuracy of laser-designated weapons. What's the straight skinny on that?"

John laughed, and his smile returned. "I like your style, Captain. You and I think alike. Now, this won't be going anyplace that might burn my backside, will it?"

"No, sir," Ya'acov answered for them both.

"Good. Gentlemen, we'll be carrying the finest aerial weapons of destruction ever made, and I'm telling you that as a career aviator who's dropped 'em. These things will hit what the laser designates within a radius of about ten feet well over 90 percent of the time."

"What about the rest of the time?"

"Nothing is perfect. If you don't designate the right target, you miss. And very occasionally the guidance fails, and the bomb could fall anywhere."

"So what's *your* prediction? Will you guys take this target out?"

John struck the map with his pointer. "Is that the target, Captain? Are you sure?"

Ya'acov nodded. "We're sure."

"Then that lab is dead meat. Count on it."

David waited until Ya'acov and Ari were seated.

"So, how are things down in the Negev?"

Ya'acov glanced toward Ari before answering. "I would say things are under control as far as operations go. The right equipment is in place, and I was quite impressed with Colonel Barker. He knows his stuff."

"Good," David replied grudgingly. "The operational guys are always griping about the quality of intelligence they get. Now that they've got some good stuff, they'd better not mess up."

Ya'acov moved uneasily in his chair. David saw it and frowned at him, giving the younger man a clear understanding of what could *not* be discussed.

"What did you think of the F-117?" David asked. "I've never seen one except in photos."

Ya'acov relaxed a little. "It's quite an aircraft. Looks like an ugly, flat, black bug — something straight out of a sci-fi novel. It has more angles than a Tel Aviv real estate developer."

David chuckled. "You have a kind word for everyone, don't you?"

"If the colonel would care to point out any inaccuracy . . ."

"Shall we stick to Intelligence matters? Are you convinced the Americans can take out the lab?"

Ya'acov pursed his lips. He knew what the colonel's stern look meant. "The probability that Colonel Barker will successfully service the target is very high, in my opinion. The amount of collateral damage will depend on two factors: the accuracy of the delivery and what the target turns out to be."

David slammed his fist on his desk. "Ya'acov! I said I didn't want to hear any more about that! The General Staff has made the decision to go forward. There will be no more discussion. Clear?"

"Very clear, Colonel."

"Very well. Anything else?"

"Have we heard anything from the archaeologists?" Ya'acov asked.

David paused and looked Ya'acov in the eye. "We haven't heard anything, but we presume they are making preparations for leaving. We, of course, know they received the message that —"

"And then we took down the satellite link," Ya'acov interrupted in irritation.

"Its purpose was accomplished, and it was deemed wise to avoid the possibility of detection."

"The link was undetectable. I verified that for myself."

"Ya'acov, let me remind you that this is none of our business."

"Have we done anything to try and contact them?" Ya'acov persisted.

"There's nothing we *can* do. We certainly can't phone them. We have to assume they're making travel arrangements. They have plenty of time."

"Any indications of trouble in Iraq?"

"None. There is absolutely nothing to indicate that the Iraqis know about our interest in their lab." David's stern expression softened. "Ya'acov, I'm aware of your concern. And regardless of what you think, I'm not unsympathetic. But once the boss makes his decision, we can only say 'yes, sir' and march right along. My honest opinion is that Moshe, Mars, and Anne are making their travel plans right now. We know they got the message. We have no indication that the Iraqis are upset. Everything points to an uneventful egress for our people."

"They aren't our people," Ya'acov pointed out. "They're ordinary citizens."

"Ya'acov, they'll get out."

Joe Enderly paid the entrance fee to the Megiddo National Park. He glanced around the museum briefly, then left the building. He walked up the winding footpath leading to the summit of the rather low hill that is nevertheless called a mountain. At the top he saw a lone figure near the northeast edge.

"Nice view," Joe said as he approached.

"One of the best in Israel," Ya'acov agreed, pointing toward the north. "The Jezreel Valley and the Plain of Esdraelon below us, Mount Tabor and the Sea of Galilee to the northeast over there."

"So, this is where Armageddon is supposed to take place," Joe remarked with a weary smile.

"So the New Testament says," Ya'acov answered.

"I'll believe it when I see it."

Ya'acov nodded. "I know what you mean."

Joe glanced around to make sure they were alone. "So, what's up?"

"Why did I ask to see you? I couldn't forget what you said about Mars, Anne, and Moshe."

"About taking care of them?"

"Yes. It may come as a surprise to know that I care about them also."

Joe thought back to what had happened during the Syrian invasion of northern Galilee. "I remember, Ya'acov. Sometimes I have a hard time separating the man from the organization he works for. You I like. It's the Israeli government I'm not so sure about."

"Just between us military guys, I agree with you, but don't quote me."

Joe laughed. "Your secret is safe with me."

"It had better be. I've already taken heat from my boss over this."

"Thank you. Anything new about Mars, Anne, and Moshe?"

Ya'acov frowned. "Yes. They helped us confirm the location of the Iraqi lab. After that we told them to leave Iraq ASAP. We've scheduled an air strike to take out the lab."

Joe's mouth fell open. "Those idiots! That's a biological warfare research lab! They'll kill not only Mars, Anne, and Moshe but everyone else in the region!"

"We don't know it's biological — not for sure."

"I think so! You think so!"

"But the operational people don't. All our evidence — *all of it* — points to a nuclear lab. The only thing that doesn't is that Kurd's story."

"Are you changing your tune?" Joe asked sarcastically.

"No, I'm not. I think it's biological, but I'm not positive. There's no way to know for sure."

"Until you bomb it, and then it's too late."

Ya'acov shrugged. "What can I say?"

"O.K., O.K. Are they on their way out?" Joe asked, trying to hide his growing exasperation.

"We think so."

"What does *that* mean?" Joe snapped.

"It means we aren't sure. We took the satellite link down after ordering them out, so we can't confirm. But we know they got the message. And we're certain there's no big flap in Iraq, so they should be on their way."

Joe cursed. "But you don't *know!* Ya'acov, this is exactly what I was afraid of! First you involve people in your operation, and now you can't tell me if they're all right or not because you think operational security is more important. Once again, nailing your enemy is more important than protecting the people who deserve it."

Ya'acov sighed. "The government sees it that way. I don't."

"I've had a bad feeling about this ever since you told me what you asked them to do."

"I can't say I've been entirely comfortable about it either."

"How long do they have to get out?"

"You know that's classified, Joe."

"How long, Ya'acov?"

"The strike's scheduled for the early

morning on Thursday. They have about thirty-six hours."

"That doesn't leave much time, does it?"

"No, it doesn't."

"And you still think they're on their way out — and I mean *you*, not Military Intelligence."

Ya'acov took a deep breath. "Joe, that's the way it honestly looks to me. We see absolutely no indication there's anything going on in Iraq concerning this."

"But you're not sure," Joe persisted.

"No, I'm not sure."

"Tell me — did you expect to hear from them before now?"

Ya'acov paused a long time before answering. "Yes, Joe, I did. But the delay doesn't mean anything. We're talking about Iraq. There are many, many reasons why they could be delayed."

"Ya'acov?"

"Yes?"

"I still expect you to watch after Mars and Anne and Moshe."

"I promise I'll do what I can."

Joe nodded. "Thanks. I'm counting on you." But Joe also knew he wouldn't just sit back and wait for others to ensure the well-being of his family and friend. It was time to make some travel plans.

★ ★ ★

Joe looked around the luxury suite in the Ishtar Sheraton. The satisfied tourist gave the bellboy a generous tip and waited until the door closed. It was nearly ten o'clock, and he was definitely travel-weary. He pulled out the itinerary the Tel Aviv travel agent had given him. A limousine would call for him at 6 A.M. in the morning and take him to the office of Babylon Tours. The tour bus would leave from there for an all-day tour of Babylon.

The suite was quite nice, Joe saw. He thought about checking out the movie offerings, but he was tired. And besides, he had other things on his mind.

The four archaeologists gathered around the table in the dining building. They had already gone over the day's work, discussing the finds and planning for the next day. Though the site continued to yield rich artifacts, the usual spark of discovery was just not there. Their *defacto* imprisonment weighed heavily on them.

Moshe's expression was long and somber, Anne noticed, most unusual for the lively Israeli. She longed to talk about their situation but knew that was inadvisable. All they could do was discuss Belshazzar's palace or

320

engage in meaningless small talk. Anne wondered if *their* lives had seen the handwriting on the wall.

Finally Mars and Anne excused themselves and returned to the Ritz. They entered their room and closed the door. Anne felt her anxiety return with even more force. It hurt far worse, she realized, that she could not even discuss their situation with her husband. One look at Mars showed he felt the same way.

Suddenly she felt a tinge of hope. This puzzled her. After all, the circumstances had not changed. They were still at the mercy of the Iraqis, with no sign of letup. But the confident feeling remained. A word formed in her mind: *Pray.* The word was as clear as if it had been uttered aloud, which she knew it hadn't.

"Something the matter?" Mars asked cautiously, looking pointedly about the room.

"No," she replied softly. She looked up into his eyes. "I love you, dear."

He smiled as he took her hand and squeezed it. He leaned over and gave her a gentle kiss. She beamed at him.

"I love you too. You're the best thing that ever happened to me. Thank you for being my wife."

She rested her head against his chest. He stroked her hair.

"Mars?" she asked.

"Yes?"

She thought about the listening ears before she spoke. "I think I need to pray."

"What?" he replied in surprise.

She looked up at him. He was not irritated, she was glad to see, only puzzled.

"Do you mind?" she asked.

"Well, no . . . I guess not." He struggled with his feelings. "You know how much I love you. Okay, if you want to do this, go right ahead."

She smiled again. "Thank you, dear."

He nodded.

She felt self-conscious as she walked to the other side of the two beds and knelt down. She didn't have the slightest idea what to do as she began her silent prayer. *Heavenly Father, You know the trouble we are in. We don't know what to do. Please help us. Please do something about that lab, and keep it from harming innocent people. I ask these things in Jesus' name.*

She felt a gentle reassurance in her soul. She sighed as she continued her prayers.

17

THE UNDERCOVER TOURIST

There was only one other person in the dining room when Joe approached the breakfast buffet. He gave the waiter his room number and went immediately to the long tables laden with food. He grabbed a warm plate and loaded it with scrambled eggs, bacon, hash brown potatoes, and two biscuits. He took these to a table for two and returned for a fruit plate and a glass of orange juice. By the time he returned to his table, the waiter was ready to serve coffee or tea. Joe selected the hot tea.

He hardly noticed the food since he ate only out of necessity, although the breakfast was quite good. Thinking about the danger his loved ones were in, he felt something cold and heavy in the pit of his stomach. Other people began to drift into the dining room, all westerners, and Joe wondered absently why they were in Iraq. That thought reminded him of what he would face that day. Despite his Navy experience and business success, he felt vulnerable. What could he do against the might and paranoia of President Hammad Talfah? he wondered.

He ate most of his breakfast and lingered over his tea. He had just poured his second cup when a bulky Iraqi in a black uniform appeared at the table.

The man touched his cap. "Mr. Joe Enderly?"

Joe forced his trademark smile. "That's me."

"I have your limousine, sir. Is there anything I can help you with?"

"No, thank you. I'm ready to go." He took a last sip of the tea.

He followed the chauffeur out the door, nodding at the doorman as they swept past. The chauffeur held the rear door of the Mercedes limousine as Joe entered, then hurried around to the driver's door and got in. He put the big car into gear and pulled smoothly into the light traffic. Fifteen minutes later they pulled up outside the office of Babylon Tours. The driver left the engine running and checked the air-conditioning controls.

He looked at Joe in his rearview mirror. "I will tell them you are here, sir."

Joe nodded.

The man got out and hurried inside. A

few minutes later he returned and got in. The driver's door closed with a solid thump that seemed to isolate the limousine's privileged interior from the harsh world outside.

"Your bus is the one in front of us. They will board in ten minutes. The front right-hand window seat is reserved for you. The tour guide will come for you when they are ready to leave."

"Thank you," Joe replied, impressed with the thoroughness of his travel agent.

"Can I get you anything, sir? Coffee? Newspaper?"

"No, thank you. I'll just wait until the tour is ready to leave."

"Very good, sir."

The chauffeur looked straight ahead and left Joe to his privacy.

The bus started loading at 6:45. The group appeared to be entirely western tourists, mostly couples but a few singles as well. Everyone was dressed casually, and they toted every kind of camera imaginable. Joe looked down at his old Pentax K1000, wondering how it measured up. Not very well, he guessed, but then he really wasn't interested in taking pictures, although the Pentax had served him well for many years.

Finally the tour guide left the office and approached the limousine. The chauffeur hopped out and opened the door. Joe stepped out.

"Mr. Enderly," the Iraqi guide said with a broad smile below his thick black mustache. "I am Mizban Ammash, guide for your tour of Babylon." His dark brown eyes were open and friendly. He was several inches short of six feet, and his thick middle said he liked his exercise in sparing amounts.

"I reserved your seat next to mine up front," Mizban said as they approached the large motor coach. "If you have any questions today, please let me know."

"Thank you. You are most kind."

"Glad to be of service."

Mizban waved for Joe to board first. The American smiled at the driver as he mounted the steep steps. The two front seats on the right side were vacant. Joe took the window seat and sat down. The guide said something to the driver in Arabic and took his seat beside Joe. The driver closed the door and pulled out into traffic.

Mizban got up and grabbed a mike. Facing his charges, he clicked the mike on and winced at the sudden squeal. He turned down the volume until the feedback stopped, then greeted the tourists in lightly-accented English. He enthusiastically described the sights of interest in Baghdad.

Soon they were out of the city and heading south. Mizban then shifted to a quick preview of what they would be seeing in Babylon, when and where lunch would be, and what they could buy. He cautioned them to stay with the group at all times. His duty done, he sat down beside Joe.

"Is this your first trip to Iraq, Mr. Enderly?" he asked.

"Yes. I've always been fascinated by Babylon — the hanging gardens, that huge gate, Nebuchadnezzar, and all that. I've wanted to come see it ever since I heard it was being restored."

"I think you will find this tour quite informative. Much of the work has already been done. Nebuchadnezzar's Southern Palace, for example, is very impressive. And we're continuing to find new ruins all the time. We have a team of archaeologists working on a site right now that they think may be Belshazzar's palace. It's right next to the Southern Palace."

Joe felt his pulse quicken. "Will we be seeing that?"

Mizban frowned. "I am afraid not. It is a closed site, so we will not be able to tour it. It is not very interesting anyway since they've only recently begun. Sorry."

"I see." Joe thought about trying a bribe

but decided it was not worth the risk.

About an hour later the bus slowed, turned left, and parked near a large, brickwork gate. Mizban sprang to his feet.

"This is our first stop, ladies and gentlemen," he announced. "Across the highway is the heart of Babylon. But first we're going to see the restored Marduk Gate, one of the entrances to ancient Babylon, named for Marduk, the chief god of Babylon. Please be careful stepping down from the bus. We will be here for fifteen minutes, then reboard the bus to drive into Babylon."

Mizban motioned for Joe to get up. The American got off and stretched his legs. He followed the other tourists as they gathered around their guide. Joe gave every indication of following the practiced spiel. But his thoughts were across the highway. He was so close now. But what could he do, especially since the site was closed?

All eyes turned to the west as the tourists reboarded the bus. Across the highway they could see the reconstructed Greek Theater and a small artificial lake. Mizban counted his charges as the driver crossed the highway and entered the main street leading into Babylon.

Their guide pointed to the right. "Over there is the Greek Theater, which seats

4,000 people. And behind that is an artificial lake. Ahead of us is the Hammurabi Museum and the Nebuchadnezzar Museum as well as a model of the Ishtar Gate. To the left are the temples to Ishtar and Nabu. We will be stopping at the Nebuchadnezzar Museum. There we will tour Procession Street, where we will see Nebuchadnezzar's Southern Palace, the Ninmah Temple, the original Ishtar Gate, and the Lion Monument at the Northern Palace.

"Afterwards, at noon, we will have box lunches under a tent near the Nebuchadnezzar Museum. Then we will enjoy free time to see the museums and visit the shops. You will be on your own until 2. But please, for your own safety do not leave Babylon or try to enter any fenced areas. This is very important, so if you have any questions, please see me."

Mizban clicked off the mike and looked down at Joe. "What do you think?"

"This is terrific," Joe replied, careful to maintain his enthusiasm. "I had no idea so much work had been done down here."

Mizban smiled. "And it's still going on. I understand the new site next to the Southern Palace is going to be spectacular once the archaeologists are finished and we can begin the reconstruction."

"I'm sure it will. That where we're going?"

The guide looked where Joe was pointing.

"Yes. That is the Nebuchadnezzar Museum."

The driver parked the bus and waited patiently as the tourists got off. Mizban waited until he had everyone gathered around.

"That's Procession Street," he said pointing. "Follow me."

He led them through towering brick arches and into the Southern Palace complex, culminating with the impressive throne room with its arched entrance and high walls. He carefully explained the function of each room before leading them across the street to the Ninmah Temple, a large brick structure with a typical high arch entrance, this one inset from the exterior wall by several steps. Further down the street they examined the original Ishtar Gate with its bas-relief bulls and dragons. The last stop before lunch was the Lion Monument at the Northern Palace.

"Was it what you expected?" Mizban asked Joe as they were walking back toward the Nebuchadnezzar Museum.

"This is fabulous. It's everything I hoped it would be, and more."

Mizban smiled. "Be sure to tell your friends."

"Don't worry, I will."

The guide turned and pointed to the striped tent. "Listen, everybody, here's where we have lunch. Go through the line and pick up your box lunches. Then we have free time until 2. But please remember what I said — stay inside Babylon and do not enter any fenced areas. This is for your own safety."

He stood to the side as the hungry tourists hurried toward the food lines.

"Don't miss your lunch," he said to Joe who was looking across the street.

"Don't worry about me. I don't miss meals." He pointed at the high fence that surrounded the parking lot beside the Southern Palace. "What's in there?"

Mizban turned around. "We won't know for sure until the archaeologists are done. But they say it's probably the remains of Belshazzar's palace."

Joe's heart beat faster. He saw a man leave one of the temporary buildings and walk toward the dig. He recognized him instantly — it was Mars.

"That sounds fascinating," he said. "They're working on it now?"

"Yes, and will be for some time."

Joe took a deep breath. "Would it be possible to see what they're doing?"

Mizban shook his head sadly. "No. I am sorry. It is too dangerous." He gave a sudden laugh. "Besides, archaeologists are strange people. They don't like us ordinary mortals poking our noses in their business."

Joe considered pursuing the matter but decided not to. He joined the end of the line and waited for his box lunch. He finally made it to the table, picked up his white box, grabbed a plastic glass of iced tea, and made his way outside to be by himself.

The lunch wasn't bad, he decided. There was a chicken sandwich, an apple, a small bunch of grapes, and a sweet roll wrapped in plastic. But the heavy lump in his stomach had taken away his appetite. He ate only because he knew he needed to. He finished the lunch and tossed the box into the trash barrel. He sipped on the tea as he looked across the street at the archaeological site.

Mars descended the ladder and stood behind Anne. She was down on her hands and knees examining the base of a wall.

"Are we down to the foundation yet?" he asked.

"I don't think so. We need to keep digging."

She extended her arms to relieve a cramp

but remained on the ground. Mars smiled, and a short laugh escaped before he could stop it. Anne whipped her head around and looked up at him.

"What's so funny?" she demanded, their situation forgotten for the moment.

"Nothing," he replied, but the glint in his eyes gave him away.

"Yeah, right."

She struggled to her feet and looked up into his eyes. "I know that look when I see it. Now, what's so funny?"

"Er, well, you are."

"Me? What did I do?"

"You didn't do anything. It's how you looked."

"And how did I look?"

"Can't we talk about something else?"

"No, we cannot. Now, out with it."

"Boy, Moshe was sure right about you being persistent."

"Mars . . ." He heard her rising tone and knew the clear warning of an approaching storm.

"Er, you looked sort of like a frog."

"A frog? Your wife looks like a frog?"

"Umm . . . Well, see, you were all hunkered down, quite compact, and the back part is kinda wide. And then, when you raised up in front, it hit me, so to speak."

She tried to keep her stern expression but felt it slipping away. He was glad to see the change in the weather. They both looked up as they heard someone approaching. Moshe smiled down on them, but they could also see the tension in his eyes.

"And how is the wall coming?"

"We're making progress," Anne replied, "but we're not down to the foundation yet."

Moshe nodded. "All in all, though, this dig is going quite well." He glanced around nervously. "Except for one technical detail."

"Is that why you came over here?" Mars asked.

Moshe tried to take on a demanding look but was only partially successful. "Actually, I came over to make sure you children are playing nicely."

"But your *yenta* duties are over," Mars pointed out.

"True, true. But I still care. Now, I caught a few words drifting up from the pit as I approached. What were you two talking about?"

"Aren't you being a little nosy?" Anne asked, fixing him with a critical gaze.

"Why, no, of course not. It would be kinder to call it interested."

"But not as accurate." Anne struggled not to smile.

"Hmm. I guess I will never learn."

"What?"

"That you can't win an argument with a female." He held up a hand to ward off her rebuttal. "O.K., O.K. I'm being nosy. So what were you two talking about?"

Anne turned to Mars.

"We could plead the Fifth Amendment," he said. "According to that amendment of our country's Constitution . . ."

"Yes, I am familiar with that expression, Mars. Now back to the question at hand . . ."

"Mars, we don't have anything to hide."

Mars examined his stained sling as if it contained the answer. "Umm, Anne was hunkered down examining the wall." He glanced at her and decided that gale warnings were not posted yet. "And, well . . . she sort of looked like a frog."

A complex expression flitted across Moshe's face. "A frog? Anne looked like an amphibian?"

"It loses something in the telling."

"Apparently." The smile returned to his bearded face. "But you are playing nicely?" he asked again.

Mars circled his long left arm around

Anne, pulled her to his side, and gave her a squeeze. She smiled up at him.

"Yes, we're playing nicely," Mars answered for them.

"Good. Now, there's something I need to see Ghanim about. If you two will excuse me . . ."

Anne waited until he was out of earshot. "A frog? You think I look like a frog?" She couldn't keep from smiling.

"Not now," he said. He leaned down and kissed her, pulling her close. "You look like my loving wife."

"That's better." Then she returned his kiss.

He sighed as he released her. "Suddenly it's quite warm down here." He glanced at his watch. "Hey, it's after 12. You ready for some lunch?"

"Yes. We're at a stopping point anyway."

Mars clambered up the ladder and held out his left hand to help Anne up. They looked toward the towering chain-link fence in the direction of the Nebuchadnezzar Museum. Mars pointed at the striped tent.

"Looks like a tour group is going through Babylon. Guess it's their lunchtime too."

Anne's shoulders slumped. "Don't you wish we could just join them and get out of here?"

"Yeah. But there's not much chance of getting past the zookeepers. We'd better . . ."

"What is it, Mars?"

She followed his gaze, at first seeing nothing but a sea of typical tourists. Then she spotted someone familiar.

"It's . . ."

Her exclamation was abruptly cut off by Mars's hand. She glanced up at him and nodded. She understood.

Mars sought out his father's face again. Did he know they were here? A thrill of excitement raced down Mars's spine. He must know — why else would he be here? And that meant he knew about the lab. Mars wondered if his father also knew it was biological.

Joe was sauntering toward Procession Street. Mars felt a tight knot grow in his stomach. He knew that his father saw him. But with all the paranoid Iraqi security in the area, what could he do? Mars watched as Joe brought both his hands up in front of his chest, palms out. He moved them about in a quick pattern and then stopped, apparently waiting.

Mars grinned as he recognized what it meant. Years earlier, while Joe was still in the Navy, he had taught his son signal flags along with Morse code. Joe had told him that Navy signalmen frequently used their hands rather than flags when communicating at close range. Mars swept his left hand around in a big question mark. After a few moments Joe repeated his message.

Mars struggled to remember the code as he puzzled over each signal. Finally he had it. "How can I help?"

Anne looked up at him, obviously dying to know what was going on. He nodded at her and turned back to Procession Street. Joe was still waiting.

"Have you seen Ghanim?" he asked Anne.

"I think he's still working in . . . Oh, here he comes now."

Mars saw him a fraction of a second after Anne did. Ghanim was obviously heading for the dining hall with lunch on his mind.

"Come on," Mars said quickly.

He hurried to head off the Iraqi while Anne struggled to keep up.

"Ghanim," Mars called out as they approached.

He looked toward Mars and slackened his pace a little. "Yes, Mars."

"I had a question about the cistern," Mars said as he approached.

"Shall we discuss it over lunch?" Ghanim suggested.

"No, it's something I have to show you. I'd like to finish my notes before lunch, if you don't mind."

The Iraqi puzzled over this. "I guess not," he said finally, with a little irritation.

Mars led the way back to the work pit nearest the Guest House and went down the ladder. He walked to the end of the pit and jumped into the rubble-strewn cistern. Then he stooped over and disappeared into the dim interior of the water tunnel. The other two followed him in.

"What is it you need?" Ghanim asked.

Mars lowered his voice to a whisper. "We have to talk. My dad is here."

Ghanim glanced around toward the cistern. "No, no, please . . . What if they hear us?"

"They can't hear us down here as long as we whisper," Mars said, hoping he was right.

Ghanim didn't look too sure. "What in the world is he doing in Iraq?"

"My guess is, he knows about the lab and the air strike. And he probably also knows we were ordered to get out and haven't been heard from."

Ghanim glared at Mars. "And what does

he think *he* can do about it — call in the Marines?"

Mars couldn't help a smile. "Well, he *was* in the Navy. But to answer your question, I have no idea. I wish he hadn't come . . ."

"That makes two of us," Ghanim grumbled.

". . . but he's here. And Dad *is* pretty good in getting what he goes after. He was involved in covert operations when he was in the Navy."

The Iraqi shrugged in disgust. "I don't see what he can do."

Mars smiled. "As a matter of fact, that's what he asked me: 'How can I help?' "

"How could he ask you that?"

Mars explained the semaphore code.

"So what do I tell him?"

"How can you signal him?"

"I'll use Morse code from inside the tent. What do I tell him?"

"We can't meet, that's for sure," Ghanim grumbled.

"Other than telling him to go home, what can I say?"

Ghanim thought it over. "I hope he is discreet."

"Trust me, he is."

"He could contact Nadhim, I guess, but I don't know what good that would do."

Mars felt a ray of hope. "Let's do it. It certainly can't hurt. What is Nadhim's address?"

"Number 47 Arbat, Al Hillah."

"O.K., I'll tell him. Anne, I think you and Ghanim should go back to the dining hall. I'll go to the tent like I have to make an entry in the computer. That should keep any of the bad guys from seeing me. I'll send the message and join you when I'm done. We'll find a way to tell Moshe later. That sound okay?"

"Yes," Anne replied.

"I suppose," Ghanim said. "Please be careful."

"Believe me, I will."

They left the pit and started walking back toward the dining hall. As they approached, Mars left them and went into the tent. He switched on the PC, flipped up the screen, and viewed a document for a few moments. He glanced toward Procession Street. Joe was still there, and no one else appeared interested in what was going on inside the fence. Mars shut off the PC and closed the lid. He picked up a flashlight and retreated further into the dim recesses of the tent. He moved the switch to flash and tested it, then pointed the light directly at Joe and slowly flashed his message. "Nadhim Shakir 47 Arbat Al Hillah." He resisted the urge to repeat it.

After a few moments, Joe signaled back, "Got it."

Mars smiled. He knew he had.

18

A DOOMSDAY TEAM

Ari Jacovy rushed into Ya'acov's office without knocking and sat down. "Your suspicion was right," he said. "He told the people at IAI that he was taking a two-week vacation in Tiberias. Someone did indeed check in at the Vered Hagalil Guest-Farm in Galilee, and there are bags in the cottage — but Joe Enderly is not there. I checked at Ben Gurion and found the copy of his landing card. He left Israel yesterday sometime after you talked to him. I traced all possible flights and missed him on first try. Then I found a passenger named Joseph Anderley."

Ya'acov snorted. "Nice touch. Different enough to give us trouble finding it but close enough to explain as a spelling error."

"We're not dealing with an amateur."

Ya'acov thought over his previous experience with the Enderlys. "I'm sure he could have made things a lot harder for us if he had wanted to. My guess is, he really doesn't care if we know where he is as long as he gets there. In fact, he probably wants us to know."

"Why?"

"He wants our help."

"But he can't change military policy."

A wry smile came to Ya'acov's face. "He's done it before." He saw that Ari remembered as well. "What else did you find?"

"He flew to Amman, then on to Baghdad. He checked into the Ishtar Sheraton last night and left this morning on a tour conducted by Babylon Tours. Guess where?"

Ya'acov rolled his eyes. "I haven't a clue," he stated facetiously. "This is great. We're missing a famous Israeli archaeologist along with his two American colleagues and now a rich American industrialist with his head chockful of Israeli and American secrets besides. What could be better."

"Nothing's happened yet."

"That won't last long. The question is, what should we do?"

"For starters, we have to tell the boss."

"True. That's our next stop. But what do we recommend?"

"Open up the satellite link?"

"Let's give it a shot. After you, Lieutenant."

The two officers found David Kruger in

his office. The colonel listened solemnly to Ya'acov's summary. The younger officer began to be concerned about his status before he was done.

"So, now we have someone else to worry about," David snapped. "And this one knows state secrets." He eyed Ya'acov. "I presume you have a recommendation."

"Yes, sir. I recommend we open up the satellite link. If they still have the computer, maybe they can tell us what's going on."

"You know we can't do that, Ya'acov. If they're on the way out — and they probably are — it would serve no purpose. They'd have no knowledge of Joe being there. If they are being held, we certainly don't want to do anything the Iraqis might detect."

"But there's nothing they can detect."

"No, Ya'acov. The link stays down."

"What about the possibility that the archaeologists are at the Babylonian site? Shouldn't we call off the strike until we know?"

David struggled to contain his temper. "Don't push me too far. I told you that was a closed subject. The strike is still on. Too much has gone into it to call it off. This won't affect our friends one way or the other. The only thing that's going to be hit is that underground lab. Moshe, Mars, and Anne are innocent bystanders. The Iraqis won't do anything to them."

"O.K. What about Joe Enderly?"

David pursed his lips as he thought. Finally he said, "That will be all, gentlemen."

The tour had been well done, Joe had to admit. But it had held no interest for him except for the chance to see his son. And that had been a heart-stopper. The guide had been very attentive and seemed disappointed at Joe's lack of attention after lunch. Joe snorted. Probably thought I was a typical American tourist, more interested in when the next meal was rather than how old the artifacts were.

Mars's message had been clear enough. Joe was to see Nadhim Shakir who lived at 47 Arbat in Al Hillah. The only problem was how to get there and find the man without bringing Iraqi security police down on his head.

The sun was nearing the western horizon by the time Joe left the lobby. He was dressed in heavy pants and a durable long-sleeved shirt and wore high-quality hiking boots. He stood on the sidewalk for a few moments. A taxi driver rushed to the curb at his nod. Joe opened the back door and got in. The driver smiled at him, revealing a mouthful of teeth that had only a few vacancies.

"I would like a drive," Joe began. "Are there any good restaurants in Al Hillah?"

The man's smile grew wider, obviously anticipating a good fare. "Oh, yes sir. Many good places to eat."

"Good. Could you recommend one?"

"Leave it to me, sir."

Joe nodded.

The driver poked the button on his meter and pulled briskly into the Baghdad traffic. They followed the same route the tour bus had taken that morning but with a little more *élan*. The dusk deepened as the western sky turned orange and then deep red before fading into violet as the stars started coming out. The cab swept past Babylon, and soon the lights of Al Hillah appeared in the distance.

The driver slowed his pace a little as the open desert gave way to the outlying houses. They continued through the city until they were near the southern edge. Finally the driver slowed and turned off the highway, continuing past several streets before making a final turn. Moments later he stopped in front of a white-painted concrete building with its name in huge red letters: *Ali Baba*. The driver turned around. Joe could not see his face very well in the darkness, but he was sure the magnificent smile was on display again. He pointed toward the restaurant.

"The Ali Baba, sir. But do not worry — the forty thieves are elsewhere. Good food. Middle-Eastern, western, whatever you want. Even pizza and hamburgers."

"Sounds wonderful."

"I can come back," the man said hopefully.

"No, that's not necessary. But I would appreciate some information. A friend of mine lives on Arbat — number 6, I think. Could you tell me where that is?"

"Surely. Go to the end of this block and turn left. You will ran into Arbat — it is three or maybe four streets. You cannot miss it."

Joe thanked him and did a quick calculation on the meter's fare. He handed the driver the equivalent in dollars plus a handsome tip. He could have paid in Iraqi currency, but, not knowing how much he would need before this mission was over, he wanted to keep as many dinars on hand as possible.

"Oh, thank you, sir. Thank you so much."

Joe got out and stood on the narrow sidewalk as the happy cabby drove away. He then entered the dim interior of the restaurant. Not feeling dietarily adventuresome, he opted for a hamburger, an order of fries, and a Coke. He smiled at the waiter when he brought the meal and ate it without interest. When he finished, he paid the bill and stepped out into the night.

The street was surprisingly well lit. He walked to the corner and turned left. By the third block he was in deep shadows. The fourth street turned out to be Arbat. He turned right and made his way slowly along until he saw number 47 painted on the side of a small concrete house. He walked up to the neglected wooden front door and knocked. When no one answered, he knocked harder, wincing at the echoing sound. This started the neighborhood dogs on a round of barking. The door opened a crack, and someone said something in Arabic.

Joe took a deep breath. "Are you Nadhim Shakir?"

The door started to close. "I am Joe Enderly, Mars's father. Ghanim Jassim sent me," he added quickly, grateful he remembered the archaeologist's name.

For a while nothing happened. Then the door swung slowly open, revealing a tall, thin young man with brown hair. His dark brown eyes told how scared he was. He motioned for silence as he stepped out and closed the door. Joe followed him toward the blackness that marked the southern edge of Al Hillah. When the last house light was behind them, Nadhim led Joe a little further into the desert scrub the sand and rocks crunching under their shoes.

"What do you want?" he demanded.

"Mars Enderly told me to come see you. I presume the message came from Ghanim Jassim."

"I know Mars, and Ghanim is my uncle. How did Mars contact you?"

Joe sensed the young man's tenseness. "I was in Babylon this morning. I saw the fence. Mars signaled me using Morse code." Joe hesitated, wishing he could see Nadhim's eyes. "I know about the lab."

"Forgive me, Mr. Enderly, but our meeting is very dangerous for both of us."

"Please call me Joe."

"Joe, do you know what will happen to us if the security people catch us?"

"I have a pretty good idea."

"So, you know about the lab. What else do you know?"

"I know it's going to be bombed sometime early tomorrow."

"And do you know what the lab does?"

"The attackers think it is used for nuclear research. But I believe it's actually working on biological warfare."

"You are right. So you also realize what will happen if those idiots bomb it."

"I do. That's one of the reasons I'm here." He paused. "The other is to try and help some friends of mine."

"I understand." Nadhim sighed. "And that is the end of it. Neither one of us can do anything about the lab or the strike."

"Mars — or your uncle — must have had some reason for me contacting you. Why?"

"The only reason I can think of is that I work there. I handle maintenance for the lab."

Joe whistled. "Now I think I understand. Could you do anything about this if you were inside the lab?"

Nadhim thought that over. "Yes, it is possible — if I were tired of living. But that does us no good. I'm not scheduled to work until tomorrow night, and that will be too late."

"Could you get in tonight if you wanted to?" Joe asked, though he already knew the answer.

"Impossible. You wouldn't believe the security."

"Oh, I think I would. Did Mars tell you anything about me? Do you know what the Navy SEALS do?"

"Some. What used to be called under-water demolition teams."

"UDT — that's right. Except the SEALS do a lot more — sort of like UDT on steroids. I've been out for quite a while, but I think I remember the basic steps. And I'm in reasonably good condition for an old codger."

Nadhim laughed in spite of the situation. "I am glad I didn't get rough with you earlier."

"Nadhim, we have to do *something*. Tell me how you get to the lab, and we'll see if that suggests any ideas."

Nadhim described his unusual daily commute. Joe kept probing him for details until he understood the entire process. There was a long silence after Nadhim finished.

"That's very thorough," Joe said at last.

"It's impossible," Nadhim added with feeling.

"Not impossible, only very difficult."

"You think you can get past all that?"

Joe laughed. "Twenty years ago, with the right people and equipment, yeah."

"What about today with you and me?"

"Harder, but it still could be done. Nadhim, this is the only chance we have. Either we get in there and do something about that lab or this whole area of the world is dead.

We don't have a choice. We have to try."

"I can't argue with that, though I am frightened about trying anything."

"If we can get in there, what can you do?"

"I could destroy the lab. That's the only thing that would work. The designers knew what would happen if we had an accident that released biological agents into the air. If containment is breached, sensors close the armored door on the entrance, the entire lab is infused with pure oxygen, and strategically-placed white phosphorus flares are ignited. The entire lab would be ashes in less than a minute."

Joe exhaled slowly. "Wow. That would do it, all right."

"All the lab wiring — power, fiber-optic, sensors — goes through the utility room where my maintenance shop is located. Induce the correct signal on the alarm circuit, and the rest is automatic."

Joe pushed the light button on his watch. "It's nearly 9. When would be the best time to do it?"

"The shift change goes from 11:30 until 12. There is time to do it before, but it would be better after."

"Why?"

"There is a good chance we will run into the maintenance man in the shop. The man on the third shift — I don't know his name — is not very sharp. But the one who is on now would be hard to handle."

"That's cutting it close."

"When is the strike due?"

"Early tomorrow — that's all I know. My guess would be between 1 and 2, but it could be earlier."

"Do you want to try it before the shift change?" Nadhim asked.

"No, I trust your judgment. When can we go in?"

"At 12:15, I would say. The subway usually runs right on the hour."

"O.K. That gives us a little time to prepare. Do you have any weapons in your house?"

"I have a pistol."

"Can't use that. Any knives? What about some sort of club?"

"I will show you what I have. Say nothing when we get back to the house."

"I understand."

They returned to the young Iraqi's home and waited to make sure everything was quiet. Nadhim let them in and led Joe into a small bedroom. The Iraqi pulled open a drawer and took out four knives. Joe picked out one with a thin, six-inch blade that looked sharp enough for shaving. Nadhim nodded at the selection. The one he took for himself had a slightly longer, thicker blade. Joe's eyes darted around the room, stopping on a three-foot stick propped up in a corner. He picked it up and hefted it. It wasn't perfect, he decided, but it would serve.

Nadhim undressed to his shorts and undershirt and pulled on his work coveralls. He motioned toward the tiny living room. The two men sat down and began their wait.

Nadhim turned off the lights and stepped to the door. He listened for a moment before turning the knob. As he and Joe hurried outside, the front of the house was in deep shadows. The stars blazed down on Al Hillah through the clear, cool desert air.

Joe reached down and put the knife in his boot. "Got any transportation?" he asked as he hefted the club.

Nadhim pointed to a motor scooter.

"Let's go," Joe said.

Nadhim removed the lock and chain and inserted the key in the ignition. The engine started on the third kick. Nadhim sat on the saddle and held the club as Joe climbed on and put his feet up. The two men then trapped the club between their legs and the seats.

They rode slowly through Al Hillah and

out onto the highway. The wind whipped about their clothes as they drove through the cool desert night. The tiny headlight bounced and jiggled as it painted an inadequate pool of yellowish light on the road ahead. Soon the blackness swallowed up all light except that provided by the scooter. Joe squirmed around on the buddy seat trying to get comfortable and avoid the annoying vibration, but it was impossible.

Finally a small oasis of light appeared on the horizon. A diesel truck roared up behind them and swept past, pelting them with gravel and grit. The freight vehicle's taillights dwindled as the driver pressed on toward the truck stop. Joe was about to nudge Nadhim when the latter switched off the lights and pulled off the road. He killed the engine and handed the club to Joe before pushing the scooter into the deep ditch running parallel to the highway.

Colonel John Barker scanned the gently glowing instrument panel as he waited. The F-117's two turbofan engines whined somewhere below and behind him as the angular black delta-shaped plane waited on the active runway. Behind him was the rest of his flight, two more stealth fighters waiting for the same thing he was. But his helmet earphones were silent. The runway lights drew parallel lines that seemed to merge at the far end, where he would be comfortably airborne with his two companions or else the source of a bright fire marking his grave. He shook off the morbid thought. The bird was full-up, max on fuel, and carrying a heavy weapon, making the takeoff less than routine. But the F-117 was a capable aircraft with an excellent safety record. True, its flying characteristics left much to be desired, and it was a hog on gas. But the radar-hiding stealth more than made up for that.

John looked up. It was a clear night. Billions of stars looked down on him, bright and unwinking. The surrounding desert was as dark as a black cat in a coal bin, except for the runway lights.

His earphones crackled. "Badger leader, your flight is cleared for takeoff."

"Roger," he said into his throat mike.

He stood on the brakes while he smoothly pushed the throttles forward. When the RPM hit 100 percent, he released the brakes. The fighter surged forward, and the runway lights began to move past, slowly at first, then in a streak. A quick scan of the instruments told him everything was operating at peak efficiency.

The airspeed indicator hit the magic

number, and John pulled smoothly back on
the stick. The plane rotated to takeoff attitude, hesitated for the briefest moment, then
lifted into the darkness. The airspeed built
rapidly as the runway lights dropped away.
Badger leader smiled to himself. *This is what
it is all about,* he thought as he felt the familiar adrenaline surge.

He made a quick check on his radar. Good
— no one behind, and the other two aircraft
of his flight were with him. He pulled back
on the throttles slightly. The altimeter continued to wind upward as they reached for
their cruising altitude. The rest of the trip
would be made in radio silence.

Nadhim led the way through the desert
brush, angling gradually away from the highway. For a long time neither man could see
anything except the black branches that
snagged and tore at their clothes and the
dreamlike glow up ahead coming from the
unseen truck stop. Then they topped a rise,
and Joe could see the main building and the
cars and trucks parked in front. The area
behind the stop was utter blackness, but a
little light reflected off the razor wire topping
the high chain-link fence.

Joe tapped his guide on the shoulder and
assumed the lead. Both men crouched as

they cautiously approached what Joe estimated to be the middle of the fence. He saw
the dim outline of the links just before he
reached it. He reached out and brushed the
metal with the back of his hand, then
breathed a sigh of relief. He didn't think it
would be electrified and was glad to find he
was right.

He looked up. Dim starlight reflected off
the coiled razor wire high overhead. He was
prepared to climb the fence as a last resort
but definitely preferred an easier way in. He
dropped to his hands and knees and started
crawling away from the truck stop, feeling
the links as he went. About fifty feet down
the line, he snagged his hand on a sharp
wire. He felt cautiously around the protru-
sion and discovered two layers of fence.

Vicious barks suddenly tore out of the
darkness. Joe whirled around in a crouch
and grabbed Nadhim, who had started to
bolt. He pulled him back down and pulled
him along into the thick brush. The dog
continued his frantic growling and barking.
An overhead light winked on, blindingly
bright after the deep darkness. Joe winced
as he lost his night vision but consoled himself with the knowledge that the guard had
also.

The two intruders watched as the guard

approached, his huge Doberman pinscher straining at the chain lead. The dog pulled his master to the fence. The Doberman sniffed around the links Joe had touched and dug halfheartedly at the ground. The guard unclipped the flashlight from his belt and panned it slowly around. Joe buried his head in the dirt as the narrow beam prowled among the dense foliage. He looked up cautiously as the beam continued on around to the fence. Then the guard clipped the light back on his belt. He said something in Arabic and pulled on the chain. The dog lunged against the lead as he continued to paw at the ground. The guard jerked the chain hard, and the dog yelped in pain and reluctantly followed his master. The light clicked out.

Joe breathed a sigh of relief as the crunching footsteps faded into the distance. He crawled back to the fence, grateful that the flashlight had shown him what he wanted to know. Joe handed Nadhim the club and began untwisting the wires holding the overlapped fencing material together. Then he pulled on the outer piece while pushing on the inner. It gave. He wriggled into the gap and began pushing his way through. It was a very tight fit, but he wormed his way along, wondering what he would do if he got stuck.

Finally he felt the constricting pressure lessen. He was almost through. He clawed at the dirt and pushed with his legs. One more effort and he was free. He turned and took the club from Nadhim before helping him through the gap.

Joe stood in a crouch and listened. He could not hear the guard or his dog. He tried to estimate where the derelict bus was and crept cautiously off in that direction. They had gone about 100 feet when they heard a low growl. Joe froze and felt Nadhim bump into him. Joe couldn't tell where the dog was and wondered absently if it was the guard returning. Then he heard a distant bark coming from near the back of the junkyard.

Joe realized this was another dog and wondered whether a guard was with this one also. Another growl, this time closer. The hairs raised on the back of Joe's neck. He knew attack was imminent. He heard rather than saw the rush of the dog's paws and the silence of the leap. His stomach went ice-cold as he brought up his club against the unseen attacker. The weapon hesitated high overhead before Joe brought it down in a brutal, scything motion. The club connected with something solid. A sharp yelp of pain pierced the darkness, and a heavy, warm body brushed past, almost knocking Joe off his feet.

A light clicked on near the back of the yard. A tall, angular piece of junk lay in between, and Joe watched in horror as the bobbing light came closer. He reached into his boot for the knife and pointed. Nadhim gulped and nodded. They ran toward the object blocking the guard's view and crouched. Joe reached down and closed his hand around something cold and heavy. He waited, then throw it to the side as the guard trotted past. The piece of metal clanged off another piece of junk. The guard skidded to a stop, his left arm extended by the taut chain. The man whirled around, the light clipped to his belt turning with him. He gasped in surprise when he spotted the dead dog and started reaching toward his holster. Joe threw the knife, hoping he had estimated the distance correctly. The thin blade flashed through the flashlight's glare and buried itself in the man's chest. He gasped and fell forward, landing on his side, then rolled over on his back and lay still. Joe winced as he saw the flashlight beam stabbing into the heavens.

The dog lunged against the chain. On the third leap he pulled the padded grip loose from the dead man's hand. The Doberman pinscher wheeled around and tore over the ground. Joe brought the heavy club down, and the threat ended with a muted yelp. Joe ran to the dead guard and flipped off the light, unclipped it, and attached it to his own belt. He then retrieved his knife, wiped it on the guard's shirt, and put it back in his boot.

Having caught a glimpse of the bus, Joe led the way toward the black shape, shuffling his feet to avoid tripping over unseen junk. Finally they reached it.

"How do we get in?" Joe whispered.

Nadhim led the way to the front. He opened the door for Joe, let him enter, and followed him inside.

"Give me a little light," Nadhim requested.

Joe clicked on the flashlight.

Nadhim hurried to the trap door and held it up. "Down the stairs."

Joe rushed down the concrete steps. Nadhim lowered the trap and joined him in front of the combination door.

"I'm not supposed to know this," he muttered as he punched in the code. "The supervisor isn't very careful." The lock clicked obediently, and Nadhim opened the door. After closing it again, he joined Joe on the small platform.

"Shine the light on the tracks. The subway

is waiting at the lab for the end of the shift. See that metal channel on the far side of the tracks? That provides the power. As long as we stay inside the rails we'll be O.K. Are you ready?"

Joe nodded. "Ready. Go ahead and step down. You lead and I'll keep my hand on your shoulder."

Nadhim jumped down between the rails, and Joe followed him. The light clicked off, leaving them in absolute darkness. "Will there be any light at the lab's platform?" Joe asked.

"Yes. Not very bright, but we'll see it long before we get there."

"Lead on."

19

TWICE DESTROYED

John Barker checked his Global Positioning System readout. They had been in the air for almost thirty minutes, and his flight was rapidly approaching the end of Jordanian airspace and the rendezvous with the KC-10 tanker, whose presence they should have spotted by now. He began to wonder if something had happened to their gas station. Such events were common, he knew, and if it happened, the mission was a scrub. And with the horsepower behind this one, heads would roll. He breathed a sigh of relief as he saw navigational lights and a dim outline up ahead, a shape that quickly grew into a huge tanker.

A bright light came on as the plane approached. John maneuvered into position as the crewman in the tail of the KC-10 guided the refueling probe down toward the fighter. He heard and felt the solid *chunk* as the probe inserted and latched. The pilot micromanaged the controls as he struggled to maintain a tight position on the tanker. Slowly the fuel gauges crept upward until the fighter was completely topped off. Barker looked up and waved at the boom operator, and the man cut off the fuel flow. A few seconds later John disconnected and moved to the side while the other two fighters took their turns.

John sighed. So far, so good. Now came the hard part. Was the stealth really as good as advertised? he wondered. He knew the statistics, the claims, and the history of the plane in actual combat. But this was his hide — his and two other aviators'.

Nadhim kept up a brisk pace, Joe was glad to see. The blackness was complete. Their footsteps echoed off the walls as they crunched their way over the track's ballast. If the one mile estimate was correct, it would take about fifteen minutes to reach the other end. Joe kept peering ahead, looking for some glimmer of light. Several times he thought he saw something, but when he closed his eyes and opened them again, there was nothing. Finally he saw a murky glow in the distance. As they got closer, they could see the dim outlines of the subway car. Joe tugged on Nadhim's shoulder.

"You said the maintenance man will be in the utility room?"

"He should be."

"And there's only one TV camera that covers the platform?"

"That is correct, and one inside the shop. If anyone is watching the platform, they'll probably think I'm the duty maintenance man, unless they also look inside the shop, which isn't likely because it's not very interesting in there. The light's dim on the platform, so if you stay on my far side, I doubt that they'll see you. If you take care of the man in the shop, I will take the camera inside the lab out of commission."

"I'm ready," Joe said with more enthusiasm than he felt.

Nadhim jumped onto the platform. When Joe joined him, they hurried toward the utility room. Nadhim quickly punched in the code and opened the door. He reached up and disconnected the TV camera's cable as Joe rushed past.

"He's not here," he whispered.

Nadhim looked around and shook his head. "Must be inside the lab somewhere. We'd better hurry. No telling when he'll be back. Watch the door while I get to work."

"What about mikes?"

A wry smile came to Nadhim's face.

"There are several in here," he admitted, savoring the look of shock on Joe's face. "But unknown to the security people, they don't work."

He opened a toolbox and took out a screwdriver and a set of nut drivers. He located the correct cable duct and removed the cover. Inside were a series of pencil-thick black cables and heavy bundles of multicolored wires wrapped with plastic ties. He ran to a filing cabinet and pulled open the bottom drawer. He flipped quickly through the folders until he found the wiring diagram he wanted. He pulled it out and rushed back to the workbench, where he examined the drawing for a few moments, then searched one of the wiring bundles.

"There's the first pair," he mumbled to himself. "And there's the second."

He inserted pins through the insulation on each of the four wires. Then he attached two alligator clip test leads to one wire of each of the two pairs. He looked at Joe.

"Are you ready? These are the signal wires from two separate containment alarm circuits. If both circuits are shorted within five seconds of each other, the lab automatically self-destructs. If either shorts, or if they both short more than five seconds apart, an alarm is activated in the control room in the Guest

House basement above us. That allows the security boss to decide if the threat is real."

Joe nodded. "So, if both alarms go off at the same time, they know it's real."

"That's what the designers decided."

"Will we have any problem getting out?"

"We shouldn't. The armored door is supposed to keep the fire inside the lab, and the guard station is inside, so we should not have to worry about them either."

"Let's do it," Joe said.

Nadhim took the loose alligator clips, one in each hand. He looked at the wires carefully, making sure he had the right ones. He attached one clip and then the other.

A loud Klaxon horn sounded outside the utility room, accompanied by an ominous rumbling noise. A muted thud told them the armored door leading to Security was in place.

"I can't hear anything," Joe said. "Is it burning?"

"You won't hear anything out here. There are several feet of concrete and steel between us and the lab. But to answer your question . . ."

He rushed to a computer perched on a small, cluttered desk. He tilted the monitor and keyed a command. His hands moved quickly over the keyboard as the program responded. A grim expression came to his face.

"No doubt about it. The lab is a cinder." He glanced at Joe.

"Thinking about the people trapped inside?"

Nadhim nodded.

"I don't like that part of it either. That was something I could never entirely shake when I was a SEAL. But given the circumstances, there's nothing else we could have done."

"I know. And it is definitely done now."

Joe pointed toward the ceiling. "Do they know?"

"Oh, yes. The containment breach sounded up there as well, and they know the lab has been destroyed."

"Will they come down here?"

Nadhim smiled. "Depends on how brave they are. What if some of the bugs got out?"

A heavy relay closed somewhere, and a deep throbbing noise came through the shop's walls.

Nadhim cursed. "Someone's braver than I thought. That's the elevator to the Guest House."

"Do something."

Nadhim ran to an access panel and threw it open. He quickly selected the correct circuit breaker and tripped it. The throbbing stopped.

"Should I clean all this up?" Nadhim asked, pointing to the exposed wiring and the test leads.

Joe glanced at his watch. It was almost 1:30. "No. We have to get out of here. The air strike could come at any moment."

Joe pulled the door open slowly and peered out. A heavy black door sealed the lab's security entrance. Other than that, the subway platform looked just as it had earlier. He and Nadhim stepped out and began running toward the subway car. When a loud crash sounded behind them, Joe whirled around in time to see a man jump down to the floor.

"The man in the elevator," Nadhim said. "He was further down than I thought."

"Come on!" Joe shouted.

The man jerked a gun out and fired, the shot shattering one of the subway's windows. Joe and Nadhim pounded across the hard concrete toward the darkness of the tunnel. The man fired twice more, and Nadhim yelped in pain. The other shot plowed into the concrete wall to their right. The fugitives sailed out into the darkness and landed heavily on the subway's roadbed, continuing into the darkness toward the truck stop without a pause.

"Are you hit?" Joe asked.

Nadhim reached down and touched something wet and warm. "Yes. In the side."

"How bad is it?"

The Iraqi cried out as he felt around. "I didn't know anything could hurt like that."

"Can you go on?" Joe asked in growing alarm.

"I think so, though I am bleeding badly."

Joe looked back toward the platform. A shadowy shape edged around the corner. "Stuff something in it. Come on — that guy won't stay back there forever."

Joe led the way as they began walking toward the distant truck stop. He didn't know how long it would take to get there, though he knew they were moving much more slowly than they had on the way in. Nadhim's footsteps were slow and faltering, and Joe began to wonder if he would have to carry his new friend out.

A solid thud echoed through the tunnel, as if someone had slammed something down hard. A high-pitched whining sound drifted down to the two men, and a dark shape blocked the dim light coming from the platform.

"He's in the subway," Nadhim gasped. "He's going to run us down."

Joe whirled around and clicked on the flashlight clipped to his belt, the need for secrecy gone. The subway was lumbering toward them, and an icy pang of terror stabbed him in his gut. There was no room on either side to stand clear of the car.

"Come on! Run!" he shouted.

"We can't outrun it."

"I said move it!"

Joe grabbed one of Nadhim's hands and started pulling him along. The Iraqi gasped in pain as he tried to keep up. Joe unclipped the flashlight and pointed it back. The car had to be doing at least thirty miles an hour. He estimated the distance to be only a hundred yards. When Nadhim stumbled and fell heavily, Joe ran back and pulled him up. A quick glance revealed the worst. The car had already covered half the original distance.

"It's no use," Nadhim said.

"Come on!"

They lurched along the uneven roadbed as fast as they could. Joe resisted the urge to look back, though he could hear the clicking of the wheels clearly now. He expected to feel a sledgehammer blow from behind at any moment. It was probably futile to keep running, but that was all they could do.

★ ★ ★

The oxygen mask covered John's broad smile. The Global Positioning System readout brought him unbelievably close to the target. He looked down as he orbited the president's Guest House in Babylon. He laid the laser designator in the center of a garden south of the house and held it there as he toggled the smart bomb. The weapon fell away cleanly and dropped toward the earth, its long, slim body being directed by its fins as the computer and optics tracked the laser spot on the ground. The pilot held the laser steady until he saw the bright flash of the explosion. Smoke billowed upward, but surprisingly little dirt and debris showered the surrounding ground. John was momentarily surprised until he remembered how deep the bomb was supposed to penetrate before exploding. Most of the explosive force had been absorbed down where it would do the most good.

He banked sharply away from the target. So far, so good. No one in Iraq had objected to their presence. He looked back. He could barely see two sinister black shapes. The next aircraft was lining up for his run. The one behind would follow soon after. John wished they weren't under radio silence. He wanted very much to say something about how well things were going.

Nadhim cried out in pain as he tripped on a cross-tie and fell heavily. Joe turned and began to reach down. The subway car, illuminated by the darting flashlight in Joe's other hand, was less than fifty feet away. Just at that instant, a deafening explosion blew a ball of red flame into the tunnel behind the car. The ground heaved with a sledgehammer blow that threw Joe against the rough concrete wall. He landed across a rail that slammed painfully into his ribs. The flames flickered for a few moments, then went out. The pungent stench of cordite blew past like a hot breath.

Joe's ears rang, and his side felt like it had been kicked in by an irate giant. He saw the dim glow of the flashlight where he had dropped it — the only light in the tunnel. He gasped in pain as he grabbed it. When he turned the beam up, he could see that the subway car had stopped less than ten feet away. He struggled to his feet and staggered over to Nadhim. He reached down and pulled him up.

"What was that?" the Iraqi asked.

"They bombed the lab. Come on!"

The flashlight bobbed and swung as Joe helped Nadhim down the tracks. A few moments later they heard a sharp sound behind them, then again. The third time was accompanied by the sound of breaking glass. Joe stopped and turned around. The flashlight's beam barely reached the car, but it was enough. The painted-over windshield was gone, except for a few jagged pieces still held by the gasket, and the man inside was clearing those away. He raised his arm, aiming at the flashlight beam. Joe clicked off the light. The muzzle flash briefly illuminated the man. The shot ricocheted off the concrete wall.

Joe clipped the flashlight to his belt, then grabbed Nadhim's hand and began pulling him along. They heard frantic scrabbling behind them. A few moments later a light clicked on, dim but enough to show them where they were.

"He's found the emergency subway light," Nadhim gasped.

"Come on!"

The two men forced their legs to obey them. They stumbled along, their long black shadows preceding them. They heard a heavy thump behind them as the man jumped out of the subway.

"Hurry up!" Joe yelled.

The gun roared again, and Joe heard the zip as it went past his ear. He waited for the next one, the one that could end his or Nad-him's life. With no immediate way out of the tunnel, they could not get away from the man.

A brilliant, red flash eclipsed the feeble light behind them. The shattering explosion did not seem quite as loud to their tortured eardrums. The ground jerked but did not throw them down. They were farther away, Joe thought, or perhaps the second bomb was not quite on target. When the afterglow died down, the tunnel was in complete darkness.

"Come on," Joe whispered. "He doesn't have any light to help him, but that won't stop him. Hurry."

They continued their agonizing way toward the distant truck stop. A minute later a third blast echoed through the tunnel, the light and noise diminished by the growing distance. Joe glanced back and thought he saw a black shadow between the rails. Then the curtain of blackness descended again.

It seemed to Joe that they were walking on a treadmill, expending waning energy but getting no closer to their destination. They hurried along as fast as Nadhim could walk, their feet crunching over the gravel between the cross-ties. Occasionally one or the other would touch a rail with his foot, forcing them to drift back toward the center. The utter blackness seemed to reach out and enfold them.

Gradually the ringing in Joe's ears diminished. When he thought he heard something, he pulled Nadhim to a stop. There it was again. Someone was coming up behind them. Joe tried to estimate the distance but had to give up. The footfalls sounded uncomfortably close, though the echoes made it hard to tell. Joe felt an electric surge of fear race down his spine. The man was definitely moving faster than they were.

He pulled Nadhim forward with renewed effort but had to slow down when the other gasped in pain.

Joe stopped again and bent very close to Nadhim's ear. "Wait here," he whispered.

He reached down and pulled the knife out of his boot. The crunching footsteps continued coming toward them, then stopped. Joe felt for the next cross-tie with the toe of his boot. Finding it, he began inching soundlessly forward, avoiding the gravel as much as he could. Silence. *How far away is he?* Joe wondered. He stopped again, listening so intently, his head hurt. Not a sound. He heard the rattle of gravel behind him. Nadhim had moved. Then he heard a sound he recognized instantly —

the click of a safety going off.

Joe estimated the distance between the ties and began stepping rapidly toward the man. He had gone about ten feet when he hit some gravel on top of a tie. He skidded to a stop when he heard the sudden clatter.

A gun roared less than twenty feet away. Seeing his adversary clearly in the muzzle flash, Joe dashed toward the man and plowed into his hard body. The man staggered backwards as he tried to regain his balance. Joe pushed harder, trying to hook a leg and trip his enemy, but his adversary was too wary. As they slid to a stop, Joe grabbed the gun arm with his left hand. Vise-like fingers circled his right wrist and started squeezing as the Iraqi tried desperately to force Joe to drop the knife, but the former SEAL held on doggedly.

The other man had the advantage of youth and conditioning, Joe realized as he was being forced back. His boots scrabbled over the gravel and ties as he gradually lost ground. As he suddenly fell backwards, he felt his assailant topple forward. Joe groaned in agony as the gravel ground painfully into his back. Realizing his momentary advantage, he brought up both feet and caught the man in the solar plexus, pulling him forward viciously with his left hand. The man continued to fall forward, unable to regain his balance. Joe pushed up hard with his feet, and the man lost his grip on Joe's knife hand and sailed over the American, landing heavily behind him. Joe whirled around and brought the knife down with all his might. The man slumped back, his gun clattering to the ground. Joe pulled out the knife, wiped the blade, and returned it to his boot, then wiped his hand on the man's trousers.

Joe unclipped his flashlight and switched it on. The swarthy Iraqi looked up at him with dead eyes, his mouth still open, mute witness to the agony of his death. Joe thought about taking the man's automatic but decided not to. He pointed the beam up the tunnel and hurried over to Nadhim, standing but staggering.

"Let me look at that," Joe said.

He took his knife, slit the side of Nadhim's bloody shirt, and brought the light close. The wound was raw and ugly and was still weeping blood. But coagulation had definitely started. Nadhim had lost a moderate amount of blood — enough to put him into minor shock.

The wound definitely needed tending — something else to take care of while avoiding the stirred-up Iraqi hornets' nest.

"How is it?" Nadhim asked.

"I know it hurts, but it's quite minor. We'll get you looked after once we get back to Al Hillah." Joe pulled out his shirt to get at his T-shirt. He ripped off a large swatch and handed it to Nadhim. "Wad this up and hold it against the wound. Think you can go on?"

"We don't have any choice. But how can we get away?"

"One thing at a time. First let's get to the truck stop."

Avraham and Abdul huddled under a table in their second-floor office until they were sure the attack was over. They had come on duty at midnight, as befitted their adjusted status. But security enforcement was like being a fireman. If there were security problems, there was much to do. Otherwise you were on call. And nothing much happened between 12 and 8 — usually.

Ten minutes after the third bomb, Avraham crawled out from under the table, taking care to avoid the glass. The lights were out, but he had no trouble seeing the devastated window.

"Where was it?" Abdul asked as he got to his feet.

"On the other side, I think. Let's go."

They hurried through the corridors until

they got to the south side of the Guest House. Avraham opened the door to a small conference room. The window was blown in, and a ragged hole ran up the exterior wall and into the roof. He walked cautiously toward the wall and peered out. All the exterior lights were out, but the damage still stood out clearly under the starlight. The formal garden and all the walkways were gone, replaced by three huge craters that blended into one.

"Were they aiming at the house?" Abdul asked.

Avraham shook his head. An icy pang of fear drove deeply into his stomach "No. They hit the lab."

"Does that mean . . ."

"We will wait for Akram. He will be here shortly."

A shiver ran down Avraham's spine. He knew exactly what it meant.

Mars yawned. The archaeologists had already discussed the nearby explosions in what they hoped sounded like innocent surprise. It didn't seem very convincing to Mars, but they had tried their best. His stomach churned with acid. They knew exactly what had happened. He wondered if his dad had been able to do anything but knew that was highly unlikely. What could he do? He could almost feel the deadly bacteria floating down on them and everyone else downwind of Babylon.

"Will anyone come around and tell us what happened?" Anne asked.

Ghanim shrugged. "I'm sure they will. But it will probably take time. Whatever it was sounded serious."

"So, do we wait here?"

He nodded. "Yes. That is all we can do."

It took Akram Rashid a little less than a half hour to arrive at the Guest House. As Avraham had predicted, their boss called for them immediately. He led them through the darkened house and down to the first floor, where he keyed in a code on a heavy steel door. Down the steep steps they could see dim emergency lighting. They entered the security communications control room and sat down at a small table. The wall-mounted emergency lanterns provided feeble lighting, but it was better than the darkness above.

"Don't you have emergency generators?" Avraham asked.

Akram scowled at him. "Yes, of course we do. But the strike hit our transformers and power distribution, which are — or were — at lab level."

Avraham shivered. "Er, did the strike release any . . ."

"I didn't bring you down here to chat! Now shut up and listen. We have a security problem here."

Avraham nodded while he choked down his anger.

Akram pointed toward the dead monitors. "You can quit worrying about your precious hides. A few minutes before the air strike, we had a containment breach. The automatic self-destruct system activated and destroyed the lab. The armored door sealed the lab, and oxygen infiltration and white phosphorus did the rest. Complete destruction was verified just before the first bomb hit."

"So there is no biological hazard?"

"Isn't that what I said?" Akram snapped.

"Please continue."

"Then came the air strike. Three bombs, each about a minute apart, hit outside the Guest House and penetrated down to the lab level — we think."

"You don't know?"

"We can't get down there with the power out. We sent a man down in the elevator when we got the containment alarm. We haven't heard from him, so either the bombs got him or he's stranded down there. The bombs probably got him, because we've listened for noises in the elevator shaft and haven't heard anything. Of course, he could be walking out to the truck-stop entrance. If so, we'll hear about it soon enough."

"How soon after he went down there did the first bomb hit?"

"A minute, maybe two. So he probably was hit."

Avraham nodded. "Sounds likely. What would you like us to do?"

"Get out to the truck stop." He gave Avraham a card. "Ask for this man. When you show him this, he'll take you to the secret entrance. Follow the subway tracks until you get back to the lab. Look it over. I want a report on the conditions down there — everything. Any questions?"

Avraham looked at Abdul, who shook his head. "We understand."

"Good. Be sure to take several heavy-duty flashlights. I'll be down here when you get back."

They hurried up the stairs and were gone.

20

ACCUSED!

Joe climbed up onto the subway platform, then reached down to help Nadhim up. The Iraqi took a few moments to catch his breath before operating the door. He pulled it open after punching in the code and staggered up the steep steps. Joe followed, ready to catch him if he fell.

They walked to the front of the old bus and listened. Joe started to push the door open when he heard voices. They were close. He reached down and pulled out his knife. His heart jumped into his throat when he heard a muffled shout. He peeked through a narrow crack and saw three men run past. The beams from two powerful flashlights moved jerkily over the ground, roughly centered on two crumpled forms. The guard and his dog had been discovered.

"Come on," Joe whispered. "But be quiet."

He pushed the door open and stepped out,

holding it for Nadhim. He carefully closed it and pointed toward the fence where they had come in. He led the way, hoping he would not ran into something in the darkness. He glanced back. The flashlights were still hovering over the fallen guard.

Joe reached the fence and held the gap apart while Nadhim struggled through. When the fence made a twanging noise, Joe looked over his shoulder. One of the flashlights was bounding toward the truck stop. The other one was approaching the bus. He could see two men open the door and disappear inside.

Nadhim gave a muffled cry of pain, and then he broke through the fence. Joe wriggled into the gap and joined his friend on the other side.

"Are you all right?" Joe whispered.

"My side . . ."

"Come on. We're almost there."

Joe led the way into the heavy brush, glancing behind frequently to make sure Nadhim was keeping up. He listened for signs of pursuit, but there were none. He knew this would change once the gears of bureaucracy started to turn. He was relatively sure of his bearings by using the stars, but he knew it would be very easy to miss the scooter. He was almost ready to admit they had passed it when he saw a dark mound in the ditch ahead.

"There it is," Joe said. "Better let me drive."

Nadhim handed him the key. Joe picked up the scooter and rolled it up to the deserted highway. He pushed it across to the other side, got on, and waited as Nadhim slowly climbed onto the buddy seat. Joe turned on the ignition and kicked the starter. The engine backfired and caught. Joe pulled in the clutch, shifted into first, and drove off toward Al Hillah.

The trip was mercifully short. Joe checked several times to make sure Nadhim was still alert. Finally they turned onto Arbat and pulled up in front of number 47. The street was dark, and none of the surrounding houses showed a light. After Nadhim climbed down, Joe leaned the scooter against the side of the house. A dog started barking somewhere nearby. He was soon joined by several more. Their chorus continued for a while, then gradually tapered off.

"We have to talk," Joe whispered. "Feel up to it?"

They walked along the same path they had taken earlier in the evening. Joe could tell by Nadhim's heavy plodding that he was near the end of his endurance.

"I think this is far enough," Joe whispered when they passed the last house. "We need to get you tended to and find somewhere to hide."

"My house . . . I have a friend . . ."

"They'll start checking all the lab personnel soon — probably before morning. They must not find you."

"What can we do?" Nadhim asked, a trace of panic in his voice.

"Can your friend be trusted?"

"Yes — I think so."

"Let's go see him first. Then we can worry about where to stay. How about some rundown hotel — someplace where they won't know you? Anything like that nearby?"

"Quite a few, actually. My family is from An Najaf, so I don't know very many people here."

"That helps. Do you feel up to another scooter ride?"

"Yes."

Avraham held the flashlight on the dead Iraqi. "Here is Akram's man." He tilted the powerful beam up. In the distance was the subway car with its gaping windshield.

Abdul knelt down. "Shine the light here, please."

When the light came down, Abdul ripped the dead man's shirt open and pulled up his undershirt.

"Knife wound — thin blade. Went between the ribs and through the heart. Whoever did this was no amateur. He really knew what he was doing."

"Enemy agent?"

Abdul thought about this. "Has to be. It happened at the same time as the air strike. I don't think that can be coincidence."

"But why send someone down here when you're going to bomb the place?"

"Good question. It's almost like there were two operations going on, neither aware of the other."

"That doesn't make sense," Avraham observed.

"No, it doesn't. What next?"

"We'd better get back to Akram. Let's see what he makes of it all."

Ya'acov and Ari stood outside the closed hangar and looked up into the early-morning sky. The stars were brilliant white dots against the jetblack night firmament. Ya'acov looked toward the east. It was too early for any signs of dawn. But three sets of navigation lights were rapidly approaching.

"There they are," he said, pointing.

"And we find out what happened — finally."

"Are you suggesting we're overdoing the secrecy bit, Lieutenant?"

"I would never criticize our superiors, Captain."

"I'll remember that."

The F-117s made a long, shallow, straight-in approach and touched down one after the other. After braking, they turned onto a taxiway and headed for the hangar. The heavy steel doors rumbled open behind the two IDF officers. Three yellow tractors emerged, each with a long towbar attached.

The stealth fighters pulled up short of the waiting crew. The six engines shut down as one, and the canopies hinged upward. The three American crew chiefs pushed their ladders up to the aircraft and bounded up to the top. Each took his pilot's helmet and helped him out of his harness and out of the cockpit. After the ladders were pulled away, the tractors hooked up and pulled the planes into the hangar.

"Show and tell time, Lieutenant," Ya'acov said.

The two officers followed the pilots into the hangar. Inside, they joined the combined American and Israeli air intelligence personnel in the conference room where Colonel

Barker had briefed them. Ya'acov and Ari took seats behind an Israeli Air Force brigadier. The three pilots gave concise summaries of the mission, from taxi out to shutdown on the ramp. The analysts recorded everything and took copious notes. When the aviators finished, the interrogators rattled off all their questions to fill in the blanks. When that was done, an American air intelligence major invited general questions.

A United States Air Force major general looked John Barker right in the eye. "You sure you hit the lab, Colonel?"

John couldn't help smiling. "Sir, if that lab was where the spooks said it was, it's history. All three bombs were right on target. The tapes will prove it."

"Did you see anything?" the general persisted.

"Nothing much to see, General. The bombs went off deep. We saw the flash and some debris. All I know is that the bombs went in where they were supposed to. Whatever is under there is *way* broken. President Talfah's going to have to get by without his nukie factory."

Ya'acov felt the blood drain from his face.

Ari saw it. "What's the matter?" he asked softly.

Ya'acov leaned over. "If that was a biological lab, we've just signed our death certificates."

The Israeli brigadier looked back at them in irritation.

Ya'acov tried to smile but couldn't.

Avraham and Abdul found Akram in his second-floor office at the Guest House. An emergency lantern sat on a filing cabinet, giving the room garish, inadequate lighting. Shattered glass littered the room below the destroyed window.

"What did you find?" he asked.

"Someone got inside the junkyard behind the truck stop," Avraham replied. "Whoever it was killed a guard, his dog, and another dog. They got past the combination lock at the subway platform, walked down the tracks, and killed the guy who was sent down to investigate the containment breech. Your man was apparently operating the subway when the first bomb hit because it was some distance from the lab's station and the front window was shattered. He was obviously pursuing the intruder or intruders when he got it."

"What! How could that happen?"

"I would say some of the security procedures are inadequate."

"The truck stop is not my responsibility," Akram snapped.

"Of course," Avraham agreed with a smile. "I did not mean to imply that it was."

"O.K., O.K. What problems did you see?"

"Many, but that won't help us now. The fence is inadequate and poorly constructed, it's ridiculous to patrol the yard with only two dogs and a guard, and someone was careless about the door combination."

Akram nodded. "You are right. Others will take care of those problems. Do you have any idea who did this?"

"None. But whoever it was knew about the lab, the truck stop, and the combination."

"Someone who works there."

"I think it is safe to assume that."

The doctor had made all the appropriate noises while cleaning and dressing Nadhim's ugly wound. Joe had spent an uneasy thirty minutes waiting outside, wondering what they would do if the security police made an appearance.

When Nadhim came out, he and Joe rode the scooter to within a block of the highway. There they left it and walked slowly toward the center of town. At Joe's direction, Nadhim led them into a section where the streets became progressively more narrow and dirty. They got something to eat at a street vendor and continued until they arrived at a narrow, three-story building.

"That's a hotel?" Joe asked.

"You said 'run-down.' "

"It's certainly that. I don't think it even rates a half star."

Nadhim smiled. "Want to go somewhere else?"

"No. This is a perfect place to hide, I guess. Remember, don't use your name." He reached inside his shirt and pulled a wad of dinars out of his money belt. "O.K., get as nice a room as they've got. Then come out and tell me where it is."

"Why not come in with me?"

"I don't want the snoop at the front desk to see a foreigner in his place."

A few minutes later Nadhim returned with the key. "Room 203," he said. "Second floor, top of the stairs."

"Excellent. Is the man on the front desk by himself?"

"Yes. There's a tiny lobby, but no one is in there."

"O.K. Go get yourself a paper. Then go unlock the room and return to the lobby to read. When the clerk steps out, come to the door. Got it?"

Nadhim nodded. He wandered off down the street and returned a few minutes later with a thin Arabic newspaper. He disappeared inside the hotel. Joe looked around the street as he tried to decide where he wanted to wait. He saw a rapid movement out of the corner of his eye. Nadhim was waving at him. Joe dashed across the street. The front desk was vacant. Nadhim hurried up the stairs with Joe right behind him. He unlocked the door and pushed it open, and they both rushed in.

"That was quick," Joe said as Nadhim locked the door.

"The clerk was gone when I came in."

"Must have weak kidneys."

"What?"

"Never mind."

Joe looked around the room. It was, as he expected, filthy. The window that overlooked the street was cracked and looked as if it had not been washed since the hotel was new. The bare wood floors were cracked and uneven and were caked with dirt. The remains of the previous occupant's dinner lay on the table. Roaches scampered across every exposed surface in the room but were especially thick on the table. Joe pulled the bed's threadbare cover back. The sheets had obviously not been changed in a long time.

There was one rickety chair next to the window and another at the table. A filthy mirror hung over the battered chest of drawers.

"You want to go somewhere else?" Nadhim asked again.

"No. That would be too dangerous. Besides, this is just what we need." He smiled. "And believe it or not, I've seen worse."

Nadhim looked doubtful. "What do we do now?"

"Rest. You've had it, and I'm not much better. We'll have clearer minds when we get up. You take the bed, and I'll sleep in the chair."

Nadhim started to protest.

"Go on," Joe insisted. "We'll talk about it when we wake up."

Akram looked up as Avraham and Abdul again entered his office. Sunlight streamed in through the shattered window, and a light breeze carried the scent of date palms. The security chief nodded toward chairs. The two men sat down.

"I received a call from Baghdad a few minutes ago," Akram began. "Why didn't you tell me about the map you two brought back from England?"

Avraham cleared his throat nervously. "You did not ask. And per our instructions, this was a secret operation — the map was to be hand-delivered to President Talfah."

"I see. Well, I wish I had known about it. I think I've seen a copy of that map — a diagram of the lab showing the Guest House as thin lines."

"Sounds like the one."

The security chief leaned back in his chair. "So, an Iraqi defector gets to England with a map of our underground lab — a map without coordinates. You two kill the guy, bring the map back, and give it to President Talfah."

"That is correct," Avraham agreed.

"And early this morning we have a containment failure, the lab is automatically destroyed, and minutes later an air strike hits the lab, at least what's left of it. Then one of the lab employees comes down the secret entrance and kills one of my men. What's going on?"

"I do not know."

"How did the Israelis know where the lab was? Was there another copy of the map?"

"I do not know that either. We brought back what we were sent for. If there was another copy of the map, we were not aware of it."

Akram played with a deactivated hand grenade, enjoying how the pineapple shape fit his hand. "Several days ago you told me that the Enderlys were involved with IDF Intelligence. Tell me more."

Abdul's eyes darkened with hate. "It was this dog of a Jew. He was the one who found me in the Dome of the Rock when I was planting the bomb. He interviewed me in jail and was there when they tricked me into telling them who I was."

"It was a little more than that," Avraham grumbled.

"Yes. But they *tricked* me. And this same man came after us in a helicopter when we were trying to escape into Syria."

"With a hostage, as I recall," Akram said.

"Yes. We had the girl in our grasp. Then her boyfriend came along, and finally this Israeli."

"You're positive the Israeli is in Intelligence?"

Avraham nodded. "I am convinced. The media said that Intelligence had found our headquarters in East Jerusalem. I'm sure that's who he works for."

"Do you know his name?"

"No."

"So, this Mars Enderly was with this Intelligence guy in a combat zone."

Avraham snorted. "I don't think he sneaked past the IDF by himself."

Akram continued to play with the grenade. "Both of *you* did, but I think I agree. Sure sounds like they were involved with IDF Intelligence. But why?"

Avraham shrugged. "I can't think of a reason, and I've thought about it a great deal."

"So, do you think they're involved with Intelligence now?"

"I don't know. But the circumstances make me wonder."

"Indeed."

"What are you going to do?"

"I'm not sure. You know about the security we've imposed on them. With all that, we have no evidence of any spying. They're doing exactly what you would expect archaeologists to do — dig up things."

Avraham smiled. "Why not bring them in for interrogation?"

Akram glared at him. "It's not that simple, unfortunately. The Enderlys and the Israeli are well-known. And Joe Enderly, Mars's father, is an influential man. We cannot afford bad publicity over this."

"What if we can prove they are spying?"

"That would be different, but the proof would have to be convincing."

Avraham nodded in the direction of the dig. "So, what do you want to do?"

"Nothing for now. Just watch them. They

can't go anywhere. We must await our opportunity, though perhaps we can help the situation along just a bit as well."

Mars and Anne approached the ladder leading down into the pit. Ghanim was examining the interior side of the wall near the cistern. He looked up when he heard them approach.

"Hello," he said with a strained smile. "Need help with anything?"

"No," Anne replied. "Mars and I wanted to see the cistern again. Do you know when we're going to dig it out?"

"It will be a while. We know basically what we'll find. I'd rather keep working on the palace itself. But come on down."

They hurried down the ladder. Mars bent down and brushed the stonework at the lip of the cistern.

"Nice work," he commented.

"Yes, it was."

Ghanim looked around nervously. The only other person in the pit was Moshe, working near the center and apparently oblivious of his colleagues. Ghanim nodded toward the tunnel. They entered the dim interior.

"What are we going to do?" Mars whispered.

"I have no idea. What about your father? Do you think he will be able to help us?"

"I don't know. But it probably doesn't matter now."

"Now that the lab's been bombed?"

"Yeah. We're probably all dead as we stand — we're right next to the blasted thing!"

"Hold it down, dear," Anne said.

"O.K.," Mars grumbled. "But what I don't understand is, why isn't the government doing something? It's almost like nothing's happened. Why aren't they evacuating Babylon?"

"Yes, that doesn't make sense," Ghanim agreed. "It's almost like the danger doesn't exist for some reason."

"So, what do we do?"

Ghanim shrugged. "Continue with the dig."

When they left the tunnel, they found Moshe standing at the ladder. "Mr. Rashid is looking for us."

The head of security watched them closely as they approached. "Good morning, everyone. Ghanim, I need to meet with you and our guests. May we?" He pointed to the dining hall.

"Of course."

Ghanim led the way and held the door until everyone was inside. They gathered around the table, and Akram waited until they sat before he did.

"I'm sure you know why I'm here," he began.

"I presume it is about the explosions last night," Ghanim replied.

"That is part of it, yes."

"What happened, if we may ask?"

The security chief appeared to give this much thought. "Yes, of course you may. We had a natural gas leak outside the Guest House. The gas was apparently leaking into an underground cavern, and something touched off an explosion. Gas seeped back in two more times before we could shut off the line. There is nothing to worry about. As you can see, everything is back to normal, or will be shortly. The explosions did some light damage to the house, but that will all be repaired shortly."

He looked around the table slowly.

Ghanim licked his lips. "That is good to hear. So we may continue with the dig?"

"You may continue with the dig," Akram confirmed with a smile. "Unless there is some reason you should not."

"What does that mean?"

The security chief looked directly at Mars. "Mr. Enderly, do you know what happens to spies in Iraq?"

"I don't understand."

"It was a very simple question, really. Do you know what the government does to spies — yes or no?"

Mars nodded. "Yes, I am aware of what your government does to people they accuse of spying."

"Ah, an amateur lawyer, the implication being that those hung for spying might not be guilty, only accused. You and your wife and Dr. Stein are guests in Iraq. And I assure you, we do not appreciate criticism of our government by foreigners."

Anne squeezed Mars's hand.

"Perhaps you should heed your wife. She seems to understand the seriousness of being honest with me."

Mars nodded.

"Good. Then perhaps you would be so kind as to tell me what you are doing helping IDF Intelligence spy on us."

Mars's mouth fell open. "What?" he croaked.

"What is the meaning of this?" Moshe demanded, glaring at Akram.

"You will be quiet, Dr. Stein. I am waiting for Mr. Enderly to answer my question."

"I h-have no idea what you're t-talking about!" Mars stammered.

"Then why are you so upset?"

"Because it's a serious charge!" Mars shot back.

"Indeed it is. I have every reason to suspect you. I am giving you the chance to prove otherwise."

"This is ridiculous. We are American archaeologists, not spies. We have no connection with IDF Intelligence whatsoever."

"Are you telling me, Mr. Enderly, that you have *never* been associated with IDF Intelligence in any way?"

Mars hesitated. "That is exactly what I am telling you."

Akram smiled. "How puzzling. According to two of my men, you are lying to me."

A heavy knot formed in Mars's stomach. "Who are these men?"

"Two friends of yours — Avraham Abbas and Abdul Suleiman."

"They're here?" Mars blurted before he could stop himself.

"Ah, so you have heard of them. Is everything coming back now?"

Mars glared at him.

"Very well, let me ask again — have you *ever* been associated in any way with IDF Intelligence?"

"Not in the way *you* mean! Those creeps kidnapped my wife — I mean Anne — she wasn't my wife at the time." He paused.

"There *was* a certain IDF officer who helped me. But I certainly wasn't working with him."

"That won't do, Mr. Enderly. You know very well you have told me an outright lie, and I caught you at it. So, are you at this time spying on us for IDF Intelligence?"

"No, I am not."

"Your denial is not so vehement this time. Are you losing your confidence? Before you answer, let me state that cooperation with the authorities is taken into consideration in espionage cases."

"I have nothing more to say."

"I guess that is not surprising. You have already said much." He smiled at them all. "Well, thank you all for your time. I must not keep you from your work any longer. Good day."

When the Iraqi interrogator had left, Mars bowed his head in despair. Anne put her arm around him and put her head against his. Moshe gaped at Ghanim, for once at a complete loss for words.

21

EMERGENCY EXTRACTION REQUESTED

David nodded for Ya'acov and Ari to take their seats.

"So," he said with an attempt at lightness, "how were things down around Beersheba?"

Ya'acov frowned. "If you mean the air strike, it went according to plan, according to our people and the Americans. No opposition, and all three smart bombs hit the target."

"So we've taken Talfah's nasty toy away from him. Sounds like cause for celebration."

"We didn't take the toy away — we broke it."

"Same difference," David said warily.

"Depends on what the toy was, Colonel."

"Knock it off, Ya'acov! I've told . . ."

"Colonel, please," Ya'acov interrupted.

"It's done now. But I think we should consider what we'll do if we start getting reports of an epidemic in Iraq, especially if we hear it's coming this way. That's only prudent, isn't it?"

David scowled at him. "Yes, I suppose it is. But I still think you're worrying about nothing. That was a *nuclear* lab. You know we've seen no unusual activity. They aren't evacuating around Babylon."

"That's true, but no one ever accused Talfah of having the best interests of his people at heart."

"Can't argue with that. But I would expect to see the government in panic if your theory is correct."

"I guess. Colonel, we still have one other loose end we need to take care of."

"And what is that?"

"We still haven't heard from Moshe Stein or the Enderlys, despite everyone's assurances that they would get out. I think they're in trouble. And I think they're in trouble because of what we asked them to do. The question is, what are we going to do about it?"

"I don't know."

"What are our superiors saying?"

"That's none of your business, Captain."

"I bet they aren't saying anything about

it. The mission's been accomplished, and everything else is collateral damage."

David slammed his fist down on his desk. "Enough! You two are dismissed."

They jumped up and hurried out of their angry superior's office.

Akram looked up as Avraham and Abdul entered his office.

"What did you find out?" Avraham asked as he and Abdul sat down.

"I am not sure. I caught Mars Enderly in a lie, but his response was reasonable. I find it very hard to believe that IDF Intelligence would recruit archaeologists to do their dirty work. After all, foreign espionage is usually the Mossad's turf, these people have absolutely no training, they have no secure means of communication — I could go on."

"All these things might make it easier for them to work. As for communications, they could take the information out with them."

"True. But we were trying to tie this into the assault on the lab. For that they needed communications." Akram looked at the Palestinians with more respect. "I appreciate your concern because these coincidences bother me also. But how do they tie together? *Do* they tie together?"

"They do," Avraham grumbled.

"O.K. But we have to find out how. Until then, we must watch them very carefully — without harassing them. If it turns out they are innocent, we do not want any bad publicity. That might not be good for *our* health."

"We understand," Avraham answered for himself and Abdul.

Ya'acov was pounding away on his laptop computer when Ari returned from a trip to the room housing the network printers.

"I got the graphs and the color picture from the F-117. Nice of the Americans to give us all that." He showed Ya'acov the crisp, color pages.

"Not bad, Lieutenant. I'm sure the heavies will be suitably impressed."

"Right you are, Captain. I wonder who David will grab to do the dog-and-pony show."

Ya'acov cocked an eyebrow at him. "Why, Lieutenant, I was going to volunteer you."

"Oh, no, sir. The colonel knows you're the best at this. And he's right — I've seen you perform."

"Thanks. I'll do something for you sometime."

The phone rang. Ya'acov picked up the receiver as he continued to admire the stealth fighter.

"Captain Isaacson."

"Is Ari in there with you?" David asked.

Ya'acov looked up. "Yes, he is, Colonel."

"Good. I need to see you both."

"We'll be right there."

"No. I'll come there." The phone went dead.

"The colonel's on the way here. How about cleaning off that chair? Just stack those reports in the corner."

David entered without knocking a few minutes later and took the chair Ari had cleared.

"I forwarded your remarks about the Enderlys and Moshe Stein. Regardless of what you think, I'm concerned about them too. I got permission to reopen the satellite link."

"Wonderful," Ya'acov said. "When will it be up?"

"It's up now. I want you to send them a message. Ask them what's going on."

"And hope they reply."

"Yes, and hope they reply."

"We'll do it immediately."

Mars was about to update the notes on

the cistern and the tunnel when he saw the telephone icon indicating they had a message over the satellite link. He glanced over at Anne, who was looking for a sketch she had made of the water tunnel vaulting. He caught her eye and looked pointedly at the ThinkPad's screen. She came over.

Mars looked around quickly to make sure they were alone. He clicked on the icon and entered the password. It took only a moment to interpret the message in the pop-up window. It was a request for a status report. Mars thought for only a moment before updating a copy of the notes on a vase fragment. In it he inserted the words "Mount Ararat" and a code for the number 2. He was requesting emergency extraction in two days.

He looked into Anne's eyes. She took a deep breath and nodded. He exited and saw the hard disk access light come on. The message was on its way. Moments later he saw the confirmation.

They left the tent and tried to remain calm as they walked past the long pit. Moshe was on his hands and knees examining something buried about a yard from the interior side of the palace wall. He looked up as they approached.

"We need your help," Mars said.

"Be glad to. What is it?"

"It's a question about the tunnel vaulting. Could you come look at it?"

"Of course." He struggled to his feet and came up the ladder.

Mars was glad to see that Ghanim was near the cistern. Mars hurried down the ladder and waited until Anne and Moshe were down as well.

"We're still having trouble dating the tunnel," he told Ghanim. "It has to do with how the masonry was done. Do you have time to look at it?"

Lines of fear constricted the Iraqi's eyes. "Yes. Show me what you're concerned about."

The men had to crouch as Mars led the way into the tunnel to where the excavation of the dried river silt and sand stopped. Anne's hair barely brushed the top of the barrel vaulting.

"What is it?" Ghanim hissed.

"They've opened the satellite link," Mars answered. "They sent us a message asking for status."

"What did you say?" Moshe asked.

"I told them we wanted emergency extraction in two days, which, according to Ya'acov, is as quick as they can do it. That would make it dawn, day after tomorrow."

"What are you talking about?" Ghanim demanded.

"Something IDF Intelligence came up with just in case. They fly in at dawn east of here and take us all out."

"So you commit us to a plan without even asking," Ghanim grumbled.

"Yes, I guess I did," Mars admitted. "Perhaps I acted inadvisedly . . ."

"Aside from the fact that the security people will probably have us in jail by then, how do you propose we get out of here?" Ghanim went on.

"I think we can use this tunnel. We're under the western edge of the fence right now. If we put a work crew in here and dig out a little more silt and sand, we'll be clear of it." He pointed up at the barrel vaulting. "The mortar is in poor shape. All we have to do is pull down a section of the vaulting and dig up through the sand and soil. The surface outside slopes rapidly. There is no more than three or four feet of soil above us at this point, and less the closer we get to the old riverbed."

"What if the whole tunnel collapses on us?"

Mars took a deep breath. "Let's be careful that it doesn't."

"O.K., O.K., so it doesn't collapse and we get out. What then?"

414

"We take your Land Cruiser and drive east."

Ghanim shook his head. "Mars, it will never work. Too much can go wrong. We'll never make it."

"Ghanim, we have to try. We know what will happen if we stay. What can it hurt? It's at least a chance."

"I think Mars is right," Anne said. "We can't give up."

"I remember worse situations," Moshe said.

Mars shivered. "Yeah, I do too."

"That was quick," David remarked after Ya'acov brought him up to date.

"Quicker than I expected," Ari replied. "Ya'acov sent me up to communications with the message. I sent it and was about to come back when the reply came in. Mars, or whoever, must have been working with the PC when the satellite transmitted the message."

"So, emergency extraction at dawn, two days from now. I don't suppose we know anything about their situation — where they are, why they didn't come out."

"No, Colonel, we don't," Ya'acov replied. "Presumably they were restrained somehow, perhaps only temporarily. But they still have the PC, and they apparently think they have enough freedom to make it to the extraction site."

"Any possibility someone else could be operating the PC and spoofing us? Or that the Iraqis know about all this and are forcing them to lure us in?"

"Colonel, Ari and I discussed this. We're convinced no one except the ones we trained could operate the PC in this secret way. However, it's possible they are being forced to do this."

"Is that what you think?"

Ya'acov thought for a moment. "No, sir. I don't think they're compromised at this point. This message is from the archaeologists. Something's wrong, but they're not under arrest."

"Lieutenant Jacovy?" David asked.

"I agree with Ya'acov. We can't tell for sure, but I don't think they were being forced."

"What if you two are wrong?"

"I think we have to try. This is why we set up the contingency plan. We told them we would come get them if something went wrong. It would be dishonorable to sit by and do nothing."

David's eyes narrowed. "We will do the honorable thing, Ya'acov. But the plan was never meant to be executed if they were captured."

"I understand. But I don't think they have been. They're telling us they need our help — desperately."

David thought this over. "Very well. The authorizing order will go out this afternoon. Any other problems you foresee?"

"The weather might be," Ya'acov said. "Meteorology says a sandstorm is brewing in that area. But they're expecting the winds to remain moderate for another forty-eight hours, so we should be O.K."

"Keep an eye on it. Anything else?"

"Only one. The resources have already been allocated. They're down at our base in the Negev — the one we used for the air strike. Same hangar, as a matter of fact. The only thing not assigned is the pilot."

David nodded. "Do you have anyone in mind, Ya'acov?"

"As a matter of fact I do. Can I have Lieutenant Joel Rabinovich?"

"The Apache pilot? The plan calls for a U-27A — a fixed-wing turboprop."

Ya'acov smiled. "Colonel, that guy can fly anything."

"You've got him. Provided we can talk his commander into it, which I suspect we can." He glanced at his watch. "Gentle-

417

men, it's nearly fifteen hundred, and I know you have much to do before tomorrow night. Keep me informed."

"Yes, sir," Ya'acov answered for them both as they got up.

"Hope you like this," Nadhim said as he placed the net bags on the table. He pulled out plastic bottles of water and a wide assortment of packaged and fresh foods.

"I'm hungry enough to eat just about anything." Joe smiled at the Iraqi. "And while I was in the Navy, I think I did. But I suppose we'd better eat the fresh stuff first, before the roaches get it."

Nadhim glanced around at the large brown insects that seemed to be conducting endless drag races over every exposed surface in the room. "That would be wise," he agreed.

Joe pulled a tipsy chair up to the table; Nadhim took the other one. They stuffed pita bread with grilled lamb chunks, cheese, lettuce, and tomatoes. Nadhim opened one of the water bottles while they each took huge bites out of the sandwiches.

"Like it?" Nadhim asked.

"Wonderful," Joe said, although he didn't particularly care for lamb. "I love pita bread."

"Do you have it in America?"

"We didn't for many years. But we do now."

"You didn't know what you were missing."

Joe laughed. "I agree with that. It's a cultural thing, I guess."

"Do you like oriental food?"

"For the most part I do. I'm used to spicy food since I come from Texas."

"Then you should feel right at home."

They wolfed their sandwiches, washing them down with large gulps of water. Joe sighed as he felt his hunger pangs come under partial control. He looked at a cellophane package containing two tan objects. The printed explanation of ingredients used a seemingly haphazard combination of Arabic and English.

"Those look like Twinkies," he said.

Nadhim glanced at them. "What is a 'twinkie'?"

Joe looked puzzled for a moment. "Well, a Twinkie is . . . It's a brand-name rather than a word. The closest English word, I guess, is twinkle, you know, like a star?"

"These things are supposed to flash?"

"No. I have no idea where they came up with the name. It's been a favorite snack food in America for years." Joe pointed at the package. "Are those cream-filled cakes?"

"Yes."

"Sounds like Twinkies to me. Do you like them?"

"Oh, yes. So, are they really Twinkies?"

"Let's find out."

Joe opened the package and took one. He bit off half and smacked his lips as he savored the slightly soggy cake and the creamy white filling. Nadhim took the other one.

"No doubt about it," Joe assured him. "Vintage Twinkies. Here I am in the heart of Iraq enjoying an American delicacy. Life is good."

"I am glad I got them."

Joe pointed at the wrapper. "What do you call them?"

"I would rather not say. Nothing so grand as 'Twinkie,' I can assure you. From now on, that is what I will call them." Nadhim's smile broadened. "Do any of your other products have unusual names?"

Joe thought about telling him about Ding Dongs but decided not to. "Quite a few. Perhaps we will talk about it later."

The Iraqi's smile dwindled. "Yes, we do have more pressing problems."

"Yes, we do."

"What should we be doing?"

"We have to just sit tight for now. We

can't move about until the security people settle down." Joe glanced at Nadhim's side. "And it would be good to give you some time to heal."

"What about Uncle Ghanim? And Mars, Anne, and Moshe?"

"We can't do a thing for them if we get caught. Which reminds me — I need you to make one more shopping trip before tonight."

"Of course," Nadhim agreed. "What do you need?"

"Some working clothes. And can you find something to make my face and hands a little darker?"

"I will take care of it."

"But for right now, let's get some rest. I think we're going to be very busy before long."

Ya'acov and Ari looked away from the assembled equipment arrayed before the two Cessna U-27 turboprops when they heard the heavy *whomp-whomp-whomp* of the approaching helicopter. They were inside the locked hangar that had housed three F-117s only hours earlier. Now they had it to themselves.

"I think I know who that is," Ya'acov commented.

"Our favorite Apache driver," Ari said. "Let's go see."

They passed the armed guard and walked out a steel door in the corner of the hangar. In the last rays of a brilliant sunset, they saw the red and green navigational lights of an AH-64A Apache helicopter, minus its usual load of Hellfire missiles. Ya'acov saw the pilot was by himself; the front seat, the home of the copilot/gunner, was empty. The Israel Air Force pilot cut the engines and continued with his shutdown procedure. The massive, four-bladed rotor slowed to a stop, its blades sagging like a huge umbrella stripped of its fabric. Ya'acov shook his head. The helicopter still looked like a gigantic, prehistoric insect.

The pilot stepped down from the helicopter and walked toward the hangar. A wide grin covered his face as he saluted Ya'acov.

"Good evening, Lieutenant Rabinovich," Ya'acov said, returning the salute. "We would have sent a car for you."

"What, and miss a beautiful flight down here in the world's finest helicopter?"

"Nice to see you haven't changed, Joel."

The pilot turned to admire the Apache. "Gentlemen, that is a tank-killing machine without peer. Can't you feel the deadliness from here?"

"Let's be fair now. We do have other things that take out tanks."

"You mean like TOWs?"

Ya'acov knew he was referring to tube-launched, optically-tracked, wire guided missiles. "For one. Our tankers think they're pretty good at this business also."

"Oh, yeah. I guess they've got their place. But neither one of them has my Hellfire missiles."

"Too bad we can't take the Apache with us," Ya'acov observed.

"I agree, Ya'acov." He looked at the helicopter wistfully.

"Can you fly a U-27?" Ya'acov asked with a smile since he already knew the answer.

"I can fly anything, Captain. I much prefer the Apache, but if it travels through the air, let me at it."

"That's what we wanted to hear. Step inside, and we'll show you the plane and what you'll be carrying. Did anyone brief you on the mission?"

Joel arched his eyebrows. "Not a word. I gather it's super-secret spook stuff."

"It's nice to know our work is appreciated, Ari," Ya'acov commented.

"Oh, it is," Joel agreed.

Ari held the door for the other two. The hangar looked cavernous with only two relatively small aircraft inside, each with identical piles of cargo spread out underneath its wings.

"Those puddle jumpers look tiny in here by themselves," Joel observed. He stopped and looked at Ya'acov. "What are we going to do?"

"I'll give you the short version. After that Ari will present the blood-and-guts version in the conference room over there."

"Understood," the pilot said, looking over the nearest plane.

"We have three people in trouble over in Iraq. Archaeologists. You know them. Mars and Anne Enderly — they're married now. And Moshe Stein."

"They're working for Intelligence?" Joel asked in surprise.

"It's a long story. They're working on a dig in Babylon, and they've requested an emergency extraction. We received the message this afternoon and confirmed it a short time later. We're committed to extracting them east of Babylon at dawn, day after tomorrow."

Joel cocked an eyebrow at this. "Have you checked meteorology?"

"If you mean the forecasted dust storm, yes. They're predicting dust later on in the afternoon."

"Hope they're right. Those things are hard to predict. I'd sure hate to get caught in one."

"I suppose we'll have to watch it."

"How many passengers will there be?"

"Four. The three archaeologists and myself." He smiled at Ari. "Ari wanted to go, but someone has to be liaison here."

Joel pointed to the other U-27. "What's the other bird for?"

"In case the first one fails." Ya'acov paused. "Or the first extraction team runs into trouble."

"Let's hope not."

"Roger that, Lieutenant."

"Gonna be snug with all that gear."

"It's all part of the equipment load."

"Including that?" Joel asked, pointing to a four-wheel-drive, all-terrain vehicle.

"The ATV most especially goes. I may need some ground transportation, and I might not be able to catch a camel."

"Or ride it if he caught it," Ari observed.

"I don't believe I was talking to you, Lieutenant."

"Sounds like fun," Joel said.

"Good. I hope it is. Shall we go to the conference room? Ari is dying to give you the details."

"Right this way," Ari invited.

22

ESCAPE FROM BABYLON?

It had been a sleepless night for the Enderlys. Mars could not forget what he had committed Anne to — what he had committed them all to. As dawn approached, he thought about what had to be accomplished that day. He was not at all sure they could do it.

He got up before the alarm and started putting on his clothes. Anne yawned and opened her eyes.

"Good morning, dear," she said with a smile.

Mars's earlier gloom dissipated a little. "Good morning." He sat on the edge of the bed and kissed her. "Mmm," he sighed.

"Spark still there?" she asked.

"Yes, indeed."

The brightness quickly dimmed as the reality of their situation came back into focus for him. Her smile went away as well. The Iraqis were like a cat playing with a live mouse. Would their captors toy with them until they'd had enough fun?

"I love you, dear," Anne said, cutting through his gloom.

"I love you, too. I only . . ."

"I know. We'd better press on. Busy day today."

He finished buttoning his shirt and sat on the bed to pull on his socks and boots.

Ghanim and Moshe were already in the dining hall. They all had dry cereal with milk and sugar, toast, and coffee. They discussed several of the finds, but their hearts were not in it. Mars knew they were all thinking about the same thing: Would their plan work?

After breakfast, Mars made a quick trip to the tent to check the PC. There were no new messages. He joined the others above the cistern. Ghanim was pointing around that end of the pit.

"We're getting close to having everything exposed. On a later dig, I want to excavate the eastern end toward the Southern Palace to see how much of Belshazzar's palace remains. But for now I want to finish what we've started. The only thing left along this southern wall is the cistern and the tunnel."

"How far down does the cistern go?" Anne asked.

"Hard to say. My guess is it's quite large and will probably take a long time to excavate. We won't be able to finish it, so let's have the crew concentrate on the tunnel."

"Good idea," Moshe agreed.

Ghanim turned to the waiting supervisor. He pointed down toward the tunnel mouth and spoke in rapid Arabic. The man nodded and waved a crew of six down into the pit.

"That will give us time to get caught up on our notes," Ghanim said. "I'll supervise here."

"Very good," Moshe agreed. "See you at lunch."

Mars and Anne worked together on finishing the notes and diagrams on the PC. Mars kept watching for new messages, but there were none. They resisted the urge to return to the tunnel to check on progress.

As they ate a quiet lunch of sandwiches and iced tea, they discussed the morning's progress, careful not to emphasize the work on the tunnel. Mars wanted very much to know how far it had gotten but knew he dared not ask. It would either be far enough or it would not. They would find out that night.

By 10 P.M. it was all done. The three Israeli officers had, all by themselves, completely loaded the Cessna U-27 with over a ton of supplies: jet fuel, camouflage netting,

Uzis, assault rifles, knives, food, water, Arab clothing, and one Yamaha Kodiak ATV. The plane's three oversized tires were noticeably flatter by the time they were done. The U-27 seemed frail standing there on its tricycle landing gear.

Joel performed a thorough preflight check of the aircraft, starting with an inspection under the engine cowling and proceeding on to the flight controls. He dragged a ladder to the leading edge of the wing on the right side, clambered up, and twisted off the tank filler cap.

"What are you doing?" Ya'acov asked.

"Checking the fuel. We're supposed to have 332 usable gallons in two wing tanks. The wise aviator never assumes anything."

He stuck a finger into the neck until he felt fuel. Satisfied, he replaced the cap and performed the same check on the left tank.

"We're ready to go," he said, stepping down from the ladder.

Ya'acov nodded toward the guards standing by at the hangar doors. The men took hold of the heavy metal doors and began pushing them to the side, revealing the coal-black night sky over the Negev. Ya'acov looked out toward the bright, unwinking stars that seemed so much brighter than they did in Jerusalem or Tel Aviv. He and Joel each grabbed a wing strut and started pushing the plane outside.

Finally they were on the deserted tarmac, and Ya'acov knew it was time to depart. He turned around to face Ari.

"As always, thanks for your help," he said with unusual seriousness.

"You're welcome." Ari paused. "You take care." He looked around the fuselage at Joel. "Both of you."

"Of course," Joel said cheerfully.

"We will," Ya'acov echoed. "We'll be back before you know it." He turned around. "Lieutenant Rabinovich? Think you can get this heap into the air without killing us?"

"Roger that, Captain. Climb aboard and strap yourself in."

"Don't I get a parachute?"

"Naw, you won't need that. You're traveling with a professional. Not scared, are we?"

"Not a bit."

"Let's go."

Joel was already in the left-hand seat and going over his checklist. Ya'acov entered through the airstair door on the right side, wended his way forward through the cargo, and climbed in beside the pilot. He started scrabbling around.

"You're sitting on it," Joel said without looking away from his checklist.

Ya'acov raised up and reached under, grabbing the parts of the seat belt. "So I am," he admitted as he buckled it and pulled the strap tight.

Joel flipped on the master switch.

"That's good," he said.

"What?" Ya'acov asked nervously.

"We didn't pop any circuit breakers, and the battery has enough juice to crank the turbine."

"Isn't that what you expected?"

Joel laughed. "Yes, but you never know. Hold on to your hat, Captain. Here we go."

The pilot flipped on the electric fuel pump, made sure the power lever was in the start position, and pressed the appropriate button. The starter/generator whined as it began spinning the turbine. Joel's eyes flitted from gauge to gauge as the Hartzell three-bladed propeller began to turn. The igniters came on at 10 percent rpm, followed soon after by fuel flow and ignition. When 40 percent was reached, the starter switched automatically to a generator. Seconds later they were ready to taxi.

"Everything looks in order," Joel said as he finished his checklist. "Are you ready?"

"Ready as I'll ever be."

Joel handed Ya'acov a series of detail maps. "Here's our course to the recovery zone. I'll need your help in keeping track of where we are." He pointed to a box mounted above the instrument panel. "That's the readout from the Global Positioning System — very accurate. Use that to plot our position on the maps. The obstacles are clearly marked. I think I have them all memorized, but I want you to double-check me."

"I'll do my best. How will I read it?"

"You can use low-light goggles or this." He handed him a penlight with a red lens. "I'd use the light. It's a little hard to see in the red light, but we need to preserve our night vision."

Ya'acov clicked the light on and then off. "O.K."

Joel peered out the windshield through the spinning disc of the propeller. "You sure I don't have to call the tower?"

"That's correct. Radio silence until we get back. This base is closed until we take off. The tower is watching us right now."

Joel looked over at it. "Sure enough, they're pointing a green light at us. Captain, I'll say this about you — every time I fly you someplace, we never have any problem with priority."

Joel released the brakes and began taxiing. He entered the active runway without a pause and braked to a smooth stop over the black-streaked white bars that told how long the runway was. He ran the flaps down to 15 degrees and started pushing the power lever forward slowly. He released the brakes while continuing to advance the power.

"Next stop Babylon."

The U-27 started rolling down the runway, and the airspeed increased rapidly.

"Aren't you going to use full throttle?" Ya'acov asked, pointing to the power lever that was short of full travel.

"That's the power lever," Joel answered. He pointed to two gauges. "We can't exceed 100 percent shaft horsepower or max turbine inlet temperature."

"Whichever comes first?"

"Right. And on a night like tonight, it's inlet temperature."

Joel pulled firmly back on the wheel, and the aircraft swept up into the nighttime sky. They climbed until they reached 10,000 feet and leveled off.

"We'll stay at 10,000 until we get near Iraq. Then we'll do nap-of-the-earth the rest of the way."

"That mean what I think it does?" Ya'acov asked.

"You'll be able to pick flowers out of your window, if there are any."

Soon they were over the Wilderness of Judea as they proceeded toward the east. The rugged mountains were indistinct shadows below them. The flat pewter-gray Dead Sea spread out ahead of them. On the far side, Jordan's military took no official notice of their presence, although they knew about the flight.

"Where are we?" Joel asked.

"Don't you know?" Ya'acov asked with some alarm.

"Of course I do. But you're supposed to be marking our position on those maps. Are you looking at the right one?" He glanced quickly. "That's the one. They're in order unless you've shuffled them. Look at the GPS and find us on the map. Look at the margins for the longitude and latitude. See them?"

Ya'acov clicked on the penlight. The dim, red light seemed inadequate, but he finally found the scales. He wrote the longitude and latitude on the map and laboriously found them. He used a clear, plastic aviator's plotter and extended the two lines to where they crossed.

"We're near 'En Gedi about to cross the Dead Sea coast."

"Very good. What's around us and up ahead?"

"More training?"

"It might be important, Ya'acov. I don't fancy flying into a power transmission line, do you?"

"Can't argue with that."

"So where are we? Tell me."

Ya'acov scanned the map carefully. "Whole lot of nothing, mostly. However, Masada is to the south of us, not too far away."

"See that plastic plotter you used to draw the lines?"

"Yes."

"You could use that to find the exact distance."

"Want me to?"

"No. Do you have a good feel for where we are, relating the map to what you can see outside? This is called pilotage. It tells you what to expect, among other things."

"I think I understand. We're about halfway down the Dead Sea, if we include the southern salt pans. Our position is right on the course you marked."

"Do I detect a note of awe?"

"Words fail me."

"That would be a first," Joel observed.

Ya'acov looked up. The Jordanian coast

was a gently curving line before rugged mountains. He flipped through the maps to see where their course took them.

"There's Jordan. After we cross the coast, our course jogs south. We pass south of Madaba, well south of Amman, and then turn more to the north."

"Right. We avoid all large towns and cities, as well as airfields. Find Amman, and then look toward the south for an airplane symbol. See it?"

"Oh, you mean Queen Alya International Airport?"

"Yeah. We probably don't want to fly directly over that. Once we're well past there, we turn north to avoid Saudi Arabian airspace. Then it's down the corridor between the Saudis and Syria. After that we enter Iraq, and we most definitely do not have permission to be there."

"Yes. Let's be careful."

"Roger that. That's where we drop down and blend into the brush. When we hit forty east, we'll be a little over halfway there."

The turboprop droned ever eastward. Their progress was marked by Ya'acov's changing charts and following their course with the GPS readouts. These precise fixes ran along Joel's plotted course with monotonous regularity. The pilot really was good at what he did, Ya'acov had to admit. That fact bolstered his somewhat shaky confidence as they flew on into the unknown.

Joel looked over at Ya'acov when they were about halfway down the neck of land between Saudi Arabia and Syria. "What do you make of the archaeologists' situation?"

"I wish I knew. We ordered them to leave Iraq, and they had plenty of time to do it. But for some reason they didn't, and we have no idea why."

"Captured and held by the security freaks?"

Ya'acov gave a short, mirthless laugh. "Who knows? That seemed likely until we opened up the link, sent a message, and got a response."

"The request for the emergency extraction?"

"Right. So if they were arrested, they were later released."

"Any possibility an Iraqi sent the message, or that our people were forced to do it?"

"We discussed that. Option one, I don't think so. The Iraqis might be forcing them to lure us in, but I really doubt it." He glanced at his watch. "If they make it to the extraction site, I guess we'll find out."

"And if they don't?"

"I'd rather not think about that," Ya'acov grumbled. He paused before continuing. "There's something else that's bothering me, something we didn't include in the briefing because it's not part of our operation."

"What's that?"

"Joe Enderly, Mars's dad, is in Iraq."

"Why?"

"Taking matters into his own hands would be my guess."

"What can he do?"

"I don't know. But he was a Navy SEAL, so I'm not going to underestimate him."

"Was he in there before the strike?"

"Yes. That's what makes me suspect he might be involved in this puzzle."

"One guy against all of Talfah's psychopathic wackos?"

"I could tell you some stories," Ya'acov began, recalling his experiences with the elder Enderly. "Maybe I will, later, although you don't have a need to know."

"You are not known for following proper procedures."

Ya'acov laughed. "Now you sound like Ari. Know any more than you did before you asked?"

"Some. Thanks. As you say, we'll know more at dawn."

About a half-hour later, Joel began a rapid

descent as they neared Jordan's border with Iraq.

"Look sharp," he told Ya'acov. "Here's where it gets real serious. Keep the map plots current. Warn me of the marked obstacles well before we get there. And keep a sharp lookout with the low-light goggles when you're not playing with the maps."

"Right. I don't see anything on the first one."

"It's pretty bleak until we get close to the Euphrates. When the map's clear, help me watch outside."

"O.K."

Ya'acov put on his low-light goggles as Joel continued to descend. A few minutes later the pilot leveled out at thirty feet over the seemingly endless expanse of sand and stunted brush.

"You weren't kidding when you said 'nap-of-the-earth.' "

"We'll get even lower at times. So stay alert."

"Roger that."

It seemed to Ya'acov that they were moving much faster now, streaking over the western desert of Iraq. He shuddered to think of what would happen if Joel bobbled the controls even slightly, or if either of them missed an obstacle in their path. He took off the goggles and reviewed the map one more time. He double-checked the GPS readout to make sure he knew where they were. Then he donned the goggles and scanned the rushing desert for anything that could snatch them out of the sky.

Mars glanced at his watch for what seemed like the thousandth time. It was 3 in the morning. Finally it was time. He threw back the covers, leaving the light off. The bed wiggled as Anne sat up. They silently pulled on their clothes and got into their boots. Mars crept to the door and opened it, and they both looked out. Two dark shapes stood by the door. Mars felt a flush of embarrassment as he realized they were the last out.

Ghanim cracked the door and gazed out. Dim light washed over the site from the two poles that supported the surveillance cameras. There were a few dark shadows around the long pit where they had found the wall, but none close enough to help them. The pit itself, however, was in deep blackness all along its southern edge.

Ghanim glanced at the camera mounted on the eastern pole. It seemed to be pointing toward the western fence, and it was not currently panning. The western camera he could not see. He squinted as he tried to locate the ladder he had left at the eastern end of the pit. Mars pointed toward the two tiny gleams marking the top of the ladder.

Ghanim nodded. He crouched down and ran for it. After reaching the ladder, he whirled around and dashed down to the comforting blackness at the bottom. Anne rushed down a few moments later, followed quickly by Mars and Moshe. They leaned against the sheer side of the pit as they waited for their pounding hearts to slow.

They crouched low to stay deep inside the shadows as Ghanim led them quickly down the pit to the tunnel entrance. They disappeared inside and began walking. Ghanim waited until they reached the end before clicking on his flashlight. He tried to shield the beam with his hand as he examined the stonework of the tunnel's barrel vaulting.

Moshe picked up the hammer and chisel they had left in the tunnel at the end of the day. He picked a large stone that was directly overhead and began working carefully around the edge, chipping out the crumbly mortar.

"Better stand back," he whispered.

The stone began to wiggle like a loose tooth. Moshe took the flashlight and examined the remaining mortar closely. He handed the light back and carefully placed the chisel. He then brought the hammer up in a ringing blow. The stone crashed to the tunnel's stone floor as if it had been shot from a cannon. Dust and sand rained down, interspersed with small stones.

"It isn't going to take much to bring that down," Moshe said. "We're still under the asphalt, aren't we?"

"I think so," Ghanim replied.

Moshe worked at the stones that had surrounded the one he had broken loose. They fell with hardly any effort. A small avalanche of dirt and sand accompanied each one as it thudded down. When he judged the hole was wide enough, he took the flashlight and looked up. A roughly dome-shaped void extended upward about two feet from the tunnel's stone ceiling. He reached past the ladder lying on its side and picked up a long broom handle. A few quick jabs brought down the rest of the dirt. The flashlight revealed the rough underside of the asphalt paving, a surface that was already beginning to sag downward. Moshe poked a few holes around the perimeter, and the sag increased quickly. The black mass thundered down, blowing a choking cloud of dust over everyone.

Anne blinked her eyes and looked up. "The stars."

"Now, if we can just make it to Ghanim's Land Cruiser."

Ghanim grabbed the ladder and began angling it up through the hole. When it stuck tight before he could get it upright, Moshe widened the hole to free it. A few minutes later they had the ladder up.

"I'll check," Ghanim said.

He hurried up the ladder. He stuck his head out and looked around. He breathed a sigh of relief as he saw that the exit was in dark shadow. The lights on the nearby surveillance pole pointed in the opposite direction, and the ones at the far end were too far away to be a threat.

"It's clear," he whispered back down the hole at the eager faces peering up at him.

He rushed up the remaining steps and steadied the ladder for the others. He held out his hand to help Anne as she stepped unsteadily off the ladder. Mars joined her a moment later. Moshe looked back at the ladder after he hopped to the asphalt.

"Leave it," Ghanim whispered. "Come on."

He led them to the north behind the Southern Palace.

23

DESERT CHASE

It was quiet in the basement of President Talfah's Guest House. Power had been restored to the security communications control room, but there was obviously no need to man the lab monitoring stations. Two bored guards and Abdul Suleiman sluggishly punched console buttons as they rotated around the surveillance cameras stationed throughout Babylon. There wasn't much to see in the early-morning hours.

Abdul yawned, then blinked, wondering if he was seeing things. His swivel chair squeaked as he sat suddenly upright. He grabbed the joystick and zoomed in on the east camera inside the fence, training it down at the same time. He caught a brief flash of something before it disappeared behind the Southern Palace. He panned back and forth for several moments but saw nothing else.

He frowned. The camera was aimed beyond the fence where it was very dark. There shouldn't be anything moving out there. He reached up and increased the sensitivity of the camera. The monitor became very blotchy. He moved the camera slowly from side to side until he saw a faint reflection. He zoomed in tighter and again increased the camera's gain. It took several moments for the distorted picture to register. He felt a sudden chill.

He picked up the phone and punched the number for Avraham's room in the Guest House.

"What is it?" a groggy voice snapped.

"This is Abdul. We have a problem. I think the archaeologists have escaped."

"What? How?"

"There's a hole in the parking lot west of the site with something sticking out of it. It's outside the fence, so they must have tunneled out. Want me to sound the alarm?"

"Wait! I want to handle this! I'll be right down."

Abdul looked up a few minutes later as Avraham stormed in with his shirttail hanging out and his shoelaces untied. The two guards looked toward the two Palestinians.

Avraham pointed a finger at them. "This

doesn't concern you. Go back to your duties!" They snapped their heads back to their own monitors.

Avraham turned back to Abdul. "Which way were they going?"

"Behind the Southern Palace, toward the river."

"That doesn't make sense. They can't get out that way. Have you tried the cameras in that direction?"

"Yes. The Iraqi archaeologist probably knows where they are, except we don't know where he is at the moment."

Avraham snorted. "Where have you looked?"

"All around the Palace, the Lion Monument, and along Procession Street."

"I doubt they would come along the Street — too many cameras. I bet they're circling around behind it to the east. Is there a camera that shows the back of the Ninmah Temple?"

"There's one on the top of the Ishtar Temple, but it's pretty far away."

"Train it around and zoom in."

Abdul looked at a list and punched in a number. The monitor's screen blurred and danced as he panned the camera around until it was pointed north.

"There!" he said excitedly.

Even zoomed out, they could see four small objects behind the temple, leaving a smeary trail of light on the screen. Abdul zoomed in as close as he could get.

"Can't tell who it is, but it's got to be them. Where are they going?"

"Probably heading for Jassim's Land Cruiser. Wonder where he parked it?"

The light blobs disappeared behind the Nebuchadnezzar Museum.

"Punch up the camera on the side of the museum," Avraham ordered.

"There they are!" Abdul shouted.

"And there's the Land Cruiser! Come on! We need some goggles and weapons!"

"I'll grab some on the way out. Do you have the keys?"

Avraham felt in his pocket. "Yes. Let's go!"

Ghanim dashed up to the Toyota, jammed the key into the lock, and twisted it. He pulled the door open and thumbed the Unlock button. Mars pulled the back door open and held it for Anne. She jumped in and scooted over. Mars got in, sat down, and pulled the door shut. Moshe joined Ghanim in the front seat.

"Where to?" Ghanim asked as he threw the gearshift into reverse.

Mars leaned forward. "Turn right at the highway and head for Al Hillah. We'll turn off the road a couple of miles down."

Ghanim nodded as he shifted into drive and pulled onto Procession Street in front of the dig. The archaeologists gazed at the high, chainlink fence as they swept on past. The Iraqi turned left at the intersection and sped toward the highway.

"Might want to hold it down a little until we're out of here," Mars said.

Ghanim backed off of the throttle a bit. He paused at the highway and turned right. He accelerated quickly to 70 and held it there.

Avraham unlocked one of the Security Land Cruisers. Abdul jumped in the passenger side, placing an AK-47 assault rifle on the floor of the backseat and two Makarov 9mm pistols on the seat between them. He held the low-light goggles in his hand. Avraham spun the tires as he backed out. He slammed the gear selector into drive and stood on the accelerator. In moments they roared past Procession Street, made the curve, and were headed for the highway. The heavy Toyota slid to an impulsive stop in a stench of rubber.

"Which way?" Avraham demanded.

Abdul looked both directions. Several tail-lights were visible going north toward Baghdad. Only one set showed to the south.

"They went to the south," Abdul said. "Turn out the lights, and put these on." He gave Avraham a pair of the low-light goggles while he put on the other set.

The dark night immediately turned into a garish green scene. In the distance they could see the fleeing Land Cruiser. Avraham pulled onto the highway and accelerated quickly.

"Are you going to take them now?" Abdul asked.

"No. Let's see where they're going. Maybe we'll find out what's been going on."

"Where are we going?" Ghanim asked as he slowed down a little.

"There's a wrecked bus by the side of the road somewhere along here."

"I remember it. I think we're only a few miles from it."

"Ya'acov says that's where we turn off the road and head east. Is that compass accurate?" Mars pointed to the large instrument mounted on top of the dash.

"Quite accurate. I use it for navigating in the desert."

"Good. We're going to need it." Mars

turned his head around. "I don't see any lights behind us."

"And none coming toward us," Ghanim said. "And I think I see the bus up ahead."

He slowed down as they approached the rusted hulk, then came to a stop. Mars looked across the highway toward the east. There was a shallow ditch on that side. The flat featureless desert fled toward the distant horizon, punctuated only by low scrub brush.

Mars sat forward in the seat. "Ya'acov said to drive on a course of 80 degrees for fifteen miles."

"We'll miss him," Ghanim said. "The odometer is fairly accurate, but I can't tell when we've gone exactly fifteen miles. Also, the wheels slip a little in the sand, and I won't be able to steer a perfectly straight course." He pointed at the compass. "And we might not be able to maintain exactly 80 degrees either. We could easily miss them by several miles."

"We'll be okay. Ya'acov said he allowed for the slippage. Our course is to the north of where they'll be. That way we won't have to wonder whether they're to the right or the left of us — they'll definitely be to the right. If it's still dark, we can wait until the sun is up and then start driving south heading 170 degrees. They'll be looking for us."

Ghanim glanced at the dash clock. It was approaching 4 in the morning. "That's comforting, I guess."

He twisted a dash-mounted dial, thus locking both differentials, turned sharply left, and drove across the highway and into the low desert brush. He made tiny steering adjustments until the red line on the compass rested on 80 degrees. He ran their speed up to 25, then backed off to a little below 20 to make the ride smoother.

"Help me watch the compass, Mars," he said.

"I will."

The sand made a faint, tinkling sound as it was thrown up against the wheel wells. This blended in with the sibilant sound of the knobby tires rolling over the desert. The Land Cruiser bounced and bobbed on its stiff suspension as Ghanim struggled to stay on course.

Mars glanced at Anne. Even though the light was dim, he could see that her head was bowed.

"Are you all right?" he asked.

Her head came up. "Yes. I was praying."

He didn't know what to say.

She reached over, took his left hand, and squeezed it. "I was praying that God would take care of us. That He would guide us to our rescuers."

"Do you think that will help? Does God really care about what happens to us?"

"Oh yes, Mars. I'm not an expert in the Bible, but I know that much. God cares for us more than we know."

Mars cleared his throat. "He has a funny way of showing it," he griped.

"Mars, do you remember when those Palestinians kidnapped me?"

"How can I forget it?"

"Did you think you would ever see me again?"

Unwanted, unbidden, Mars felt hot tears brim in his eyes, then spill over and run down his cheeks. He started to speak, but his voice cracked. He struggled for composure. Finally he said, "No."

"I became a Christian while they held me. I read the Bible Zuba gave me. I kept thinking about the Temple veil we found, torn in two, just like the Bible said, and I knew it was all true. Everything my mom and dad told me all my life was true. That's when I prayed for Jesus to save me."

Mars struggled with emotions he did not understand. There was something about what she was saying that drew him. But at the same time, he was afraid. Of what, he didn't know. But the fear was very real.

"I know all this," he said finally. "I remember you telling me."

"I had a lot of time to read and pray. Mars, I prayed that God would do something — that somehow He would bring us back together. And He did. How else can we explain what happened?"

"I don't know."

She reached over and touched his face. He closed his eyes and leaned toward the comforting hand as he struggled with his emotions. He opened his eyes a few moments later. Moshe's head was turned to the side as if he were about to say something. Then, without a word, he faced forward again.

Ghanim gripped the wheel with both hands as he guided the husky Toyota through the desert on a course of 80 degrees magnetic.

Avraham began to slow down as they approached the derelict bus. He glanced to the left. A small green blob, trailing a plume of dust, danced in his goggles.

"Look for where they turned off," he ordered.

Abdul looked across the highway. "There it is," he said, pointing.

Avraham slowed further and turned across

the highway. He locked the Toyota's differentials as they passed through the shallow ditch.

"Plain as day," Avraham agreed as he followed the twin lines. "How far away would you say they are?"

Abdul squinted at the indistinct image in his goggles. "A little more than a mile, I'd say."

"Do you think they have low-light goggles?"

"Extremely unlikely. That sort of thing is closely guarded by the government."

"So they can't see us back here."

Abdul glanced back. Their dust trail rose no higher than the roof and quickly settled to the ground. "It's possible. I recommend we drop back a little. We can definitely see better than they can. And there's no way we can lose them out here."

Avraham slowed down and let the distance widen before resuming his pace. "We can't let them get too far ahead. I don't want them to get away."

"Think they are meeting an airplane?"

"Couldn't be anything else with them heading toward Iran. Keep a sharp lookout. Let me know if you see anything."

"I will."

The Land Cruiser followed the distinct

trail through the desert brush.

The desert brush flashed underneath the wings of the U-27 in a blur of green. The plane was lower now, something of which Ya'acov was nervously aware. The sky was still black, but it did seem a little lighter to the east.

"How are we doing?" Joel asked.

"We're coming up on a dry *wadi* according to the GPS." Ya'acov looked up.

Joel pointed down. "There it is. Good work. Aren't we nearing the course change?"

"We are. About five miles."

"Can you tell me why we're changing our course?"

"Well, we've been angling a little to the south since we entered Iraq. Now we're heading almost due east through a big open area south of Al Hillah. Avoiding towns?"

"That's it."

Ya'acov flipped to another chart. "We're not far from the Euphrates. Once we're past there, we turn north to the extraction site, which is in the big fat middle of nowhere."

"Correct. The better to not meet people we would rather not know."

"Think we'll see them on our way in?"

"I doubt it. We're well to the south of where they're supposed to be. That and how low we're flying means we won't see them until they approach the site."

"There's the Euphrates," Ya'acov said, pointing.

Joel pulled up sharply to clear the date palms that dotted both sides of the river. He then ducked down to his former altitude. The minutes ticked off on the aircraft's chronometer as they penetrated deeper into Iraq. Ya'acov spent more of his time watching the GPS as they drew near their final turn. When the longitude readout reached the magic number, Joel pulled up slightly and banked the plane around in a tight left turn, settling down on a due north heading.

"Won't be long now," he said.

"Right." Ya'acov wiped his sweaty hands on his trousers. He looked out his window. It was definitely getting lighter to the east.

Ghanim looked down at the odometer. He took his foot off the gas and stopped. "Mars, we've gone fifteen miles. What now?"

Mars looked toward the gray of the approaching dawn. "The plane should be landing about now. Turn around until we're pointed 170 degrees. Once the sun is above the horizon, we'll drive south until we see them."

"I hope they get here."

"I do too."

"How far away is the plane supposed to be?"

"I don't know. Enough so they can see us before we see them, I would guess."

"Do you regret how this has worked out?" Moshe asked Ghanim.

The Iraqi gave a brief, mirthless laugh. "You mean leaving my country forever? I don't have much choice. I don't hold it against you, if that's what you mean."

"I can promise you interesting work," Moshe said.

"I know. But I'll never see Iraq again."

"That is true, and for that I am sorry."

"Ultimately it's Talfah's fault. All this mania for nuclear and biological weapons to pamper his ego." He thumped the steering wheel. "It is done. I will not worry about it anymore."

Anne leaned her head on Mars's shoulder. Smiling in spite of their situation, he reached over with his left hand and found hers. It was small and soft and warm. He gave it a squeeze.

"I love you, dear," she whispered.

"I love you, too. We'll be out of here soon."

"Yes. I'm glad."

He felt her shiver.

"What's the matter?" he asked.

"I hope we're not carrying a biological bomb back with us."

"I don't think we are. Something happened to take away the danger. We haven't shown any signs of illness, and the security people at Babylon sure aren't worried."

"But what happened?"

"I don't know."

Avraham and Abdul stared through the windshield. They still had their low-light goggles on, but the fast-approaching dawn would soon take away their value.

"What are they waiting for?" Avraham asked in irritation.

"Their ticket out, I guess."

"Do you think they can see us?"

Abdul took off the goggles and put them on the seat. The predawn gray was quite bright now, but the desert was dark by contrast. He could not see the distant Land Cruiser even though he knew exactly where it was.

"Not yet. They might see us once the sun is up, especially if we are moving. At some point we are going to have to take them. Then it won't matter, unless they reach the plane before we get there."

"This is it," Joel said as Ya'acov read off their final GPS position. "At least we don't have a long approach to make."

"No chance of running out of runway either," Ya'acov observed.

"Right you are."

The pilot lowered full flaps and pulled back on the power lever. He started applying gentle back pressure on the wheel as the speed began to bleed off. He held the Cessna off with increasing elevator. The stall indicator began an intermittent chirp as if it weren't sure but then came full-on. The plane quit flying and dropped to the waiting sand and brush. The fat, oversize tires crunched through the stunted growth as Joel started applying the brakes. He breathed a sigh of relief as they rolled to a stop.

"Nice landing," Ya'acov said.

"You know the aviator's definition of a good landing, don't you?"

"No."

"One you can walk away from."

Ya'acov grinned. "I think you're a little better than that."

"I could tell you some stories, but I think we have other things to do."

"Right. Cover the plane."

"That and refuel."

Joel's skilled eyes made a quick circuit of the instruments. Then he killed the engine. The turbine's high whine started descending as the propeller gradually slowed.

Ya'acov opened the airstair door and jumped out. He circled the U27, opened the cargo doors, and felt for the large plastic bag containing the camouflage net. He pulled it out and dropped it on the ground while Joel started pulling out the five-gallon jerry cans of jet fuel.

"Which first?" the pilot asked.

"Net first, then refuel. It'll be harder that way, but we can't take any chance of being seen."

Joel helped him pull the net out and unfold it. Ya'acov reached in and started pulling out the pole sections.

"When will they get here?" Joel asked as he and Ya'acov started pulling the net over the tail.

"Anytime after the sun is up."

"We'd better hurry, then."

They used the poles to lift the camouflage over the long wings. Joel made a circuit of the aircraft as Ya'acov finished tugging the net into place.

"Looks good to me," the pilot reported. "Help me with the refueling?"

"Right."

Joel placed a folding stepladder on the ground below the right wing. Ya'acov propped up the net with a pole and waited as the pilot bounded up the ladder. He reached over, removed the filler cap, and placed a large plastic funnel in the tank's neck.

He turned his head. "Hand me one of those jerry cans."

Ya'acov removed the cap and lifted the can to where Joel could reach it. The pilot hoisted it up as if it weighed nothing and began pouring. After he emptied ten cans, the two officers hurried around to the left wing and repeated the process. When they were done, they pulled out two aluminum folding chairs.

Ya'acov nodded toward the north. "That's where they should come from, but we need to keep a watch all around. Why don't you take the south, and I'll keep an eye out for our friends."

"O.K. I hope they're on time. I want to get out of here."

"You and me both."

Joel took his chair and walked around the plane's nose. Ya'acov picked a spot under the left wing and sat down. The sand crunched as the chair's legs dug in. A red glint flashed in the corner of Ya'acov's right eye. He turned his head and saw the narrow rim of the sun sitting on the horizon. It was much lighter now, and he had no trouble seeing in the clear desert air. But something else was coming up with the sun. What looked like a long brown cloud straddled the entire eastern horizon. Ya'acov felt a cold chill settle in his stomach. It looked like the dust storm would be ahead of schedule.

24

IN PRISON, YET FREE

The deep, red sun sat on the horizon, a full circle that was dimmed significantly by the approaching dust cloud.

"Time to go," Mars said, sitting on the edge of the backseat.

Ghanim started the engine. "Hope we get there before the dust storm."

"Me too," Mars said, looking out the left window.

Ghanim accelerated up to an uncomfortable 40 miles an hour. He struggled with the wheel as the Land Cruiser bounced and swayed over the desert. They roared over the stunted scrub brush as Ghanim tried to avoid the bigger bushes. Occasionally he wasn't quick enough, and the heavy vehicle would plow through one. The resulting crash and explosion of branches was alarming but apparently did no harm. Ghanim only hoped they would not hit a hidden rock.

This area of the desert was fairly level,

with only an occasional gentle hill or shallow *wadi*. Mars and Anne were leaning on the back of the front seat, peering out over the bounding hood. Moshe glanced into the mirror on his side.

"We're leaving quite a dust plume," he remarked.

Ghanim's eyes flicked toward the rearview mirror. "Shouldn't matter. There's no one out here but us and, I hope, our rescuers."

Anne turned around. She watched their dust trail boil up and then start dissipating. She was about to turn back when she saw a bright flash through the thinning dust. She watched for several moments, but it did not repeat. A chilling jolt raced down her spine as she tried to convince herself there couldn't be anything or anyone out there. Yet, she knew there was.

"Someone's coming after us," she said, facing forward.

"What?" Ghanim shouted.

"I saw a flash behind us — the sun reflecting off something."

"Can you see what it is?"

"No. Our dust trail is hiding whoever it is."

"Could it be our rescuers?" Moshe asked.

"Can't be," Mars answered. "They're in front of us somewhere."

"What do we do?" Ghanim demanded, almost in panic.

"If we keep going, we'll give our friends away," Mars said.

"How do we know for sure we're being followed?" Ghanim inquired, hoping they weren't.

"Turn right. Once we're clear of our plume we should see them."

"What then?"

"I don't know."

Ya'acov lowered his binoculars. "I think they're coming, but we've got a problem."

Joel pushed the flapping camouflage net away from the plane's nose and joined the Intelligence officer. "What is it?"

"Someone's following them." He handed him the glasses and pointed. "There's a second cloud of dust merging with the first one."

Joel focused the binoculars. "All I can see is one now. Could they be coming in two cars?"

"I guess that is possible, but I doubt it. Besides, when the second one started out, it was some distance away. If they were in two vehicles, they would've been together the whole way."

"This is bad. They'll be here in a couple

of minutes. We've got to get out of here. Help me with the net."

"Wait a minute."

"Wait nothing! We have to get in the air!" The pilot started pulling down poles.

"I said wait, Lieutenant!" Ya'acov shouted.

Joel dropped a pole and glared. "If we get caught on the ground, your goose is cooked! Not that it will matter with us rotting away in a Baghdad jail."

"They're turning to the west," Ya'acov said. "They've apparently seen their pursuers."

"Have they seen us?"

"With our camouflage? I doubt it."

He lowered the glasses and glanced toward the east. "That dust storm is going to arrive soon."

"And we need to take off before it does."

"We can't do that as long as they're still out there."

"They've seen us," Abdul shouted, pointing.

The Land Cruiser had been invisible a moment before, hidden in its dust roostertail. Now it thundered out of the murky cloud heading toward the west at a right angle to its previous course.

Avraham cursed as he turned hard to the right. He floored the accelerator as he homed in on their prey. Slowly the gap between the two cars began to decrease.

Abdul reached into the backseat and grabbed the AK-47. He checked the weapon quickly, chambered a round, and set the safety.

"Cross over behind them," he said.

Avraham glanced over and nodded.

Mars and Anne looked out the back.

"Where are they?" Ghanim shouted.

"About fifty feet back," Mars replied. "They're about to enter our dust."

The pursuing Land Cruiser disappeared for a few seconds, then reappeared on the other side.

"They're going to shoot at us!" Mars yelled.

Ghanim twisted the steering wheel sharply to the right. The vehicle shuddered as the tires slid over the sand, and the rear end started to break loose. Ghanim eased the wheel to stop the spin but held the tight turn.

"Can you see what they're doing?"

Automatic gunfire sounded behind them. Twice they heard something heavy slam into the back of the Toyota. The other vehicle was lost in the curve of dust behind them.

"They can't see us," Anne said.

"That won't last long," Ghanim responded with a scowl.

He continued the tight turn until they had turned in a complete circle. He snapped the wheel straight when the compass neared 270 degrees. He floored the accelerator, hoping the car would hold together.

Mars searched the confused dust cloud behind them.

"Ghanim, they're behind us again on your side, just outside our dust trail. They're about 150 feet back now. Any chance we can outrun them?"

The Iraqi shook his head. "I doubt it."

Mars saw the flashes coming from the passenger side of the other vehicle. "They're shooting at us again."

Ghanim jogged left sharply, then began a gentle curving turn to the right. The other car disappeared behind an obscuring wall of dust.

"Look out!" Moshe shouted, pointing straight ahead.

Ghanim jerked his head down, but it was too late. The hurtling Land Cruiser soared out over the dry *wadi*. The left front hit the opposite bank and began crumpling like wet cardboard. Both front-seat air bags deployed, pushing Ghanim and Moshe back against the seats. Mars and Anne flew forward as the vehicle started a rapid roll to the left. The windows fractured, then crumpled as the roof dented in. They looked out in horror as a kaleidoscope of desert tans swept past interspersed with flashes of blue.

Finally it was over. The Toyota bounced to a stop right-side-up. Ghanim and Moshe stared in shock through the open hole where the windshield had been, the deflated air bags lying on their laps. Moshe blinked and looked back.

"Are you two all right?" he asked.

Anne was sprawled on top of Mars, who was on the floor. She pushed herself up and looked down at her husband. He was dazed but conscious.

"Are you okay, dear?" she asked.

"I think so," he said as he cautiously moved. "How about you?"

"I banged my arm on something, but that's all." She helped pull him up into the seat.

"Thanks." He checked the sling on his right arm. "I think I'm more or less in one piece."

The pursuing vehicle slid to a stop on the bank of the *wadi* in a shower of sand and pebbles. Mars felt a momentary urge to try to escape but knew it was futile. Two men got out of their car and jumped down into the dry streambed.

"It's Avraham and Abdul!" Anne gasped.

"That figures," Mars grumbled. "That Security honcho said they were here." He glared at Abdul. "Looks like His Ugliness hasn't learned to smile since the last time we saw him."

Abdul held the AK-47 on them as Avraham approached the driver's door, his Makarov 9mm pistol leveled on Ghanim.

"Keep your hands where I can see them," he ordered. "Get out."

Ghanim tried his door, but it was jammed. Moshe forced his open with his shoulder and climbed out. He walked around to the other side and helped Mars and Anne make their exit from the ruined vehicle. Ghanim slid over and went out the passenger's door. Avraham was waiting for him.

"So, Doctor Jassim, perhaps you could tell us what you are doing out here and why you were running from us."

"I have nothing to say."

"Oh, I think you will change your mind once we get back. Why not save yourself the trouble — and the pain?"

Ghanim shook his head.

"My, how brave. I am very impressed."

Avraham motioned toward the south with his pistol. "Who were you meeting out here?"

The Iraqi remained silent.

"Perhaps I should be asking the Enderlys, since they and Dr. Stein are Jewish Intelligence agents."

"We are not!" Mars shot back.

"Don't lie to me!" Avraham thundered, his gun hand shaking. "We know you are out here to be picked up. Now, where are they?"

"We don't know," Anne answered softly.

Abdul whispered in Avraham's ear. They both looked toward the east. The towering dust storm was only a few miles away and approaching rapidly.

"Get in the car," Avraham ordered. "We will sort this out later."

Abdul ushered the archaeologists to the back door and watched them as they got in. Moshe lowered the right-hand middle seat so he and Ghanim could climb into the two seats in the back while the Enderlys took the middle seats. Abdul closed the door and got in. Avraham put the Land Cruiser into gear immediately and turned toward the west. He took it slow until he found the clear trail the two vehicles had made only a short time earlier. Then he accelerated up to 40 since he knew there were no obstacles in front of them.

Ya'acov lowered his binoculars and sighed.

"What happened?" Joel asked.

"The first Land Cruiser crashed. The other one stopped, and everyone got in it. Now it's hightailing it toward the west."

"So they've been caught."

"Looks like it."

"What happened?"

"Who knows. Our people were probably followed."

"Which means the bad guys know we're out here somewhere."

"I'm sure they do," Ya'acov agreed.

Joel glanced back to the east. "We'd better get a move on. I think we may be able to get out ahead of that storm."

Ya'acov glanced at the towering brown cloud. "We're staying put."

"Captain, if we don't leave now, we'll have to stay put until the storm's past."

"Is the net secure?"

"I think so."

"Let's check it one more time. Then I suggest we try and get comfy inside the plane."

"If you're thinking of escaping the dust,

472

forget it. You can't keep it out."

Ya'acov started checking the pegs on the left side of the aircraft. Joel finally shrugged and took the right side. A few minutes later they were sweltering inside the cabin as the wall of brown swept over them, reducing visibility to a few feet.

Avraham drove toward the long shadows of early morning. Up ahead the sky was blue, and the desert was bathed in beautiful warm colors. But an ugly, brown cloud blocked out the view to the rear.

"Are we outrunning it?" Avraham asked.

Abdul turned around and looked out the back. "Hard to tell. It's still several miles back. If it doesn't catch us now, it will when we hit the highway."

"Better there than out here."

"Yes," Abdul agreed as he turned back. "Where are we taking them?"

"Back to the Guest House. Akram will be glad to see them, I am sure," he said with a laugh. "A little interrogation, and then a trial, if any of them are still alive. And finally, a hanging in Baghdad."

Avraham kept up the pounding pace as their car plunged and rocked over the desert wilderness. The angry, brown cloud followed them relentlessly, gradually narrowing the gap. Finally they sighted the highway. Avraham took his foot off the accelerator as he slowed for the ditch. The cloud swept over them like a shroud, rocking the Toyota like a toy in a giant's hand. Anne sneezed as the fine dust permeated the interior. Avraham jammed on the brakes, and the car slid from side to side as it skidded to a stop on the highway shoulder.

Avraham pounded the steering wheel. "I can't see anything." Everything beyond the front of the hood had disappeared.

"Follow the stripes on the highway," Abdul suggested.

Avraham crept forward until he could see the pavement. Tendrils of sand and dust danced over the surface like brown snow. A dim painted line crept into view. Avraham cranked the wheel hard to the right and drove slowly to the north, watching the stripes that repeatedly appeared and disappeared.

The sand made a dry rattling noise as it pinged off the curved Plexiglas windshield, barely audible over the moaning of the wind. The camouflage netting appeared and disappeared as it flapped like a muffled bedsheet in a storm.

"No one is going to find us while this is

going on," Joel said.

"I think that is a safe assumption," Ya'acov agreed.

"What do we do when it clears?"

"I'm not sure."

"At the mission briefing we were told to get out ASAP if it became impossible to achieve the objective."

"The objective can be achieved," Ya'acov said quietly.

Joel turned his head in disbelief. "I can't believe you said that. The Iraqi security creeps have captured our people, and we're stuck in a sandstorm. We couldn't rescue them now if we had an entire armored division. And all we have is us."

"We're not doing anything as long as the storm lasts. I'll decide what to do when it quits."

Joel shook his head and turned back to the endless dust.

Avraham sighed in relief when he finally spotted the edge of the drive leading into the rear parking lot behind President Talfah's Guest House. He guided the Land Cruiser into one of the vacant Security slots. He and Abdul herded their prisoners in through the rear entrance, where they took the service elevator to the basement.

"Take them in there," Avraham said, pointing to a small conference room near the security communications control room.

He ascended to the second floor and hurried to Akram's office. His boss looked up in irritation.

"Where have you and Abdul been?" he demanded.

Avraham compressed his lips as he struggled with his anger. "The archaeologists tried to escape."

"I know that! I got the report immediately after you two disappeared. Why didn't you notify me instead of taking off on your own?"

"There wasn't time. If we had delayed, we would have lost them. Is that what you want?"

"Both of you are under my command! I do *not* allow independent action! Is that clear?"

Avraham glared at him. "It is."

"Very well. What happened?"

"We saw them sneak around on the other side of Procession Street and take Jassim's Land Cruiser. We followed them as they headed south, and after a few miles they turned east and drove out into the desert. They stopped a little before dawn and waited. After the sun was up, they drove off toward the south. But they apparently saw us, because they turned back and tried to get away. We captured them when they wrecked their car and brought them back here. I told Abdul to watch them while I came to tell you."

"So, they were meeting someone out there."

"I think that is obvious."

"Did you see who it was?"

Avraham shook his head. "No. But whoever it was had to be nearby. I was hoping to catch them as well, but unfortunately we were seen."

Akram glanced out his window at the blowing sand. "As soon as this lets up, I will ask for an air search."

"It is probably too late for that. I am sure they have escaped."

"Maybe. But it's possible the sandstorm caught them before they could take off. If they are still there, we stand a good chance of catching them. Meanwhile, we will interrogate the archaeologists."

"Abdul and I have considerable experience in this."

Akram snorted. "We are quite proficient, I assure you. But we must proceed carefully. This whole situation is very sensitive."

"Because of what was going on in the lab?"

"That, and also the archaeologists are well-known."

"But they were certainly involved with the attack."

"Yes, I know that," Akram snapped. "But how? What did they do? We have to convince the media of their guilt — without revealing what the lab was doing."

"That may be hard to do."

"But we *will* do it. I won't let them go until I know exactly what happened. Are they all together now?"

"Yes. Abdul is holding them in the basement conference room."

"Good. I will question them separately and see how their stories hold together." A cruel smile crossed his face. "And then we shall see what we shall see. Come with me."

They took the elevator to the basement. Akram paused outside the room, then pushed open the door. He looked at each of the archaeologists in turn, waiting until their eyes met his. He stopped on Anne. The cruel smile grew wider.

"Anne Enderly," he said, "you will come with me."

Mars started forward. "You can't do that!"

Akram nodded to Abdul. The Palestinian

intercepted the American, bringing his Makarov around in a vicious backhand blow. Mars crumpled to his knees and slumped forward. Moshe moved toward him but stopped when Abdul trained the gun on him.

"Mars!" Anne screamed as she fell to her knees. "Mars, are you all right?" She cradled his head in her hands. Tears squeezed out of her tightly shut eyes as choked sobs wracked her body.

Akram took two quick strides, grabbing her upper left arm in a vise-like grip and jerking her to her feet. She whipped her right hand around, but he easily grabbed it. He laughed as she made an inept attempt to knee him in the groin. He let go of her arm and slapped her hard.

"Enough of this!" he shouted. "As spies, all of you are under a death sentence! If you cooperate, the courts may show leniency — provided you get that far. Many spies, unfortunately, do not survive interrogation. Forget about any childish games of honor. There is only one thing that can save you — and that is to cooperate with me fully. Now, Dr. Enderly, you will come with me."

Akram took her to a small room in the corner of the large basement, a room he had often used. He opened the door loudly and pointed toward the single chair.

"Sit down," he growled.

She looked down at the scarred surface. It had numerous gouges and deep scratches. Large brownish stains covered most of the surface, as well as much of the floor. The chair tipped on wobbly legs as she sat down. She grabbed the filthy tabletop to steady herself. Akram slammed the door shut.

"There," he said. "Now we will not be disturbed. Feel free to make as much noise as you please."

He stepped to a spotlight mounted on a stand, clicked on the powerful beam, and focused it on Anne's face. She put up her hand and squinted. Akram stepped to the table, towering over her.

Anne lowered her head to her hands. The prayer was in her mind before she understood where the urge had come from. With her eyes tightly shut, she silently implored the only One who could help. *Dear God, help me — help us all.* Another thought rushed in upon her. *And please, God, reach out to Mars. Show him You are real. Save him, dear God.* After her silent amen, a wave of despair washed over her. But a deep sense of peace forced it to retreat. She smiled, knowing the source of her reassurance.

"Look up!" Akram demanded.

He gaped at her transformed face, not understanding the change. Doubt edged his eyes for a few moments as his self-confidence wavered. Then the steel resolve returned.

"Listen to me carefully. All of you are in serious trouble. After we confronted you about your association with IDF Intelligence, you tried to escape. I believe that you drove into the desert to meet an airplane the Israelis sent to take you home. But we found out about that as well, and now you are here." He paused to let his words sink in. "And there is no escape for you now. You are all under a sentence of death for espionage. Your only hope is to tell me everything."

"I have nothing to say," Anne said without emotion.

Akram pounded the table. Anne jumped and looked up at him in irritation.

"Where is the plane they sent to pick you up?" he demanded.

"I said I have nothing to say."

Akram glared down at her for almost a minute, then realized he would get no information from her. After he took her back to the conference room, he interviewed the other archaeologists, starting with Mars and ending with Ghanim, who returned with a swollen left eye that was already turning black. Akram watched them from the door.

"We will continue this later. I would advise cooperation. Once you leave here, you won't have another chance." He slammed the door.

Ghanim slumped down in a chair.

"How badly are you hurt?" Anne asked.

"It is nothing," he replied, revealing the bloody gap where he had lost an upper tooth.

"What did he hit you with?"

"His fist. It does not matter."

"Yes, it does!" Anne snapped.

"What can we do?" Mars asked.

Ghanim glanced pointedly up at the ceiling.

Mars grimaced in embarrassment, remembering that the walls had ears. The others took seats at the table as they began their wait.

Moshe's face displayed deep sadness, but Anne couldn't help smiling in spite of their situation. His somber expression changed to one of puzzlement.

"A shekel for your thoughts," she said.

The puzzled scowl grew deeper. "That's quite a bit more than a penny."

"I couldn't remember what you call your fractional currency."

"Agorot."

"Thank you. So what are you thinking about?"

"How sorry I am that I invited you two along on this dig." He glanced quickly at Ghanim. "This has nothing to do with you, my friend. I'm just sorry it happened."

"I am sorry as well," Ghanim agreed.

Anne felt a sense of encouragement she could not explain. Even though she knew their situation was serious, for some reason that fact did not penetrate to her innermost being. Her thoughts drifted to what they had found in Babylon, and further back to their earlier discoveries in Jerusalem.

"I'm grateful for what we've found here," she said.

"How can you say that after what's happened?" Mars asked.

"Because of *what* we found — the inscription on the wall: '*mene, mene, tekel, upharsin.*' It's a comfort to me to know how accurate the Bible is."

Anne saw the familiar look of irritation in Mars's eyes, but there was something else there now, something she had not seen before.

"Mars, on our last dig we found the Temple veil — the one hanging in Herod's Temple the day Jesus was crucified. It was torn in two, from top to bottom, and no one could explain how. That was something out of the New Testament. Now we find this, out of the Old Testament." She glanced at Moshe. "Or I guess I should say the *Torah*."

Moshe made a steeple out of his hands. "Many refer to the Old Testament books as the *Torah*, but the precise term is the *Tanach*. The *Torah* is the five books of Moses."

Anne smiled. "You are never lacking in precision."

"I would thank you, but I fear a compliment was not intended."

"Moshe, you are such a dear. It *was* a compliment." She could tell that embarrassed him.

He looked down and cleared his throat. "Well then, thank you."

She turned back to Mars.

"I know where you're going with this," Mars said quickly.

"Don't be angry with me, dear. I just want you to discover what I've found. I can't tell you how important it is — not only to me but to you."

"I'm not angry. I understand your concern, and I appreciate it. It's very loving of you." He smiled suddenly. "And believe it or not, I have thought about the things you've told me ever since you . . ."

"Became a Christian," she finished for him.

"Yes. That. I have began to wonder if there could be a part of the universe we can't see. A lot of people think so, and many of them are intelligent. I used to find that puzzling, but now I wonder."

"I'm glad you're at least considering it."

"I've heard people say there are many ways to God — that all of us get there eventually."

"Oh, Mars," she cried in anguish, "that's not true. There is only one way to God, and that's explained in the Bible. I wish I knew the New Testament better."

"But, dear, how could God be so narrow that He only allows one way? That's not kind or loving."

"Mars?" Moshe said.

"Yes?"

"If you were my student and I told you to conduct a dig in a certain way and you refused, what do you think would happen?"

"I guess you'd flunk me."

"Why?"

"For going against your instructions."

"What stands behind my instructions?"

"The fact that you know more about archaeology than I do." Mars frowned. "O.K., I see where you're going with this. But it's *not* the same thing."

"Of course it's not," Moshe agreed. "The difference between God and us is much greater."

Anne touched her husband's arm. "Mars, if we've found things that prove the Bible accurate in places where skeptics claim it's wrong, doesn't it make sense that what it says about Jesus is right also? I wish I knew the Bible better so I could show you."

"You mean the stuff about the only way to be saved is by believing in Jesus Christ? Where does the Bible actually say that?"

"Your wife is telling you the truth," Moshe said. "The New Testament says *exactly* that, over and over. The Gospels — Matthew, Mark, Luke, and John — would be a good place to look, as would the book of Romans. There's a very good example in the third chapter of John starting at verse 17: 'For God did not send His Son into the world to condemn the world, but to save the world through Him. Whoever believes in Him is not condemned, but whoever does not believe stands condemned already because He has not believed in the name of God's one and only Son.' "

Anne looked at him in awe. "Thank you, Moshe. I'm surprised you knew that."

He grinned sheepishly. "I am somewhat familiar with the Bible — the Old and the

New Testaments. As you would say, Zuba Rosenberg has been on my case over the years."

Anne smiled. "How sweet of him."

Moshe arched his eyebrows. "I assure you, I did not think so at the time."

"But you do now?"

He sighed, deep in thought. "Yes, I do."

"Moshe, are you telling me . . ." Anne began.

The Israeli's serious expression softened and drifted into a self-conscious grin. He brushed his beard forward with his hand. "Yes, I believe that Jesus is God's Son. Except I call him Yeshua, which is Hebrew for Jesus — He is the same person. Yes, I am a Christian."

"When did this happen?" Anne asked.

"While Avraham and Abdul were bringing us back here. To be honest, I have recognized the truth for several months, but I avoided doing anything about it. Then the strangest thing happened when we started back. This thought popped up in my mind: 'You know the truth — what is your decision?' That got my attention. I rationalized for a while, but I knew where the thought had come from — God. In that moment I accepted Yeshua as my Messiah. Then I prayed."

"Moshe, I had no idea," Anne stammered.

"Why should you? The Bible says that salvation is a personal thing. No one can do it for you." He turned toward Mars. "Your dear wife is telling you the truth, Mars. This is something you have to choose, and refusing to accept means turning down God's offer. And the Bible is very clear on what happens to those who do that."

Mars scrunched up his face. "Hell."

"Yes. Being banned from God's presence forever, with no second chance."

"What about all the people who say there are many ways to God?"

"I think you know the answer to that. But in John chapter 14, Jesus Himself says, 'I am the way and the truth and the life. No one comes to the Father except through Me.' That sounds clear enough to me." He paused. "Mars, may I ask you a question?"

"I guess so," he replied cautiously.

"You have heard my story. You know that what we are saying is true. The Bible is accurate — we've seen that for ourselves. And what it says about Jesus is easy to understand — without Him we're doomed. This is *all* true."

Anne felt her stomach tighten into a knot as she watched her husband. She shot an arrow prayer to heaven. *Dear God, help him make the right decision.*

Mars flicked his eyes back to Anne. For a long time she thought he would say nothing. Then he cleared his throat. "Yes. I believe what you're telling me is true."

"Oh, Mars," Anne began but stopped when she saw Moshe's cautionary glance.

"So you know this is true," he rumbled. "Good. But that won't do you a bit of good unless you choose. You either accept Jesus or you are dead where you sit."

"That's awfully hard," Mars said with a frown.

"They are God's rules. So, what do you choose?"

Anne watched the complex play of emotions on her husband's face. She longed to hear the right words but feared she would not. And the longer she waited, the more sure she became of his refusal. His eyes crossed hers, and she thought she saw fear there, as if something were after him. Then she sensed a resolution, though she couldn't tell what it was.

"I want to accept," he said, his voice barely above a whisper. "What do I do?"

Moshe and Anne traded glances. "I would like to help, if I can," he said.

She nodded.

Moshe suggested a prayer to Mars and

explained what each point meant. He then waited as his American friend prayed to receive his salvation.

"I'm glad that's done," Mars said when he finished. "Anne, I appreciate you putting up with me. I just couldn't see it until today. But now it makes all the sense in the world." He smiled at her. "Thank you, dear."

"You're welcome, Mars. I only wanted you to find the truth like I did."

He shivered.

"What's wrong, dear?" Anne asked.

"I was thinking of what would have happened to me if I hadn't accepted Christ."

Moshe nodded. "You have passed into life." At that moment he remembered Ghanim and turned to see the Iraqi's reaction. The other had a puzzled expression on his face.

"Does any of this make any sense to you?" Moshe asked.

"I am not sure," Ghanim replied.

"Are you a Christian?"

"My whole family is. We are all Christians, going back many generations."

Moshe's eyebrows arched in concern. "But did you ever pray a prayer like Mars did? Did you ever personally accept Jesus as your Savior?"

"I do not know what you mean. My family

is Christian, just like other families are Muslim. They choose one way, our family chooses another."

"I don't think you understand," Moshe said gently. "Would you like me to go over it with you?"

"No," he replied quickly. "I do not wish to discuss it."

Moshe nodded.

Anne wondered at his rejection. How could you look at the truth and turn it down? Then she looked at Mars and thanked God for answering her prayer — for saving her dear husband.

25

RESCUE PREPARATIONS

Ari met the staff car at the hangar's side entrance. He saluted as Lieutenant Colonel David Kruger got out.

"Enjoy the flight down?" Ari asked as they walked inside.

"I was too preoccupied with our mission to notice," he replied as they passed the spare Cessna U-27. "I presume we still haven't heard anything from Ya'acov."

"I would have said first thing, Colonel."

"I know you would. Just hoping."

"I understand."

David stopped abruptly. "No, Ari, I don't think you do. Ya'acov and Joel are inside Iraq on my orders. Regardless of what you guys think of the 'old man,' I *do* care what happens to you." He saw the lieutenant's shocked expression and almost smiled. "Bet you and Ya'acov thought I had a heart of stone."

"No, Colonel. Of course not."

David looked at the young man critically. "Mendacity does not agree with you, Ari."

"But, Colonel . . ."

"That's all right, Ari. When I was a junior officer I also thought all my superiors were blockheads. Now, where can we talk?"

"The conference room is convenient."

Ari led the way and flipped the lights on. David waved him to the head of the table and took the seat next to him. The hum of the fluorescent lights was very noticeable, and one bank flickered on and off.

"Review for me your understanding of the mission."

Ari got up and walked to the wall map. "Ya'acov and Joel were to fly the U-27 to the extraction site here and land before dawn." He pointed to a spot a little east of Babylon and Al Hillah and about midway between them. "The archaeologists were to wait until sunup and then drive down to meet them. Then Joel would fly everyone out."

David nodded. "And something obviously went wrong because they haven't returned. The question is, *what* went wrong?"

"Since they're completely cut off, it's hard to say. If we could borrow a bird, we might be able to see what's at the site, if anything."

"No dice. I asked for the loan of a satellite

and was turned down flat. Now that the lab's been taken care of, suddenly we don't rate." His eyes bored into Ari. "What's your opinion? What happened?"

"That's a difficult question, Colonel."

"You're paid to answer hard inquiries, Lieutenant."

"Yes, sir. Well, I think there are three main possibilities. One, they may have crashed either on the way in or out. Two, they may have been captured on the ground either on landing or when the archaeologists were approaching. Or, three, Ya'acov and Joel are okay and are sitting on the ground in Iraq."

David frowned. "We can't do anything about one or two. And I really don't think they're the most likely. I think the Iraqis would have screamed by now if they had captured our people. The third option is what worries me. Why would they still be on the ground?"

"Only two reasons I can think of. The most obvious is that the plane's disabled, although that seems unlikely. The other possibility is that the archaeologists have been delayed getting to the extraction site, and Ya'acov is waiting for them."

"It better not be the latter or I'll have his hide. He knows he is not supposed to wait."

Ari paused before answering. "That wasn't expressly covered in the briefing, Colonel."

David pounded the table. "Well, it was *supposed* to be! Some things shouldn't *need* explanation. You don't get briefed on what to do in the latrine, do you?"

"No, sir."

"Ari, what worries me is the possibility that the plane is disabled. I know it's unlikely, but I'd hate to be sitting here and allowing them to die or get captured when I have what it takes to save them sitting right in this hangar."

"I thought that was strictly for backup in case the first bird couldn't take off."

"Technically that's true. We never envisioned it as a rescue vehicle for the rescuers. Nevertheless, Ari, I want to send you and an IAF pilot into Iraq to see what's what. But this is on a volunteer basis only. You don't have to do it."

"I'd be glad to go, Colonel."

David smiled his gratitude. "Thank you. I thought you would. I've already ordered Lieutenant Eitan Hoffmann down here. He's been briefed. Basically you two will be going to the same site. If they're still there, they'll signal you."

It was a little after midnight when the

Apache AH-64A attack helicopter landed outside the hangar. David and Ari watched through the hangar's side-door window as a tall IAF officer climbed down from the front cockpit and ran out from under the blurred rotor blades. David opened the door, admitting wind-borne grit along with the young airman. The Apache lifted off and flew into the night sky.

"Colonel Kruger?" the man asked.

"That's me. Eitan, this is Lieutenant Ari Jacovy. We're with Military Intelligence."

"Yes, sir."

"I know you've been briefed on the mission. Any questions?"

"No, sir. Is that the bird?" He pointed to the U-27 sitting by itself under the mercury vapor lights.

"That's it. When can you and Ari be ready to go?"

Eitan took a deep breath. "As soon as I preflight the aircraft."

David glanced at Ari. "I'll leave it to the two of you then." He retreated to the conference room.

"Are you one of Joel's friends?" Ari asked as Eitan began checking the engine.

"Never met him. I heard about what he did up in Galilee though. That was *some* mission."

"Yes, it was. Are you an Apache driver also?"

"Oh, no. I fly Phantom 2000s."

Ari glanced at the Cessna. "I suppose this is a big step down."

Eitan stopped and looked the craft over. "Yeah, I guess it is. I'll miss my two engines and especially the afterburners. We're going to be plodding along at around 200 miles an hour. That makes us a sitting duck."

"Don't say that."

A smile returned to the airman's face. "Then again, flying is flying. We will carry out the mission."

He conducted a rapid but thorough preflight, ending with a peek inside the fuselage.

"It looks like an Arab market back there. Do we really need all that junk?"

"Want to see the manifest?" Ari asked with a grin.

Eitan whistled. "I'll take your word for it. Only thing I'm interested in is those jerry cans. I count twenty. Are they full?"

"Checked them myself. A hundred gallons of fuel."

"O.K. I'm convinced we're ready to fly. If we can get the engine to light off, I'd say we're in business."

They turned as they heard someone round the front of the aircraft.

"That's what I want to hear," David said as he ran a hand over the smooth paint on the engine cowling.

"We can leave anytime you're ready, Colonel," Eitan said.

"Both of you, take care."

He stepped back and waved at the guards who started opening the hangar doors, revealing a rectangle of black, nighttime sky. Eitan and Ari pushed the heavily loaded U-27 outside. They climbed in and strapped down. Moments later the powerful Pratt & Whitney turboprop was spinning the three-bladed Hartzell constant-speed propeller. The burners in the turbine stage ignited, and the engine accelerated rapidly.

"There's the green light from the tower," Eitan said, pointing.

"Right. You ready?"

"If the officer in tactical command is."

Ari turned his head and saw the aviator's wide grin. "So go, already. I'll be in my cabin if you need me," he said sarcastically.

"Yes, sir."

The U-27 rolled down the taxiway, bouncing on its oversized tires. They turned onto the active runway without stopping and immediately took off.

David watched from the ground as the plane's navigational lights began to dwindle in the distance. He glanced down at his watch. It was a little after 1 in the morning.

At first Ya'acov thought he was imagining things. He checked the chronometer on the U-27's instrument panel. It was a little past 2 in the morning, and another beautiful day in Iraq was approaching. He peered through the sand-scarred windshield. All he could see was an occasional flap of the camouflage netting. But it was not flapping as hard, and the irritating shriek of the wind seemed to be moderating. He punched Joel, who was sleeping. He jerked awake.

"What is it?" he asked, breathing hard.

"The storm's dying down," Ya'acov replied.

"Can't be. The meteorology guys said it would last at least a week." He chuckled.

"It seems they were wrong." Ya'acov smiled. "But that wouldn't be a first."

Joel smiled as he listened. "I think you're right. When it dies down a little more, we'd better gather up everything and get out of here."

Ya'acov looked at the GPS box, still faithfully indicating their position. "Right. The Iraqis will probably send out air search to look for us as soon as this clears." He grabbed a map and illuminated it with a penlight. "I want you to take us down around here." He stabbed the map with a forefinger.

"Nothing doing, Captain. We're taking this crate back to the Negev as fast as it can go and hope we don't run into any nasties on the way out."

"Do you understand our operational orders, Lieutenant?"

The pilot rocked his head back and closed his eyes. "I presume you mean the part about the officer in tactical command."

"You got it first try. And since we're under radio silence, we can't ask for advice."

"This could get us killed, Ya'acov."

"I'm aware of the danger, I assure you. But some people are in trouble because of us. We were sent to bring them out, and that's what I intend to do."

"But the mission's blown. The bad guys got them, and there's nothing we can do about it."

"We don't know that for sure — not yet. Now, what about this?" Ya'acov pointed again to the map.

Joel looked across, squinting to see the map in the dim, red light. "South of Al Hillah. Ya'acov, that's very close to town."

"The map says there's a ridge here," Ya'acov pointed. "Wouldn't that hide us from prying eyes in that direction?"

Joel grabbed the map and light. "Yeah, I think it would, as long as no one comes snooping around down there."

"I don't the think the Iraqis would expect us that close to a city."

"No, I don't expect they would. They probably think we have better sense than that."

"That sounded like criticism."

"Oh, no. Nothing like that." Joel examined all the surrounding terrain. "It might work, Ya'acov. I sure wouldn't look for some goofball spies down there."

"When can we leave?"

Joel watched the camouflage net flap in the wind. "In a bit. We need to go as soon as we can see. Help me saddle up?"

The officers jumped out of the plane and started taking down the net. The wind was down to gentle gusts, but the air was still thick with dust. Joel rolled up the net while Ya'acov took down the poles. They stored it all inside the plane and made a quick check, using the low-light goggles to make sure they had left nothing behind.

"Help me dig these wheels out," Joel called from the other side of the plane.

The fat, oversized tires were almost completely buried in the sand, with only the very tops sticking through. Joel and Ya'acov scooped the fine sand away until there were three long troughs in front of the wheels.

"We can take off now," Joel said, peering toward the east with his low-light goggles. "The visibility is increasing rapidly."

They stepped into the aircraft and banged the doors shut. Joel went through the checklist quickly and brought the turbine to life. He breathed a sigh of relief as it lit and climbed rapidly toward 100 percent. The plane bounced across the sand as the airspeed slowly crept up. Joel pulled back gingerly on the wheel, and they staggered into the air. He leveled off scant feet over the scraggly brush as he waited for the airspeed to build.

"We'd better stay low," he said. "Help me keep an eye out."

Ya'acov gulped as he saw they weren't going any higher. "Right."

They came around in a wide turn to the right until the magnetic compass read 210 degrees. The air continued to clear rapidly as the wind fell. Soon the lights of Al Hillah winked in the distance and appeared to do a slow crawl toward the approaching airplane. But they disappeared suddenly when the long ridge interposed itself, as if a giant hand had flicked off the power. Joel glanced at the GPS readout and pulled the power lever. The plane touched down, bounced once, and stayed planted. When it came to a stop, the two officers hopped out and set up the camouflage net. Twenty minutes later they were back in the aircraft waiting for dawn.

Eitan and Ari had their heads on a swivel as the GPS indicated they were approaching the extraction site. The western horizon supported a thin line of gray heralding the approaching sun, but the desert floor lay cloaked in black. The low-light goggles transformed the blackness into a grainy, green image, reminding Ari of a surrealistic painting.

"See anything?" he asked.

"There's something large off to our left."

"Where?"

"See that *wadi* about 300 yards at our ten o'clock?"

Ari looked where he was pointing. "Yeah. Let's check it out."

Eitan pulled up a little and banked steeply to the left. When he centered the wheel and dropped back down, they were headed right for it. They watched as the object grew rapidly in size before disappearing in a smear of green.

"Looked like a wrecked Land Cruiser," Ari said.

"That's what it looked like to me," Eitan agreed. "We'll make another pass to be sure."

The pilot brought the Cessna around in a tight circle and crossed the wreck from the northwest.

"That's what it is all right," he confirmed.

"How far to the extraction site?"

Eitan glanced at the GPS readout. "Less than a mile. Let's fly over and see if anyone's home."

He dropped down until it seemed the wheels were skimming the stunted brush. Eitan made tiny adjustments to the flight controls to maintain a precise course.

"That's it," he said moments later. "We passed right over the site. They're not there."

"What if they're under the camouflage netting?"

Eitan pointed at the GPS box. "We flew within yards of where they were supposed to be. We would have seen the hump of the net. What's under us is absolutely flat. Besides, they'd come out and wave if they were down there."

"They might not know it was us."

"You're grabbing at straws, Ari. Joel knows a U-27 when he sees one, and Iraq doesn't have any of them. We'll fly over a few more times to make sure, but they're not down there."

The next two passes revealed nothing new.

Eitan glanced at the Intelligence officer. "What now?"

"What?" Ari said. "Oh, sorry. I was thinking. This makes no sense. They're not at the site, but they haven't returned."

"Shot down or crashed on the way out?"

"I doubt it. The Iraqis haven't said a thing, and Joel's too good a pilot to crash."

"O.K., so what do we do?"

Ari looked out at the gathering dawn. "Land."

"Here?"

"No. Too close to that Land Cruiser." He glanced at the map in his lap. "Fly due south until we're abeam of Al Hillah. That should put us far enough away from any air search pattern."

"You've got it."

Eitan turned to the south, and minutes later they landed. The two officers set up the camouflage netting. The next half hour was occupied with refueling the wing tanks from the jerry cans. Once the empty cans were secured in the cabin, they brought out two folding chairs and placed them under the left wing.

Joe examined his face in the filthy mirror and looked down at his hands. The dark makeup that Nadhim had found seemed to do the job, and the work clothing looked natural. The thin knife was secure in his right boot.

"How do I look?" he asked.

"Like my brother," Nadhim answered with a grin.

"I guess we're in business."

The Iraqi walked to the window and looked down. It was 7 in the morning, and people were beginning to show on the narrow street below.

"How is your side?" Joe asked.

"Much better. When are we going to do something?"

"Today," Joe said with more confidence than he felt. "Things are probably as settled as they're going to get. I wish we had more time for you to heal, but we don't."

"I understand. I can't stand hiding here doing nothing. What do we do?"

Joe took a deep breath. "That depends on where Mars, Anne, Moshe, and your uncle are. Do you suppose they're still in Babylon?"

"I think so. It depends on whether Security has proved they had anything to do with the bombing. Security is probably going slow because Mars and Anne are well-known. However, if they've been taken to Baghdad, there is no hope."

"Since we're not sure, we need to get a quick look at the dig to verify they are still there. After that, we will buy some equipment and stage a strike."

"Just you and me?"

"Unless you know some people we can absolutely rely on. You know what happens if someone gives us away."

"But can the two of us do it?"

"The odds aren't good," Joe admitted. "But it's the only hope we've got. Are you with me?"

Nadhim clenched his jaws in anger. "Yes."

"Good. Now, what's the best way to get to Babylon for a quick looksee?"

"The safest way would be to flag down a truck on the highway."

"O.K., let's eat a little something and then be on our way."

They had both been working since the long, red rays of dawn. Joel had finished fueling and checking the Yamaha Kodiak ATV, while Ya'acov concentrated on his equipment and his Arab disguise. The Intelligence officer applied his makeup carefully before donning a flowing robe and checkered *keffieh*. He examined the broad mustache in a mirror, making sure it looked natural.

Joel stood by the ATV as Ya'acov crawled out of the plane with two loaded Uzis and four extra clips. He put it all in a heavy nylon bag and returned for the knives. One he strapped to his right leg while the other joined the submachine guns. He strapped the bag to the ATV's front luggage rack.

Joel shook his head. "You're really going to do this?"

"I have to try."

The pilot looked toward the north. "What if you don't return?"

"You don't get rid of me that easy," Ya'acov replied, trying to keep it light. The smile faded. "But if I'm not back by dawn tomorrow, leave without me."

He gathered the lower part of his robe and swung his leg over the ATV's saddle. He sat heavily and propped up his feet on the foot pegs. He gripped the handlebar grips as if he were afraid the machine might come alive unexpectedly.

He glanced up at Joel and forced a smile. "How do I look?"

Joel shook his head, his eye lingering on the name Yamaha emblazoned on the seat. "Like Lawrence of Tokyo."

"Glad you like it." Ya'acov pressed the electric starter, and the ATV's engine roared to life. The Israeli grinned as he jazzed the throttle. "If you will hold up the edge of the camouflage net, I will be on my way."

The pilot pulled up three pegs and held the net. Ya'acov carefully edged past and out onto the desert. Long, black shadows fled away from him, pointing toward the west. He twisted the throttle and turned the ATV in a big circle around the camouflaged plane until he was heading a little west of north. He charged up the gentle ridge that hid them and paused at the top. There in the distance were the low houses and buildings of Al Hillah. He could barely see a thin line off to his left, the highway leading to the city and to Babylon and Baghdad further to the north.

He twisted the throttle and accelerated swiftly until the Yamaha was bounding through the sand and rock in a way that was decidedly uncomfortable. But the four-wheel-drive vehicle was surprisingly stable, and the suspension and fat tires smoothed out most of the bumps.

Ya'acov concentrated on riding in as

straight a line as the scrub brush and dry *wadis* would permit. After a few minutes he topped a slight rise and saw the highway clearly. He slowed as he came up to it and stopped. There was one truck coming from the south, but it was still several miles away. That was the only traffic. Ya'acov eased onto the highway and wound the ATV up through its gears.

26

INFILTRATION

Even though he was shielded by the wing and the camouflage net, Ari squinted at the map in his lap. A light breeze rattled the edges of the map and threatened to blow it away. Ari held it down with his hand.

"I think I know what happened," he said, looking up.

"My hat's off to you. So far this makes about as much sense as Israeli politics."

Ari smiled. "The Colonel likes to stay away from comments like that."

"Guess that's what happens when you get a little rank. So, what happened?"

Ari's eyes took on a faraway look as he glanced to the north. "The archaeologists were being chased in that Land Cruiser, and when they crashed, the Iraqis captured them. Ya'acov and Joel saw it happen but couldn't do anything."

Eitan nodded. "That sounds reasonable,

I guess. So, what happened to Ya'acov and Joel?"

"I think they moved to avoid an Iraqi air search."

"Why not fly out?"

"Ya'acov feels personally responsible for the archaeologists being in trouble. I don't think he'll leave until all hope is gone."

Eitan shook his head. "Sounds plenty hopeless to me."

"You don't understand Ya'acov."

"Guess not. Assuming you're right, any idea where he and Joel might be?"

"His only hope would be if the Iraqis take our friends back to Babylon. If they're in Baghdad, there's no way. And if they're in Babylon, he would want to be somewhere the Iraqis won't look but still close enough so he could travel into Babylon."

"That's what the ATV is for."

Ari smiled. "That's not what the Colonel intended it for, but Ya'acov might use it for that. He is fluent in Arabic, and we have the proper clothing and makeup."

"You think he went to Babylon?"

"I don't know, but it's possible."

"O.K., so where do you think the plane is?"

Ari traced a ridge with his forefinger. "I think they moved close to Al Hillah, behind this ridge. It's an unlikely place for the Iraqis to search, but our men would still be hidden from the city."

"It would be nice to have some proof."

"That's the next step. I'll need your help with the ATV."

Ari and Eitan wrestled the Yamaha Kodiak out of the plane. The pilot began preparing it while Ari worked with the makeup. An hour later, Ari adjusted his *keffieh* and checked his robes.

"Does this look O.K.?" he asked.

"I'm no expert, but it looks good to me. Want any weapons?"

"Yeah. Let me have one of the Uzis and a couple of spare clips." Eitan checked the gun, put it and the extra clips into a nylon bag, and fastened it on the front luggage carrier.

Ari got on the ATV. "If I find Joel, I'll stay there until sunset, unless something happens. If I'm not back by midnight, take off without me. Any questions?"

Eitan shook his head. He held up the camouflage net to let him out.

Joe and Nadhim walked slowly through Al Hillah, apparently in no hurry. Their path was random but steadily toward the Baghdad highway. Fifteen minutes after leaving the hotel, they walked onto the road's gravel shoulder. A beat-up Toyota pickup rattled past heading south, trailing a swirling blue cloud that gradually dissipated in the early-morning air. Both men looked south.

"See anything?" Joe asked, shielding his eyes from the glare to the east.

"Looks like a truck and something else in front of him. Too small to see what it is. Get ready. I'm going to try and get the truck to stop."

They waited as the two vehicles slowly approached.

"The one in front is an ATV," Nadhim said. "They're handy for getting around in the desert."

"And for playing," Joe suggested.

"That too," Nadhim replied with a grin.

Soon they could see the man clearly. His flowing robes flapped madly behind him, making it seem he was going faster than he was. His head was lowered, and he was hunched over the handlebars. He looked them over as he roared past.

Joe turned back to the truck. Nadhim was already waving at the driver. His brakes squealed, and he began edging onto the shoulder. But just then a sharp screech of rubber sounded behind them. Joe turned his head and saw the ATV making a sharp U-turn. The rider was accelerating rapidly toward them as the truck came to a stop. Nadhim looked at Joe with a wordless question. The American glanced back toward where they had come from, but there was no time to retreat. The ATV rider cut in front of the idling truck and parked on the shoulder. He directed a quick question to Nadhim in Arabic.

Joe looked at Nadhim.

"He wants to know if you would like to buy some pictures."

Joe glanced up at the truck driver, who was waiting patiently as if there were nothing unusual in this type of transaction. He leaned close to Nadhim's ear. "Tell him no, and let's get on that truck."

Nadhim rattled off a polite reply to the man who was grinning broadly behind his bushy mustache. But this only evoked another question.

Nadhim sighed. "He says he has special pictures. Pictures of Babylon, pictures of the night skies. He says he even has a picture of the planet Mars."

Joe had opened his mouth to tell Nadhim to get rid of the pest when he stopped. He looked closely at the Arab. The man's right eye winked.

"What is it?" Nadhim whispered.

"Tell the truck driver he can go."

"What? You're going to buy some pictures?"

"Tell the driver to go," Joe repeated, stressing each word.

Nadhim looked up into the truck's cab and delivered the message. The man shrugged and drove off.

"Ya'acov, is that you?" Joe asked in English.

"Yes. We need to talk, but we can't do it here. Climb on."

Ya'acov sat forward in the saddle while Joe and Nadhim squeezed on behind. The Israeli pulled onto the deserted highway and rode rapidly toward Babylon. When Al Hillah was small and indistinct, Ya'acov pulled over and stopped.

"What are you two doing?" Ya'acov asked, stepping off the ATV.

"I am tempted to ask you the same thing," Joe replied. He quickly introduced Nadhim and explained his relation to Ghanim. "We, or rather Nadhim, destroyed the lab just before the air strike."

"Was it . . ." Ya'acov began.

"Biological? You bet it was. We all had a close call on that one."

"How in the world did you manage it?"

"We'll tell you later. We were on our way

516

to Babylon when you happened by. We are going to try to get our people out of there."

Ya'acov whistled. "Good thing I came along. I'm afraid they're under arrest."

"What happened?"

"They requested emergency extraction. We were waiting for them east of Babylon. They were apparently followed because when they started coming toward us, this other vehicle chased them down and took them off."

"That's bad," Joe said. He turned to Nadhim. "Where would they take them?"

"I'm not sure. Initially back to Babylon, I would guess. If there's going to be a spy trial, which I think is likely, they'll be transported to Baghdad soon."

"Assuming they're still in Babylon, where would they be held?"

"There's only one place — the president's Guest House. In the basement would be my guess. There's a conference room down there that would work."

"Can we get them out of there?" Joe asked.

"Getting them out of the dig would have been hard enough. Getting them out of the Guest House? That would be practically impossible."

"But is there any chance?"

Nadhim sighed. "Some, I guess. I know how the security works, where the cameras are and all that. But we would have to get past the surveillance cameras, break in, go down the elevator to the basement, overpower the guards down there, get our friends, and make our escape."

"What do you think?" Joe asked Ya'acov.

"I think all three of us are crazy. But I can't leave our friends without trying to save them, not after getting them into this mess."

"Are you freelancing on this?" Joe asked.

Ya'acov snorted. "Do my superiors endorse what I'm doing? I'm in command, and I'm not in a position to ask them right now."

"I appreciate what you're doing," Joe said with a husky voice.

"I wish there was more than just me. I have two Uzis and two knives, but that's nothing compared to what we're going up against. What do you suggest, Nadhim?"

"We have to find some way to get past the cameras. If the alarm goes off, we don't stand a chance — they'll get us all."

Joe nodded. "Do you know of a way we can do that?"

Nadhim looked off toward the north. "There is only one way I can think of. Let them capture me."

"What?" Joe exclaimed.

"You can bet they're looking for me. I think they would throw me in with the others if they caught me. If they did, I know a way to temporarily knock out the security monitors in the basement."

"No. There's got to be another way."

"There isn't," Nadhim insisted. "I know the security setup better than anyone else. If we don't disable the security monitors in the basement, the alarm would go off before we got within a hundred yards of the Guest House. And that would be that."

"He's right, Joe," Ya'acov agreed.

"Yes, I know. But the thought of them getting one more of our group bothers me." He turned to Nadhim. "All right, assuming this works, what next?"

Nadhim spent fifteen minutes explaining his plan. When he finished, he looked at Joe, then at Ya'acov.

Joe shook his head. "Everything would have to go just right or we'll all get captured. But I think you're right. I don't see any other way."

"I agree," Ya'acov said.

Joe and Ya'acov set their watches according to Nadhim's.

Joel saw the thin line of dust from a long way off. "This is all I need," he muttered as he ran to the cargo doors. He threw them open and scrabbled inside until he found the compact binoculars. He returned to the nose of the Cessna and looked out through the netting. Checking his holster to make sure his Beretta 9mm was ready, he adjusted the focus on the binoculars. He saw an Arab riding an ATV heading in the general direction of the plane. He lowered the glasses.

What's Ya'acov doing coming from that direction?

He brought the glasses back up. He could tell the rider was going to miss the plane by several hundred yards. He tried to see the man's face, but he was too far away. But the ATV was the same model. It had to be Ya'acov.

Joel ran to the edge of the net and crawled out. He ran a little way toward the rider, waving his arms. For a long time the ATV continued its course. Then it turned as the rider saw Joel. The pilot felt the sweat pop out on his forehead. If he was wrong, he'd be forced to kill the Iraqi. Finally the man stopped about ten feet away.

"Ya'acov?" Joel asked tentatively.

"Nope. It's me — Ari."

"What in the world are you doing here?" Joel demanded.

"Help me under the net, and I'll tell you."

The pilot pulled up some stakes and held the net as Ari pushed the ATV through. He parked it by the Cessna's rear cargo doors.

Joel set up another chair by his under the left wing.

"Where's Ya'acov?" Ari asked when he was seated.

Joel told him what he knew. Ari listened with resigned understanding. He knew why his friend had done it, and he was inclined to agree, up to a point. He looked into the distance toward where Eitan was waiting with the other plane.

"Colonel Kruger thought you two might be stranded," Ari explained. "I thought it might be a little more like this."

"You were right. What do we do now?"

"I'll stay here until sundown, then return to where Eitan is waiting."

"What about me?"

"That's not for me to say. Ya'acov is in tactical command."

"What if he's dead?"

Ari smiled. "What if I wasn't here?"

"Oh."

"You'll have to decide that for yourself, Joel."

"Do you think he'll make it back?"

"You've seen him operate before."

"Yeah, and I'll never forget it."

"Then let's not count him out yet."

Anne squirmed around in the chair. Mars straightened up and turned her way.

"What's the matter?" he asked.

"I can't get comfortable."

He saw her feet dangling about an inch above the concrete floor. "Chair too high?"

"Yes," she confirmed with a frown. "No one makes furniture for short people."

"They're uncomfortable even if your feet *do* touch the floor."

"I bet it helps keep their meetings brief," Moshe observed. "But perhaps comfort is not a concern for Iraqis." He glanced quickly at Ghanim.

"I am not offended," the other replied with a weary grin. "I am well aware of the shortcomings of my government and the ways we do certain things. And, yes, these blasted chairs are uncomfortable."

Mars turned to Anne to say something but stopped when he saw her head bowed. He felt a strange reassurance come over him as he watched her pray, not willing to interrupt her time with her — with *their* Lord. Finally she looked up and saw him. She smiled self-consciously.

"Amen," he whispered, taking her hand. "What were you praying for?"

"For us. I asked the Lord to get us out of here. And . . ."

"And what?"

"And I was thanking Him for my sweet hubby."

This obviously pleased Mars.

"And I especially thanked Him for saving you," she added.

They both became aware, at the same time, of the other two in the room. Ghanim looked at them, a puzzled expression on his face. Moshe had a broad smile on his. He was looking up toward the ceiling humming a familiar tune from *Fiddler on the Roof*.

Nadhim approached the tall fence with dread. A solitary guard patrolled along the long pit. Periodically he stopped and looked down on the thick wall below, only to resume his boring walk toward the three temporary buildings. Taking a deep breath, Nadhim waved for him to come over.

"I am Nadhim Shakir, and I am looking for my uncle, Ghanim Jassim. Do you know where he is?"

"Stay where you are," the guard ordered. He quickly unslung his AK-47 and centered the barrel on Nadhim's chest.

The man pulled out a hand transceiver and called for help. In less than a minute

Avraham and Abdul showed up in a Toyota pickup. Abdul got out, leveled his assault rifle, and ordered Nadhim to get in. As soon as the door slammed shut, Avraham wheeled around with a screech of rubber and drove back to the Guest House.

Nadhim watched the palm trees approaching and beyond them, the Euphrates. They turned left just before the river and pulled into the parking lot. The Palestinians escorted him toward the security entrance at the rear of the house. Someone opened the door, and they rushed in.

Akram smiled. "Ah, our wandering maintenance man returns. I have some questions for you, but that will have to wait for a while. We are still working out some details with Baghdad."

The smile melted into a sneer. "You are asking about your uncle? Come. I will take you to him." He turned to Avraham and Abdul. "I will take it from here."

Akram pushed Nadhim into the small elevator, and they descended into the basement.

"You remember this, of course," Akram said as he led Nadhim past the security monitors. The two guards sat up straight and made a show of calling up different surveillance cameras. Akram opened the conference room door and checked the inside knob to make sure it was locked.

"Here is your uncle," he snarled, "and some more of your friends. I'm sure you remember what happens to spies and traitors?"

Nadhim only stood there.

"Get inside!" Akram shouted.

He entered, and the door slammed shut.

"What are you doing here?" Ghanim asked.

"I came looking for you at the dig. I wanted to know if you were all right."

Ghanim started to speak but stopped.

"That wasn't a good idea," Mars said.

"Perhaps so." Nadhim glanced at his watch.

Mars felt his pulse quicken. He looked into the Iraqi's eyes but could read nothing there. But the man was clearly preoccupied as he kept looking at his watch. Then he got up and started pacing the room.

"What is that?" he asked his uncle.

Ghanim held up a bent piece of metal. "Paper clip, or what's left of it. Something to play with."

"May I see it?"

Nadhim took the thick wire and examined it. "That was some paper clip."

He bent it into a rough U shape as he

525

continued his slow walk around the table. He sneezed and pulled a large handkerchief out of his pocket. After blowing his nose, he carefully folded the handkerchief into a small, thick rectangle. He glanced at his watch and dropped suddenly to the floor by the wall. He wrapped the handkerchief around the paper clip and shoved the two ends firmly into the electrical socket above the baseboard. Blue flames shot out accompanied by a sharp zap as the lights winked out.

"Stay where you are!" Nadhim shouted as he jumped up on the table and leapt off on the other side. He slid to a stop against the wall near the door. He felt with his hand until he touched the handle. Outside he could hear the two guards stumbling around in the dark.

Something bumped into the door. Nadhim felt the knob vibrate, and the bolt clicked. As soon as Nadhim felt the latch release, he pulled the door open as hard as he could. The unseen guard let out a yelp of surprise and stumbled forward. Nadhim grabbed the man's left hand and twisted it tightly behind his back. He then pulled the guard's Makarov 9mm pistol from its holster and brought it down hard on the back of his head. The man collapsed with a moan.

"What's going . . ." Ghanim began.

"Be quiet!" Nadhim commanded.

He checked the Makarov by feel. It was cocked. He clicked off the safety and checked to make sure a round was in the chamber. Satisfied, he walked through the open door into the inky blackness that swallowed the entire basement. A dim glimmer of light winked on inside the utility closet. Nadhim rushed across the floor. The lights flashed on briefly, then went off once more as the breaker tripped again. But in that brief moment, the guard had seen Nadhim.

The flashlight's glare blinded him. Nadhim heard the man fumbling frantically at his holster. Nadhim brought his pistol up and pulled the trigger. The guard cried out in pain and tumbled to the floor. The flashlight bounced on the concrete and spun into the room, its beam ending up on one of the chairs in front of the dead monitors.

Nadhim grabbed the flashlight and returned to the conference room. He pulled out the paper clip that was shorting the circuit before returning to the utility closet. Moments later the lights came back on.

"It's time," Ya'acov said.

His watch disappeared under his robes. He unstrapped the nylon bag from the luggage rack and pulled out the Uzis and the spare clips. He handed one of the guns to Joe along with two of the clips.

"I don't suppose I have to tell you how to use that," Ya'acov said.

"No, sir. I get along with these just fine." The American checked the weapon quickly, chambered a round, and set the safety before jamming it under his belt.

Ya'acov checked his quickly before it disappeared under his flowing robes. "Let's go."

He straddled the ATV and cranked it while Joe climbed on behind.

They sped north on the highway and turned left at the main entrance to Babylon. They were nearing Procession Street when Ya'acov had to stand on the brakes. They swerved to a shuddering stop under the driver's window of a tour bus that had pulled into the intersection unexpectedly. The window slid open, and a round, swarthy face glared down on the two riders. A torrent of Arabic flowed down from the position of power. Ya'acov gave the man a blistering retort, then engaged reverse and backed the ATV to allow the bus to complete its turn. The driver smiled smugly as he drove past, drowning the two in a swirling cloud of diesel smoke.

"What did you say to him?" Joe whispered.

"Oh, we traded observations on family genealogies. It was expected, so I obliged him." Ya'acov twisted the throttle and accelerated rapidly toward the Guest House.

"I sure hope Nadhim knocked out the monitors."

Ya'acov turned his head so he could be heard over the wind. "Me too. We're dead if he didn't."

27

DEADLY PURSUIT

Akram used the joystick beside the keypad to train the surveillance camera. The large monitor on his desk showed an ATV carrying two men rapidly approaching the Guest House. This was unusual. He knew they weren't on his staff and couldn't be employees working in Babylon. But not all tourists came on buses. He punched a button on the intercom.

"Samal?"

There was no answer.

Akram used the keypad to select the camera on the northwest corner of the Guest House. He cursed when he got a wide view of the Euphrates drifting past the date palms. He moved the camera around with the joystick. The two men were definitely heading for the house. Akram tried the intercom again, but there was still no answer. The ATV made a sliding turn into the parking lot, heading for the back door.

Akram opened a drawer and grabbed a Makarov pistol before jumping up and running for the stairs beside the elevator. He threw open the door and dashed down, taking the steps two at a time. He dashed into the first-floor rear entryway and glanced up at the monitor.

Ya'acov pulled up beside a Land Cruiser and stopped. He and Joe jumped off the ATV and rushed the door. They paused on the concrete stoop. A TV camera pointed in their direction.

"Sure hope Nadhim took care of that," Joe said.

"We're done if he didn't. Think these will open it?" Ya'acov pointed to the Uzis.

"Don't know. That door looks pretty substantial."

A muffled sound came through the thick metal.

"Look out!" Joe shouted.

He jumped to the right and did a shoulder roll to the ground. Ya'acov fell heavily off the left side of the stoop. The door crashed open, and a gun roared three times. Ya'acov, flat on his back and in pain, struggled to bring his Uzi up. He wondered why Joe had not fired, but decided to wait as well. He heard quick footsteps, then silence. He saw a shadow on the wall inside the door. Ya'acov aimed the Uzi at the doorjamb and squeezed off a short burst. The bullets pinged off the metal as they ricocheted inside.

A man screamed. Joe bounded to the stoop and brought his Uzi up in one smooth motion. The muzzle delivered death. Ya'acov heard the man fall down.

"Come on," Joe urged.

The Iraqi lay sprawled on the floor, a pool spreading under him as his life's blood drained out. Joe thrust his hands into the man's pockets.

"Here they are," he said, holding up a ring of keys.

He ran to the elevator and punched the Down button. The door opened, and they ran in. Joe inserted the elevator key, twisted it, and punched the B button. The door closed, and the elevator began its leisurely descent into the basement.

Avraham looked up from the newspaper he was reading. "What was that?" he asked.

Abdul looked toward the hall. "Don't know. Sounded like gunfire."

"Let's go," Avraham ordered. He opened a drawer and grabbed a Makarov 9mm. Abdul stuffed his under his belt and also took two AK-47s with extra magazines. He looked around for the low-light goggles.

"Come on!" Avraham shouted.

Abdul followed his boss out. They ran past Akram's office and down the stairs to the first floor. Ignoring Akram's corpse, Avraham dashed through the door and stopped. Abdul checked outside quickly.

"No one out there," he said after coming back in. "Either they're gone or they're inside somewhere."

Avraham looked up at the elevator indicator. "They're in the basement."

He pressed the Down button, but the elevator remained where it was.

"They've got it turned off," Abdul said.

"Then we wait. The elevator is the only way out."

"Unless they go down to the lab level and escape through the subway tunnel."

"We'll see it if they try." He pointed to the "X" below the "B" indicator. "And if they go out that way, a simple phone call will take care of it. If the elevator starts back up, you take the outside, and I'll wait down at the corridor. I'll hit them as they come out. Any I miss, you get."

They watched the indicator as the "B" continued to glow.

Both Ya'acov and Joe leveled their Uzis as

the elevator door opened. Nadhim's grinning face greeted them.

"It worked!" he shouted.

"So far," Ya'acov agreed.

The Israeli glanced quickly around. One guard lay dead on the floor beside an open closet. The archaeologists were clustered tightly behind Nadhim. Ya'acov could see the legs of another man through the open conference room door.

"What happened upstairs?" Nadhim asked.

"A guard jumped us as we were trying to get in," Ya'acov replied. "Must have seen us coming somehow."

"Probably a monitor upstairs. Killing the power down here didn't affect the cameras themselves, just the monitors down here. Only one man?"

"Yes."

"Sounds like Akram Rashid. I think there are more security people upstairs. They'll probably ambush us on the way back up."

"Wish we had known you had things under control," Joe said. "I could have stayed up there."

"But we didn't know," Ya'acov reminded him.

"Is there another way out of here?" Joe asked.

Nadhim shook his head. "The elevator's the only way. It goes up to the first floor and down to the lab — what used to be the lab."

"Too bad we can't go out the subway tunnel."

Nadhim snorted. "You can bet they've beefed up security at the truck stop. And if they knew we were coming . . ." He snapped his fingers. "Wait a minute. What if they thought that's where we were going?"

· "What do you mean?" Ya'acov asked.

"Everyone stay here. I'll be back in a few minutes."

Ya'acov started to protest, but Nadhim was already in the elevator. He punched a button, and the door closed. The "B" winked out on the overhead indicator, and moments later the "X" illuminated.

"What's he doing down at the lab?" Anne asked.

Silence was her answer. She glanced toward the flickering monitors. "Look." She moved closer for a better view. Two men bolted out of the rear entrance and jumped in the Land Cruiser beside the ATV. The vehicle backed up rapidly, then made a noiseless exit.

"That's eerie without any sound," Mars remarked as the car moved out of the camera's field of view.

A few moments later the elevator doors opened. Mars looked up and saw the "X" was still illuminated on the indicator.

Nadhim grinned. "In case anyone remains upstairs, they'll think the elevator is still down at the lab."

"O.K., everybody on the elevator," Ya'acov ordered.

It was a tight fit. Joe and Ya'acov were the last on, each holding his Uzi in front of his chest. The elevator hummed and started up. The car stopped with a jolt, and the doors opened.

Ya'acov and Joe jumped out and turned opposite directions, their guns at the ready. But the corridor was deserted except for Akram's body. Nadhim held up the dead man's key ring.

"Car keys," he announced.

They scrambled out of the house. Nadhim headed for the Land Cruiser that was closest to the rear entrance. He tried the key on the door and found that it fit.

"How considerate," he said as they piled in, with Ya'acov joining him in the front seat.

He cranked the engine as Mars lowered the right-hand center seat to let Ghanim and Moshe into the rear seats. Then Joe, Anne, and Mars scrambled into the center seat.

Nadhim jerked the Cruiser into reverse and backed out. He drove quickly through Babylon, pausing only briefly at the highway. Then he turned right and headed south toward Al Hillah.

Avraham held on to the steering wheel so hard, his knuckles were white. Abdul wondered briefly why his leader had not called the truck stop to warn them, but he realized he knew the answer. Avraham wanted to take care of certain unfinished business. The three archaeologists — especially the Americans — were a festering sore in his side. Abdul snorted. They were a sore in *his* side as well.

He watched the desolate landscape sweep past while the truck stop grew larger in the distance. He frowned.

"Why would Nadhim take them out through the tunnel?" he asked Avraham. "He knows what they'll find at the other end — especially since we know that's what they're doing."

"What other choice do they have?" Avraham countered.

Abdul felt a quick chill in the pit of his stomach. "I don't think that's where they are," he said, looking back the way they had come.

"What are you talking about?"

"I think they tricked us. I think they ran the elevator down to the lab level to make us believe they went out that way. They probably came back up after we left."

"What if you're wrong?"

"Pull in at the truck stop. I'll warn the manager just in case."

Avraham scanned the rearview mirror. Nothing was coming southbound. "Make it quick," he snapped as he turned onto the gravel apron.

Avraham turned the Land Cruiser around and waited. A vehicle was approaching from the north, but it was too far away to tell what it was. Abdul returned and jumped in.

"They'll be ready. The manager also phoned Security in Al Hillah to set up a roadblock in case they get that far."

Avraham pointed as he turned north on the highway. "Something is coming."

"I see it. Slow down when he goes past."

The distance closed quickly. Avraham took his foot off the gas and braked.

"It's a Land Cruiser, so it could be one of ours," Abdul said, looking past Avraham. "See if you recognize them."

The other vehicle drew abreast.

"It's them!" Avraham shouted. "The maintenance man is driving."

He jammed on the brakes and made a tire-screeching U-turn. Abdul reached into the backseat and grabbed his AK-47. He checked the weapon and set the safety before rolling down the window.

"Trouble!" Nadhim announced, glancing in the rearview mirror.

Joe and Ya'acov turned and looked back.

"Sure enough," Ya'acov agreed. "Move it! We have to outrun them."

Nadhim pressed harder on the gas pedal. The heavy Toyota quickly accelerated until the stunted roadside brush became a blur.

"I don't think this is going to work. They're too close."

"Are they gaining on us?" Ya'acov asked.

"Hard to tell. I don't think so, but we're not leaving them behind either. If we have to slow down, they'll be on us in a hurry."

In the center seat, Mars turned and looked out the back. "Did you see who it was?" he asked with a sinking feeling.

"Yes," Ya'acov replied. "Unfortunately, I did."

"Avraham and Abdul," Mars said in resignation.

"Right."

Mars turned back to Ya'acov. "Can we beat them to the airplane?"

The IDF officer shook his head. "Not unless they crash or something."

"What about facing them with our weapons?"

"It will probably come to that. But I suspect they've got more firepower. And those two are the deadliest men I've ever come across."

"Plus they hate our guts," Mars added.

"That they do — especially mine. This is not good. Not good at all."

The city of Al Hillah drew rapidly closer. Soon they were on the outskirts, and the local traffic began to build.

"Slow down," Ya'acov said.

"They'll catch us if I do," Nadhim replied.

A taxi pulled out of a side street directly in their path. Nadhim clamped down on the horn as he swerved around the startled driver.

"Look up ahead!" Joe shouted. "It's a roadblock!"

Nadhim cursed as he stood on the brakes. Blue smoke billowed up behind them as the Land Cruiser fishtailed from side to side. He hesitated for a moment, then cranked the wheel hard to the left and made a screeching turn into a side street. It was moderately wide and lined with one- and two-story shops and restaurants. Nadhim continued to hold down on the horn as the startled pedestrians scattered for their lives.

"They're turning in behind us," Mars announced.

"Give me some good news," Ya'acov grumbled.

People shook their fists at the speeding Toyota. Nadhim twisted and turned as the congestion forced him to slow down. Half a block ahead, a small white and blue bus backed suddenly into the narrowing street, completely blocking it. School children packed the vehicle. All the windows were down, and the children were clapping and singing. One was playing a large drum. The boisterous sounds carried clearly over Nadhim's frantic honking. The bus driver looked surprised, but it was obvious he had no intention of moving out of the way.

"Can we go down that alley?" Anne suggested, pointing to the left.

"Looks tight," Nadhim replied, "but I don't see any other choice."

He made the turn and slowly eased into the alley. The mirrors cleared the buildings by less than an inch. Trash littered the filthy dirt track. They jounced through deep potholes and over the discarded garbage. Anne looked through the back at the alley's narrow entrance.

"They're following us in," she said.

"So they are," Joe agreed as he faced forward. "Turn right at the next street and let me out."

"What are you going to do?" Ya'acov demanded.

"Just do what I say!" Joe snapped. "They're going to catch us unless we do something."

"This is my call, Joe."

"Don't argue with me, Ya'acov. I'm the only one who's qualified for this. Nadhim, after you let me out, go down about a block and I'll catch up with you."

The Land Cruiser bounded over a final pile of garbage and turned right. Nadhim continued until they were clear of the alley and stopped.

"Joe . . ." Ya'acov began.

"I know what I'm doing."

Joe opened the rear door and bounded out like a man twenty years younger. He slammed the door, and Nadhim pulled away from the curb and continued down the street.

Joe ran to the building next to the alley and flattened against the wall. He brought up the Uzi and checked it. A round was chambered, and the weapon was cocked. He pushed the safety off with a decisive click.

He could hear the rise and fall of the other Land Cruiser's engine as the vehicle struggled through the mired alley. They were getting close. He inched forward and peered around the corner, exposing as little of himself as possible. Just a few more feet. He pulled back and waited.

Abdul felt the familiar jolt of ice in his guts. "There's someone behind that building!" he shouted, pointing to the right. He instinctively touched the AK-47 at his side.

Everything seemed to be in slow motion. Abdul saw the thin line begin broadening into the man waiting in ambush. He knew what was coming as surely as he knew his own name. And he knew it would succeed unless he acted immediately.

"Get down!" he shouted. He leapt toward Avraham before the other had time to move. He grabbed the other Palestinian's head and pulled him down with all his strength. Avraham cried out in surprise.

Joe snapped around the corner, bringing the Uzi up in one smooth motion. He cursed as he saw two heads disappearing below the windshield. He squeezed off a short burst. The slugs stitched a precise series of holes at the base of the windshield. The Land

Cruiser crashed into the back of a building and ground to a screeching stop.

A dark muzzle appeared above the dash, held up from below. Joe ducked back as the assault rifle roared a short burst. Most of the shots went wild, but several hit the cinder block beside the former SEAL's head, spraying him with sharp chips.

Joe glanced down the street. A man in uniform, several blocks away, was running toward the disturbance. Joe whirled around and started running. He saw their Land Cruiser idling at the curb about a hundred yards away. Joe wrenched the rear door open and jumped in.

"Go!" he shouted.

Nadhim pulled away from the curb.

"Did you get them?" Ya'acov asked.

"No! Those two are the wiliest characters I've ever seen."

"Tell me about it," the Israeli griped.

"Where should I go?" Nadhim asked.

"They'll be coming out of that alley as soon as they discover I'm gone. You know the city better than they do. Do whatever it takes to lose them."

Nadhim drove one more block, then turned right.

Abdul opened his door, slamming it into

the back of a building. He cursed and reached for his AK-47. He waved the weapon above his head, half-expecting to draw more fire, but silence greeted him. He cautiously raised his head above the dash. The end of the alley was deserted.

"I think they're gone," he said as he sat back up.

Avraham got up and looked around. He put the Toyota in drive and pulled up to the street. A block away, a policeman was running toward them. Avraham turned right and sped away.

"Do you see them?"

"No. But they can't be far away."

"Are we being followed?" Nadhim asked.

"Not yet," Mars answered as he watched the intersection behind them. "Wait a minute! They just went past. They're stopping and backing up. They've seen us!"

Nadhim cleared a young man on a motor scooter by inches. The traffic ahead seemed to be traveling in every direction at once, totally oblivious of the danger hurtling down on them. Nadhim clamped down on the horn as he twisted the wheel and alternated between the accelerator and frantic stabs at the brake. Behind them, the other Land

Cruiser followed in their wake.

"They're gaining on us," Joe said. "Do something!"

Nadhim turned left at the next street, cutting off a delivery truck coming from the opposite direction. The other driver shook his fist at them as they swept past. Despite all Nadhim's efforts, the pursuing vehicle drew steadily closer.

"Look out!" Anne shouted as they approached the next intersection.

Nadhim cursed as he saw a truck and trailer pull into the intersection from the right. He held down the horn as he turned into the opposing lane of traffic. The truck continued to come, belching a thick cloud of diesel smoke. Nadhim floored the accelerator as the gap on the left continued to narrow.

Ya'acov pointed. "We're not going to make it!"

Nadhim twisted the wheel. The Toyota jumped up on the curb and plowed over a street sign. They bounded off the curb and around the front of the truck. The other driver hit his horn and finally applied his brakes. Blue smoke billowed up from the tires as the heavy truck slid through the intersection. Nadhim swung the wheel back to the right. The truck's right fender clipped their rear bumper. Nadhim cranked the wheel hard left to prevent a spin.

Mars looked back. "Ha! He's blocked the entire intersection. Let's see the deathmeisters get past that one."

He watched as the other car slid up to the stalled truck. The frantic honking gradually faded into the distance. Nadhim made a series of random turns, gradually slowing when it became apparent they had lost their pursuers. Finally he stopped outside a fenced construction site near the eastern edge of Al Hillah. He got out and walked quickly to the fence, stepping up on a large box to look over the fence. He turned and motioned for Ya'acov to get out.

"Help me move this," Nadhim said as he removed the loop of rope holding the gate shut.

The two men dragged the gate open. Nadhim got back in the Land Cruiser and drove it inside and down a steep path, stopping behind a thin cement wall. He shut off the engine and motioned for everyone to get out. Ya'acov pulled the gate shut and walked down to join them. Nadhim ushered them into the bare, concrete basement.

"We should be safe here for a while," he said. "Whoever was building this apartment abandoned the project over a year ago. I don't know what made me think about it."

"I believe God guided you," Anne said.

A puzzled expression came to Joe's face. "However it happened, I'm glad you remembered it. This should keep us safe while things cool off a bit." He turned to Ya'acov. "When should we head for the plane?"

"I think near sunset would be best. Since we don't have any lowlight goggles, I'd like some light to make sure we're on the right course. If we're close, Joel will signal us."

"About a half hour before the sun goes down?" Nadhim asked.

"That sounds about right," Ya'acov agreed.

Avraham's angry, black scowl showed no signs of moderating. Abdul knew that mood and had no desire to draw lightning down upon himself. He looked out at the crowded streets on the east side of Al Hillah as they continued their aimless patrol, Avraham unwilling to admit they had lost their prey. Several times they had stopped, and Abdul had asked pedestrians if they had seen the other Land Cruiser. Most were sure they had not. A few thought they had, but beyond this were little help. The trail was definitely cold.

Avraham turned south on a street they had

been down several times before. Most of the buildings were one-story houses and shops since they were near the eastern perimeter of the city. They passed the fenced-off building site and traveled two more blocks. Avraham turned right, then right again at the next street and began another northward beat.

28

WILDERNESS WARFARE

David Kruger ran a hand over his day-old stubble. He struggled up from the well-worn, green vinyl sofa that graced the rear wall of the hangar's conference room. He walked to the venetian blinds and held them open so he could see out. Both guards were at their stations, protecting the brightly-lit, empty hangar. David let go of the blinds and walked to the coffee-pot. He filled a Styrofoam cup, tasted it, and made a face. It was hot and bitter, but he knew the caffeine would help him stay awake.

He had thought several times about checking in with base housing so he could get a place to sleep. But each time he decided not to. He knew he wouldn't truly rest until he knew how it went with his men — and the archaeologists.

He made his weary way back to the couch and sat down.

★ ★ ★

Eitan looked toward the west. The sun was a brilliant, yellow ball that would dip below the horizon in less than an hour. Although he knew it was too soon, he scanned the endless desert for Ari's return.

When he first saw the dust plume, he thought it might be a small whirlwind. But after a minute he knew something was approaching, although its present course would take it past to the north by several hundred yards. Eitan brought up the binoculars and focused them. The image danced and bobbed as the aviator struggled to keep it centered.

He frowned as he lowered the glasses. It had to be Ari. It was a man in flowing robes, and he was riding an ATV. It was coming from the direction Ari had taken that morning, so it couldn't be anyone else. But why was he was off course?

Eitan snorted. Actually, that wasn't all that puzzling. Ari was a desk jockey, and he was in Intelligence to boot. The pilot could easily understand him getting off course. Unless something was done, he would miss the aircraft entirely. That would never do.

He scrambled out from under the net and faced the approaching rider, waving his hands over his head. For several seconds nothing happened as the ATV continued steadfastly on its course. Then Eitan heard the throttle cut back, and the rider turned toward where the plane was hidden. The aviator lowered his hands to his hips as he waited for Ari to approach.

The ATV bounded along until it was about thirty feet away when it turned abruptly toward the west and stopped. The man looked toward the pilot but appeared in no hurry to come closer. Eitan felt cold sweat break out.

"Ari?" he called out hopefully.

The rider shifted into first and twisted the throttle. In a moment he was hunched over and driving the ATV away as fast as it could go.

Eitan resisted the urge to leave immediately. Others depended on him, although his usefulness would evaporate if the Iraqi returned with a bunch of his friends, which was very likely. The Israeli cursed his stupidity as he retreated beneath the camouflage net.

"Time to go," Ya'acov announced as he got up.

The unfinished basement was in deep shadow as the unseen sun approached the horizon. The others stood and brushed themselves off, walking around to get rid of the stiffness of inactivity.

"I'll get the gate," Ya'acov said.

Ghanim and Moshe climbed into the rear seats while Joe, Anne, and Mars took the center. Nadhim started the Land Cruiser and waited.

Ya'acov dashed up the hill, flipped off the loop, and pushed hard to start the gate moving over the rutted dirt. The top hinge groaned and ripped out the two rusty nails holding it to the post. The heavy wooden gate jerked out of his hands before he could grab it and fell with a crash, twisting the bottom hinge loose as well. Ya'acov pulled the gate to the side so the Toyota could exit.

"Come on," Nadhim urged through the open window.

"I need some help."

Joe jumped out and took the other side. Together they raised the gate, but they found there was no way to repair the hinge damage. They propped the gate against the fence, leaving about a two-foot opening into the construction site.

"That's the best we could do," Joe said as he and Ya'acov got back in.

"It will have to do," Ya'acov agreed. "We have to get to the aircraft." He turned to Nadhim. "Can you get us out into the desert east of Al Hillah?"

"Yes. We are very near the edge of the city now. Almost any left turn will get us there."

"Take your pick. Once we're well clear of town, we'll have to circle around to the south. I'll show you."

Nadhim nodded as they sped down the street and turned left.

Abdul frowned but kept his irritation to himself. He had lost count of the number of circuits they had made in the eastern sector of Al Hillah. He felt like he had every detail of every street memorized. His eyes trailed along the dilapidated wooden fence to his right. He turned slightly to keep it in sight as they reached the end of the abandoned construction site.

"Wait a minute," he said as Avraham drove into the next block. "Back up."

"Why?" Avraham demanded as he stepped on the brake.

"I don't remember that gate being that way. I want to take a look at it."

Avraham put the car in reverse, backed up to the corner, and stopped.

"I'll be back in a minute," Abdul said.

He got out and waited for a delivery truck to pass before running over to the gate. He looked down and saw the clear tire tracks in the loose dirt. He ducked through the narrow gap and descended the hill to the unfinished basement. Tire tracks were down here as well, along with fresh footprints.

He ran back up the hill, crossed the street, and jumped into the car.

"A bunch of people and a car have been down there recently. And that gate wasn't broken the last time we went by."

"Do you think it was them?"

"I don't see who else it *could* be. That's an abandoned construction site."

"Where do you think they went?"

Abdul looked out through the windshield toward the left. "Toward the east — out into the desert."

"What do you suggest?"

"Go down a mile or two and head east. I'll bet we see them by the time we get out of the city."

Avraham pulled out into traffic.

Ari glanced at his watch. "I need to start back. Would you help me with the net?"

Joel pulled up a few pegs and helped Ari out with the ATV. They stood for a few moments looking at the sun sitting on the western horizon.

"Take care of yourself," the pilot said.

"I will. Hope to see you back at Beersheba — all of us."

"Yeah," Joel said without much enthusiasm.

"We've been in worse spots, or at least you have."

The pilot looked off in the general direction of Baghdad. "Yeah, I guess so. But I think I'd rather be pounding on T-72s with Hellfire missiles than doing this."

Ari felt a knot grow in his throat. "Ya'acov will make it back."

"I hope so."

Ari cranked the ATV. With a nod, he shifted into first and opened the throttle. In a moment he had the sun at his back, and his long black shadow pointed his course to the east and the hidden aircraft.

He tried to relax as the wind whipped past him. The ATV bounced and shook its way over the desert floor and through the stunted and seared brush. He tried to regain his earlier optimism, but it wasn't possible. Nothing seemed to be going right!

The houses became smaller and further apart the closer they came to the edge of town. Finally, without any warning, the dirt street ended and the desert began. Nadhim locked the differentials and dropped back in speed a little.

"Where to?" he asked.

"Let's get well clear of town, then circle back around," Ya'acov said. "The plane is almost due south of us now, but I want some more distance between us and Al Hillah."

"Sounds good to me. How far do you want to go?"

"Oh, two or three miles. I'll tell you when."

Moshe glanced out toward the south and pointed. "What is that?" Mars and Anne turned their heads.

"Nadhim . . ." she said.

"What?"

"There's another car to the right of us."

Joe looked south. "They've found us! I don't know how they did it, but they've found us!" He turned to Ya'acov. "We can't turn toward the aircraft. They'll cut us off if we try it."

"I know."

"What are you going to do?"

Ya'acov glanced at the gas gauge, which was around half full. "Keep going for a while. Maybe they will hit something."

"Yeah. Or we might. Or they might have help on the way."

"If we can't shake them, we'll have to

fight. But I'd like to avoid that if we can. I suspect we're outgunned. AK-47s against Uzis isn't exactly a fair fight."

Joe grunted. "Depends if you're close-in or not. But in this case, I think I agree. It'd be nice if we could sucker them around to where the aircraft is and catch them from both sides."

Ya'acov looked out the window. "No chance of that. Not with those two."

Moshe tapped Ya'acov on the shoulder and pointed. "There's another cloud of dust out in front of their car."

Ya'acov followed Moshe's direction. "Yes, I see it. Something smaller — a motorcycle or ATV."

"ATV? You don't suppose . . ."

The sun was almost down, and the vehicles were getting hard to see.

"There was a second rescue plane back at Beer-sheba, but it's too much to hope for that. It's probably another Arab anxious to help us out of this life."

Ari looked across at the plumes of dust boiling up behind the two vehicles to his left. One had a slight lead on the other, and both were running parallel to him. As long as this continued, he would reach the plane while the nearest car was about a mile away.

Enough time to get on board and get away — maybe. But who were they?

The two cars were definitely not together. One presumably was Ya'acov's, hopefully with the archaeologists, but what about the other?

Ari continued on for another minute, then turned toward the nearest car.

Eitan lowered his binoculars. The smaller dust plume, presumably Ari's ATV, had just turned toward the other two vehicles. Whatever was going to happen would be over very quickly. He ran around the camouflage net, pulling up all the stakes. He quickly removed the net and left it in a wad behind the aircraft. Throwing the chairs in through the cargo doors and closing them, he climbed in the pilot's door and went quickly through the checklist. The bird was ready. All he had to do was start the engine.

The sun was gone now, and the vehicles were beginning to meld into the darkening background. He picked up his low-light goggles and put them on.

"That ATV has turned toward us," Joe announced. "Man, is he closing the distance!"

"It has to be Ari," Ya'acov said. "Nadhim,

turn toward the other car. Let's try and catch him in a pincers move."

Mars leaned forward in the backseat. "Don't forget, that's Avraham. He's crazy enough to do anything."

"I *know*, Mars," the IDF officer snapped.

Nadhim brought the Land Cruiser around in a tight turn, throwing everyone off balance. He straightened out on a course that intersected the other car.

"Hey!" he said a few moments later. "They're turning toward us!"

Ari felt his heart sink when he saw the two cars turn toward each other. He reached inside his robes and pulled out his Uzi. Flipping off the safety, he brought the submachine gun up and tried to aim it onehanded, but the sight danced all over the place. He squeezed off a short burst in the right general direction, hoping to scare their enemies, but he couldn't see where the bullets actually hit. He held down the trigger and pulled the muzzle toward the car in front of him. He saw the puffs of dust walk near the car.

Ari saw something dark appear in the driver's window. He twisted the handlebars sharply to the right just a moment before the assault rifle spat death at him. He cleared the car's dust trail and looked to the left in horror.

Nadhim was trying to decide which way to dodge to avoid a collision when the other car swerved to the left. He wrenched his wheel to the right and watched as the other car swept by only inches away. Brilliant muzzle flashes illuminated the other car. Nadhim winced as he felt and heard the heavy slugs tearing into the side of the car.

"Look out!" Ya'acov shouted, pointing straight ahead.

Nadhim stood on the brakes as the ATV cut directly in front of them. He saw the dark shape of the rider and vehicle passing into danger with agonizing slowness. The heavy Toyota rocked from side to side as it slid over the sand and brush.

"We're going to hit him!" Anne screamed.

The dark image crept past the right fender and then the front of the car as the distance rapidly diminished. Nadhim turned the wheel even further to the right, but the car barely responded since the wheels were sliding. As Ari approached the car's left fender, the bumper hit the rear of the ATV and shoved it out of the way. Ari twisted the handlebar to regain control and continued turning toward the south.

"That was close," Nadhim breathed as he released the brakes and got back on the accelerator.

"Where are Avraham and Abdul?" Ya'acov asked.

Mars looked back. "They're turning around and coming down on our right side."

"How far back?" Nadhim asked.

"About a hundred yards."

"We still can't make a run for the plane."

"Not until we do something about those two," Ya'acov agreed. "Where's Ari?"

Mars turned to the other side. "He's dropping back on our left." Muzzle flashes illuminated him for a moment. "He's firing at Avraham and Abdul."

"It'll be sheer luck if he hits them," Joe said.

"They're firing back now. Ari's moving further away."

"Wise move."

A dark shape appeared in the distance, seeming to rise out of the desert floor.

"What's that?" Nadhim demanded.

"Stop!" Ya'acov shouted.

"What?"

"I said stop! It's Ari's plane."

The Land Cruiser skidded from side to side as it ground to a stop. The angular shape of the waiting plane was unmistakable.

"Get out, Ya'acov!" Joe shouted. "The rest of you, get down!"

Ya'acov opened his door and jumped out.

"Follow my lead!" Joe ordered as he got out.

He flipped the Uzi's safety off as he sprawled over the hot hood. Ya'acov joined him on his right. The Palestinians' car rumbled toward them, circling wide to the east. Ari was driving hard, trying to close the gap. The Uzi's muzzle flash illuminated him briefly as he fired. This was answered by angry flashes from the driver's window.

"Get ready," Joe said.

Ya'acov lifted the Uzi and sighted along the barrel as he waited for the car to come into view. The black shape came into sight trailing a dark, boiling cloud. The smaller shape of the ATV drifted rapidly to the side to get away from the pounding of the AK-47.

"Wait until they're closer," Joe advised.

Finally the car came broadside.

"Now!" Joe shouted.

Both men clamped down on their triggers. The muzzle flash made it hard to see. They could barely hear the flat, tinny sound of the slugs tearing into the car over the noise they were making. Yellow flashes illuminated the passenger's window.

"Get down!" Joe yelled.

Heavy slugs crashed into the far side of their car. Ya'acov felt the body vibrate and shake as it absorbed the pounding. Suddenly it swayed as the two opposite tires were shot out.

"What has he got, a cannon?" Ya'acov asked.

"AK-47. Does a pretty good job, doesn't it?" Joe took a peek under the car. "Run around the back! Stay low! They're coming around the front."

Joe stayed in a crouch and dashed around the back of the car. Ya'acov joined him a moment later. They watched as the other car roared around in a tight turn, trailing a dark rooster tail.

"Right between us and the plane," Ya'acov muttered. "Hope they don't hose that down."

"They'll concentrate on us first. The plane isn't firing at them. Get ready to move to the other side."

The Palestinians continued their turn. Joe and Ya'acov ran down the far side and leaned over the mauled hood. The Israeli sighted and pulled the trigger. The muzzle roared twice, and the magazine quickly emptied. He ejected the clip, inserted a new one through the handle, and brought the gun back up. Joe sprayed the retreating car with his Uzi until his clip was exhausted. Ya'acov pulled his trigger and tried to steady the sight on the indistinct target. Return fire erupted from the other car. Ya'acov and Joe ducked as more slugs pounded the car.

"Did you see Ari?" Ya'acov asked.

"No. I lost sight of him when we were on the other side."

"I don't think we're doing any good with these."

"Hard to say since we can't see very well. But we did slow them down a little."

"I'd rather stop them."

Joe shrugged.

Ari let go of the throttle so he could concentrate on changing the clip in his Uzi. He ejected the old one and inserted his last clip through the handle. He jacked a new round into the chamber and grabbed the throttle again. He twisted it open and turned toward the departing Land Cruiser. It was headed north at a slower pace.

Ari knew what would come next. They would turn and come back down on his friends unless he could do something about it. He snorted. What *could* he do? He had fired two full clips of forty rounds each, and it hadn't done a thing except make them mad.

He twisted the throttle against its stop and held on as the ATV bounced and screamed over the desert. He thought briefly about turning on his headlight — only briefly. He drove just to the side of the car's dust cloud. The dark shape grew larger rapidly. He saw it start veering to the right.

He's coming around. It's now or never.

Ari let go of the throttle and grabbed the Uzi with his right hand. As the ATV coasted, he brought the gun up and clamped down on the trigger. He saw a flash of light under the car as the magazine emptied. A moment later the vehicle erupted in a ball of flame as the gas tank exploded.

Ari swung the handlebars over to the side and squinted at the sudden glare. The car swerved sharply to the right and started to roll. The Israeli could clearly see the silhouette of the man on the passenger's side. The driver he couldn't see. The car rolled and bounced, spreading flames over the desert floor. Finally it came to rest on its side in a crackling wreck.

Ari turned around and headed south.

"Don't shoot," he shouted as he came within range. He came to a sliding stop, killed the engine, and got off.

"Nice work," Joe said.

"Sheer luck," Ari replied.

"The results are what counts." He turned back and stuck his head in the passenger's window. "Everyone O.K.?"

There were muffled gasps and grunts as they untangled limbs and struggled to sit up.

Joe counted the right number of heads with relief. "Anyone hurt?"

"Guess not," Mars replied. "Banged my arm, but I don't think I broke it. Hurts like the dickens though."

Anne turned in concern, although she couldn't see anything. "Are you sure, dear?"

"I'm fine. Are you all right?"

She smiled. "Yes, dear."

Ya'acov heard the sound of a starting turbine. "Joe . . . The plane."

Nadhim opened his door and got out.

Joe grabbed the handle on the right rear door and pulled. It was jammed. "Ghanim, try your side."

The door made a horrible sound, but it opened. Anne stepped out followed by Mars, Ghanim, and Moshe.

"Listen, everybody," Ya'acov shouted. "Go around the tail of the aircraft. Ari will show you where the door is."

"You want me to stay with you?" Joe asked.

Ya'acov looked at the flaming wreckage. "I don't think so. I'll be there in a minute."

Abdul opened his eyes and looked up into the heavens. The first thing he saw was a few stars in the deep blue, almost black sky. For a few moments he didn't know where he was. Then pain returned and with it his memory. He reached up and touched the knot on his head. He looked back at the torched car, now resting on its left side. The passenger door gaped open.

I was spared for some reason. But Avraham is dead. The Palestinian Revolutionary Force is dead. Hate welled up deep within him. *Not that our Arab brothers cared. But why am I still here?*

He staggered to his feet and turned toward the south. Dark shapes were moving toward the aircraft. He started running, ignoring the blurred vision and the throbbing pain in his head.

29

EMERGENCY EXIT

Ya'acov stood at the U-27's airstair door at the right rear of the aircraft. "Ari, go forward and take the right seat." The lieutenant hurried inside. "Everyone else, take any seat."

Mars and Anne ducked down, climbed up into the snug cabin, and started forward. Moshe followed them. Ghanim and Nadhim were next.

"Are you two ready?" Ya'acov asked.

"We have no choice," Ghanim replied for them.

"I am sorry. I didn't want this to happen any more than you did."

"It is done now. There is no more to say." He and Nadhim stepped inside.

"Need me for anything?" Joe asked.

"Don't think so. Get aboard. I'll be right behind you."

Joe entered the cabin and took one of the rear seats. Ya'acov climbed aboard and shut the airstair door.

"Ya'acov?" Eitan called from the front.
"Yes?"

"Would you check to make sure the camouflage net is clear of the tail? I'd like to be sure the wind hasn't blown it back over our tail feathers."

"I think it's clear, but I'll check."

He opened the door, admitting sand and grit. He stepped down and looked back. The propeller blew swirling sand past him. The vertical fin and the right-hand horizontal stabilizer were clear. That only left the other side. He crunched through the sand and rounded the tail. The net was well clear. They were ready to go.

He started to turn back when he saw a black blur out of the corner of his eye. Icy fear stabbed deep into his gut. The man landed on his back and pitched him forward. Ya'acov cried out as he hit the ground hard, the air bursting out of his lungs. He twisted hard and looked up at the man sitting on him. He couldn't see his face, but with dreaded certainty he knew who it was. Then something colder than death settled over him. He knew those in the aircraft could neither see nor hear him back at the tail.

"Abdul?" he asked in shock.

The other did not reply. Instead, those powerful hands circled Ya'acov's throat.

The Israeli brought up his hands and struggled to reach his opponent. Abdul released his right hand briefly and brought his fist down in a powerful right cross. Ya'acov's vision exploded in stars, and he felt his consciousness slipping. The choking grip was back, and he could feel the hate that was behind it.

"You lost," Ya'acov gasped.

The grip relaxed slightly.

"Avraham's dead, and you might as well be. You lost again — to a Jew."

Abdul howled in rage. He released his grip and clenched both hands over his head. Just as he started down, Ya'acov twisted to the side and with a strength borne out of desperation struggled partway up. Abdul, caught off-guard, fell backwards. Ya'acov scampered to his feet and jumped to the side to avoid a vicious swipe. Abdul leapt upward at him.

Ya'acov whirled around and ran forward into the propeller blast, ignoring his dizziness, squinting to try to keep the sand and dust out of his eyes. He barely saw the wing strut, ducking under it at the last moment. A dull thump behind him indicated Abdul had not been so fortunate. Ya'acov didn't look back, his only thought being to round the front of the aircraft and get some help.

He glanced to the side as he went past the cockpit. He thought he could see the outlines of two heads, but he couldn't see their faces. As Ya'acov brushed past the unseen disc of the propeller, he felt it snag and rip his robe. Clear of that danger, he dodged right.

Ya'acov heard a loud ripping sound followed by a heavy thump. He whirled around expecting to face Abdul, but instead he saw a shapeless hump sprawled on the ground. The engine abruptly began to wind down. Eitan opened the pilot's door and jumped down. He took one quick look at the dead Palestinian and joined Ya'acov.

"He ran right into the prop," he said.

Ya'acov glanced at the rapidly slowing propeller. The disc had a pronounced wobble.

Eitan cursed. "It's wrecked."

"Will it hold together long enough to get us home?"

The pilot shook his head. "Not a chance. That bent blade would come off the first time we went to full power. We're stuck."

Ya'acov looked toward the west. "No, we're not."

Ari stepped cautiously past the slowly turning propeller and looked down. "Wow! I never thought I would see that. Couldn't happen to a nicer guy."

"Except it wrecked our prop," Ya'acov snapped. "Where is the ATV? I've got to go get Joel."

"Come on. I'll show you."

Ya'acov got the GPS coordinates of their current position and joined Ari for a walk in the desert. Finally they located the dark hummock amid the black brush.

"Dark night," Ari remarked.

"That's to our advantage, I guess, as long as I can find Joel and get back before the Iraqis discover us."

"Do you remember where he is from here?"

"Yes, I think so."

"I wish you sounded a little more confident."

"I hope you're smiling, Lieutenant."

"Oh, yes, sir. Can't you tell?"

"Not in this darkness." Ya'acov straddled the ATV. "Keep everyone together. Be ready to board the instant we land."

"We will," Ari said, his tone somber again. "And good luck."

"Thanks."

Ya'acov selected first gear and accelerated smoothly into the night.

He thought about trying to navigate by using the stars but wasn't confident he could pick the right ones. Finally he set his course based on the glow of Al Hillah in the distance. He thumbed the light on his watch and tried to estimate his estimated time of arrival.

The desert brush whipped past the lightless ATV as Ya'acov pushed it as hard as he could. Every so often he sailed through the air after hitting an unseen hummock. He was grateful for the balance of the ATV every time he landed safely. Once he almost flipped over when he careened through an unseen *wadi* on a diagonal. The right wheel came off the ground and started over. Ya'acov stood and leaned right, barely stopping the roll-over.

He was beginning to think he had missed the plane when he noticed a dark ridge rising to his right. He turned to parallel it and slowed down a little. Soon he could see a large dark shape rising abruptly out of the desert floor. He stopped the ATV about a hundred feet away and shut it down.

He dismounted and listened.

Silence.

He thought he saw a slight movement next to the shape.

"Joel?" he said in a harsh whisper.

"That you, Ya'acov?"

The Intelligence officer rushed forward.

"Come on, we've got to go. Everyone's at the other plane, and it's down."

"What happened?"

"Long story. Prop's busted. Let's move it."

They quickly removed the camouflage net. Joel stepped up into the cockpit while Ya'acov entered through the airstair door and made his way forward to the copilot's seat.

"Wind's picking back up," Joel remarked as the engine lit and began its rpm buildup.

"Dust kicking up yet?"

"Hard to tell as dark as it is. But it's bound to if this keeps up."

"Let's move it."

"Right you are."

Ya'acov gave the pilot the GPS coordinates. Joel nodded and smoothly advanced the power lever until he reached max turbine inlet temperature. After a short takeoff roll, they were airborne and flying low over the blackened desert.

"Looks like trouble," Joel said after he leveled out.

"The wind?"

"No." He pointed out the left window. "Company on the ground."

Ya'acov craned his neck and looked out and down. Two tiny headlights were cutting a path that pointed directly at the extraction site.

"Can we beat them there?" Ya'acov asked.

Joel glanced at the GPS readout. "We'll land before they get there, but by the time we get everyone on board, they'll be on us."

Ya'acov slammed his fist against his armrest. "Nothing's going right!"

"What do you want to do?"

"Land! We don't have any choice."

"What about our guests?"

"I'm thinking about it. Just get us on the ground."

"Yes, sir."

A minute later Joel pulled back on the power. They touched down, and the pilot slowed the plane rapidly with the brakes. He watched the GPS readout carefully as he taxied.

"I could use a little help," he muttered.

"What?" Ya'acov asked.

A tiny green light winked on, then off.

"Thank you," Joel said, advancing the power lever slightly. "Eitan flicked on the navigational lights for a second."

"Stop here!" Ya'acov ordered.

Joel stood on the brakes.

Ya'acov looked toward the approaching lights. "Stay here. The other plane is between us and that car."

He stumbled his way to the back and opened the airstair door. He stepped down, then ran around the tail and over to the other aircraft.

"Get aboard the other plane!" he shouted. "Move it."

The car's yellow lights were beginning to illuminate the nearby brush.

"Eitan, fire that thing up and set it to taxiing that way." He pointed to the north. "And flip on the navigational lights."

"The prop may not take it."

"Just do it! We're no worse off if it breaks."

Eitan ran around to the pilot's door and climbed in. Moments later the turbine lit and started accelerating. The damaged blade could be clearly seen as it made the propeller's disc wobble. The pilot locked the left brake and pivoted the plane to the north. Then he advanced the power lever as much as he dared and flipped on the navigational lights. He jumped out as the plane began rolling and bouncing over the sand.

He and Ya'acov watched for a moment.

"Will it take off?" Ya'acov asked.

"No. Fast taxi at best. But it looks like it faked out our friends."

The yellow lights started curving away toward the north.

"Come on!" Ya'acov ordered.

They ran back to the idling plane and through the prop wash. Ya'acov rounded the tail, then dashed up the airstair door and into the aircraft. Eitan jumped in and closed the door.

"Sit down!" Joel yelled.

"Take off!" Ya'acov answered. "Now!"

The pilot pushed the power lever forward. The plane picked up speed rapidly as it bounced over the unseen desert. The stragglers found their seats as the U-27 became airborne.

"Things going a little better now?" Eitan asked.

"Yeah," Ya'acov admitted.

The pilot brought the plane around in a wide turn until they were flying west.

"Joel?" Ya'acov called out.

"Yes, sir?"

"Just like old times."

"Indeed it is. I vote we call it quits after this."

"I agree with that," the Intelligence officer said with a laugh. "Who's up front with you?"

"Ari. You want to come up?"

"No. I think I'll relax back here. Send the cabin attendants back once we reach cruising altitude."

"We're at cruising altitude. And the service you've got now is all you're going to get. Anything else?"

"Just keep us right-side-up."

"Roger that."

Ya'acov sat back and tried to relax. But his racing mind refused to cooperate. What would Colonel Kruger make of *this* operation? he wondered.

All the normal airborne avionics came to life once the U-27 entered Israeli airspace. Joel finished by flipping on the navigational lights and checking his transponder code. He set the transceiver's frequency and sent a short, coded message.

"They're expecting us," he relayed back to Ya'acov.

"Can't wait," Ya'acov grumbled.

Less than half an hour later they landed and taxied into the hangar. Joel shut down the engine and turned to watch his passengers deplane. When they were all off except Ari and Ya'acov, he opened his door and got out.

The two Intelligence officers stepped down to face an unshaven Lieutenant Colonel David Kruger. They saluted. David returned the salute.

"How did it go?" their boss asked.

"We got them all out," Ya'acov replied.

"Good. I'm glad for that. I would guess there were some problems."

"That there were, Colonel."

David nodded. "Time for the debriefing. Military Intelligence first with all four of you, then IAF for the pilots." He turned to Ari. "I've arranged for your transportation back to Jerusalem, Ari. Ya'acov will be coming back with me. Are we ready?"

"Yes, sir," Ya'acov answered for both of them.

"Let's get it over with. I'm beat."

They disappeared into the conference room with Joel and Eitan.

"I'm so glad that's over," Anne whispered as she stood under the hangar's harsh mercury vapor lights.

Mars pulled her close and looked into her eyes. "Me too." He kissed her. "Did you think marriage would be this exciting, Mrs. Enderly?"

A twinkle came to her eye, and she poked him in the ribs. "Not *exactly* in this way."

"Ow. You play rough, ma'am." He kissed her again.

"How sweet," a familiar voice rumbled.

They turned to see Moshe beaming at them. Ghanim and Nadhim were standing a ways off, and Joe was talking to the younger man.

Mars cleared his throat. "Yeah, I guess it is." He smiled at Anne.

"Since you two obviously have everything under control, I need to have a word with Ghanim. Carry on."

They watched him go.

"He's a sweet man," Anne observed.

"Better not let *him* hear you say that."

"Well, it's true."

"Yeah, I guess it is. He's been a true friend, as well as a colleague."

"He's more than that," Anne said.

"What?"

"We're all Christians now. He's our brother in Christ."

Mars's expression turned thoughtful. "You're right. But that's going to take getting used to. Everything is so different now." He shook his head. "I don't know why I couldn't see all this before."

"I know what you mean. I remember my own experience." Tears came to her eyes. "Mars, I'm so glad you accepted the Lord. You have no idea how much that worried me."

He lowered his head. "Yes, dear. I know — now. I'm sorry I worried you so. Will you forgive me?"

"Of course I will." She wiped at her tears. "I feel like the Lord has given you to me a second time."

He grinned. "I guess He did."

She rested her head on his chest as he stroked her hair. He leaned down and tenderly kissed her forehead.

Moshe came up behind Ghanim and put his hand on his shoulder. The Iraqi barely moved as he stared at the hangar's smooth concrete floor.

"How are you, my friend?" Moshe asked quietly.

Ghanim shrugged. "Like a man without a country. I can never go back."

"I know."

"What will I do? I am in your country illegally and without a job."

"All this will be taken care of, I assure you. Because of the circumstances, the government will make you most welcome. And I meant what I said about you continuing your work. I know of an opening the Hebrew University has for a Ph.D. archaeologist. You fit the bill perfectly."

Ghanim gave him a weak smile. "I know how you operate, Dr. Stein. Just how long has this opening existed?"

The bushy eyebrows shot upward. "Whatever do you mean?"

"You know very well." He wiped at his eye. "I appreciate your kindness, Moshe."

"Kindness, nothing. We need a scholar of your caliber. And I think we can find some worthy digs to keep you occupied. I think you'll enjoy the academic freedom we have here."

"That *will* be a relief," Ghanim admitted.

"Will you let me help?"

"Do I have a choice?"

"Now, now, only Jews get to answer questions with questions. But, no, you don't have a choice. Please let me do this for you."

Ghanim nodded. "Thank you, Moshe."

"You are welcome." He looked around. "Where is your nephew?"

"Mr. Enderly came and got him. I think they're talking on the other side of the airplane."

Moshe looked around. "Hmm. So they are."

Nadhim looked at the American in disbelief. "*You* are offering *me* a job? Just like that?"

"Yes, I am."

Nadhim sighed in exasperation. "There are a few problems in the way."

Joe laughed but became serious when he

saw the other's dark look. "I'm not laughing at your situation, Nadhim. Believe me, Moshe and I can make all those problems disappear for you. Do you know what I do for a living?"

"No, I don't."

"I own a company called Dallas Heuristics. We're working on an artificial intelligence project with Israel Aircraft Industries. How would you like to work for my company? I promise I can offer you a responsible, interesting job."

"I have no degree."

"I couldn't care less. I've seen you work, Nadhim. I'd love to have you with us."

"I don't know."

"I know you need time to think about it. Come to Jerusalem with us." He nodded toward Mars and Anne. "Let me put you up in the American Colony Hotel. Then we can take our time going over the proposal. Give me a chance to take you to Lod and show you what we're doing. Will you do that?"

"Yes," he said with a tentative smile. "Thank you."

"Good. Now let me check with the others about arranging some transportation."

30

WHAT'S MOST IMPORTANT

Anne opened a reluctant eye when the alarm went off. It had been a short night. She poked Mars to make sure he was awake. They hurried through the bathroom ritual and finally left the room. Mars took Anne's arm, and they walked down the corridor to Joe's suite at the American Colony Hotel. Mars knocked.

"Come in, you two," Joe said, opening the door. "Get enough sleep?"

Anne saw her husband begin to grin, and she gave him a little pinch. The grin disappeared.

"We're quite refreshed," he said.

Joe seemed oblivious of the exchange. "Good. Shall we call room service or would you two like to go down to the restaurant?"

Mars looked at Anne.

"I think I'd like to go to the restaurant," she said.

They found the room nearly empty when

the waiter seated them at a corner table. They selected the breakfast buffet and made their trips to the heavily laden tables. Three steaming cups of coffee were waiting for them when they returned with their heaping plates. Mars helped Anne with her chair. Joe waited politely while they gave thanks for the food.

He took a sip of his coffee. "I know you're glad to be out of there, but did you find anything on the dig?"

Mars glanced at Anne, then looked at his father. "Yes, we did. It was as significant, in its own way, as finding the Temple veil in Jerusalem. Have you ever heard of the story from the book of Daniel about a disembodied hand writing a message on King Belshazzar's wall?"

"Ah, no, I don't believe so."

"It's where the expression 'the handwriting's on the wall' comes from," Mars explained.

"Oh."

"Anyhow, we found that inscription. We unearthed what we think was a wing of Nebuchadnezzar's Southern Palace. And the words *mene, mene, tekel, upharsin* were burned into it in a way we couldn't explain. It looked like someone used a laser to do it."

"When did this supposedly happen?"

Mars glanced at Anne. She had her eyes closed.

"I don't know what biblical scholars would say, but archaeologists place the end of his reign at around 540 B.C."

"Don't you mean B.C.E.?" Joe asked with a smile.

"No, Dad. I mean 'before Christ.' I'm a Christian now. I found the same thing Anne did. The Bible is an historically accurate book. As Moshe says, it's the most accurate ancient book there is. Anyhow, if it's reliable, then the things it says about Jesus Christ must also be true. It doesn't make sense for the Bible to be accurate about everything except for one subject."

"I see," Joe said slowly.

"Dad, have you ever thought about these things yourself? What if the Bible is right? What if the only way to avoid eternal punishment is to believe in Jesus?"

"With all due respect, this is not something I want to discuss, son."

Mars felt his eyes sting. "I wish you would, Dad."

"If this new belief helps you, I'm glad. But I believe in what I can touch, see, and hear."

He glanced at Anne and saw her stricken expression.

The famous smile returned to full brilliance. "Now, now. We're celebrating your miraculous rescue." He turned toward Anne. "And your marriage. I can't tell you how happy I am for you both. And how delighted I am to have a daughter."

Mars sighed. He knew he couldn't choose for his father. He turned to Anne and smiled as he saw her green eyes caressing his.

She returned his smile as a peace she did not fully understand swept over her. She knew her Lord was responsible. She was grateful for her relationship with Him, His present of Mars to her, His saving her husband, and His Lordship over them and their marriage. Yes, life really could be good. And she and Mars would have to trust Joe to the Lord.

ABOUT THE AUTHOR

When he's not working on a novel, **Frank Simon** is a technical writer and computer consultant. He has a Master of Business Administration degree from Southern Methodist University. He and his wife, Laverne, live in Texas.

Veiled Threats and its sequel, *Walls of Terror*, are suspenseful adventures occurring in international settings.